NORMA
AND THE
BLUE
HOUR

NORMA AND THE BLUE HOUR

CHRIS DELYANI

ACKNOWLEDGMENT

The author wishes to express deepest gratitude to the team of editors who helped bring this story to life: Charlotte Cook, Mark Spencer, Erin McClary, and Lottie Hayes-Clemens.

For Dan

CHAPTER 1

ACCIDENT

Norma McKinsey had plans to drive from her home in the Oakland Hills to San Francisco's Palace Hotel for a lunch meeting, to talk about selling off her clothes. Her favorite charity, a Bay Area food pantry, was throwing its holiday gala in a few months, one week after her eightieth birthday. She was meeting with the charity to decide which designs she would donate to the silent auction. Hard to believe that her life's work—suits and dresses she'd created over five decades of a prosperous, some might even say legendary, career—could be dispersed in a single night. But she'd grown tired of keeping them in storage.

She was prepared to let go of the dresses she'd designed for her sister Julie's wedding. The bridesmaids' dresses—form-fitting, daringly cut; two done in gold lamé, two in metallic-gray satin—would still look chic on a young woman today. The charity could also claim one of her earliest achievements, the cornflower-blue evening gown inspired by a Corot painting on a visit to the Louvre as an eighteen-year-old design student. She could even part with the prototypes for the fairy costumes she'd designed for *A Midsummer Night's Dream* at the San Francisco Opera. But she would never budge on what the charity coveted most, the creations that had catapulted her to fame: the prom suits she'd made for her son Kevin and his boyfriend. If the charity wanted those suits, they'd need to ask Kevin. Wherever he was.

Before she left the house, she finished writing the last of her invitations for her annual summer barbecue. Then she practiced shots at her pool table. Her favorite challenge was to sink all fifteen balls in a row without missing, saving the 8-ball for last. No luck after five tries. On the sixth attempt, while she stared at the table, deciding whether to send the 3-ball to the side pocket or the 11-ball to the corner pocket, her eye caught the clock on the fireplace mantel. Her hair appointment with Mavis was in half an hour. She'd finish the game when she came home.

The sky hadn't yet cleared when she left the house—disappointing weather, given it was mid-June. Fog shrouded the laurel tree towering over her driveway. She backed into the street a shade too quickly. Before she had a chance to turn, something heavy and hulking shoved her car from the side. The laurel tree careened toward her. A spinning sensation. A spray of shattered glass. An odor of spilled gasoline. A deathly silence. She realized someone had T-boned the car before terror had a chance to rip through her.

Voices floated above her head. Urgent, sharp, panicked. Someone shouted at her as if from across a field. A man's voice. Could she hear him? Could she move? A wail of sirens drowned out the voice, smothered the car.

The sound of metal grinding against metal. Someone prying open her rumpled door. A rush of chilly air. Exhaustion washing over her. Blackness. Her eyes opening to the ceiling tiles of a darkened hospital room, her leg held captive in a cast.

The 3-ball and 11-ball must still be sitting on the pool table, waiting to be guided to their pockets. The unsent barbecue invitations must still be sitting on the passenger seat of her ruined Porsche Boxster. What had the nurses done with her saffron-colored pumps? Would she ever be able to wear a four-inch heel again? What about her hair? How long would it take before Mavis could cut it? She recalled the charity's offer to send a car to fetch her, pictured herself gliding to the Palace in plush but insipid comfort. She had no regrets.

Two weeks crawled by in purplish twilight. Day and night congealed into a mass of time. Doctors operated on her leg three times. Maybe four. Between surgeries, she lay in bed motionless. Wiggling a toe sent agony tearing through her. She drifted through a painkiller-induced mist, too weak to sit up or lift a glass of water. Her French-language fashion magazines piled up unread on her nightstand. The view from her window offered a sliver of sky no broader than the spine of a phone book. She lamented that her last view from her picture windows at home had been a wall of fog.

The surgeries proved successful. Norma graduated from Intensive Care to rehab. If physical therapy went well, her doctor said, she could be home in three months.

"Two months if you work hard," the doctor said, his voice sprightly and patronizing. He looked barely older than her own grandsons.

"Thank you, sir," she told him. "You'll be sending me home in one."

A steady stream of visitors came to her bedside. Friends from her fashion days. Bridge friends. The woman from the charity, assuring her the auction would go on. All expressed amazement at her progress, her toughness. This was her reputation. These people expected no less.

Her sister, Julie, fluttered about her room like a moth. She was even set to cancel her trip to the Galápagos tomorrow to keep housesitting for her and bringing her mail. Norma wouldn't hear of it.

"What if something happens while I'm gone?" A panicked look passed over Julie's face.

"The worst already happened." Norma spoke with crisp certainty.

"But Kate called to say she can't go with me," Julie said, her tone frantic. "Liam caught a terrible cold."

"Poor Liam," Norma said dryly, reaching for a magazine. She had a low opinion of Julie's eldest daughter and her needy husband. "You're boarding that plane tomorrow, whether you like it or not."

Norma's oldest son, Charles, came to visit at least twice a week. He always entered her room with a thousand-watt smile and a sanguine determination to make each visit worthwhile. And indeed, his visits were pleasant, or at least not awkward, so much so that she found herself—to her surprise—looking forward to seeing him. They watched baseball games and the news together, shared Chinese takeout, talked about going to Seattle to visit Jonah and Maria, Charles's oldest son and his wife, expecting their first baby in November. Charles helped her buy a chair lift for her main staircase and a mini refrigerator to put in her sitting room, in anticipation of her going home. Her accident had given him purpose now that he was retired.

But on his most recent visit, Charles brought her a brochure promoting a nursing home, or, as he put it, a "senior facility," near his home in Orinda, a few miles east of Oakland. He dropped it on her bed with casual calculation on his way out, as if passing along a newspaper he'd finished reading. Even glancing at the brochure was enough to make her stomach turn. She stuffed the brochure in her bottom nightstand drawer.

Julie's younger daughter, Olivia, living in Tokyo with her latest boyfriend, sent her a gift basket of gourmet Kit Kat bars in exotic flavors: green tea, wasabi, *Otona no Amasa* strawberry. Joanie, one of her oldest seamstress friends in New York, sent her a bottle of Campari tied with gold ribbon "*to celebrate with a Negroni once you're on your feet.*" Then there were the flowers. Roses from Paris, chrysanthemums from Rome, queen proteas from Milan. Birds of paradise from her bridge club occupied prime space on the table by the window, enfolding the bottle of Campari. Flowers pulsating with color, defying the mousy walls. But the flowers she craved most were flowers she hadn't yet received. From Kevin.

Kevin was a constant visitor—in her imagination. He sat talking to her in the sagging easy chair by her bed, no matter the hour. Sometimes he bantered with the floor nurses. Other times he looked over her shoulder as she flipped through her French-language *Vogue*. She imagined telling him about the auction, pictured him smiling and telling her he was okay with donating his prom suit. *Give it to them,* he'd say. *The sneakers that went with the suit too. What good is that old stuff doing in my old closet?*

Where was Kevin now? Was he clean and sober? Was he working? Was anyone looking after him? She asked this of the imaginary Kevin. He merely smiled, shrugged, and assured her he'd survive. *I always do,* he said. *You know that, don't you, Mom?*

Charles had to know where Kevin was living. He must have told his little brother of Norma's close call. Considering how serious her accident had been, Kevin might be tempted to visit her. Every time her door opened, she looked up with a flitting sensation through her heart. But the person coming through the door was a doctor, a nurse, a friend stopping by. Never Kevin.

And he sent no flowers.

It was now the middle of August, a Sunday, four days since Charles had given her that brochure. The walls of her room were closing in on her. The starched white pillowcases crunched as she leaned against them. Daylight struggled through the drawn blinds and glowed against the wall as if cast through prison bars. But the room wasn't the prison. The pin in her left leg was. Thank heavens, the doctors had cleared her to go home on Friday.

A nurse came to take away her lunch tray and give her that afternoon's pills. This nurse's name was—Norma glanced at her name tag—Soo-jung. So many nurses came and went, their faces half-concealed by blue paper masks, that she had trouble keeping track of them. At least Soo-jung had sparkly greenish-blue eye shadow streaking out from the corners of her eyes. A touch of glamor for an unglamorous job.

"Shall I raise the blind?" Soo-jung looked at Norma, her hand grasping the cord.

"Please," Norma said, glancing up from her magazine.

The blinds went clattering up. Sunlight flooded the room. The flowers on the table burst forth like a parade float. The strip of sky made her ache for her terrace, with its sweeping views of Oakland and San Francisco Bay. How she longed to behold tonight's sunset and Blue Hour, those enchanted minutes when daylight yielded to the night sky, from home.

"That's pretty," Soo-jung said, her eyes brightening above her mask.

She was looking at an opal pendant around Norma's neck. The pendant had slipped from beneath Norma's blue hospital robe. Blood squeezed out of her heart.

"You mean this?" Norma glanced at the opal as if she were only now noticing it. The afternoon light caught the iridescent threads shooting through the milky green.

"Yes," the nurse said, taking a step toward Norma's bed. "I don't think I've seen you wear that necklace before. Is it new?"

"I've had this pendant for years."

"Pretty," the nurse said. "Modest but classy, you know? Where did you get it?"

"I don't remember," Norma said. She picked up her magazine. "Thank you, Soo-jung."

The nurse nodded and left. This was the trouble with hospitals and rehab centers; all the patients wore the same blue robes, must all look alike to the nurses. Otherwise, Soo-jung would have known who Norma was, wouldn't have dared be so forward with her. The opal was indeed a gift—from Kevin. She'd had Julie bring the pendant to her from home. If Charles saw the opal, he'd be sure to gush over the jewel with even more cloying insistence than Soo-jung had. He should be here any minute for his usual Sunday visit. She slipped the pendant beneath her robe and reached for the TV remote.

Her ears pricked to Charles's voice echoing down the hall. He must be saying hello to the nurse behind the front desk. By now Charles was no doubt on a first-name basis with all the floor nurses. That was the real estate salesman in him. The nurse, most likely, was also taking note of Charles, admiring his square build, his welcoming smile, the dimple in his left cheek. Aside from traces of gray in his wavy brown hair, some wrinkles around his large dark eyes, he remained as striking as ever. But if Charles ever noticed the way women—and some men—looked at him, he never showed it. He was nothing like the man he resembled: his father, Robert. Otherwise, Charles would be doing more than saying hi to those nurses.

Charles appeared at her doorway with his usual radiant smile, clutching a glossy ivory-colored shopping bag. A shopping bag? What was Charles planning to spring on her now? She leaned against the crunching pillows. The TV was turned to the sports channel, showing a championship pool game.

"Hiya, Mom." Charles's voice was as insistently cheerful as his white polo shirt and AstroTurf-green golf pants—clothes his wife, Debra, must have ordered for him from some catalogue. "How's it going?"

"Going nowhere, that's the problem." She lowered the TV volume.

"More candy from Japan?" Charles's eyes strayed to the magenta foil wrapping of an opened chocolate bar on the nightstand.

"South America this time. Chocolate with chili peppers, courtesy of your Aunt Julie." Norma arranged the collar of her robe, making sure the pendant's chain was concealed. "She came home from Ecuador two days ago. Now she's talking about going to Australia next year."

"What's in Australia?" Charles gave a surprised smile.

"Two Australian women she met on the Galápagos tour. They want her to meet them at the Great Barrier Reef. Now that they're experts at snorkeling. They've also talked her into going skydiving."

"Aunt Julie's going *skydiving*?" Charles's smile went from surprise to astonishment.

"Your late Uncle Phil had wanted to go skydiving this year

for his birthday," Norma said. "Turns out these Australian friends had gone skydiving in February—summertime for them—and loved it. Now your aunt wants to go, as a tribute to your uncle."

"Ecuador, Australia, skydiving. *Man*." Charles settled into the chair, the shopping bag in his lap. "Aunt Julie won't go through with it, will she?"

"Probably not. You know how scattered your aunt can be." Norma felt a moment's irritation at Charles, despite her own doubts about Julie's skydiving plans. "I bet by next week she'll forget all about it."

"Well," Charles said airily, "I'm glad to hear Aunt Julie is moving forward with her life."

"Did Maria have her ultrasound appointment?" Norma held in her disapproval of Charles's slick tone. He should be making more of an effort to keep tabs on his aunt, considering Phil had died only this January.

"She did. But sorry, Mom," Charles said, taking the chocolate bar from the nightstand and holding it out to read the Spanish on the wrapper, "she and Jonah told the doctors they don't want to know the gender until the baby's born."

"For the love of humanity, what are those children thinking?" After two sons and three grandsons, she itched for her first great-grandchild to be a girl. She watched Charles puzzling over the chocolate wrapper. "Take that home if you want. I thought the wasabi Kit Kats Olivia sent me were strong. What you have in your hands is inedible."

"Oh, Mom, stop exaggerating." Charles smiled as he broke off a stamp-sized square and popped it into his mouth. Instantly his eyes watered, and his face went red. Still, he chewed and swallowed. "*Man*."

"The people at the store in Quito told your aunt it was one of their milder chocolate bars."

"If this is mild, then a hot one must have you writhing on the floor." Charles blew out of his mouth and leaned back in the chair to catch his breath. Once he collected himself, he held up the shopping bag. "I brought you a present."

He pulled from the bag a flat rectangular box wrapped in yellow-and-blue striped paper. His smile widened with anxious cheer. She took the box from him. The box, though not much larger than a folded newspaper, felt heavy in her hands. What could he have bought her? And why would Charles think of buying her something now, when she'd be home in less than a week? She set the box on her lap and hesitated.

"Should I open it?"

"If you want."

Studied indifference was in his tone. Charles was terrible at studied indifference. Whatever gift awaited her was more likely to benefit him, not her. She ripped open the wrapping. Inside the box, nestled in a cloud of powder-blue tissue paper, sat a laptop. She stared at her distorted reflection on the laptop's pearl-white surface.

"I know you're no fan of computers," he said. "But I thought you could use one while you're recovering at home."

"Looks state-of-the-art," she said in a hesitant voice, looking up at him. "I hope this didn't cost too much."

"I had store credit." Charles shifted to pull out his phone from his front pocket. "You can use the laptop here, assuming the rehab center has Wi-Fi."

"What's Wi-Fi?" Not that she had the slightest interest in learning the answer to this question.

"Oh good, they *do* have Wi-Fi." Charles was looking down at his phone, pressing buttons. "I need the password, though. Let me ask the nurse."

"Ask them later."

"I'll only be a couple minutes," Charles said, already rising from the chair.

"Just stay," she said, her patience running thin, and Charles sat down. On the TV, a young man in a black tracksuit surveyed his options on the pool table. "Come on, kiddo, that 13-ball is begging to be hit."

"You have Wi-Fi set up at home, you know," he said a couple of minutes later.

"I don't even know what Wi-Fi is." Norma was watching the TV, half listening.

"Wi-Fi is how you connect to the internet," Charles said, in a voice *he* would describe as patient, but to *her* ears came across as condescending. "Wi-Fi comes as part of your cable package."

"A waste of money, cable." She thought of the phone calls she would make, the letters she would write, the Blue Hours she would witness instead of squandering her time to vapid television programming. She'd stared at enough television here.

"You could play online bridge with your friends," Charles said, talking over her. "Right from your lounge chair."

"Bridge only makes sense in person." She glanced at the birds of paradise on the table, the glowing orange Campari bottle.

"All your friends overseas must have email." Charles spoke as if he'd anticipated her answer about online bridge. "You'll never have to step foot in a post office again."

"Email is no substitute for a written letter." She longed to sit at the circular table in her sitting room, feel the sweep of her blue-enameled pen against personalized stationery paper.

"Email has its uses." Charles glanced at the laptop. "If I set you up with Wi-Fi, I could create an email address for you today."

"Maybe later," she said, renewing her focus on the television.

For the next half hour, they watched the pool game in silence. Now and then, she made a comment, or he asked her a question about strategy. The player in the tracksuit didn't look much older than Charles had been when she'd started giving him and Kevin pool lessons. The billiard game finished, switched to a golf game. She reached for a magazine and settled it on her lap.

"So, Mom," he said in an offhand voice, his eyes fixed on the golfers, "what did you think of that brochure?"

"What brochure?" A zinging sensation went up her leg with the pin in it.

"You know what brochure." Charles gave her a sideways look with a knowing smile.

"Haven't looked at it," she said, turning a magazine page.

"Aw, man. Really?"

She looked up. A hurt look appeared on his face—he'd switched off his smile as if switching off a lamp.

"I'm not ready to move," she said, her tone matter-of-fact.

"But you don't use half the space in that house. The extra bedrooms upstairs. The home gym. Dad's old study with his Africa carvings gathering dust."

"One of those bedrooms is my sewing room," she answered, an edge in her tone. "I hold bridge parties in your father's old study. The cleaners dust those carvings once a week."

"Then there's Kevin's bedroom." Charles's voice was low. "What are you using *that* for?"

"For guests." The sound of Charles saying Kevin's name out loud sent a jolt through her. She tightened her hold on the magazine.

"No guest has slept in Kevin's room since he moved out." Charles sat up in the chair. "That room is exactly the way he left it twenty-five years ago. His bed. His furniture. Magic's old cat scratcher. What are you thinking, Mom? That Kevin's coming back?"

"Of course I don't think that." A burning sensation ran across her chest. "How *is* Kevin, anyway? Have you talked with him recently?"

A futile question. One that she wouldn't have asked if she weren't so incensed. Charles looked at the TV, his expression hardening. A man in a blue baseball cap tapped a putt into a hole. She reached for the remote and switched off the TV, forcing him to look at her.

"Even if I knew where Kevin was," he said with a shamefaced look, "he wouldn't want me telling you."

"Then you know where Kevin is."

"I didn't say that."

"Charlie, I almost died." She leaned forward, her voice sharp and imploring. "How would you like to pass away without ever knowing what happened to one of your own sons?"

Silence. Norma reached for her magazine, stared at a random page. A reedy young woman in a plaid bikini top and pink linen maxi skirt pouted on a sailboat in turquoise water, looking as if she'd never know hardship in her life. What Norma would give to join that model now, to slide into the fantasy of that photo. To think she had looked forward to spending more time with Charles once she returned home. And all he wanted was to manage her, tuck her away. If this accident had taught her anything, it was that she could trust only herself.

"I'd better be going," he said, glancing at the wall clock.

"Thank you for the visit," she said primly, flipping a magazine page.

"I'll come Wednesday." Charles rose from the chair. "And—if you have a chance—maybe take a moment to look at that brochure."

"Tell me something," Norma said, a thought occurring to her. She put down the magazine. "Does that nursing home have a website?"

"Probably," Charles said in an offhand tone, ringing with fraudulence.

"And is that the reason why you bought me that toy over there?" She looked at the laptop in disgust. "Not for me to play bridge with friends. But for me to look up that nursing home online?"

"It's not a nursing home," he said peevishly.

"See you Wednesday, Charles." And she picked up her magazine, withdrawing into the refuge of its pages.

She pretended to read until she was sure Charles had left. Her chest felt as if it would cave in. She reached for her heart pills in the top drawer of her nightstand and took two without a sip of water. The doctors hadn't wanted to give her this prescription, saying they couldn't determine the cause of her chest pains. What did they know?

A room at a nursing home would be as small and sterile as this one. Her world diminished to four drab walls. A droning television bolted to the wall across from her bed. Fading light through window slats. The sky no wider than the view she had here. And Norma left unattended, wondering what had happened to her younger son.

She wouldn't be thinking about nursing homes—or Kevin— if that idiot in the other car hadn't plowed into her. Before the accident, Kevin's absence had receded to the background, a ragged thread in the fabric of her busy life. She couldn't have known that her existence, one she'd built and curated over decades, could fall apart as instantly as a car crashing into her. But to hell with what Charles wanted. She was going home Friday. She'd show *him*.

CHAPTER 2

SOUVENIRS

JULIE PONTONE JUMPED from her kitchen chair and rushed to the window at the sound of footsteps going down the front stairs of her back unit. The cockatiels stirred in their cage. Down in the yard, her tenant, Alex, reached up to pluck a lemon from her ancient lemon tree. She hadn't seen him since she'd come home from Ecuador. The wall clock by the fridge read a few minutes past ten. He must not have landed a job yet. Her idea might work after all.

Pratyush, Alex's husband, had left for his job a couple of hours ago. Now was as good a time as any for her to give Alex and Pratyush the gifts she'd brought from Ecuador. And ask Alex if he might have the time to take on a certain assignment, to take care of a certain older sister recovering from a certain car accident. Assuming he said yes—and why wouldn't he, since he was still out of work?—she'd be able to pitch the idea to Norma this afternoon. Norma needed a home nurse, whether she wanted to admit that or not.

★

The scent of baking wafted down to her as she climbed the steps of the rental unit. Alex's baking reminded her of her nephew Kevin. As a little boy, Kevin had loved baking with her whenever she and Phil babysat him. He used to say that he planned to live in Uncle Phil and Aunt Julie's rental unit when he grew up. With Alex, Julie had a sense of what Kevin might have been like as a neighbor.

"Anyone home?" she called into the house, peering through the screen door.

"Hey, Julie! Welcome home!" Alex's voice came from the direction of the kitchen.

The sound of the oven door opening and closing, the clatter of a plate on a counter. Alex came to the screen door and opened it, a smartphone in one hand, a kitchen timer in the other, a blue-checked tea cloth slung over his shoulder. He was smiling as usual, but he was slightly out of breath, looking stressed. He'd never say that now was not a good time.

"I can stop by later," she said, drawing back.

"No, come in," Alex said, opening the door further.

She followed Alex through the door and into the unit's small but cozy living room. The lemony aroma was as merry as the sunlight slanting through the picture window. On the coffee table sat an open laptop playing jazz music. She often imagined Alex and Pratyush curled up together, spending the kind of quiet evening she used to enjoy with Phil.

"I came to bring you and Pratyush a couple of things I picked up in Ecuador," she said, unstrapping her canvas bag from her shoulder. "To thank you for looking after Rick and Ilsa."

"We only gave them water and birdseed." Alex's cheeks flushed pink.

"I saw Pratyush in the driveway on my way out the door yesterday." Julie smiled. "He said you sat at my kitchen table every night for an hour."

"I didn't want them to be lonely," Alex said with a modest shrug.

She pulled out her first gift, a small carving of a blue-footed booby. She hadn't seen the carving since the store clerk on Santa Cruz Island had engulfed it in tape and cotton wadding. What did that carving look like again?

Alex put his cell phone on the coffee table, took the gift, and extracted the bird from its cotton shell. The carving was pure white save for the bird's feet, painted sky blue. Seeing the booby perched on Alex's outstretched palm, in the glow of his smile, made Julie glad she'd taken the trouble to bring the carving home.

"They call it ivory, but it's not," she said. "They carve all sorts of things from a tree nut that comes out white."

"I've always wanted to see a blue-footed booby," Alex said. He turned and placed the carving on the mantel of the unit's small fireplace, next to a raft of framed family pictures.

"You should watch them dive." Julie glanced up at the ceiling, reminiscing. "Like missiles from the sky. They'd fly a wide circle to pick up steam. Dive straight down and vanish into the water. Then they'd come to the surface, take off with a splash, and make the same circuit all over again. I could've watched them all day."

"And are their feet this blue?"

"Bluer, even."

"That must've been a sight to see."

Alex looked at the carving as if he wished the booby would take off and fly around the living room. Then he turned to her, beaming. The light caught his bare arms, his curly reddish hair.

"And this is for Pratyush," she said, reaching into her bag.

She brought out a magenta-wrapped chocolate bar and held it out. A warm glow spread inside her. She'd never have gone to Ecuador if Alex and Pratyush hadn't offered to keep an eye on the place. She should've brought home ten carvings, ten chocolate bars.

"I know you said Pratyush likes spicy things," she said, "but I hope this won't overwhelm him. I gave the same chocolate bar to my sister, and she says it's inedible."

"Nothing is too spicy for Pratyush." Alex took the chocolate bar and looked at her as if with new eyes. "Is that dress from Ecuador?"

"Sure is," she said, swishing the hem of her dark purple sundress, embroidered with orange and yellow flowers above the high waist.

"I'm so glad you didn't cancel that trip," Alex said with a gratified smile.

"I'm glad you talked me out of canceling," Julie said, flushing.

"How about your daughter? Did she have a good time too?"

"She didn't go." Julie darted her eyes away.

"Kate bailed?" Alex's smile faded. "Why?"

"She called me the night before I left for the airport." Her face grew warm. "Her husband came down with a cold or something."

"Oh." Alex must be thinking the same thing as she'd been thinking—that Kate had reached for an excuse to renege. Then his face brightened as he said, "Well, ain't that a shame for Kate. She missed out on those blue-footed boobies."

If Kate had gone with Julie on that vacation, she would've spent half her time calling home and posting selfies. She wouldn't have let Julie watch the boobies for as long as she had. All it took was for Alex to point this out. She should have asked Alex, not Kate, to take Phil's place on that trip.

The kitchen timer went off. Alex excused himself to pull cookies out of the oven. As soon as he was out of the room, she turned to examine the framed pictures crowding the fireplace mantel. The blue-footed booby sat next to a photo of an older woman with long russet hair at a restaurant table. Her warm smile radiated from the frame. Alex's mother. If Julie ever met this woman—and she hoped she would someday—she'd be sure to tell her how proud she must be to have Alex for a son.

"You're sure you can't stay for a cookie?" He held out the plate as he returned from the kitchen. "Lemon cardamom. Pratyush's mother's favorite."

"I have to run a few errands," Julie said with regret. "After that, I'm going to see my sister at the rehab center."

"Nice. How's Norma doing?"

"Growing crankier by the day, which means she's almost better," she said, noticing with approval that Alex had remembered Norma's name. He'd remembered Kate's name too.

"Any idea when they'll be releasing her?"

"Friday." Now was her chance to spring her idea on Alex. "But her house is awfully big, and I think she could use—"

Alex's smartphone buzzed on the coffee table. He put the plate of cookies on the table and snatched up the phone. She wasn't sure if she was annoyed or relieved at the interruption.

"It's Pratyush," Alex said. "This'll only take a second."

His voice, as he spoke to his husband, had a hushed intimacy to it. Phil used to use that voice with her. Perhaps she should step outside.

"Sorry about that." Alex turned off the phone and placed it on the mantel, his face flushed. "I'm waiting to hear any minute from that clinic downtown. I had my third interview with them on Friday. They said they'd be calling today."

"Exciting." Julie blinked and forced a smile.

"They've all but offered me the job," Alex said.

"That's wonderful." She spoke in as upbeat a voice as she could manage. "I'm so happy for you."

"Thanks." Alex gave a relieved smile. "This job search has dragged on long enough."

He led her into the kitchen, insisting she take a few cookies for Norma. The lemony aroma made her want to park herself on a kitchen chair and do nothing but gorge on cookies all day. But she had errands to run before going to the rehab center. She hated being late for her big sister.

So much for her grand plan for Norma to hire Alex. Maybe he'd be willing to work weekends? Let him land the job first, then she'd decide what to do.

But even if the job failed to pan out, Alex would eventually find work. Once that happened, she wouldn't see him anymore. No more saying hi to him on her way out the door. No more chatting with him in the driveway. If only Kevin lived in that rental unit. If only his childhood promise to be her neighbor had come true.

She went to the pet store to pick up birdseed for Rick and Ilsa. Then she drove up the winding streets to Norma's house to collect her mail. Her first trip to the house since returning from Ecuador. The turn onto Norma's narrow street—the scene of Norma's accident—brought Julie a routine sensation of dread. She turned into the driveway and stepped out of the car into heavy stillness.

Once inside, she deactivated Norma's burglar alarm and headed to the terrace, looking for Harry Winston. Harry was a large orange tabby cat who'd been hanging around Norma's house for the past few weeks. No collar. Friendly. Someone's lost cat. Julie hadn't seen Harry since before her trip. Had he found his way home? Or would he be out there?

Ah, there he was. The cat sat on the retaining wall of Norma's flagstone terrace, looking out on the city of Oakland like a king surveying his realm. The treats she'd bought on a whim at the pet store wouldn't go to waste after all. She reached into her bag and tapped on the glass with her knuckle.

At the sound of the tapping, Harry Winston leaped down from the wall and raced, meowing, to the sliding door. She slid open the door, careful not to let Harry sneak past her into the house. The purring cat rubbed his nose against her ankles as if he'd been waiting for her the whole time she was away. Poor Harry, all alone in the world.

She walked into Norma's air-conditioned room at the rehab center about an hour later. Norma sat propped up against a throne of pillows. Her black-framed cat-eye reading glasses sat low on her nose as she flipped through one of her bridge books. With their mother's large brown eyes and soft features, her electric-silver hair piled high above a blue headscarf, her little opal pendant around her neck, Norma looked as striking as ever, even in her hospital gown.

"You've come in time, my head hurts from reading," Norma said, looking up. She removed her glasses, opened her nightstand drawer, pulled out a sheet of paper, and held it out. "What do you think of this?"

Julie took the paper, a drawing of a young man in a dark green collared shirt and black apron. A sketch of a uniform, a server, most likely. Not Norma's drawing though—her own style was looser, more confident. She gave the paper back to Norma.

"Looks fine to me," she said in a hesitant voice. How was *she* supposed to know about these things?

"Diana dropped by this morning. Her son is opening a

new restaurant on Piedmont Avenue and wants my input on the waiters' outfits. I told him if the restaurant is dark enough, they might as well walk around in their underpants." Norma's eyes narrowed, taking in Julie's new dress. "You bought that in Ecuador, I presume."

"Yes, in Quito," Julie said, her tone modest. Was her dress, with its vibrant embroidered flowers, too boastful for this drab hospital room, too much a symbol of her freedom? She sat in the chair next to the bed and spread the dress over her two good knees. "They had the same design in pink, but I liked the purple better."

"You know how I feel about pink," Norma said with a faint look of disgust. "But pink or purple, that dress is too loose around the shoulders."

"I don't mind," Julie said. But now that Norma mentioned it, the right shoulder strap had begun to chafe her, always slipping down.

"I'll fix the dress once I'm home," Norma said.

"Aw, Norma, you have more important things to worry about than altering one of my dresses."

"I've been altering your clothes since you were in the eighth grade, Jules. No car accident is about to change that." Norma gave Julie an arch smile. "I still have your measurements from the time I altered that red dress of yours last year, so it won't be a problem."

No use in arguing. Besides, the faulty dress gave Norma an added incentive to leave rehab. Julie had been right to wear it. She pulled the September *Vogue* out of her canvas bag.

"This was lying on the floor beneath your mail slot," she said, holding out the magazine.

"Good, it came early. I have the August issue memorized." Norma took the magazine, glanced at the cover, and dropped it on the bed next to her. She glanced out the window and added, "It's a sunny day out there. Your feline friend, I presume, must have availed himself of my terrace today."

"Since you're asking, he did," Julie said, giving Norma a pert smile. "I was thinking I'd never see Harry Winston again after leaving for Ecuador, but there he was, waiting for me."

"For the love of humanity, Jules. Stop calling him Harry Winston."

But Norma wouldn't have asked about the cat if she wasn't interested in his welfare. Naming him after the renowned jeweler was having its effect. Couldn't push the matter too far or too fast, though. Julie pulled out the foil-wrapped plate from her bag.

"Lemon cardamom cookies," she said, lifting the foil. "My tenant baked them this morning."

"Alex, you mean." Norma leaned forward, perhaps to breathe in the plate's lemony aroma.

"You know Alex's name?"

"Of course. You mention him every time you visit."

Julie ignored this comment by plucking two tissues from the box on the nightstand and setting a cookie on each of them. Norma took one and bit into it. If Norma made the slightest criticism of one of Alex Wolsey's cookies, Julie would take the plate home and eat the rest of them herself.

"Lemon cardamom, not bad," Norma said. "They should make a Kit Kat out of that flavor."

"He's a physical therapy nurse, you know," Julie said and took a careful bite of her cookie.

"So you've told me." Norma put down her cookie onto the magazine. "Is he still looking for work?"

"He's expecting an offer any day now. I hope they hire him. He's been looking for a job—gosh, it must be six months already." Julie sighed. "I don't know how he maintains his positive attitude. I never see him not smiling. Never an unkind word. Must be the nature of a nurse."

"Must be." Norma leaned back against her pillow-throne. "I'd make a terrible nurse."

"Have you given any thought about hiring someone to help you once you're home?" Julie glanced at Norma.

"The rehab center will be sending someone to check in next week." Norma sat up and reached for her cookie.

"Maybe Alex could help you on weekends," Julie said, her voice careful. "He could probably use the extra income. And you wouldn't have to disturb Charles."

"Don't talk to me about Charles," Norma said in an undertone, putting her fingers to her forehead. "I had a less-than-ideal visit with him yesterday afternoon."

"Oh, no. What happened?" For weeks Norma had been talking about how helpful Charles had been since the accident.

"A difference of opinion," Norma said with a scowl. Her expression softened as she added, "He was duly bowled over by your plans to go skydiving. He doesn't think you'll go through with it."

"Neither do you." Julie recalled the look of mute skepticism Norma had given upon hearing of her plans.

"Now I *hope* you go skydiving, if only to prove Charles wrong," Norma said with an adamant look. "What is wrong with our children, Jules? They think we're too feeble to do anything."

"Goodness, Norma," Julie said, leaning forward. "What happened between you and Charles?"

"His latest brainstorm is for me to sell the house—" Norma said, pausing for dramatic effect, "—and move into a nursing home."

"Move into a *what*?" Julie stared at Norma, aghast. "But your whole life is in that house."

"Maybe you should call him so you can tell him that. He might listen to *you*." Norma gestured toward a white laptop sitting on the table by the window. "He bought me that toy over there. Wouldn't you know, the nursing home has a website."

"You won't move into a nursing home, will you?" Julie asked this as much for her own sake as for Norma's. Heaven help her if Kate and Olivia began nagging her to move into one of those places. They were already hinting that her current home, a fixer-upper she and Phil had bought for a song over fifty years ago, was becoming too much for her.

"Rest assured, dear sister," Norma said, scoffing in the regal way Julie knew well. "The doctor put a pin in my leg, not through my head."

"Do you really think you can manage all by yourself in that house?" Julie glanced with apprehension at Norma's knee underneath the bed sheet.

"The doctors wouldn't have agreed to discharge me otherwise," Norma said.

"I know, but—"

"The chair lift is in," Norma said. "A new refrigerator is installed in the upstairs sitting room. The meal service is set to start deliveries the day before I come home. Mark my words, Jules. In a few weeks I'll be able to finish that pool game I started on the morning of the accident. Those billiard balls haven't moved, correct?"

"Last time I checked," Julie said, nodding.

"Good," Norma said with grim confidence. "I'm finishing that game."

"I was thinking of dropping by on Saturday morning." Julie glanced at the opal around Norma's neck. "Maybe bring Alex with me. No harm in meeting him, right?"

"I'd hate to inconvenience your tenant on a Saturday.

Especially when I have no intention of hiring him." Norma reached for another cookie on the plate. "But, yes, please come and visit. You can give me that dress to alter."

"You may think this strange," Julie said, hardly believing she was about to say this. "But sometimes Alex reminds me of—Kevin."

A lightheadedness came over her. She finally dared to say what had been weighing on her mind for weeks. This must be what it felt like to jump out of a plane, to take a step into the unknown.

"How do you mean?" Norma frowned.

"I don't know if I can describe it in words," Julie said, glancing again at the opal and then looking away.

"Do they look like each other?"

"No, not really." Julie looked straight at Norma, to keep herself from looking at the pendant. "And Alex is quite a few years younger than Kevin. Somewhere in his thirties is my guess. But his can-do spirit makes me think of Kevin. He remembers little things, you know, to let me know he's thinking of me. Like culling the lemon tree. Making these cookies. Marmalade too. And volunteering to take care of the cockatiels while I was away. You know what I mean?"

"I wish I knew better, what you mean," Norma said, her voice low.

"Maybe it's because Alex lives in the back unit," Julie went on. "Remember how Kevin used to say he meant to live in that apartment one day?"

"Yes, Jules, I do remember." Norma let out an irritated breath through her nostrils. "But I'm sorry. The last person I need in my home is a man who reminds you of Kevin."

"Forget I said anything," Julie said, rubbing her sweaty palms against her dress.

"Thank you," Norma said and blinked a few times, as if to

regain her composure. "Jules, would you mind going into the top drawer of my nightstand and giving me my pills?"

Julie opened the drawer. A small orange pill bottle she'd never seen before sat on its side. When did Norma start taking these? Julie picked up the bottle and gave it to her.

"What are those pills for?" she asked as she watched Norma shake a white capsule into her hand.

"Heartburn," Norma said, and gave a wry look. "I shouldn't have had that second cookie."

"Do you want me to pour you a glass of water?" Julie made to rise from the chair.

"No need," Norma said. She opened the bottle and popped the capsule in her mouth as if it were a Tic Tac.

"I'm glad you're not moving to a nursing home," Julie said. "It's bad enough Phil is gone. I wouldn't know what to do if you weren't close by."

"Not to worry, Jules," Norma said with the casual reassurance Julie had depended on all her life. "I'll be in that house for the rest of my days."

She left Norma at three thirty. The sun felt hot after sitting for over an hour in that air conditioning. How insensitive she'd been, prattling on about Alex. But here in broad daylight, she realized why she'd hoped Norma would hire him. To keep a connection with him—especially now that he wouldn't be hanging around her own house once he took that job downtown.

The clinic must have offered that position to Alex by now. He wouldn't have wanted the weekend side job anyway. Time for her to let him go. She squinted up at the wide blue sky, fringed with gossamer clouds, and remembered how lucky she was to be able to see the horizon, to walk on two good legs.

CHAPTER 3

A PROJECT

ALL MONDAY LONG, Alex kept his phone within reaching distance. The clinic should be calling any second. By four o'clock he put his phone face down on the kitchen counter. The apartment felt unbearably hot. He slipped on his sandals and went outside to take a walk.

His feet were throbbing by the time he came home. He walked calmly, not to his phone but to the bedroom, to remove his sandals and massage his feet. The soles of both sandals were ground to sandpaper. He'd treat himself to new sandals with his first paycheck.

He walked into the kitchen, went to the counter, and turned the phone right side up. Five o'clock on the dot. No text. No voicemail. Not even a missed call message.

Pratyush would be home any minute. Alex needed to start dinner. He wasn't supposed to be making dinner tonight. He'd been imagining himself and Pratyush going to a restaurant to celebrate the new job. Celebrating more intimately later. Pratyush hadn't touched him since Alex had been laid off in February. Worries about money had robbed Pratyush of his mojo. A new pair of sandals wasn't the only postponement.

Alex brought out a Bosc pear and a package of spinach from the refrigerator. Perhaps the clinic would call tomorrow. And wouldn't he feel foolish if they did? All this despair for nothing. He'd already managed six months—six months!—without his husband's touch. One more day wouldn't kill him.

His cell phone sprang to life at twelve past five. The clinic's phone number glowed on the screen. A call this late could mean only one thing. He lifted the phone off the counter, cleared his throat, and brought the phone to his ear.

"Hello?" He stared out the window over the sink. His calm tone surprised him. "Yes, this is Alex Wolsey."

Apology and regret filled the woman's voice at the other end of the line—an admin from human resources, not the manager who had interviewed him. She said the staff had been impressed with his qualifications, his ten-plus years of experience, and his passion for nursing. All the same, they'd chosen the other candidate. In his most buoyant voice, Alex said he understood how hard their decision must have been. The woman agreed and thanked him. He thanked her for the call and gently laid the phone face down on the counter. Then he gazed out the window at the pillowy-white jasmine tumbling into the backyard over the neighbor's fence.

His mother had taught him this trick in his boyhood, to look for something beautiful to appreciate in times of stress or disappointment. He didn't need reminding that he'd endured far worse in his life. *It's only a job,* he imagined his mother saying to him. *You'll find another one. A better one. You'll see.*

But the rejection stung. Rejection was all he'd known since his layoff. And this dead end felt more wrenching than all the other ones put together. What had happened between Friday and today? What had changed their minds? His vision blurred. The jasmine thickened into a floating blob of white. Then he blinked and looked around the kitchen, as if he'd snapped awake from a coma.

Footsteps in the driveway reached him through the front screen door. A lock unbolted beneath Alex's feet, the sound of Pratyush putting away his bicycle in their little storage room below the rental unit. For a moment, Alex wished he'd never met Pratyush, to spare him the pain of letting him down. Then he turned to the sink and tore open the package of spinach, determined to compose himself before he had to face his husband.

Footsteps echoed up the front stairs. The screen door opened and closed. Alex focused on making salad as he listened to Pratyush enter the kitchen. A feeling of dread passed through him. He brought out a colander from under the sink and dumped spinach into it.

"You made cookies," Pratyush said, shuffling envelopes.

"I did," Alex said over his shoulder, above the sound of running water.

He turned off the water and cut the pear into chunks. This was stupid, not being able to look his own husband in the eye. He put down the colander and turned to face Pratyush.

Pratyush stood in the middle of the kitchen in a red pinstriped work shirt and blue jeans, his silver belt buckle comically oversized against his slight frame. He had two lemon cardamom cookies sticking out of his mouth. Large dark eyes, flat and expressionless. Pratyush at his most deadpan. Alex turned away and burst into laughter verging on tears, his hands gripping the counter edge.

In a moment, Pratyush was putting his arms around Alex,

no more cookies in his mouth. Alex turned to Pratyush and leaned into him, his head on Pratyush's shoulder. A wave of shame crested inside him. Comfort was so much easier to give than to receive.

"You know, don't you," he said. The warmth of Pratyush's body spread through him.

"I figured when you hadn't called," Pratyush said. He always had a simple explanation for knowing everything.

"I have other leads," Alex said, his eyes feeling heavy. "No need to worry."

No response. Pratyush's body tensed up against Alex's. Alex listened to the soft beating of Pratyush's heart.

"Richard Chen called me today," Pratyush murmured into Alex's ear.

"Richard Chen?" Alex said. The name sounded familiar but not in a good way. He pulled away from Pratyush and looked at him.

"The CFO at my old job," Pratyush said in a small, almost ashamed voice. "He wants to have lunch with me on Sunday. At a restaurant of my choosing."

"They want to hire you back?" A foul taste filled Alex's mouth.

"It would solve a lot of problems if they did."

"In exchange for new problems," Alex said, indignant. "Or should I say the same old problems."

"We can barely afford this place as it is." Pratyush darted his eyes around the kitchen as if he were expecting Julie to come knocking on the door at any moment, brandishing an eviction notice. "If I don't take my old job and you can't find one yourself, we'll have to move. Again."

"But you love your new job."

"Not enough to risk losing this place," Pratyush said with a pleading look. "We've only been here a year."

"Think of the day you walked out on them," Alex said, breaking his own rule of never bringing up that awful day. "Do you want to put yourself through that again? You can't go back to those people, Pratyush. They abused you."

"But if you don't find work soon?" A helpless look came into Pratyush's eyes.

"We'll manage," Alex said, his tone firm with resolve. "I'm the one who talked you into changing jobs. I'm the one who's going to fix it. Okay? I'm fixing it."

A rapping on the screen door. Alex held Pratyush's gaze then went to see who it was. Julie, of course. Her face showed through the screen. Alex's stomach flipped. How much had she overheard?

"I saw your front door open," she said, squinting at Alex in the sunlight, jingling her car keys. "I thought I'd pop in to ask if that clinic hired you."

"They called a few minutes ago," Alex said, half-opening the door. "Not good news, I'm afraid."

"You're kidding." Julie looked at him, slack-jawed.

"I wish I was," he said in a shrinking voice, giving his bravest smile. He remembered Julie's visit that morning. How could he have expressed such confidence then?

"I'll be darned," Julie said, her voice and expression turning thoughtful. "Hmm. Would you happen to have a moment to talk right now?"

"Pratyush is home," Alex said, glancing over his shoulder.

"He is?" Julie glanced at her tiny wristwatch. "Okay, no biggie."

"Are you sure?" He didn't want to seem rude, especially not now that he needed Julie's kindness more than ever. He opened the screen door wider. "Come on in."

Julie walked into the apartment, clutching her bag strap as if someone would snatch the bag from her. Her movements, along with her shock of teased white hair, made Alex think of one of her cockatiels: sharp-eyed, restless, jumping from perch to perch. She glanced around the living room as if to find a place on which to settle herself. What could she want now?

"Hello, Julie," Pratyush said, appearing in the living room doorway with his usual formal reticence. "Is that a new dress from Ecuador?"

"Yes, thank you for noticing," Julie said with a smile, using a less familiar tone than she'd used with Alex earlier. She adjusted one of the dress's straps, which had slipped.

"Julie brought us that carving," Alex said to Pratyush, nodding at the blue-footed booby figurine on the mantel. "And a spicy chocolate bar for you."

"Be careful, though," Julie said, wide-eyed. "I've been told it's too spicy to eat."

The chocolate bar sat on the coffee table, its reddish-purple foil wrapper glinting in the sun. Alex picked up the bar and held it out. Pratyush took the bar from Alex and scanned the Spanish-language label, then flashed Julie a smile. So rare for him to smile nowadays. He unwrapped the foil, broke off a square, and popped the chocolate into his mouth as if it were as harmless as a Hershey bar. Classic Pratyush.

"Thanks, Julie," Pratyush said, snapping off another square. "Even if it was Alex who did all the work."

"How long have you had this laptop?" Julie walked up to the laptop on the coffee table.

"Couple years," Alex said. The laptop's screen, in screensaver mode, showed yellow and purple bubbles, floating and fizzing.

"Is it easy to use?" Julie turned to look at Alex.

"Couldn't be easier." Alex wondered if Julie was thinking of buying one for herself and wanted help. He'd taught her how to use Phil's desktop not long after Phil's funeral in January.

"I'll be darned." Julie studied the floating bubbles then straightened up and darted her eyes around the room, apparently lost in thought. Alex swapped a look with Pratyush. In a moment, she collected herself and looked at Alex. "They were fools not to hire you. But I'm glad they didn't. Because I think I have a solution. A project that will help us both."

"What kind of project?" Alex swapped another glance with Pratyush.

"My sister." Julie drew herself up and clutched the bag closer to her. "They're releasing her from rehab on Friday."

An image of Julie's sister appeared in Alex's mind. A small, imperious-looking woman sitting in the front pew at Phil's funeral, now and then glancing over her shoulder as if she were expecting someone important to arrive. She'd worn a smart black dress with a double string of pearls and a black pillbox hat. Julie, sitting hunched and devastated next to her in barely any makeup, let alone jewelry, could have passed as the woman's personal assistant. Pratyush had whispered in Alex's ear that Julie's sister had managed to upstage Julie at her own husband's funeral. *She* was Julie's solution?

"I'm surprised the doctors would release your sister," Alex said, choosing his words carefully, "if she can't manage at home."

"Knowing Norma, she probably cajoled them into signing the release forms."

"But is that safe?" Alex already had visions of Norma heading straight to the emergency room within an hour of returning home.

"Trust me, she wouldn't do it if she wasn't sure she had everything under control," Julie said, nodding as if to convince herself. "That said, she's going to need help around the house. Nothing too strenuous. Help her with physical therapy. Run an errand or two. She's at her best when she's directing things…and she can't do that unless she has someone to direct. She'll go stir-crazy with no one to talk to in that house."

"Norma wants to go home," Alex said, "even if it means she might go stir-crazy?"

"She'll go more stir-crazy if she stays in rehab," Julie said. "Plus she misses the view from her terrace. Right now her only view is the building next door to the rehab center."

"I see." Alex glanced out his own front picture window at the lemon tree.

"She loved those cookies I brought her this afternoon," Julie said. "Positively gushed over them."

"Glad to hear it." Alex couldn't picture this older sister of Julie's gushing over anything. The glance Pratyush gave him showed he must be thinking the same thing.

"And her son gave her a laptop yesterday. Just like this one here. Close enough, anyway." Julie watched the floating yellow and purple bubbles. "If you could set up her new laptop, she'd thank you a million times over."

"Be happy to," Alex said, not quite following. If Norma's son had given her the laptop, shouldn't the son be the one to show her how to use it?

"She'd pay you, of course," Julie went on. "I couldn't give you a precise figure, but...she does have money, Alex."

Alex glanced at the floorboards and visualized Norma in her swanky black hat, her double string of pearls. A diva, no doubt. The worst kind of patient. But he'd nurse an opera season's worth of divas, if it meant saving Pratyush from returning to his old job.

"No harm in meeting her, I suppose." He glanced at Pratyush, then he looked at Julie and smiled. "Do you want to give me her number? I'll call her tomorrow and set up an interview."

"She doesn't like me sharing her number," Julie said with a

slight wince. "But I'm supposed to see her Saturday morning. How about you join me? I'm expected at her house at ten thirty."

"Ten thirty, no problem."

"Perfecto. I was thinking a casual visit, not a real job interview." Julie smiled, turned to leave, and then turned back. "And would you mind…baking something for her? Maybe not cookies, though. Something she can have for breakfast with coffee."

"Like blueberry muffins?" Alex thought of the muffins his mother used to bake on those special occasions in his childhood, when she had extra money for fresh mountain blueberries.

"Better yet, chocolate chip," Julie said. "My sister has two weaknesses: jewelry and chocolate. She calls chocolate the Correct Flavor."

"Chocolate chip muffins, no problem."

"I have an extra bag of chocolate chips in my cabinet. I'll bring them over tomorrow." Julie laid her hand on his forearm. "I'm so glad you're doing this, Alex! You have no idea how relieved I'd be to have you working for her."

"Sure thing," he said graciously. But he was already regretting agreeing to this foray to see Julie's sister.

"Your girlfriend saves the day," Pratyush said in a teasing voice, after Alex had closed the door on Julie. He popped another chocolate square in his mouth and wrapped the bar in its foil.

"If it'll keep you from saying yes to your old CFO." Alex turned from the door to face Pratyush.

"Doing odd jobs for Julie's sister is beneath you," Pratyush said, his expression turning serious.

"And the way your old job treated you isn't? Your old manager reaming you out in public isn't?"

A despairing look showed in Pratyush's eyes—the same look

he'd had on that awful November afternoon, nine months ago already, when he walked off his job. The day Alex had to leave his shift to pick him up at the BART station. He'd found Pratyush on a circular bench, staring straight ahead, looking at nothing. The first truly frightening day of their marriage.

"Hey, hey," Alex said, already regretting what he'd said. He walked up to Pratyush and put his arms around him. "I'm sorry. It's all right. But, babe, you haven't forgotten what happened, have you? Do you honestly think you have a future at that place?"

"Even if Julie's sister takes you on, it's only temporary," Pratyush murmured into Alex's ear. "Once she's better, then what?"

"I'll have a job before then," Alex said with confidence, even though, deep down, he was anything but confident of this out-come. "And if nothing comes along, I'll find something to make money. I'll walk dogs, do housesitting. Anything to stop you from returning to that godforsaken place."

He brushed the back of his finger against Pratyush's cheek. Pratyush's breath smelled of spicy chocolate. How badly he wanted to kiss Pratyush now, to have his husband again.

"It's free lunch at least." Pratyush pulled away from Alex, eyes on the floor.

"He could take you out to lunch every day for a year," Alex said. "Even then, it wouldn't be worth going back there."

"I'm seeing him on Sunday, Alex." Pratyush's face was set. "I can at least hear what he has to say."

"Fine. Hear him out," Alex said. "But if I land that gig with Julie's sister, you're not taking that job. Deal?"

Pratyush gave him a side eye, then reached for the chocolate bar. His way of saying there was no point in arguing until after Alex met Norma.

Alex's thoughts turned to the job he'd come so close to

landing, to the people he wouldn't be helping at that clinic. Those patients must be far needier than his landlady's wealthy sister. But what about the people at Pratyush's old job? The CFO? The rest of management? Those jerks had to be at least as rich as Julie's sister. Pratyush had squandered enough of his life on them. The folks at Pratyush's current job—a nonprofit that paired low-income children with tutors and mentors—were undoubtedly more worthy of his services. And had hired Pratyush in January, only two months after he'd quit the corporate job. Was that karma or what? Out of the question for him to leave that non-profit. It wasn't *his* fault that Alex had been laid off in February, so soon after Pratyush had switched jobs. Hopefully Julie's sister would take Alex on, long enough for him to land a new job, and that would end the discussion.

There, settled. Now, what was he doing before Julie showed up? That's right—the pears.

CHAPTER 4

SURPRISE VISITORS

IRST THING ON Saturday morning he ripped open Julie's bag of chocolate chips and poured them into a bowl. Gritty white coating covered the chips like fungus. He checked the bag wrapper. The chips had expired three years ago.

He slipped on his sandals and rushed to the corner market. Instead of chocolate chips, he bought two bars of artisanal baking chocolate that he'd melt and then chill to make homemade chocolate chunks. A small bag of demerara sugar tempted him. Was it worth the extra eight bucks to sprinkle demerara on the muffins? If it landed him the job, then yes.

The finished muffins came out of the oven at nine thirty. They were still warm when Julie rapped on the front screen door. He packed a few muffins on his best serving plate and left two for himself and Pratyush. For the celebration, later.

"Smells like chocolate," Julie said, her bag slung over her shoulder. She wore a blue flower-print sundress and a green kerchief around her neck. "How did those chips work out?"

"Perfect," Alex said with his best smile.

"Oh, dear," Julie said, looking down at Alex's feet.

"Something the matter?" He followed Julie's gaze to his toes sticking out of his sandals.

"You see, um," Julie said, her tone delicate. "My sister doesn't care much for a man in sandals."

Of course she wouldn't, the prima donna. Then again, his sandals did look gnarly. The torn strap, the fraying threads, the leather that had faded to the same color as those expired chocolate chips. He should've known better than to consider wearing them for his audience with Julie's sister.

"One second," he said, and slipped into the bedroom.

"So where are we headed this morning?" Alex settled into the passenger seat of Julie's Honda sedan.

"Up the hill," Julie said, fussing with her seat belt.

She drove down Claremont Avenue, crossed College. At every light he expected Julie to turn onto a side street and park in front of one of those charming Craftsman houses he'd hoped one day to share with Pratyush, but whose prices kept rising further out of reach. A few more winding roads upward, and Julie turned onto a narrow street shrouded by laurel trees whose branches dripped silver-green leaves. She turned into the sweep of a towering Spanish-style mansion with green-painted shutters and an oaken front door. A laurel tree's branches embraced the orange-tiled roof like a shawl. He climbed out of the car and took in first the house then the stillness. The air felt different up here—cleaner, fresher, smelling of lavender, bay leaves, and freshly turned earth.

Julie walked to the front door and unstrapped her bag. She plunked the bag down on the front step and rooted through it. Either she'd come here so many times that she'd grown used to the house's splendor, or, perhaps, she didn't want to give off airs. Was that her dark purple sundress from Ecuador sitting at the top of her bag? Was Julie planning to change into that dress when she got here?

"I remember dropping the housekey into my bag before we left," she said, half to Alex, half to herself. "It has to be in here somewhere."

Alex gazed up at the house. The massive front door, made of dark, deep-grained wood, was as imposing as a castle's entrance. Eight green-painted shutters glowed in the sun like a spider's eyes, watching him, waiting for him, daring him to walk inside. The other houses on the street—equally lavish, equally impos-ing—had a hushed quality in the mottled shade of the laurels, looking down on him as if they knew he had no business here.

"Oh, for Pete's sake." Julie brought out a key on a silver ring from the pocket of her sundress. "I'd slipped the key in my pocket at the last second, thinking I'd never find it in the bag."

She fitted the key into the front door lock and opened it with a stealthy air. Alex followed her into a cavernous front hall. Black-and-white tiles spread out in every direction. A glass chandelier loomed over the tiles, casting shards of muted light. A staircase, fitted with a chair lift, extended into the hall like the train of a wedding gown. The sheer size of the room filled him with an overwhelming sense of emptiness. And driving the emptiness home was an eight-foot-tall carved wooden giraffe by the wall next to the staircase, gazing across the tiles as if longing for the herd that had abandoned him.

"Yoo-hoo?" Julie called up the stairs, the key in her hand. "Norma? Are you awake?"

Her voice echoed off the walls, leaving a silence that hung like the dust motes hovering in the sunlight. A less than heartening sign. Alex felt an urge to leave this house before he took another step inside.

"She didn't make it home until late yesterday evening," Julie whispered to him, her voice apologetic. "She must be sleeping in."

"Maybe you should check on her?" Alex glanced at the walker sitting at the bottom step of the grand staircase, then looked up the stairs to the shadowy landing.

"Let's give her a few more minutes," Julie said. "I can show you the rest of the house."

She led him past the giraffe and down a long corridor whose walls bore framed sketches of women in designer dresses. In each drawing, only the dresses were depicted in color or detail—a pattern of daisies, a swishing orange skirt, the peacock-blue ruffles of a floor-length gown. Wearing these designs were simple female figures done in black chalk, faceless and featureless, mere ovals for heads. Even so, the models stood with heads at an angle, hands on hips or holding up a cigarette or phone receiver, twirling a skirt, or turned to reveal a plunging backline. Alex slowed his pace, studying them.

"These are something," he said, stopping in front of the drawing of the peacock-blue gown.

"What?" Julie turned around and looked at the picture. "Oh, these. Norma drew them."

"She did? Is she an artist?" He leaned forward to take a closer look at the gown. Somber gray stripes ringed the gown's hem—an intriguing choice, considering the vividness of the blue.

"Norma's a fashion designer. Or used to be. She sold her label and retired a few years ago." Julie turned pink and tittered. "Listen to me talk, 'she sold her label.' Who gets to say things like that? Every now and then I stop and think to myself, *Is that my own sister I'm talking about?*"

"Norma's famous?"

"Not super-duper Coco Chanel famous," Julie said, looking down the row of drawings. "But in the industry, she's well-known, I think. I'm not too familiar with that world. Have you ever heard of her?"

"No. But that doesn't mean anything." He gestured toward his brown Oxfords with a smile. "I mean, you saw my sandals. Do I look like I know anything about fashion?"

"She designed my wedding dress. My bridesmaids' dresses, too. And the prom suits for her son Kevin and his boyfriend—the suits that put her on the fashion map." Julie pointed to the last framed picture along the corridor. "That's the suit Norma had designed for her son's date."

Alex walked up to the picture. The faceless figure of a tall, thin man in a crimson suit and black shirt, his shoulders narrow, hands folded in front of him, returned Alex's gaze. From the hunched shoulders and folded hands, Alex sensed shyness in the boy, as shy as Alex himself had been in high school. Hmm. Norma had a son who took another boy to the prom. Was this the reason why Julie thought Alex would make an ideal nurse for Norma?

"I don't see the drawing of the suit Norma designed for her son." Alex peered down the corridor. The young man in the red suit was the only drawing featuring a male model. "Where is it?"

"Upstairs in her sitting room," Julie whispered. "I'll show you later."

She led him into a sprawling, high-ceilinged space that included a kitchen, dining room, and living area combined. Against one wall hung a row of carved African masks bearing frozen blank stares. A row of floor-to-ceiling windows took up the wall opposite these masks, giving out onto a flagstone terrace and a panoramic view of Oakland and San Francisco. Hard to believe a single person controlled all this territory. Mind-blowing. Indecent. He put the muffins on the black granite-topped kitchen island, crowded with get-well cards, a bottle of Campari, and a large basket filled with…were those Kit Kats? With Chinese or Japanese writing on the wrappers? Who gave Norma those?

At the far end of the living area, beyond an enormous leather L-shaped couch, sat a pool table. Colored balls lay scattered like discarded jewels on the table's emerald-green surface. The only evidence that a human being made use of this museum of a living area. He walked up to the table.

"Don't touch those billiard balls!" Julie said, coming up to him with a wide-eyed look. "Norma's in the middle of a game."

"Who's she playing?" Alex looked at the balls, wondering how a woman with a broken leg could manage a cue stick.

"No one," Julie said. "She likes to practice. She was in the middle of that game on the morning of her car accident. Nothing has been moved since. She wants to finish hitting those balls into the pockets as soon as she can stand on her own."

"I won't touch a thing," Alex said, edging away from the table and folding his hands behind his back. Norma would probably notice if he so much as breathed on those pool balls.

"You should've seen the parties Norma used to throw here." Julie rested her hand on the edge of the pool table and looked around as if conjuring those parties from memory.

"Looks like she could host half of Oakland in here," Alex said, turning to the stone fireplace behind the pool table, big enough to fit a witch's cauldron. His rental unit behind Julie's house must be less than half the size of this living area.

"She was active in philanthropy," Julie said, "so she was always throwing some benefit or fundraiser. Her and her husband, I mean."

"Oh. Her husband." Alex's eyes strayed to the fireplace

mantel, looking for a framed photo. Nothing there but a brass clock flanked by blue glass candlesticks, beneath a painting of daisies and doves sprouting from a crystal vase. It looked like a Chagall painting. Whoa, wait a sec. Was that original?

"Is that a Chagall?" he said, gazing up at the painting.

"Cha-*gall*, that's the guy's name," Julie said, slapping her thigh. "I'm always forgetting, and I don't dare ask Norma because I've asked her so many times. Yes, it's an honest-to-goodness Chagall. She and Robert bought it on their honeymoon. Six weeks driving around Europe, two weeks each in France, Spain, and Italy. She was pregnant with Charles the whole time. My mother and I both thought she had a screw loose."

"Sounds like a lot," Alex said, unable to imagine what a six-week vacation in Europe would cost. He and Pratyush had to scrimp to afford a week at a Sheraton on Maui for their own honeymoon.

"He passed away twenty-five years ago this September. I can't believe it's been that long." She sighed and looked out the wall of windows. "He died out there, as a matter of fact. On the terrace. Heart failure."

"Oh." Alex turned and looked out at the flagstones shining harmlessly in the sun.

"It happened while Norma was hosting one of her bridge parties," she said, her voice hushed. "I was here when he died."

"Yeesh," Alex said, eyes on the flagstones.

"We were all in the study. Norma goes to check on dessert while someone deals. Five minutes later she comes into the room, sits down across from me, arranges her cards, bids one heart. Next thing I know, blue police lights are streaking into the room. And then Norma rises from her chair and tells us Robert is dead."

She peered out the window as if she thought her brother-in-law was still out there, slumped over in one of the patio chairs.

A shiver passed through Alex. He gazed at the array of billiard balls gleaming in the field of soft green fabric.

"My stepfather liked to play pool," he said gingerly. "He taught me how to play while I was a teenager."

"You had a pool table growing up?"

"The bar down the road from our house had one." He forced a laugh. "We'd go every Friday."

"The bar let you in, even though you were only a teenager?"

"The pool table was in a game room next to the barroom. The game room had its own entrance. They'd let me stay so long as I used the game room entrance and stayed out of the bar itself. Of course, that didn't stop me from driving us home if my stepdad got too drunk."

"Did you have a driver's license?" Julie looked astounded.

"License? Please. For a while I wasn't even old enough to have a permit," he said with a shrug and a smile. "Our house was three minutes away. Better an underaged driver than a drunk driver, right?"

A funny feeling passed over him, the way it always did whenever he recounted that memory. But it was true. The fourteen-year-old he was talking about, the one steering his stepfather's Oldsmobile in darkness, really had been him.

"Were you any good at pool?" Julie glanced at the billiard balls.

"Good enough for my stepfather." Alex remembered the relief he used to feel every time he sank a shot—and every time he pulled into their driveway afterward. "I must be godawful now."

"Maybe Norma could teach you some pointers."

"You think she'd go for that?" Alex asked, less than enthusiastic about the idea. He'd rather stick to nursing.

"Couldn't hurt to ask her. She's always complaining she has no real competition."

Alex had let his stepfather teach him pool to preserve the peace at home and to keep a roof over his and his mother's heads. This time around, he'd be playing pool not for his mother's sake, but for Pratyush's. He could think of worse ways to save Pratyush from falling into the clutches of his old employer.

The meowing of a cat on the other side of the windows shook him out of this memory. On the terrace, a long-haired orange tabby cat peered through the glass, his eyes expectant. Alex smiled and walked up to the window.

"Looks like we have a visitor," he said.

"That's Harry Winston." Julie walked up to the window and stood next to him.

"Hi, Harry," he said, squatting down. The cat writhed around on his back, exposing an expansive belly. "Whose cat is he?"

"No one's." Julie's voice touched on mournfulness.

"Then how do you know his name is Harry Winston?"

"Harry Winston is the name I gave him." Julie looked at the cat with sad eyes. "I was hoping Norma would find the name cute and adopt him."

"Since Norma has a weakness for jewelry," Alex said, looking with a smile at Harry Winston. He wanted to tap on the window but that would leave fingerprints. "I've always wanted a cat. Pratyush is allergic, though."

"Jules?" The groggy but commanding voice of Norma McKinsey boomed through the room. "Is that you?"

Julie gave Alex an apprehensive look and walked to an intercom next to the sliding door. He stood up with a sinking feeling in his stomach. Oh, good God—Norma had no idea that he was coming. Julie must've lied to him, or at least stretched the truth.

"Hiya, Norma," Julie said with forced merriment.

"Who are you talking to down there?"

"A friend." Julie turned to Alex with a disingenuous,

bright-eyed look of optimism, raising her finger as if to say, *Everything's okay, this won't take more than a minute.*

"What friend?"

"My neighbor."

"The nurse?"

"Yes, him." No high spirits in Julie's voice now. She turned her back to Alex.

"What did I tell you about bringing him here?" Norma's voice was thin with impatience.

"Norma, please."

"Oh, Julie. For the love of humanity."

Silence. Julie let go of the intercom and looked at Alex with a what-can-you-do shrug. He looked out the window at Harry Winston, his cheeks going warm.

"How about if I come upstairs for a few minutes," Julie said into the intercom.

A second or two of silence. Then: "No need."

"But then you'll be here by yourself all day."

"Charles is coming later."

"But he brought you home last night."

"He's coming again," Norma said, her voice clipped.

"Okay," Julie said. "Call you tomorrow."

Julie must be thinking the same thing as Alex was—that Norma had lied to rid herself of them. The orange cat put his paws up on the glass.

"Julie?" Eerie, the way Norma's disembodied voice issued from the intercom. "Are you still there?"

"Yes, Norma, right here." A hopeful look appeared on Julie's face.

"Did you bring the dress?"

"It's in my bag."

"Drape it over one of the dining chairs." Norma's tone was

less harsh now, one might even say sisterly. "I'll have alterations done in a couple days."

✳

No birds sang as they left the house. No wind rustled the leaves of the laurel tree. The sky above the tree line looked bleached in the searing sun. The plate of muffins felt heavy in Alex's arms. The smell of melting chocolate and demerara sugar rose to his nostrils, making him sick. How was he going to explain all this to Pratyush? Fatigue washed over him. He leaned against Julie's car.

"Alex?" Julie walked around the car and touched his arm. "Are you okay?"

"I think I forgot where I was for a moment." He snapped to attention and trained his gaze on the laurel leaves. Green and silver streamers, hanging limply against pale blue.

"You have no idea how upset I am with my sister right now," Julie said. "She'd take such a shine to you, if she gave you a chance."

"You did everything you could." He willed himself not to be angry with Julie for wasting his time, for giving him hope.

"But that's the thing, Alex. I'm not sure if I did do everything." Julie turned and looked up, frowning, at the house, a calculating look in her eyes. "Sometimes it takes some massaging for my sister to see sense."

Her cunning expression made clear that she was concocting a new stratagem. Good Lord. Now what?

"I have an idea." Julie turned to him and held out her hands. "Give me those muffins."

"Julie, it's been a long morning."

"You can't give up now," she said, grasping the edge of the plate with both hands. "Trust me when I tell you all isn't lost. All you have to do is persist."

"Persist?" Alex said, his face burning in the punishing sun. "She's refusing to see me."

"That's where the muffins come in," Julie said. "Trust me on this."

He let her take the plate and go inside. A car whooshed by and disappeared around the corner. Eerie silence. No one else around. He gazed up at Norma's house. Silent. Forbidding. Would he even want to work here?

Then the front door opened, and out came Julie. No muffins. No plate. She held in her hands the wadded-up foil that Alex had used to cover the plate. The confidence in her smile as she strode toward Alex sent a wave of uneasiness through him. Her expression was more than self-satisfied, almost smug, like a teenager who'd swiped a packet of cigarettes from the corner store.

"What did you do?" was all he could think of saying.

"Get in the car," she whispered. She held out the wad of foil.

"Where's my plate?" He took the foil wad, his eyes darting to the front door.

"On her dining table, where she can't miss it." She beamed at him. "Your muffins are sitting beneath the crystal dome of Norma's best cake dish. They look like works of *art*."

"Pratyush's mother gave me that plate." Alex swallowed, holding in a rising sense of panic. "She'll be disappointed if I lose it."

"You won't lose your plate," Julie said with a wave of her hand.

"Can't you transfer the muffins onto one of Norma's plates?"

"But that would defeat the purpose." Julie stared at him.

"What purpose are you talking about?"

"*Your* purpose, Alex," Julie said with a significant nod and the trace of an impish smile. She pointed at his chest and added, "*You're* coming here tomorrow to retrieve your plate. And that won't be your *only* errand."

"It won't? What do you mean?" Alex looked at Julie, psyching himself up for her answer.

"I'll explain in the car," she said, opening the driver's side door. "We're going to the pet store."

"The pet store?" Alex opened the passenger side door. "Why are we—"

"And we don't have a moment to lose," Julie said, cutting him off. "My sister is still moving slowly, and has everything she needs to be comfortable in her sitting room. I bet she'll be in that room for a while longer. And we have a much better chance of pulling this off if I can make it back here and leave again *before* she comes downstairs."

"Pull *what* off?" Alex stared at her, his head pounding.

"You'll see."

And Julie's smile widened as she got in the car.

CHAPTER 5
AN EVENING WITH HARRY

NORMA STOOD WITH her walker, inching her way from the intercom back to the circular table in the center of her sitting room, where she'd been writing thank-you cards. A noise came from downstairs. A door opening and closing. The front door, most likely. Julie must have returned for some reason. Was the nurse with her? If so, would they come upstairs and berate Norma for her rudeness? She stood stock-still, listening for footsteps heading toward her.

He's only a nurse, Mom. What are you so afraid of?

No footsteps came. The front door closed again. A car revved up and drove off. Silence settled over the house. Norma composed herself and completed her journey to the table.

★

Forty minutes later, the front door opened and closed again, right as she was finishing writing the last of her thank-you cards. The food-service people? Charles? She leaned forward, straining to listen. The footsteps downstairs were stealthy. Julie's footsteps. Jules, again? What would compel her to return to the house for a second time?

You're asking me, Mom? She's your sister, not mine.

She traced her finger along her pen, listening to Julie putter around the house. Julie's footsteps seemed to be coming from directly below her. Which room? The weight room? The laundry room? Kevin's old bedroom? What business would Julie have in Kevin's bedroom? Norma reached for her walker and hoisted herself up with a groan.

The front door opened and closed before she could make it to the intercom. Then came the sound of a car driving off. Silence. She stood in the middle of the sitting room, clenching her teeth. Only Julie could do this to her, make her stand flummoxed like this. She hobbled back to the circular table.

About twenty minutes later, a sound drifted up from down-stairs. Not footsteps this time. More like a displacement of air. A spirit passing through the walls. An intruder must have sneaked into the house. Was now making his way toward her. She put down her pen and reached for her heart pills, listening. The backs of her wrists prickled. She swallowed a pill and looked at her phone on the escritoire across the room, distressingly out of reach.

Come on, Mom. Your house has been empty all summer. Why would the bad guys wait to break in now?

A hearty meow sounded from the corridor. Then a large orange tabby cat appeared at the doorway, his green eyes round and yearning. Her intruder. Her face grew warm with exasperation.

"Good afternoon, sir." She spoke with offended dignity. "Mr. Winston, I presume."

The cat, apparently mistaking her tone for friendliness, trot-ted up to her with a blithe look and a twitching tail. He made to jump into her lap. She gasped, "Don't you dare," and thrust out her hands. The cat settled for leaping onto the table and tiptoeing along the edge, eyes fixed on her lap. This cat was determined, this Harry Winston.

No, she shouldn't call him that. *Harry Winston* was Julie's sobriquet for him. The cat was only an animal. One who didn't belong here. And who had to leave this house. At once. She pulled herself up on the walker, struggled her way to the escritoire, and sat on the swivel chair. Once she regained her poise, she reached for the phone and dialed Julie.

"Hiya, Norma!" Julie spoke with bogus exuberance. "Feeling better?"

"An orange cat," Norma said without preamble, "is taking up space on my sitting room table."

"Oh—oh, dear." Julie's fake-sounding delight shifted to fake-sounding concern. "You see, I went to water the geraniums as I was leaving earlier. When I opened the sliding door to go back inside, Harry Winston popped up out of nowhere and ran— *vroom*—into the house, and disappeared."

"For the love of humanity, Jules." Norma swiveled in her chair away from the cat, unable to tolerate him staring at her. "How long did it take you to prepare that speech?"

"But that's what *happened*." Julie's tone was defiant but trembly. Not remotely convincing.

"How is the cat supposed to go outside again?" Norma laid a hand on her tender knee.

"Maybe you can let Harry out yourself. Later."

"You expect me to pick up a cat and manage a walker at the same time?" Norma's hand tightened around the phone receiver as she swiveled to face the cat again. He was now reclining across the table, paws hanging off the edge, like Cleopatra floating down the Nile.

"Oh, dear," Julie said. "I didn't think of that."

"Sure you didn't," Norma said acidly. "You need to drive over here now and let him out yourself."

"I can't leave the stove," Julie said, her tone pleading. "I'm making cookies for tomorrow's coffee hour at church."

"Then when can you come?"

"Maybe tomorrow afternoon?"

"Tomorrow afternoon!"

Norma's shout spooked the cat off the writing table, leading him to jump onto the credenza beneath the picture window. He sniffed around the coffee maker and poked his nose in Norma's dirty coffee mug. She watched him with burgeoning antipathy. Soon the cat lost interest in the mug, suddenly captivated by a moth on the other side of the window. This sitting room must be an amusement park for him.

"Maybe Charles can let the cat out," Julie said in a rush of breath.

"Charles?" Norma said sharply. "You want me to ask Charles to come all the way here, all because of a cat?"

"But Charles is coming to see you later." The innocence in Julie's voice held an edge to it. "Isn't that what you'd said over the intercom?"

"Well, he isn't. He called ten minutes ago to say he can't make it." Norma's voice quivered with anger—at Julie for catching her in a lie, and at herself for being caught. "For the love of humanity, Julie. Just swing by and let the cat out."

"But I *can't*. After I make the cookies, I'm expected at a friend's house for dinner. Then, when I get home, I'm supposed to call Olivia in Japan. It'll be the middle of the day over there. I haven't talked with her since I came home from Ecuador."

"Fine then," Norma said, her tone sharp. "Tomorrow."

"Church starts at nine," Julie said. "Coffee hour is after

services. I already promised to help clean up afterward. So I don't think I can come any earlier than one o'clock—"

The cat put his paws up on the glass, eyes fixed on the moth. Then he caught sight of the dangling cord of the Venetian blinds and took a swipe. The blinds were only halfway down.

"Hey," Norma snapped. "Cut that out."

"Cut what out?" Julie said.

"Not you." Norma put a hand to her forehead. "Your friend, the cat. He's leaving paw prints on my picture window."

"I'll come as soon as I can tomorrow afternoon. Promise."

"How is he supposed to manage in the house until then?" Norma's voice rose with her indignation. "Without food? Without water? Without a litter box?"

"No need to worry about that." Julie's tone strained for reassurance. "I brought some supplies from the pet store."

"You *what*?"

The cat, alarmed by Norma's shout, dashed off the credenza, but not before snagging a claw on the cord and yanking it. Norma barely had time to register this when the blinds came crashing down, knocking over the coffee maker and breaking the carafe against the mini refrigerator. She flinched and squinched her eyes shut, then opened them. Sunshine poured through the naked picture window. Glass shards spread out on the eggshell-colored rug. The blinds lay in a heap on the carpet. The cat pulled and tugged and disengaged his claw from the cord, and then he was gone in a flash, racing out of the room like an orange bolt of lightning.

"What was that?" Julie cried.

"That was the cat pulling down my blinds and breaking my brand-new coffeepot!" Norma blinked in the sun.

"You're kidding! Oh, no." This time, Julie's voice sounded genuinely dismayed. "I'm so sorry, Norma. Let me take care of this for you. I'll come tomorrow as soon as I can. Unless..."

"Unless what?" Norma shaded her eyes, thinking, *Here it comes.*

"I could send someone to come earlier."

The hint in Julie's tone was unmistakable. A tightness came into Norma's chest, a fist closing over her heart. Her heart pills sat on the circular table, the bottle glowing orange in the sun.

"Who do you have in mind?" Norma kept her tone calm and rational, even as she seethed. "Your tenant?"

"Alex is often on his porch or in the backyard when I leave for church." Julie spoke as if put off by Norma's dismissive use of the term *tenant.* "I could give him your house key. He can come first thing, and be in and out in no time."

"For the love of humanity." The wall clock read two in the afternoon, but already Norma wanted to crawl into bed. "You let the cat inside on purpose so your tenant could come and shoo him out?"

"Norma Caroline, that is the most *ridiculous* thing I have ever heard."

But Julie's lack of conviction all but told Norma otherwise. So this was Julie's plan, typical in its staggering inanity. Norma yanked open a desk drawer and reached for her spare sunglasses, white with square frames, an accessory she'd never wear in public.

"All right then," Norma said. "You can stop by when you're home from church tomorrow."

"Those coffee hours sometimes run late," Julie said. "You're sure you don't want Alex to come earlier in the day?"

"I don't. I mean—I don't know." Norma slipped on the sunglasses. "Maybe I can figure out a way to lure the cat out myself. Let me think about it."

Her heart was buzzing by the time she finished with Julie. If there was ever a time she needed a second pill, it was now. She went to the writing table with her walker, popped open the bottle, and swallowed a pill without a swig of water.

She looked around the room, contemplating what she should do next. She could always call Charles, ask him to track down and eject the cat. But Charles would likely take one look at the ruined blinds and the broken carafe and lecture her that this was proof the house was too big for her. The cleaners would be coming on Tuesday—they could clean up the glass and maybe shampoo the carpet. And with luck, she could have someone come re-install the blinds before Charles laid eyes on them in shambles.

Already a quarter to three, for heaven's sake. If Julie had come alone like she should have, Norma would have gone downstairs sooner. Julie must have counted on that when she'd hatched her plot to foist the cat on her.

She made her way to the top of the stairs and glided down the chair lift to the foyer. A second walker waited for her at the bottom of the stairs. From the hall, she inched her way to the living area, readying herself for evidence of feline destruction. But the lamps on the end tables stood upright. The leather couch and dining chairs sat unravaged, free of fur and claw marks. The only sign of a cat was a handful of dry food strewn on the floor in front of Magic's old food bowl, next to her cat scratcher. This must be what Julie had been doing when she'd returned to the house for the second time, hauling out Magic's old things. Perhaps she had assumed that Norma, by holding on to these items for over twenty years, might want to put them to use again. A feeling of sorrow passed through Norma's heart.

A large plate of chocolate chunk muffins sat on the dining table, ensconced in her William Yeoward cake dish with its elegant crystal dome. The platter the muffins sat on—white with a pattern of gold elephants marching around the crimson-trimmed edge—didn't look like the food service's. Had Julie made those muffins? But Julie had trouble following instructions on a cake box. *He* must have made them. No doubt, Julie had told her tenant that Norma called chocolate the Correct Flavor. Her mouth watered against her will.

Now, Mom. All you've eaten today is a cup of yogurt with your coffee. You can't let those muffins go to waste. Can you?

No, she couldn't. But eating one was out of the question. To enjoy one of the nurse's muffins and then shun his company would be unseemly. Julie must have depended on that too.

Norma would give the muffins to the cleaners when they came on Tuesday. But Tuesday felt a long way away. She reached for a strawberry Kit Kat from the gift basket.

Julie's new Ecuador dress was draped over the back of a dining chair. Norma maneuvered herself to sit at the dining table and spread the dress in front of her. Coarse linen, dyed aubergine. Hand-embroidered orange and yellow flowers above the empire waist. Painstaking work by whoever did this. Skirt hem likely to fray, however. She brushed her hand along the fabric and imagined Julie finding this dress at a stall in Quito, forgetting Phil, if only for a moment. With Phil gone six—no, *seven*—months already, Julie deserved a new dress. An ache of regret vibrated through Norma. She shouldn't have been so brusque with her sister on the phone earlier.

She rode the chair lift upstairs to her sewing room, the dress in her lap. For all of Julie's machinations today, at least she'd given Norma a couple hours' employment. A far more worthwhile gift from Ecuador than that five-alarm chocolate bar. She retrieved dark purple thread from the thread drawer, along with scissors, pins, measuring tape, and erasable chalk from the alterations drawer. Measure, snip, and a run through her beloved sewing machine, a used Singer she'd bought with her own money at age sixteen. Should she do something about the hem? A rummage through her miscellaneous drawer yielded a coil of honey-colored satin ribbon that matched the yellow embroidered flowers on the bodice. But perhaps this was too much, imposing her own flair on another dressmaker's creation. She mended the hem with purple thread.

There. Done. What a pleasure, to work on a dress on her first full day home from rehab. And the Blue Hour yet to come.

She rode the chair downstairs with Julie's altered dress. The microwave clock read 5:27. Early for dinner, but by now she was starving. She resolved to take better care of herself tomorrow.

All she had to do now was bring out a single serving of tandoori chicken with red lentils from the fridge and heat it up. Here she was, a woman who'd traveled the world and run her own business, steeling herself to let go of her walker long enough to open the refrigerator door. How degrading. This lack of mobility had better be temporary.

She let go of the walker and opened the door. After much careful maneuvering with the walker and a serving spoon, she slid her dinner onto a plate and heated it in the microwave. Victory. Charles should be here to witness this. Or perhaps he'd cite her difficulty as yet another reason for her to move into a nursing home.

She ate the chicken at the kitchen island with her back to the muffins. Julie's dress sat on a corner of the island, folded and ready for her to take home. After dinner, Norma made her way to the sliding door, leaving her dirty plate on the island. As she slid open the door, the cat trotted up from out of nowhere and slipped past her onto the terrace. Was that a lucky break or what? She closed the door behind her with a satisfying slam. No need for the nurse to come over tomorrow. She'd call Julie later and tell her not to send him. But an empty feeling stole over her, catching her unawares.

Admit it, Mom. You're curious to meet that nurse.

She made her way to a lounge chair and settled into the cushions as if sinking into a warm bath. The sun descended in a cloudless sky, indescribably vaster than the meager view her hospital window had afforded her. The diamond pattern of her red-and-gold ikat sundress, purchased in happier times on a trip to Bali with Robert over fifty years ago, dazzled like rubies and topazes. She'd chosen red and gold for their boldness, their brilliance, to celebrate her first sunset at home since the accident. Colors that proclaimed—if anyone happened to spot her from a window—that she'd overcome the odds and triumphed.

The sun hovered an inch above the horizon. The sky's color deepened. Here it was, the Blue Hour, those precious minutes when every shade of blue, from ultramarine to indigo, showed in the sky. She brought out the opal from beneath her dress. The sea-green stone glowed as if from its own inner light. The kaleidoscopic threads pulsed through the green, shimmered as if by an electrical charge. The opal never glowed like that at the hospital.

Her eyes then turned to the spot where Robert had died. To think that after all these years, after what had happened—what Robert had done to her—she still sat out here, admiring the Blue Hour. A feeling of satisfaction spread through her. He hadn't yet succeeded in driving her out of this house.

Harry Winston leaped onto the stone wall and looked down on the spreading city. His silhouette showed against the darkening sky. A slight breeze ruffled his fur. Norma watched him as he cleaned his paw, paying no attention to her. The cat had an air of *sprezzatura*—a casual confidence about his allure, a consciously unthinking way of moving—that only the rarest of models possessed. He was proving oddly appropriate company for her first Blue Hour since the accident.

What made Julie think Norma could take care of that cat

by herself? With a broken leg besides? She was almost eighty, for heaven's sake. If the cat was as spry as he seemed to be, he'd likely outlive her by years. An animal this noble deserved to have someone take care of him to the end of his life, just as she had done with Magic.

Keep him inside for the night, Mom. The nurse can take care of him tomorrow.

That nurse. Hard to believe she didn't know what the man looked like, considering he lived in Julie's back unit. Had he gone to Phil's funeral? She couldn't recall anyone who bore even a passing resemblance to Kevin at Phil's funeral—and she should know, since she'd spent most of the service glancing over her shoulder, thinking Kevin might have the decency to show up. Then again, Julie had said it was the nurse's "can-do spirit" that reminded her of Kevin. A can-do spirit wouldn't exactly manifest itself at a funeral. Oh, well. Norma would have to reconcile herself to the reality that if she wanted to know what the nurse looked like, she'd have to meet him herself.

Just let him come here, Mom. You'll have to meet him sooner or later, if he keeps on renting Aunt Julie's back unit.

The cat jumped onto her lounge chair, jarring her, then crept onto her lap. She lacked the heart to push him away, even if it meant cat hairs on her red-and-gold dress. Did she dare touch him? To do so would only encourage him. But only a woman with ice in her veins could resist a purring cat. She scratched Harry Winston behind his ear. He leaned into her hand and closed his eyes as if in ecstasy. Fur as soft as vicuña wool. A wobble in her chest. This was all Julie's fault.

Stars winked open like the streetlamps glowing beyond the retaining wall. A crescent moon looked as sharp as a scythe against the sky. The wind had grown stronger, colder. Norma nudged the cat off her lap and reached for her walker.

The cat followed her to the sliding door. He rubbed his nose against her walker as soon as she parked it. She slid the door open a crack. The cat went to the door and waited. Unlike with the refrigerator door, she wouldn't be able to let go of the walker long enough to prevent the cat from going inside. The cat looked at her as if he knew this.

She opened the door wider and made a halfhearted effort to block the cat with her walker. The cat slipped past into the house and clawed at the cat scratcher. Then he turned and looked at her, as if impatient for her to follow him in.

"You can't live here, Mr. Winston." Norma's tone was firm but gentle. "I know you want to, but you can't."

CHAPTER 6

SEARCHES

THE CAT LEAPED onto her bed later that night, at the precise moment when Norma, lying in the dark waiting for the painkillers to kick in, sensed his presence in her room. He made his way, purring, toward her face. His cold nose bumped against her cheek. She nudged him away. He settled himself beside her and immediately fell asleep, stretching out and taking up more space than she had thought possible for one cat. By morning he had decamped like a faithless lover, leaving nothing but shed fur on her comforter. At least he'd made her feel less guilty about dispatching him to a shelter.

The ordeal of showering took only forty minutes. A five-minute improvement from yesterday. Her dress—orange ikat in a zigzag pattern, bought on that same trip to Bali—slipped easily over her shoulders. A matching kerchief to tame her hair. Then Kevin's opal, tucked beneath the dress in case the nurse popped by. On her way to the stairs, her eye caught her ruined Venetian blinds and shattered coffeepot in the sitting room. She shut the sitting room door and rode the chair lift downstairs. The cat was nowhere in sight.

Now was her last chance to catch Julie, before she left for church, to forbid her from sending her tenant. What good would come of such a visit? Still, she hesitated. If the nurse came this morning, she'd be rid of the cat sooner. And she'd have a sentient being to talk to, if only for a few minutes.

Aha! I caught you, Mom. Now will you admit you want to meet him?

Breakfast was a luxurious if cloying rice pudding, courtesy of the meal service. She ate the pudding with coffee at the kitchen island, once again showing her back to the nurse's muffins. After breakfast she inched her way outside, leaving the sliding door open. The gauzy mist clinging to the trees had a sickly yellow hue. Not fog. Wildfire smoke. She'd heard from the nurses at the rehab center last week that a blaze had ignited somewhere near the Oregon border. Incredible to think the smoke had drifted all the way down here. She sniffed the air, sad and frustrated.

The magazines she'd left for herself sat on the low table next to her favorite lounge chair. She settled into the chair and flipped through one of them, looking up every now and then for any sign of the nurse. French sentences swam on the page, rendering them as unintelligible as cuneiform. Half an hour passed. Forty-five minutes. No sign of the cat. No sign of the nurse. Something jagged moved across her chest. What was that? Relief? Disappointment?

Disappointment, Mom. You and I both know it's disappointment.

Then the side gate swung open, and through it came a red-haired, boyish-faced man in a faded blue V-neck T-shirt and sagging tan cargo shorts, holding her Sunday paper. Faint lines around his eyes suggested a man in his mid-to-late thirties, as Julie had said, but his muscular arms and trim waist suggested the frame of a younger man. He looked nothing like Kevin. But he must be the nurse.

"Good morning," the man said, walking toward her with determined gracefulness. His toes protruded from a pair of decrepit leather huaraches.

"Good morning," Norma said, putting aside her magazine.

She spoke in the formal tone she used to establish professional distance. Already she regretted wearing sunny orange, a more inviting hue than last night's imperial gold and scarlet. Thank heavens she wasn't stuck in a hospital gown. Otherwise, the nurse might not realize he was talking to a lady.

"Sorry to barge in on you like this." The young man had the strained smile of someone unsure of his welcome. "My name is Alex Wolsey. I'm a friend of your sister's."

"Yes. I'm aware." Norma wished she was wearing her sunglasses instead of her reading glasses, to help her hide her expression. She smoothed out the zigzags on her dress then looked him in the eye, hands folded on her good knee. "You rent the apartment above her garage."

"She asked me to check in with you this morning." The young man looked down at the flagstones in evident embarrassment, an amateur actor delivering unrehearsed lines. "To see about the cat. I hope you don't mind that I've come."

"Any friend of my sister's is welcome in this house." Norma kept her tone cordial but guarded, resolving not to repeat her severity over the intercom yesterday. She thought it only fit to add, "She speaks well of you."

"Oh," Alex said, with a surprised expression. "She speaks well of you too."

"She does, does she?" Norma could only imagine the amount of praise Julie must have heaped on her, to sell her to this stranger, this Alex Wolsey.

"She also told me you were expecting me this morning." An uneasy look passed across the nurse's face. "You *were* expecting me, right?"

"I didn't forbid her to send you, if that's what you mean." It occurred to Norma that the young man must have been as irked with Julie yesterday as she had been herself.

"Ah. Good." Julie's tenant looked relieved. He held out the newspaper. "I found this on your doorstep."

"Thank you." She took the paper and thumbed through the sections, glad to give employment to her fingers.

"I'd also like to apologize." The young man gave her an earnest look. "For showing up at your house uninvited yesterday."

"I should be the one apologizing, Mr. Wolsey." Norma smoothed the paper on her lap, unable to pretend to keep arranging it. "I wasn't at my best yesterday morning."

"Mornings can be hard when you're in pain." A sympathetic smile from Julie's tenant.

"Yes, they can," she said, happy to blame her ill temper yesterday on her condition.

"And the cat?" Alex Wolsey turned to the open sliding door. "Is he inside the house?"

"Harry Winston, you mean?" Norma arched her brow. "You mean the cat my sister intentionally let inside?"

"That wasn't my idea," the young man said with lowered eyes.

"I have no doubt it wasn't." She folded her arms, satisfied her instincts had been correct. "Perhaps you've noticed, Mr. Wolsey, that my sister can be something of a busybody."

"Please. Call me Alex." A kind look showed in the nurse's eyes.

"Alex." Norma listened to herself say his first name out loud and realized she couldn't unsay it.

"I can't blame her," Alex said. "I think she has a fair amount of time on her hands, now that Phil is gone."

"Too much time on her hands." Norma looked down and opened the newspaper on her lap, trying to decide if she should elaborate. Then she looked up and said, "Did you know my sister was once an accountant?"

"I did," Alex said with a smile. "I was helping her figure out Phil's desktop in his study once, and I couldn't help remarking on the accounting ledgers on the shelves."

"Over forty years' worth," Norma said with a nod. "All by hand. She used to keep the books for a number of small businesses along with her husband's carpentry business, right up until he sold it last year. I used to think they were out of their minds, working into their seventies. But now the business is gone, Phil is gone, and my sister needs to keep herself occupied. And here we are, chasing after cats."

"Speaking of cats," Alex said in a lowered voice, glancing down at his sandals, "I was thinking I can take him to the shelter for you. He's so friendly, he must have owners who are worried sick about him."

"That isn't necessary, Mr.—Alex." Norma disliked the idea of giving the nurse permission to enter the house, even though he'd already been inside the house yesterday. "The gentleman will emerge on his own."

"I could wait out here for him if you like."

"He'll never let you pick him up and put him in your car without a struggle. Did you bring a cat carrier?"

"No," Alex said, his voice fading. "I didn't think of that."

"Even if you did, you can't sit out here all day." Norma refrained from saying that she had Magic's cat carrier stowed somewhere in her storage room. "He could be sleeping in some cubbyhole for all we know."

"I suppose you're right." Alex sighed then gave her a look of smiling resignation. "Lovely to meet you, Norma."

"Likewise." Norma was less than pleased he'd called her by her first name, but at least this conversation was drawing to a close. "I regret I can't offer you work. Julie tells me you've been looking."

"I have. Something will come along eventually." Alex made as if to leave then turned around. "But if you need an errand done, I'm only fifteen minutes away. You wouldn't even have to pay me."

"Not pay you?" Norma couldn't remember the last time anyone offered their services free of charge. "That hardly sounds fair."

"I owe it to Julie," Alex said. "She's been a wonderful help."

"She has?" Norma frowned. "My sister gives me the impression that you're the one helping *her*."

"Which is how she helps *me*." Alex smiled. "I like keeping an eye on her. Especially now that Phil's gone. He was a good guy, Phil. I keep looking out my kitchen window expecting him to be out there weeding or watering plants. And I know he took good care of her. Watched out for her, if you know what I mean."

"I do know what you mean," Norma said with a melancholy feeling. "Thank you, Alex. I'll keep your offer in mind."

"Good." Alex looked satisfied. "I hope you won't be too hard on Julie for letting the cat inside your house. Her heart was in the right place."

"My sister's heart is always in the right place." But Norma couldn't resist adding, "It's her head I sometimes wonder about."

Alex let out a laugh. His smile was warm, his skin glowing, his blue eyes clear as lake water. His overgrown red hair looked like it would catch fire in the sun. A decent-looking fellow, in an ordinary, unthreatening, disheveled way.

See, Mom? What were you afraid of?

Just then, Charles came through the sliding door holding a half-eaten chocolate chunk muffin. Charles, in his white polo shirt and brick-red golf pants, his gelled hair parted to one side, looked as tidy as Alex looked unkempt. He usually called before coming—in fact, he *should* have called before coming. He must have used his key to let himself in. Norma's fingers stiffened, wrinkling the newspaper in her hands.

"Hey, Mom." Charles's mouth was full. "I nabbed a last-minute tee time at twelve thirty at Tilden, so I figured I'd swing by."

"Charles." Norma kept her tone placid. No need to let Alex suspect tension between herself and her son. "I didn't realize you were coming."

"My buddy called me about a half hour ago," Charles said, chewing. "And I knew you'd be out here, nowhere near a phone."

"Mm."

If the friend had called a half hour ago, Charles wouldn't have had the time to pull himself together like that. A lie of that caliber would insult someone with a hundredth of Norma's intelligence. First Julie with the cat, now Charles and his golf game. When had her family deemed subterfuge an acceptable way of dealing with her?

"Man, did the food service send you these muffins?" Charles held up the muffin in his hand. "They're great."

"Glad to hear that," Alex said. "I made them."

Charles turned to Alex as if he had only now noticed him standing there. Norma recognized Charles's detached expression as one he might have bestowed upon a waiter. Charles's boat shoes made Alex's huaraches look that much shabbier. Or did Alex's huaraches make Charles's boat shoes look that much snobbier? Either way, Charles couldn't be pleased with Alex's presence.

No nagging her about nursing homes with a witness standing there. Her fingers relaxed their hold on the newspaper.

"This is Alex Wolsey." She nodded at Alex, slipping into hostess mode. "He lives in the apartment above Aunt Julie's garage. Alex, this is my son Charles."

"Pleasure to meet you." Alex extended his hand the way a nurse would, friendly but professional.

"Likewise." Charles shook Alex's hand with something less than pleasure. He sniffed the air and added, "Man, it's not too smoky out here for you, is it, Mom?"

"Smoky? I didn't notice." Norma couldn't decide which grated her nerves more—listening to Charles fret about wildfire smoke or watching him wolf down a muffin Alex had baked for her, not him. "Alex came here yesterday with Aunt Julie. He's a nurse."

"Ah." Coolness crept into Charles's tone now, an awareness, perhaps, that Alex might represent competition. "Will you be assisting my mother?"

"No. But I'm a phone call away if she needs me," Alex said to Charles. He turned to Norma and added, "Would it be all right if I grab my dessert plate? It's a gift from my mother-in-law."

"It's on the dining table." Norma recalled that Julie had once mentioned that Alex was married. "And if you don't mind, Mr. Wolsey—Alex—you'll see a purple dress sitting on the corner of the kitchen island. If you could deliver that dress to my sister, I would be most appreciative."

Self-consciousness came over her the instant Alex disappeared into the house. Here she was, alone with Charles, sitting in smoky silence while listening to the running kitchen faucet through the open sliding door. Why was Alex running the faucet? And how long would Charles stay after Alex left? Would he harp on nursing homes then?

"Okay, I think that's everything," Alex said, coming out onto the terrace with the washed-clean plate in his hand, the folded dress on top of the plate. "Isn't this the dress Julie was wearing the other day? The one she'd bought in Ecuador?"

"Correct. The dress needed alterations." Norma was surprised to hear that Alex had known the dress's provenance.

"Yeah, I heard you ask her yesterday to leave the dress here for you to alter," Alex said with a nervous smile. Then he sighed, as if he were glad to be leaving, and said, "Nice to meet you both."

"I like the elephants on your dessert platter," she said. Not the most elegant way to prevent him from leaving, but it would suffice.

"Thanks. I'll let Laranya—my mother-in-law—know you said that." Alex looked pleased. "The first time my husband took me over to his parents' house for dinner, I made a batch of sugar cookies and brought them on a paper plate. The next time I was invited to dinner, Laranya presented me with this dish so that I wouldn't have to serve her from paper again. Now I'm always bringing her cookies on this plate. It's a running joke between us."

"Ah." Norma felt a moment's flattery that Alex had brought the chocolate chunk muffins on a valued serving dish—and a moment's envy to hear him speak fondly of his mother-in-law. Perhaps she had a son-in-law of her own, one she knew nothing about. "Alex, are you in a hurry to leave? Since both you and Charles are here, you might as well look for that cat together."

"Cat? What cat?" Charles looked at her, confounded.

"A stray cat sneaked into the house yesterday," she said, deeming Julie's involvement unnecessary.

"You're sure you want me to help?" Alex said, looking baffled.

"Well, you did take the trouble to come up here." She folded the newspaper and laid it on top of her magazines on the table.

"If you find him, maybe you could take him to the vet instead of the shelter. As it happens, I have a cat carrier in my storage room. If he's chipped, you might be able to reunite him with his owners by evening. If not, then bring him back here, and we'll consider our options. My sister won't forgive me if I consign the gentleman to a shelter."

"Do you like cats, Charles?" Alex's tone was deferential to a fault. "If he has no owner, then maybe you'd like to adopt him."

"Me?" Charles laughed. "My wife would never allow a cat in the house."

"I might as well go inside too," Norma said, reaching for her walker. "The gentleman has shown a propensity to pop up out of nowhere when I'm there."

"Here, let me help you." Charles took a proprietary step toward her.

"I can manage," she said, turning up her chin.

"Can I bring the newspaper in for you?" Alex gave her a winsome smile, the kind only a man who'd been taught proper manners would give.

"If you insist."

She gripped the walker handles and hoisted herself up, visualizing herself at a fashion show where she'd been asked to acknowledge her crowd. Once on her feet, she gave first Alex and then Charles a small nod. Charles looked as if he were straining to hold in his impatience, while Alex returned her nod with a smiling expression of confidence in her, as if he knew—and understood—the trauma she was going through. In that split-second, Norma grasped what Julie had meant when she'd said that Alex reminded her of Kevin. A pang shot through her, and she followed the men into the house.

She settled into a dining room chair with the newspaper while Alex and Charles embarked on their search. The island had been cleared and wiped down. Alex must have put her dirty dishes in the dishwasher when he'd collected his plate and Julie's dress.

How considerate of him, Mom. Picking up the dishes is something I would've thought to do. Looks like he neatened your get-well cards, too.

Alex and Charles crouched and checked under chairs and tables, as well as under the sofa. Hopefully, they wouldn't find the cat right away. The sooner they found him, the sooner Alex would leave, and the longer she would have to spend alone with Charles. But they couldn't find the cat in the living area.

Time to split up. Charles headed toward the home gym and Kevin's old bedroom past the kitchen, Alex for the storage room and study past the fireplace. Norma could only hope they found that cat downstairs somewhere, to avoid the possibility of the two of them going upstairs and finding her sitting room in disarray. She surveyed the living area, taking in its hollowness, its lack of animation. The carved masks on the wall opposite her stared out at nothing. She needed to fill this room with guests, soon.

The sound of clicking pool balls made her sit up and turn. And there he was, Harry Winston, tiptoeing among the billiard balls, sniffing each one. From what hiding spot had he materialized?

"Get *down*," she commanded.

The cat looked up at her with yearning in his eyes and sprang off the table, kicking pool balls as he went. The configuration she had preserved for over two months, annihilated with a swipe of the paw. Not that this fazed the cat. He sprang into her lap and writhed around as if he knew she couldn't move her legs to expel him. He looked up at her with naked adoration. She scratched him behind his ear, even if he didn't deserve it.

"You're lucky you're cute," she murmured.

"For a cat as big as he is," Alex said, walking into the living area, "Harry Winston sure knows how to make himself invisible—oh, hey! There he is."

"He appeared out of nowhere," Norma said. "Like I thought he would."

"The way cats manage to hide." Alex walked up to pet the cat. "Come on, dude, let's go see if you're chipped."

"The vet is probably closed on Sunday." Norma felt the vibration of the cat purring on her thighs.

"Let me check," Alex said. "They can't all be closed today."

He pulled out his smartphone and pressed a button. Norma watched Alex standing turned from her, his brow furrowed as he worked the phone. He handled the device with beguiling ease, holding it in front of him like a pocket mirror. His hands looked soft and capable. His wedding ring glinted in the sunlight.

The way he stood there reminded her of—was it Kevin? No, not Kevin. Someone close to Kevin. Then it hit her. Kevin's high school boyfriend. The one who had worn the red suit. Zack was his name. Zack Patterson. A lanky young man, a runner, brown hair and rimless glasses. Had gone to Kevin's school on a scholarship. An alternate story unspooled in her mind, one where Kevin and Zack had stayed together, got married, and settled in the apartment behind Julie and Phil before buying their own house nearby. Zack bringing her cookies on a plate she'd bought for him. Zack on a smartphone, searching for a vet.

"I've looked everywhere," Charles said, walking into the living area, and stopped short at the sight of the cat in Norma's lap. "Oh, man. He was here the whole time?"

"I turned, and there he was on the pool table." Norma stroked the cat, indulging her hand in his fur.

"I found a twenty-four-hour pet hospital in Berkeley," Alex

said, slipping his phone into his pocket. "It's probably a circus there, but we'll see."

"That's too much stress on the cat." Norma shook her head. "No need to cart him around like luggage. Monday must be a quieter day at that vet. Harry Winston might as well stay here until tomorrow."

"The cat has a name?" Charles looked at her puzzled.

"Yes. Harry Winston," she said. "Your Aunt Julie named him."

"Five minutes ago, you wanted him out of here. Now you're letting him stay the night." Charles gave her a sideways look. "What if you can't locate his owner? You won't keep him, will you?"

"Not yet." She brushed fur off her hands and held in her pique at Charles's failure, yet again, to take anything she said at face value. "First, we need to determine whether Mr. Winston is chipped. If he isn't, then why not provide the gentleman with room and board? He seems resolved to live here."

"You know you can't take care of a cat by yourself, Mom. Especially not while you can't walk without help."

"But I won't be taking care of the cat by myself." A thrill rushed through her. "Alex will be helping me."

Now it was Alex's turn to look dumbfounded. He opened his mouth to say something along the lines of, *Didn't you say you didn't need my help?* She smiled at him with all the grace at her command, willing him to accept the offer without protest.

"I will?" Alex eventually said.

"Since you live only fifteen minutes away. And seem eager to help the fellow." Her chest felt as light as air. "And when you're not assisting with the cat, you'll be assisting with my physical therapy."

"You're hiring me?"

"Starting tomorrow," she said. "Does ten o'clock suit you?"

"Whenever you want suits me." Alex gave her a dubious look. "Should I count on being here for the day?"

"I would think so," she said, her tone as smooth and serene as her smile. "We can work out a schedule later."

Charles looked first at Harry Winston then at her. The reproach in his eyes all but asked, *Have you lost your mind?* Fortunately, she didn't have to endure Charles's look for long. In a moment, he glanced at his watch and said he had to head out. A guilty sensation, as abrupt as a break of billiard balls, passed through her at the thought that she couldn't wait to be rid of her own son.

Alex said he should be going too. His husband should be coming home at any moment. She could already feel herself favoring Alex's company over Charles's. To have someone out-side the family come to her house every day. A nice man, an intelligent man, a man who would listen and not judge her. A son-in-law for hire.

Once they were gone, she looked down at Harry Winston. He returned her look with indolent green eyes, drifting off to sleep, as heavy as a sack of flour on her lap. Now that she'd made the decision to keep the gentleman—assuming she failed to find his real owner—she felt free to think of him as Harry Winston. Julie would be pleased to learn she'd achieved her objective.

Eventually, the cat's bulk grew too burdensome. She nudged the cat off her, pulled herself upright with the walker. Beneath the crystal dome, nine chocolate muffins sat on a plain white platter. She'd never seen that platter before. Only the caterers used those plates. It was humbling to realize she had no idea what items were stored in her own cupboards. She leaned against the island, removed the crystal dome with difficulty, selected the muffin with the most chocolate, and took a bite.

She thought of Alex typing on his smartphone. How easily he'd found that pet hospital. If it was that easy to look up a pet hospital, how easy would it be to look up, say, a person's life? Kevin's life? For twenty-five years she'd resisted the urge to hire a private investigator to find Kevin. She'd made a vow to herself never to stoop to Robert's level. But surely some trace of her missing son could be extracted from the flood of information sloshing online. If anyone with a smartphone could find him, why couldn't she?

Her thoughts traveled upstairs to Charles's laptop in her sitting room. What was a laptop, besides a large smartphone? Except she had no idea how the contraption worked. Charles would be livid if he knew what she was thinking. But Alex could help her. And he wouldn't have to know why.

Mom, you met the guy for the first time this morning. Are you sure you can trust him?

True enough. She'd have to play the harmless invalid with Alex, learn more about him, study his habits, discern how well he could guard a secret. Let him work here for a few days, a few weeks, before asking for his help.

Wasn't Mavis coming tomorrow afternoon to do Norma's hair? Didn't Alex look like he needed a haircut? Mavis was adept at drawing people out. Perhaps Alex could be persuaded to let Norma treat him to a new look. Neither he nor Mavis would have to know the real reason behind her offer.

CHAPTER 7

CAREER PATHS

ALEX FOLLOWED CHARLES out of Norma's house, not daring to look back. The sun's heat sank into his skin at the same time the truth sank in that Julie's harebrained scheme had worked. He stowed the dessert platter and Julie's dress in the trunk of his car and pulled out his phone. A quarter past twelve. Pratyush was probably at the end of his lunch. Alex typed the word *HIRED* and sent the text on its way. Hopefully, Pratyush would see the message before he made any commitments to his old boss.

Meanwhile, Charles walked to his own car, a black Cadillac Escalade that looked like it had been issued by the Secret Service. Alex and Pratyush's gray Ford, with its grimy windshield, dented front fender, green fuzzy dice dangling from the front mirror, and tourniquet of blue duct tape holding the side-view mirror in place, looked even more abject next to that SUV. Alex kept his eyes on his phone, waiting for Charles to pull out first.

Charles opened the driver's side door of the SUV then stopped, as if a thought had occurred to him. He walked around

79

the car toward Alex. Alex couldn't pretend to keep fiddling with his phone. He looked up.

"Alex." Charles addressed him with the casual confidence Alex often associated with straight guys, especially ones like Charles, large, good-looking, and wealthy.

"Yes?" Alex tightened his grip on his phone.

"How about I give you my number." Charles's tone was courteous, but he still sounded as if he were giving an order. "In case of emergency."

"Uh, sure. No problem." Alex held out his phone. "Why don't you enter the number yourself."

Charles took the phone as if it belonged to him and typed his number into Alex's contact list. With Charles's attention sidetracked, Alex allowed himself a good look at this older son of Norma. Sixty at the oldest, most likely. Tall frame, wavy hair, high cheekbones. The look of a retired all-star quarterback. Someone who would've turned to Alex in high school and said, *Hey, what're you looking at?* Assuming, of course, that Charles would've taken the trouble to notice him in the first place.

Then Alex remembered where he'd seen Charles before. Phil's funeral. Charles had sat behind Julie and Norma, wearing a brown tweed suit. Pratyush had noticed him first and asked Alex if he knew who the hunk in the second pew was. Charles appeared different in the sunshine, dressed in loud golf clothes. But his look of seriousness, as he frowned over Alex's phone, remained the same.

"Thanks." Charles handed the phone back with a direct smile, as if he expected a call from Alex already.

"Glad you thought of giving me your contact info." Alex looked down at Charles's number. The area code was one of the affluent bedroom communities east of here, Orinda, Lafayette, Moraga.

"If you need anything, please don't hesitate to call," Charles said, glancing at Norma's front door. He shrugged and gave an awkward smile. "Even if it isn't an emergency. My mom can be, well, you know."

Wistfulness colored his words, the tone of a man who wants to take control but finds himself sidelined instead. Alex wished he could do more for Charles. But Norma would have to be at death's door before Alex ever called him.

"I'll keep you in mind if something comes up," he said smoothly. He slipped the phone into his shorts pocket. "Thanks, Charles."

"Would you mind giving me your number?" Charles brought out his own phone, as sleek and black as his Escalade. "Just in case?"

"Uh, sure," Alex said, and recited his number.

"Thanks." Charles typed in the number then looked up from his phone with a smile, one designed, perhaps, to put Alex at ease. "I'm glad you'll be helping my mother."

"Thanks, Charles. I'm sure she's going to be fine."

Alex played with his phone, waiting for Charles to pull out of the driveway. No return text from his husband. He visualized Pratyush sitting across from his old boss at some fancy restaurant, perhaps even down the road at the Claremont Hotel. Linen tablecloth, waiters in bow ties, eggs Benedict for lunch and chocolate mousse for dessert. Pratyush's phone was likely turned off, lying face-down on the table. He would have turned it off on purpose, to keep Alex from interrupting.

Meanwhile, Charles got into his SUV and started it. The car's engine purred like a well-fed kitten. Alex couldn't help looking up. Charles's expression was darker, perhaps because he didn't realize Alex was watching him. Charles finessed the SUV into the narrow street and drove off. The laurel branches rustled as if they, too, were as relieved as Alex that Norma's son was gone.

★

Alex was in his driveway, about to climb the steps to his apartment, when the sliding back door to Julie's house opened. Out came Julie in a maroon suit with a ruffled white blouse—she must've just come home from church. She walked down her steps wearing a worried expression and fuzzy pink slippers. He should have known that Julie would be peeking out her windows, waiting for him to show up.

"Hi, Julie," he said with a smile. "How did those sugar cookies work out at your coffee hour?"

"Um. The less said about them, the better." Julie looked at him with wide eyes, taking in his shirt and shorts and sandals. "Did you go see Norma?"

"Sure did." He held out the dessert plate with the dress sitting on top of it. "Your Ecuador dress."

"Norma altered it already? Goodness." Julie took the dress and held it out in front of her. "Oh, I *knew* she'd neaten the hem. She doesn't think I notice these things, but I do."

"I start working for Norma tomorrow," Alex said.

"You what?" Julie looked at him, the dress going limp in her hands.

"Not only that," he said, smiling. "She's prepared to adopt Harry Winston."

"You are *kidding*." Julie draped the dress over her shoulder, her mouth half open.

"For today at least," he said. "I'll take him to the vet tomorrow. If it turns out he's not chipped, Norma says she'll take him in."

"Goodness," Julie said under her breath. "Even though you wore those sandals."

"A risk, I know. But something about the way she spoke to

you on the intercom yesterday had me thinking she'd rather see me dressed as my real self."

"Huh," Julie said. "All through church I had visions of Norma calling 911 on you."

"I admit things looked dicey at first. She *was* about to ask me to leave," Alex said as his lips curled into a smile. "But then her son dropped by."

"Charles?" Julie looked taken aback.

"He came to check in on her before his golf game," Alex said, his smile growing wider. "A half hour later, Norma changed her mind about both me and Harry Winston. Like she wanted to stick it to him."

He stole a glance at Julie, looking to see how she'd react. Her alarm at Charles's surprise visit already intrigued him. She must have some insight into Charles that might prove useful with Norma.

"My girls used to adore Charles," she said, her voice thoughtful. She was looking over at the lemon tree, a contemplative smile on her face. "Their strapping older cousin. Kate and Olivia loved having him over for the weekend. On clear nights, Phil would set up tents for them in the backyard. And at bedtime, Charles would sit outside the tents in his cowboy hat and sheriff's badge and play lookout until the girls fell asleep. He couldn't have been more than twelve."

"And now Charles is on the lookout for his mother," Alex said, recalling how Charles had behaved in the driveway. Did Charles think he needed to protect his mother from Alex?

"They never did click, Norma and Charles. I think it's because Norma had him at such a young age. Only twenty when she had him. But that's not your problem." Julie sighed and flashed a smile. "Enough about my sister. Have you ever gone skydiving?"

"Skydiving?" Alex stared at her.

"There's a skydiving place up in Sonoma County. Wild Blue Yonder Adventures. Phil always wanted to go. Now I want to go, for his sake. But I don't want to go alone."

"Oh." Alex pictured Julie in her church clothes and fuzzy pink slippers, floating down from the sky in a parachute.

"You know my new Australia friends, the ones I met on the trip? *They* went skydiving in February. Then, last night, they sent me an email telling me they're going *again* in two weeks. They're only a couple of years younger than me!" Julie's eyes were shining. "I can practically hear Phil telling me to go for it. Just like the Galápagos trip."

"A trip to the Galápagos is less drastic than jumping out of a plane." Alex remembered what Julie had said about the blue-footed boobies, divebombing from the sky.

"Skydiving is safer than driving a car," Julie said, nodding emphatically. "It says so on the internet. What do you say, Alex? Do you think you might want to go skydiving with me?"

"I don't know, Julie. I don't think I'm your guy," he said with a slow shake of the head. Since that sounded lame, he added, "Pratyush would never let me."

"Maybe Pratyush would want to come too."

"Pratyush? I doubt if I could talk him into riding the roller coaster at Six Flags." Alex was grateful, for once, for having such a prudent husband. "How about Kate?"

"She'd only end up trying to talk me out of it," Julie said, her voice falling. "Olivia might be game—she was always the adventurous one—but I can't imagine she'd fly all the way from Japan to go on a skydive."

"Sorry," Alex said. Couldn't Phil have encouraged his wife to do something less outlandish?

"No worries," Julie said, her cheery tone no doubt masking

her disappointment. "I'm sure I'll find someone bonkers enough to do it."

"Best of luck," he said to assure her, though he couldn't imagine anyone in Julie's acquaintance consenting to jump out of a plane.

"You have no idea how glad I am Norma hired you," Julie said, putting a hand to her chest. "I'd be heartbroken if she had to give up that house."

"Your sister's tough," he answered with certainty. "She's not going anywhere."

Her look of gratitude was enough to set his heart glowing. Poor Julie. In less than a year she'd lost her husband to a bout of pneumonia and almost lost her sister to a car accident. By taking on the job, he'd be helping not only himself and Pratyush, but Norma and Julie as well. How could he think he'd lost his purpose in life?

He walked into a silent apartment. Five past one on the wall clock by the fireplace. So much for the idea of finding Pratyush stretched out on the couch, waiting for him with a glint in his eye. Where *was* Pratyush? He must've left for that lunch over two hours ago. Either he'd finished early and had gone on a walk or an errand, or—God forbid—he was being held hostage, sitting defenseless while his boss wheedled him into accepting his old job. Alex checked his phone again. No response to his text. He closed the front door and plopped onto the sofa, the dessert plate on his lap.

How long would he have to sit here? All day? Then Pratyush came through the door, clutching a small brown paper grocery bag. This was typical Pratyush, making him wait while pretending nothing was wrong.

"Hey," Alex said, suppressing his impatience. He put the dessert plate on the coffee table and rose from the couch.

"I bought blackberries." Pratyush held up the paper bag. A peace offering?

"Did you see my text?"

"Not until after lunch." Pratyush placed the bag of blackberries onto the dessert plate. Nothing in his manner to indicate how lunch might've gone. "The old lady hired you, huh?"

"Yep."

"Julie saves the day again. She's a force of nature, our landlady." Pratyush sighed and looked out the picture window.

"You should meet the sister." Alex looked at his husband and braced himself. "So. How did lunch go?"

"As you might expect." Pratyush shrugged, with only the slightest change in his expression.

"They want to rehire you," Alex said, keeping a steady gaze on Pratyush.

Pratyush shrugged again, still looking out the window. He must've said yes to those people. Oh, God.

"Someone from the State of California came to the office last month." Pratyush turned to face Alex. "Surprise audit. The company's facing a fine. A hefty one. Richard says our payroll records are in disarray."

"Not *our* payroll records, Pratyush," Alex said, his voice hard with disgust. "*Their* payroll records. And so that's why they're wining and dining you. To make those records yours again."

"They fired Donna, at least."

"Too late."

He'd heard too many of Pratyush's ordeals with his previous supervisor to avoid thinking of her as the meanest, pettiest, most incompetent of managers. Memories of her were no doubt the primary reason—if not *the* reason—why Pratyush had lost his mojo. To hear that she'd been fired brought Alex zero satisfaction.

"Still, she's gone. And audits don't last forever." Pratyush stood up straight, as if expecting Alex to scold him. "That's the offer. My old job's waiting for me if I want it."

"More money?"

"We didn't talk money."

"New responsibilities, then?" Alex put a hand to his temple and rubbed it.

"We didn't talk about a career path." Pratyush lowered his eyes.

"Because there *is* no career path," Alex said with a sharpness he instantly regretted. In a softer voice, he asked, "What did you end up saying to what's-his-name?"

"I said I wanted to discuss it with you first."

"You had to know what I'd say about this, Pratyush."

"Not even if it's more money?"

"Not even if they opened their vault and offered you their last penny." Alex stepped toward his husband. "Come on, Pratyush, remember that day you walked off the job? Me coming to pick you up at the BART station? You haven't said anything to convince me I won't get another phone call from one of your coworkers, telling me you're—having an episode."

He placed a hand on Pratyush's shoulder then dared trace his knuckle along Pratyush's cheek. For once, Pratyush didn't turn away. Alex needed all his willpower to keep himself from going any further. *Easy does it.*

"Turns out the day I left was the beginning of the end for Donna," Pratyush murmured, laying his head against Alex's shoulder. "Or so Richard told me. Apparently, all the managers had to undergo sensitivity training."

"Barf, sensitivity training," Alex whispered into Pratyush's ear, drawing him closer. "These are grown people with fancy degrees, making gobs of money. And they need someone to teach them the basics on how to talk to people?"

"Richard couldn't stop saying how sorry he was," Pratyush said in a near-monotone. "He sounded as if he meant it."

"I'd be sorry too," Alex said with a snort, "if I had the state of California breathing down my neck."

"He promised things would be different."

"My stepfather used to pull that line on my mother," Alex said. "I told you how that turned out."

No response from Pratyush. What could he say? He had to know that Alex was right about this.

"You don't have to give in to those people," Alex said, stepping back to look Pratyush in the eye. "I know you love working for that nonprofit. And now I have this gig with Julie's sister. That should buy us enough time until I land a real job. You don't have to sacrifice your future, Pratyush. Your well-being. Okay?"

He let his palm rest on Pratyush's cheek, feeling the warmth of his skin. Pratyush turned his eyes to the picture window again, his chest quivering with each exhale. Alex brought Pratyush close and wrapped his arms around him. Did Alex dare hope that this was the end of their drought?

"How long is the assignment with Julie's sister?" Pratyush pulled away from Alex, a worn-out expression on his face.

"Until she's better, probably. I'd put it at a few weeks."

"And the pay?"

"We haven't discussed that yet."

"Jesus, Alex."

"You heard from Julie yourself that Norma has money," Alex said, his cheeks growing warm. He'd been so anxious to flee Norma's house that he'd forgotten to hammer out the employment terms. "If her house is any indication, she must be loaded. You should see her terrace. I bet you can see all the way here from that terrace."

"I doubt that." Pratyush gave the trace of a smile.

"You can, honest to God. I'll take you up there one day and show you."

"Okay. Sure." Pratyush bowed his head. "I'm supposed to give Richard my answer by tomorrow. I don't think I can bring myself to say yes."

"Then tell him no. Promise me you'll say no?"

"Promise." But a hopeless look appeared on Pratyush's face, as if he was certain he was making the biggest mistake of his life.

"Thank you," Alex said and put his arms around Pratyush again. "I swear to God, you won't regret it."

He kissed Pratyush on the side of his neck and felt Pratyush's body press against his own. His warmth flooded through Alex like the sunrise from an endless arctic night. The blinds were up. If Julie looked through her kitchen window, she'd see them holding each other. But Alex didn't dare let Pratyush go.

"Those berries need to go into the fridge," Pratyush said, pulling away.

He picked up the dessert plate holding the paper bag and slipped out of the room. The sound of the back door opening and closing, Pratyush's footsteps going down the stairs to their little basement behind Julie's garage. The strains of his cello wafted up from the floorboards. Their moment of intimacy had come and gone so quickly that Alex had to wonder if it had happened. He rose from the chair and walked into the kitchen to fix himself a bowl of blackberries.

CHAPTER 8

A NEW LOOK

T TEN O'CLOCK on Monday morning, Alex stepped out of the gray Ford and stood in the shade of the laurel tree. Norma's house had shrunk since the weekend. The orange roof tiles looked less lofty, the green-shuttered windows less menacing, the oaken front door less imposing. Still no key to let himself in, though. He walked around the house to the terrace.

Norma sat in a lounge chair, the same spot as yesterday, absorbed in a magazine bearing a photo of a twiglike young woman in a fringed black minidress. The bamboo-leaf pattern on Norma's scarlet dress shimmered, while a gold handbag—the same shade of gold as the bamboo leaves—sat on the flagstones by her ankles. Only her leg brace, peeking coquettishly from the hem, gave any hint of disability. She must've set her alarm to dress this way.

"Good morning, Mr. Wolsey," she said and looked up. "Excuse me. Alex."

She laid her magazine on her lap, pulled off her black-framed Jackie O sunglasses, and gave him a languid expression, as if he

90

were a cocktail-party acquaintance whose face she vaguely recognized. Alex allowed himself to take a good look at his newest patient, something he'd lacked the courage to do yesterday morning. Her eyes were a darker shade of brown than Julie's, her gaze more open and direct. With her high cheekbones and heart-shaped face, she must have been stunning when she was younger. A small greenish pendant hung around her neck. Were those diamonds on her wristwatch? Alex doubted she'd wear costume jewelry, even at home on a Monday morning.

"Good morning, Norma. How are you feeling today?" He kept his tone low and respectful, figuring anything perkier would irritate her.

"I took a shower and dressed myself." Norma rested her hands in her lap, diamonds nestling like dewdrops among the bamboo leaves. "I'll settle for that."

"I can always help you shower and dress, if need be," Alex said, glancing at the headline on the open magazine on her lap. *Inspirations Mode Pour Été.*

"I'll make a note of it." The downward turn in Norma's voice suggested she'd sooner jump into an active volcano. She sat up in the lounge chair. "We need to take Mr. Winston to the vet."

"I can drive him there now."

"A cat carrier is sitting at the bottom of the front stairs." Norma spoke as if she'd been long used to giving clear, precise orders. "I'll be surprised if he isn't chipped."

"And if he isn't?"

"Then go to the pet store and buy him a collar and whatever else you think will make the gentleman more comfortable." Her tone held a decided unconcern that Alex couldn't tell was real or fake. "Here, you'll need money."

She picked up the handbag at her feet, zipped it open, and brought out two crisp hundred-dollar bills. The folded bills were wedged between her scarlet fingernails—the precise shade as her dress—as if she were proffering a cigarette. Alex walked up and took the money. Had she rehearsed that gesture, or was doling out hundred-dollar bills a talent that came to her naturally? He imagined hundred-dollar bills tucked in purses all over Norma's house.

"You'll also need this," she said as an afterthought, reaching into her bag again.

She pulled out a key. A front door key. Alex now had access to this kingdom—or should he say queendom—of a house.

He found Harry Winston on the desk chair in Norma's sitting room. The room was done up in daunting shades of white—not that this fazed the cat, resting with his paws hanging over the side of the chair as if he were waiting for a manicure. Harry looked at Alex with complacent eyes. Alex put down the cat carrier and felt a pang at the thought that this might not be Harry's home for much longer.

Wooden blinds sat in a heap on the floor in front of the credenza. The picture window was bare. Was that broken glass by the mini refrigerator? What happened? No matter—Alex saw an opening to be helpful. The blinds looked like they snapped into brackets. He picked up the blinds and went to the window. Snap, snap, done. Then he picked up as many pieces of glass as he could and dropped them into a wastepaper basket by Norma's writing desk. He'd vacuum the carpet when he returned from the vet.

"All right, you," he said to Harry Winston.

He bent down to pick up the cat but stopped short at a framed drawing on the wall. The drawing's faceless male model wore a sea-green tuxedo with yellow, pink, and purple stars swirling up one of the pant legs to the jacket like a rainbow-colored Milky Way. This must be the prom suit Julie had talked about on Saturday. The prom suit Norma had designed for her other son—Charles's brother. The model's hand was buried in his front pocket. He leaned on one leg. A posture of confidence, of attitude.

Why did the drawing make Alex feel sad? Perhaps it was the model's isolation, hanging apart from his brethren downstairs. Or perhaps his cocky pose, no doubt struck to intimidate people, served as a cover for deep insecurity, deep loneliness. No time to ponder that. He picked up Harry Winston and brought him squirming to the cat carrier.

He languished in the vet's waiting room for forty-five minutes before anyone could see Harry. The cat peered out of the carrier, looking befuddled and betrayed. Eventually, a young doctor came through a door and took the cat to the back. Alex watched Harry go with a sense of despair. He'd met Harry Winston only two days ago—how could he have let himself grow attached to him? At least he could take comfort in knowing he'd be a good Samaritan, reuniting some owner with their lost cat.

The doctor came out with Harry about twenty minutes later. The cat was about a pound or two overweight but otherwise healthy. Yes, the cat was chipped. But the vet had looked up the identification number and learned the cat's last registered address was in Los Angeles. The phone number on the chip, with an LA area code, was disconnected. Turned out Harry Winston's original owner was more negligent than Alex had imagined.

He headed to the pet store, bought what he needed, and returned to Norma's house to find Norma still out on the terrace. She sat at the patio table in the shade of the umbrella, writing with a confident hand on cream-colored paper. Was that a *letter* she was writing? Who wrote letters anymore?

"The verdict?" she said, her attention on her writing.

"He's overweight, but otherwise he's healthy."

"Humph. No doubt he's been mooching off everyone in the neighborhood." Norma put down her pen and looked up. "And does he belong to someone?"

"The cat was chipped but no way to find the owner." Alex put down the carrier and unlatched the door. Harry Winston crept out and sniffed the ground by Norma's lounge chair. "His previous owner is someone from LA. Phone number disconnected. If you want, we can write a letter to the LA address and see what comes up. Or maybe the owner moved from LA up here. We could show him around the neighborhood, see if anyone is missing a cat—"

"We're not doing that." Norma, her face inscrutable behind her sunglasses, leaned down to let Harry Winston rub his nose against her finger.

"You're adopting the cat?"

"It appears we have no choice," Norma said. She stopped petting the cat and looked up at Alex. "Does it?"

"I had a feeling you'd say that." He pulled out from his pocket a plastic collar shaped like a piece of sushi. "Here you go, sir. I christen thee Harry Winston."

"Your Aunt Julie will be delighted," Norma said in a sour voice to the cat. "I suppose we'll have to update the information on his microchip."

"I'll schedule a checkup for Harry," Alex said. "We can update the info then."

Harry jumped onto a lounge chair, next to his new mistress. Alex smiled at them both. His odds of staying here for a longer stint just shot up, now that he had two divas to look after.

☆

But his first physical therapy session with Norma, for an hour on the terrace after lunch, brought home a sobering truth.

The damaged knee, though tender, could bend with much more dexterity than he'd thought it would. Not only that, but Norma powered through her exercises with the single-mindedness of a decathlete training for the Olympics. Forget about this assignment lasting a month. At this rate, she'd be off and running in two weeks, maybe even one. No need to tell Pratyush *that*.

His eye caught sight of the pool table in the living area. He remembered what Julie had said on Saturday. Another opportunity to make himself indispensable. Here went nothing.

"Julie tells me you're an ace at pool." He was crouched on the ground next to Norma's chair, focusing on her knee. "Do you play often?"

"I practice more than I play." Norma glanced at the pool table through the plate glass.

"My husband plays gigs at a bar that has a pool table," Alex said, using his most upbeat voice.

"Gigs? What kind of gigs?"

"Jazz combo," Alex said. "Pratyush plays bass viol. He plays cello too, but nowadays he mostly plays bass viol for this jazz band. They play at the Thirsty Raven on Piedmont Ave. Any chance you've been inside there?"

"No," Norma said with surprise and a trace of revulsion.

"I used to play pool as a teenager." He cringed inwardly at the phony gusto in his voice. "My skills have grown rusty since then. I'd love to be able to play a halfway-decent game at the Thirsty Raven, next time I'm there. Maybe you could give me a lesson or two?"

"I could be persuaded," Norma said. She pushed in her sunglasses.

"We could practice today if you want," Alex said, drawing hope from Norma's answer. Then he felt a twitch of guilt. He should be paying *her* for pool lessons, not her paying him to *receive* pool lessons.

"Today won't work." Norma put her foot down, smoothed bamboo leaves over her knee, and yawned. "My hairdresser is coming at three."

"Tomorrow, then." Alex stood up. "Uh, is there anything else you'd like me to do before I call it a day?"

"Call it a day? But there's work to be done." She looked at him with a slight frown then reached over and picked up the sealed letters on the patio table. "I need you to go to the post office and mail these. They're international and I have no stamps, so you'll need to wait in line. After that, I need you to go to Peet's and buy a pound of coffee. You still have money from this morning?"

"More than enough." He reached into his pocket and felt the crispness of the remaining hundred-dollar bill she'd given him, along with the change from the first hundred-dollar bill. "What kind of coffee do you prefer? Light? Dark?"

"The darkest they have." She held out the letters, red nails gleaming against the creamy envelopes. "Make sure it's free trade, or my youngest grandson, Jeff, won't let me hear the end of it. He's in Vietnam right now, teaching English for the Peace Corps. The next time I write him, I want to be able to say I buy free trade coffee."

"Dark, free trade, no problem." Alex took the letters from Norma, surprised at their heft. Two were headed to France, one to Japan.

"Don't bother buying the coffee if the line is too long," she said. "I'll need you here no later than four."

"Is there something in particular you need me for?"

"One thing at a time," she said. She gave Alex the hint of a smile beneath the sunglasses.

✶

At a quarter to four, he let himself in through the front door to the sound of chatting voices drifting down from upstairs. Norma and her hairdresser, most likely. Maybe he should leave the coffee on the kitchen counter. Let them be. But Norma had said earlier she'd wanted him back early. What if she needed his help now? He headed up the stairs.

He walked into the sitting room to find Norma in a chair near the window, her leg propped up on a footstool. A buxom middle-aged woman with crow-black hair and cherry-red lipstick was putting the finishing touches to Norma's hair. A tattoo of a B-52 bomber showed below the hairdresser's collarbone, dropping pink hearts into her cleavage. The stylist had transformed Norma's hair into gray feathers around her face, making her look softer, more approachable. Poor Norma—she deserved more people than himself to see her look so classy.

"Sorry for interrupting, Norma. Should I leave this here or downstairs?" He held up the Peet's bag and caught sight of Harry Winston lounging on a chair by the circular table, watching the snipping of the hairdresser's scissors with sharp-eyed focus.

"Downstairs." Norma looked up at the hairdresser. "Are we finished, Mavis?"

"Finished, *madame*," the hairdresser said with a smile. She removed the apron around Norma's neck and folded it, expertly preventing any hair from falling onto the carpet or Norma's scarlet dress.

"Now it's your turn," Norma said to Alex.

"My turn for what?"

"A haircut."

"Now?"

"Yes, now." Norma's voice was curt and businesslike. "I've already settled it with Mavis."

"Hiya, doll," Mavis said, looking at Alex with a frank expression.

"Hi," he said with an uneasy smile. Was this the reason why Norma had wanted him to return early to the house? For a *haircut*?

"It's to thank you for cleaning up my broken coffee carafe. And fixing my blinds," Norma said. She nodded at the window. "Both disasters were courtesy of Mr. Winston, in case you were wondering."

"All I did was pick up a few pieces of glass," Alex said. "And snap those blinds into place."

"Mavis, how much do you think the window people would have charged me if I had them come fix them?"

"A hundred bucks at least."

"More like two hundred," Norma said with a hint of indignation. "Those are custom blinds."

"They're *gorgeous*," Mavis said, beholding the blinds with an admiring expression. "And with cords. *Very* retro."

"I had to pay extra for corded blinds, so that I could pull them down from the top without reaching. I commend your modesty, Alex, but I really must insist on paying you back." Norma's eyes strayed to his hair with an expression of distaste, as if she'd grown tired of the subject of window blinds.

"How long's it been since you've had your hair cut, ginger snap?" Mavis's eyes glowed as if she were burning to take on a challenge.

"Can't say," he said, reaching for a lock of hair growing over his ear.

"How long it's been is beside the point," Norma said. She slid her foot off the stool, grasped her walker, and hoisted herself up. "I refuse to spend a chunk of my day beholding that pile of spaghetti on your head."

"Have a seat, ginger," Mavis said, gesturing at the empty chair.

True, Norma wasn't exaggerating when she declared he needed a haircut. But his overgrown hair was most likely not the only reason—or even the main reason—for this impromptu appointment. Norma wanted something. He settled into the chair while Norma took a seat by the circular table, next to Harry Winston. The drawing of her faceless younger son gazed down at him.

"You have spectacular curls," Mavis said, running her fingers through his hair. Her nails were perfect ovals, painted the same cherry red as her lipstick.

"The curls stay," Norma said, not looking up from her magazine. "The rest goes."

"Do I have any say in how I look?" Alex laughed, hoping to sound carefree and not at all suspicious of Norma's motives.

"Technically, you do." Norma gave him a serious but amiable look. "But, in situations such as this one, it's best to defer to people who know what they're talking about."

"Sit tight, Red Hot." Mavis held up her scissors like a magic wand. "By the time I'm done with you, you'll need a security detail to protect you from hordes of women chasing you down the street."

"I'm married to a man." Color rushed to Alex's face.

"That'll only make the ladies run after you harder," Mavis said. "They'll want you to make an exception for them."

"For the love of humanity, Mavis," Norma said with a roll of her eyes. "Just cut. The man's. Hair."

Like nearly everyone who ever cut his hair, Mavis liked to talk. She asked him where he lived, what he did for a living, what he liked to do for fun. Norma, her eyes scanning her French-language *Vogue*, now and then scratching Harry Winston behind his ear, must be absorbing every word he said in response. Her son in the flowery green tuxedo looked as if he were listening, too. This must be Norma's ultimate purpose for this haircut.

"Okay, ginger snap, you're all set." Mavis held out her hand mirror.

Alex raised the mirror. The hairline around his ears had been neatened into semicircles, bringing out his face, his eyes. His curls glowed in the sunshine from the window. A feeling of joy rushed through him.

"You don't like it?" A look of uncertainty crossed Mavis's face.

"Don't like it?" He turned to look at Mavis, aware that what he was about to say would likely make Norma look up. "I haven't looked this good since my wedding day."

Sure enough, Norma looked up. Her eyes met his. No change in her expression. Then she looked down at the magazine and stretched her hand toward Harry Winston.

"Not since your wedding day?" Mavis smiled at him, but her tone was disbelieving. "Where do you usually have your hair cut?"

"Nowhere special," he said. "But on the morning of our wedding day, Pratyush and I went to his mother's beauty salon. Her treat."

"What did you say your husband's name was?"

"Pratyush." He didn't dare glance at Norma, but no doubt she'd taken note of the intriguing name.

"Prat-yoosh," Mavis repeated, pouting her cherry-red lips.

"It's Hindi for 'dawn.'"

"Sexy," Mavis said. "Is your husband as handsome as the dawn?"

"For the love of humanity, Mavis." Norma looked up from petting Harry Winston.

"See for yourself," Alex said, pleased that Norma had been listening.

He pulled out his phone. Scroll, scroll, and—yes, here was his favorite photo. Morning of the wedding. Pratyush sat up straight in the barber's chair, head poking out of a black apron, hair freshly cut. Laranya and Lorraine, Alex's own mother, beamed behind him. Sunshine poured into the salon. Pratyush's mouth was open, laughing at something. Alex wished he could remember what had made Pratyush laugh like that. With a proud smile, he handed the phone to Mavis.

"Your man is *hot*," Mavis said. She held out the phone to Norma. "Wanna check him out?"

"Some other time." Norma's tone was polite but terse, as if to establish that she was above checking anyone out.

"The lady on the left is Pratyush's mom. She came with us that morning." Alex took the phone from Mavis. "She invited my own mother to join us. So, there we were, the four of us packed in this tiny salon, plus the photographer. I think I had more fun that morning at the salon than I did at the wedding itself."

"Better than the wedding?" Mavis said with facetious skepticism. "Come on."

"Of course the wedding was fabulous," Alex said. "But we'd planned the ceremony and the reception to the last detail. The fun we'd had in the salon hit me by surprise. Kind of like—well, kind of like now. You know?"

"You need to send your husband to my salon sometime," Mavis said.

"Awesome! I will." But he'd never send Pratyush to see Mavis, not on their budget. He rose from the chair, thinking he'd passed Norma's test, if this business of having his hair cut really was a test. "Thanks for springing for the haircut, Norma."

"Thank you for straightening up my sitting room." Norma cast a careless glance at his hair.

"I can vacuum the rug before I go," Alex said, "in case there's still glass."

"That won't be necessary. The cleaners can take care of it tomorrow."

"Mavis, you won't mind if I offer you a tip?" He fumbled in his pocket for his wallet, fished out a twenty-dollar bill.

"I never mind being offered a tip." Mavis beamed and took the money, wedging the bill in her cleavage, beneath the airplane tattoo. "See you next time, Red Hot."

"I'm sorry it's not my wedding day again." He picked up the hand mirror and looked at himself. "A haircut like this deserves a special occasion."

"Then make it one." And Mavis's eyes shone wickedly.

It would be nice if Pratyush were already home by now. He could be on the couch with his laptop, maybe. His eyes would drift up and widen first with surprise then with appreciation at Alex's new look. What should happen next? Should Pratyush stand up and put his arms around him at the door? Should he put the laptop on the coffee table, invite Alex to join him? Either way, the fantasy would have to wait. Pratyush almost never came home before a quarter past five.

Alex walked into an empty apartment. Last night's leftover white bean soup sat in the fridge. Blah. His first day on the job with Norma—a resounding success—seemed to demand something snazzier than reheated soup.

Pratyush's footsteps sounded on the front stairs. Alex tensed up. But as soon as Pratyush shuffled into the kitchen, Alex knew at once that there'd be no restaurant, no romance, no change in their lives at all. His heart shrank inside his chest.

"You got a haircut?" A vague, questioning look on Pratyush's face.

"At Norma's house," Alex said, embarrassed. "Long story."

"Looks nice." A flicker of interest passed over Pratyush's face. Then he lowered his eyes. "I'm sorry, Alex."

"You don't have to be sorry." Alex stepped forward and put a hand on Pratyush's shoulder.

"You know I want to, don't you?" A beseeching look came into Pratyush's eyes. "I just can't stop worrying. I know you don't like me worrying. I try hard not to. But I can't stop the thoughts from buzzing around in my head."

"It's okay, it's okay," Alex said and brought Pratyush in for a hug. "This is only temporary. Soon I'll have a real job, and all this will be behind us."

"I hope so."

"It will, sweetie. It will."

Pratyush hugged Alex tightly as if to assure him that none of this was Alex's fault, that his feelings were as true as ever. Alex would have to accept this as consolation. Of all the men he'd ever been with—and he'd been with many, especially right after he'd moved to the Bay Area as a twenty-year-old nursing student—Pratyush remained by far the kindest, most considerate, and until very recently, most attentive and energetic in the bedroom. What else could Alex do but be patient?

Then Pratyush sighed and said, "I'd better go practice."

Alex brought out the soup after Pratyush left the kitchen. His eyelids felt heavy. The wall clock read twenty past five. Way too early for dinner. Way too early to feel this burnt-out. He put down the soup and looked out the window, gazing at the jasmine tumbling over the neighbor's fence.

CHAPTER 9

UNDER PLASTIC

THE NEXT MORNING, he found Norma on the terrace swathed in cranberry-colored satin, pen in hand like an artist's brush, Jackie O sunglasses in place. Harry Winston reclined in a patio chair like one of the stone lions in front of the New York Public Library. Her only jewelry was that pea-sized opal pendant. She'd apparently given the diamond watch the day off.

Only after he cleared his throat and said good morning did Norma tilt her gaze toward him. She already had the day's agenda mapped out for him—a grocery list, a claim ticket for dry cleaning, specifications for a new coffeepot to replace the one that had broken. Errands, good. He took the list and said he'd be back by lunchtime.

Later that afternoon, after the cleaners had come and gone and he'd finished with her knee exercises on the terrace, Norma asked him if he was still interested in burnishing his pool game. She feigned otherwise, but the glint in her eyes—even behind the sunglasses—suggested a keenness to teach him. They moved inside and settled by the pool table.

He spent a pleasant afternoon learning how to stand, how to hold a cue stick, how to sink one or two basic shots. The tougher work lay ahead. How to strategize, how to plan two or three shots in advance. Norma watched him play with a tranquil expression and spoke to him with more patience than he would've thought. He drove down the hill at five o'clock feeling more relaxed than he'd felt in months.

If the exterior of Norma's house struck him as less imposing than last week, so did the house's interior. Less space separated the kitchen island from the pool table and fireplace. The giraffe in the front hall greeted him with a jolly expression, as if the animal had made a new friend in Alex. The faceless models in the corridor regarded him with less scorn. Why should those models bother him? Wasn't Alex the one who could see?

But there was one sketch he couldn't help noticing every time he walked past—and only when his patient was safely out of sight. The drawing of the model in the crimson suit. Unlike his date upstairs, with his hand stuffed down his pocket and an arrogant tilt of his head, the young man in the red suit looked straight out, hands clasped, posture stiff, looking as shy, self-conscious, and vulnerable as if he were naked. Alex could imagine introducing himself to this guy at a house party, in the same way he'd introduced himself to Pratyush on the December night they'd met, eleven years ago already. Leaving his clutch of friends to walk up to this stranger and say hello, sorry to see him standing in a doorway by himself. The young man in the drawing—like Pratyush that night—would doubtless be full of surprises.

The suit itself had an understated classiness. The deep reddish-purple, like autumn leaves. Black edging around the lapels. If Alex had gone to his own prom, he would have chosen to wear this suit, not the starry extravaganza upstairs. But he didn't go to his own prom, did he? No use dwelling on that now.

Where were the family photos? None hung anywhere in the living area. Not a single framed photo graced an end table. If Norma used this living area for large parties, perhaps she'd rather have her guests admiring the Chagall and the carved masks than scrutinizing family history. Then again, the haunted look on Julie's face on Saturday suggested a deeper reason for the lack of photographs.

He might never have looked around for a family photo if he hadn't felt an itch to know what Kevin McKinsey looked like, a face to fill the blank oval on the model upstairs. Pictures of him might be floating around somewhere on the internet. All Alex had to do, probably, was type "Kevin McKinsey" and "famous prom suit" into a search engine. But to look up Kevin online would be admitting too much interest in him. Alex couldn't bring himself to do that.

And if Norma's progress was any indication, Alex would be out of here in a matter of days, not weeks. Friday's physical therapy went so well that he prepared himself for her to announce at the end of the day that she no longer needed him. Rent was due in little more than a week. What would he say to Pratyush?

At the end of that afternoon's pool lesson, Norma reached for the black handbag at her feet. If Norma planned to let him go, now would be the time. She pulled out a folded slip of paper and proffered it to him between scarlet fingernails. A check. He took the paper and slipped it into his pocket, making a silent promise to himself not to unfold it until after he reached home.

"Oh, and Alex?" Norma's expression betrayed no sentiment, just her usual observing look.

"Yes, Norma?" He turned to face her. Honestly, if she was going to let him go, couldn't she have said something sooner?

"I have an assignment for you this weekend." She zipped her purse shut and laid it in her lap. "Go to the shoe store and buy yourself a new pair of huaraches."

"A new pair of what?" Alex looked at his sandals then looked up. "You mean these?"

"Yes. Those." Norma glanced at the sandals with the same subtle but pointed look she'd given his overgrown hair on Monday. "I added an extra hundred dollars to your check so you can buy a new pair."

"I—uh—you didn't have to do *that*," he stammered. "I was thinking of buying new sandals this weekend anyway."

"Now you don't have to think about it." She nodded and gave a polite smile. "When you walk through that door on Monday, I want you wearing new huaraches. Do I make myself clear?"

"Yes. Loud and clear." A thrill passed through him at the sound of *Monday*.

"I was also thinking you might like to take advantage of my home gym," she went on. "Before you start the day's work. Do you belong to a gym?"

"I used to." He hadn't worked out in months, not since he'd let his membership lapse to cut down on expenses.

"My husband had that gym built for himself and my sons," she said. "Later on, my grandsons would come to work out. No one has used that gym since my youngest grandson left to teach English in Vietnam. I don't like those machines sitting idle."

"I'll bring my gym bag on Monday." Alex gave the smile he thought was called for. "Thanks, Norma."

He turned and headed for the front door, expecting her to summon him back to offer yet more perks. Forget about waiting to look at the check until he reached home—he pulled it out of his pocket as soon as he stepped out of the house. Even taking the extra hundred for the sandals into account, the check was fifty dollars more than what they'd agreed upon. Haircut. Pool lessons. Money for sandals. Use of her home gym. So much for worrying that she'd been preparing to let him go.

But none of this was normal. He would gladly have shown up for work on Monday with or without extra money for sandals, with or without permission to use the weight room. Norma wanted something from him, something other than a friendly face and a billiards student, more than a pair of hands guiding her through physical therapy. But what?

Best not to overanalyze. No need to relay his suspicions to Pratyush, either. Norma needed his services. Alex needed a paycheck. That was enough for now. He slipped the check into his pocket and drove home.

The weight room turned out to be smaller than he'd thought. Well-equipped, though. A full set of free weights. Two weight machines. A treadmill with a control panel that looked like it belonged at NASA. The gym even had its own bathroom, stocked with citrus-smelling liquid soap and fluffy white towels. How strange it felt, to have all this equipment to himself. No waiting for a weight or a machine. No risk of catching a cold— or worse—from the germs of other gymgoers. But working out alone was creepy. No one to talk to. No other guys to check out, or to check him out in return. All the same, he was content.

His second and third weeks of work fell into an agreeable rhythm. He'd arrive at Norma's at seven thirty for a workout. While in the gym, he'd hear her come downstairs and pass through the sliding door. After working out, he took care of Harry Winston's food dishes and litter box and put on a second pot of coffee for Norma. If he had the time and was feeling ambitious, he baked something, arranging muffins or cookies or banana bread on his elephant plate in case a friend stopped by. Then he'd change from his gym shoes to his new leather sandals—*huaraches*—and walk out onto the terrace to tend to his patient.

She wore something different every day. Sage green, butter yellow, scarlet, turquoise, peach with raspberry trim. Everything designed by her, no doubt, right down to the patterns and the seams. Alex imagined closets bursting with dresses, enough to clothe a parade of well-dressed women. The only similarity her outfits shared was their comfort—something she could easily drape over herself, no buttons or straps or zippers. More elaborate getups would have to wait, presumably, until after she could walk again.

If the outfits changed daily, the woman wearing them didn't. Norma always sat in the same chair by the patio table wearing the same opal pendant around her neck—a disappointingly modest habit, he had to admit, considering her reputed weakness for jewelry. Always scratching out a missive with extravagant sweeps of her pen. Harry Winston usually slept in a nearby chair or eyed the birds chirping in the trees beyond the retaining wall. Her tone of voice was never unkind, but still she said little. Her expression rarely moved behind her gigantic sunglasses as he guided her through her exercises. Her clothes were all he had to go by, to guess what she might be thinking.

By the end of the fourth week, Norma was doing so well that Alex couldn't believe that she wasn't walking on her own already. Yet when he hinted that perhaps she'd like to attempt a step or two without the walker, she refused. Perhaps she didn't want to let him go any more than he could afford to leave. He wasn't about to insist.

On Friday afternoon, he went upstairs to collect his check. His feet moved heavily up the stairs. The usual Friday dread of losing his job. At least he'd saved enough to cover next month's bills. He also had an initial phone interview next week for a clinic up in Vallejo, though it would likely be weeks before that clinic hired anyone. He walked to the doorway of Norma's sitting room and rapped gently on the door.

"There you are," she said, turning. "I was concerned you'd left already."

"I made brownies," Alex said. "They're on the counter."

"I thought I smelled the Correct Flavor." Norma reached for her purse, pulled out a check, and smiled at him. "See you Monday."

"Thanks." He slipped the folded check in his shirt pocket, relief flooding through him.

"But before you go," she said, as if it were an afterthought, "I need you to do me a favor."

"Of course."

A quarter to five on a Friday afternoon was an odd time for her to be giving him a task. She darted her eyes away. That, too, was unusual. She almost always held his gaze when she spoke to him.

"I have a new laptop." She nodded at a box sitting on the credenza. "Can you help me set it up?"

"Oh." He walked over to the credenza and lifted the box lid to reveal a white laptop, undoubtedly the store's priciest and most powerful model. This must be the laptop Julie had talked about—the laptop Charles had bought for Norma. "Sure, no problem."

"I've been told I can use the internet on it," she said. Her tone was vague, similar to the way Julie sometimes talked.

"You want to use the internet?" He looked at her. She'd never spoken of the internet in anything other than disparaging terms.

"Maybe. I'm not sure." She cast a distrustful glance at the laptop.

"You'll need Wi-Fi for the internet." He brought out the laptop and opened it, bringing the machine to life. "Do you know if you have Wi-Fi?"

"Charles says that I do."

"Do you know your Wi-Fi password?"

"Wi-Fi password?" She twisted the chain of her pendant.

"Wi-Fi usually requires a password. Whoever set up your Wi-Fi must've set up the password. That must've been Charles, right?"

"Yes. I believe so." Her stricken expression suggested she was regretting asking him this favor.

"I can call him and ask," Alex said, pulling out his phone. "I have his number."

"Don't do that," she said, holding out her hand. Then she collected herself and said, "I'd rather not trouble him for such a trifling thing."

Alex knew better than to push the issue. But something was off. An uneasy feeling sank in as he realized that whatever Norma wanted that laptop for, she didn't want Charles to know.

"If Charles says you have Wi-Fi, then there must be a Wi-Fi router somewhere in the house," he said. "Maybe he left the password with that router. Let me look for it."

He went downstairs without the slightest notion of where to search first. The router probably wasn't hiding in the kitchen or the living area, or else he would have spotted it by now. No router in the pantry or the laundry room. Nothing in the gym, of course. The storage room? The study? But those rooms were at the other end of the house.

His eyes traveled down the hall from the gym to the closed door of another room, between the laundry room and a side door that led outside. Another storage room? Maybe the router was hiding there. He walked up to the door and opened it.

The room wasn't a storage room but a bedroom, smaller than the guest bedrooms upstairs. The room held a bed, a bureau, and not much else. Plain gray-blue walls. A framed photo of a canal in Amsterdam by the window. A small mirror above the bureau. An unusual place to put up guests for the night, nowhere near any other bedroom in the house. Then it dawned on him. This must've been Kevin's bedroom.

The room was a few degrees cooler than the rest of the house. Alex soon saw why. The room had its own thermostat, set to seventy degrees. A portable humidifier hummed away next to the closet, whose door was tantalizingly ajar. Maybe the router sat on a shelf inside? He walked to the closet and opened the door the rest of the way.

Two suits hung smothered in translucent garment bags. In one bag, a riot of colors competed to dominate. The other bag was solid red. Alex's breath left him. Could these be The Suits? That would explain the room's climate control. He unzipped the garment bag of the red suit.

The fabric was a bolder crimson than its framed drawing in the corridor. A fleur-de-lis pattern covered the jacket, so subtle that he had to peer closely to make out the black thread tracing the velvety cloth. Wide black lapels. If clothes made statements, then this suit's statement ended with an exclamation point. A clashing contrast to the diffident model in the drawing.

Now for the second suit. The suit was a sea green so luminous that the fabric seemed to glow from within its threads. Tiny, embroidered stars in motley colors crowded the lapels, trailed down the jacket, and spiraled down one leg of the charcoal-gray pants like pixie dust. On the closet floor sat a shoebox. Alex bent down and opened the box to find a pair of black Nike sneakers, painted with little dots that matched the stars on the suit. He knelt on the carpet and held the box beneath the pants. The effect was stars bubbling up from the sneakers and swirling up the suit to the lapels. At least a hundred hand-embroidered stars adorned that suit. Norma must've sewn those stars herself. No wonder the woman was famous.

What a shame that these two dazzling suits—so patently meant to be worn and looked at, admired and celebrated—hung neglected in this forgotten room's closet. Alex stood up, stepped back, and regarded the starry sea-green dinner jacket, the shoebox in his hand.

"Alex?" Charles's voice said from behind.

Alex froze then turned around. Charles's frame filled the doorway. His white polo shirt was blinding in the sun streaming in from the window.

"Charles." Alex smiled as if he'd been waiting for Charles to show up. "Your mom didn't tell me you were coming today."

"She didn't know I was coming." Charles's tone was as dull as the bedroom's gray-blue walls. "I thought I'd surprise her with a barbecue."

"Should be a nice evening for a barbecue." Alex put the shoebox on the bed, his palms itching. "So—um—I was looking for your mom's Wi-Fi router. I need the password."

"Mom wants to use Wi-Fi?" Frank suspicion clouded Charles's face.

"Actually, I'm the one who needs Wi-Fi." Alex glanced over Charles's shoulder at the open door. "I've been eating up my data plan all this time."

"Password is 'fashion'." Charles's voice was unbelieving. "All lowercase."

"Thanks." Alex pulled out his phone and typed in the password, glad to have something to focus his eyes on.

"What's that?" Charles's eyes strayed to the shoebox on the bed.

"Sneakers." Alex picked up the box and held it out.

Charles walked up and peered inside the shoebox. A glimmer of a smile passed over his face. He reached into the box, brought out a sneaker painted with stars, and held it up to the light.

"Look how the colors change." Charles turned the shoe in his hand. The dots on the sneaker winked silver before blushing pink then vermilion.

"They look hand-painted." Alex was grateful that the sneakers had engrossed Charles.

"My brother painted them." Charles gazed at the shoe then looked at Alex with a shade of melancholy in his eyes. "I didn't realize my mom kept a pair in this closet. Or these suits, for that matter. I thought she kept everything in storage."

"Your brother designed those sneakers to go with that suit?" Alex couldn't resist asking.

"My brother didn't design the sneakers to go with the suit." A reminiscing smile spread across Charles's lips. "My mother designed the suit to go with the sneakers."

Charles nestled the shoe inside the box in Alex's hand, laying it alongside its twin like an infant in its cradle. Alex set the box on the bed and covered it with the lid.

"I couldn't resist looking," he said in a contrite voice to Charles. "I let my curiosity get the best of me."

"Then you must know about the splash those suits made." Charles was looking at the garments with a stiff, cool expression, as if he were running into insufferable relatives he hadn't seen in years. "I never cared for the designs myself."

"Not everyone can pull that look off. I know I couldn't," Alex said, hoping that response sounded tactful enough. He glanced at his phone.

"My brother could pull that look off," Charles said with a hint of sorrow in his tone, and then he shrugged.

Charles zipped up both garment bags. A guilty feeling coursed through Alex for unzipping the bags in the first place, for peeking into Kevin's closet. No doubt Charles would report all this to his mother. The humidifier emitted a soft whooshing sound.

"I should be going," Alex said, slipping his phone into his pocket.

"You haven't called me once since you started here." Charles turned to look him in the eye, though not with an unfriendly expression. "I take that to mean Mom's doing well."

"She's making amazing progress." Alex was thankful to hear Charles referring to Norma as *Mom* and not *my mother*. A sign of a thaw in his attitude, perhaps.

"Glad to hear. I'm available if you need anything," Charles said, his tone half-hearted, and he gave Alex a modest smile and left the room.

Alex listened to Charles's voice echoing from the kitchen area as he talked to Norma through the intercom. Soon his footsteps headed upstairs. Alex let go of the breath he was holding and scurried down the hallway to the kitchen.

What about the Wi-Fi password? Now that he knew the password, how was he supposed to tell Norma? He didn't have Norma's phone number. He rooted through the kitchen drawers, found a package of yellow sticky notes and a pen, and wrote *Wi-Fi Password: fashion (all lowercase)*. Now, where to leave the note so that Charles wouldn't see it?

Not the counter. Not the refrigerator. Beneath the dome of the crystal cake dish, under the elephant plate holding a pyramid of brownies? What if Charles wanted a brownie later? Alex's scalp itched with sweat.

Out on the terrace, Harry Winston lay asleep on his back on Norma's favorite lounge chair, exposing his prodigious orange belly. A fashion magazine lay open on the cushion next to him. Alex slipped through the sliding door and crept up to the magazine, open to a photograph of a young woman in a feathery pink ball gown. He stuck the note next to the model's pouty lips. Then he closed the magazine, tickled Harry's belly, and hustled around the house to his car.

CHAPTER 10

BARBECUE

NORMA SAT UP, palms flat on the circular table. No mistake, that was Charles's voice downstairs. He and Alex were talking. The open laptop on the credenza gaped at her.

There was no way to discern what Charles and Alex were saying, but they must be talking about her. What else did they have in common? Perhaps that was why Charles had shown up unannounced. Not to ambush her, but to ambush Alex. *How is my mother doing—really?*

Now, Mom. Charlie isn't the one who's up to something. You are.

If Alex was as discreet and quick-thinking as she knew him to be—as she knew he *should* be—he'd keep his mouth shut about the Wi-Fi router. No time to think about that. The laptop needed to go into a drawer, now. She could already hear Charles's voice if he saw that laptop sitting there. *So, you decided to use the laptop after all? What for?*

She reached for the walker and hoisted herself up. Her hand slipped on the handle. She gasped, tottered, grabbed the edge of

117

the circular table. The walker tipped over on its side. But that wasn't what shocked her. What shocked her was... Could it be true? No pain in the injured leg?

She pressed her foot on the carpet, waiting for her knee to buckle or a spasm to shoot down her leg pin. Nothing. She let go of the table edge. Both legs on the floor. A negligible twinge in the bad knee. Nothing else.

See that, Mom? Now you don't need Alex anymore. That's your reward for working so hard.

"Mom?" Charles's voice crackled through the intercom. "Are you there?"

On past visits, Charles insisted on coming up and escorting her downstairs. If she didn't reach that intercom to stall him, he'd take that as permission to come up. No time to right the overturned walker. She pressed her foot onto the carpet and took a step. A second step. She crept to the intercom as if walking a tightrope.

"Charles?" Her finger pressed the intercom button so hard that her French-manicured nail went even whiter.

"Hiya, Mom." Charles had a bounce in his voice, manifestly artificial.

"I didn't realize you were coming today."

"I have some time this evening, so I thought I'd swing by and cook on the grill. Can I come up?"

"Is Alex downstairs?"

"He's on his way out." Charles's tone took a turn for the frosty—no doubt a more accurate reflection of his state of mind.

"Give me two minutes." Norma glanced at the laptop. "And then you can come up."

She let go of the intercom button. Not a moment to spare. She crept to the credenza, shut the laptop, stashed it in a drawer. Never mind the walker. She managed to settle into the chair right as Charles tapped on the door and walked in.

"Are you okay?" He looked with concern at the overturned walker.

"Yes, thanks," she managed to say. "The walker tipped over as I was sitting down."

"Honestly, Mom." Charles went over and picked up the walker. "Imagine if you'd knocked this over when no one was home. Then what would you have done?"

He placed the walker in front of her. His smile was admonishing but good-natured. A more inquisitive mind might have noticed that for the walker to have landed on the carpet that far from her chair, Norma would have had to shove it, maybe even throw it. Fortunately, Charles's mind didn't work that way. He'd surely tell Debra later that he'd saved Norma from spending the weekend sitting confined to a chair, unable to reach her walker.

Be nice, Mom. He brought dinner.

"I have salmon and a couple of veggie skewers from the market." Charles's expression was one of affected good humor. "I thought we'd eat outside and watch the sunset."

"Wonderful. I haven't used the grill all summer," Norma said. "Where's Debra tonight?"

"Hosting book club," Charles said, with a forced upturn in his voice that suggested, perhaps, that he'd been run out of his own house. He must drive Debra crazy, hanging around the house all day.

For once, she took the arm Charles offered to pull herself up to the walker. She took care as she made her way out of the sitting room and down the corridor to the main staircase. Under his attentive eye, she made sure her every step was one an invalid would take.

Downstairs, she fake-hobbled toward the living area. What if Alex had written the Wi-Fi password on a slip of paper? Stuck the paper to the fridge with a magnet? Now that would be mortifying.

Especially since Charles must know the password. *Why didn't you ask me, Mom? Why do you want that password, anyway?*

Her eye caught a packet of yellow Post-it notes on the counter. The meal service used those notes to label food containers. Those Post-its weren't sitting on the counter—she was sure of that—before she'd gone upstairs. *Ipso facto*, Alex must have written the password on one of those notes. She inched her way toward the counter. The top note was blank.

"What's that you're looking at, Mom?" Charles called out behind her.

"Nothing."

Either Alex had missed his chance to write down the password, or, more likely, he'd written down the password and hid the note somewhere only she would look. Leaving the packet of notes on the counter must have been his signal to let her know he'd completed his task.

Of course, she could call Alex later and ask him for the password. But he was off duty. To disturb him over the weekend was the sort of thing only oblivious rich people did. Norma couldn't avoid being rich. But she *could* avoid being oblivious.

"The veggie skewers are mushrooms and peppers and onions," Charles said, opening the refrigerator door. "Some have green peppers, I'm afraid. I asked if they had ones with only red peppers, but no such luck."

"Green peppers are fine, Charlie." She peered over Charles's shoulder into the refrigerator. No password on any of the sticky notes in there.

How about that, Mom? Charlie remembered you don't like green peppers.

Everyone knows I don't like green peppers.

I didn't know.

Of course you know.

You think I'd remember something like that? After all this time? I'll remind you when I find you.

She had forgotten how much Charles enjoyed barbecuing. The scrubbing of the grill and the turning of food over the flames kept him happily occupied. The salmon glistened in a glaze of soy sauce and brown sugar. And she couldn't have asked for better weather to eat outside. The sky was robin's-egg blue, the setting sun a gold medallion, the air warm and inviting, free of wildfire smoke.

Implausible, though, that Charles would happen to be passing through the neighborhood with salmon steaks and vegetable skewers. As happened so often these days, he couldn't be telling her the whole story. Perhaps he'd bought the food to grill for himself and Debra tonight, forgetting that Debra already had plans. If so, then no wonder he'd decided to pay his mother a surprise visit. Seeing Alex here would have ruined everything for him. Alex was a walking, talking reminder that Norma could manage without him during the day, reducing him to seeing her only at night.

Her eye fell on the *Marie Claire* magazine lying on the chaise longue next to a somnolent Harry Winston. When she'd gone inside earlier, she'd left that magazine lying open. Now the magazine was closed. The sticky note with the password must be inside. Something Kevin would have thought to do.

Ouch, Mom. Now you'll spend dinner waiting for Charlie to leave.

Charles's buoyant mood as they sat down to dinner suggested he'd forgotten about his run-in with Alex. He chatted about the cabin at Tahoe he'd rented for next weekend, his intention to visit Jonah and Maria in Seattle once the baby was born, his annual trip to Cabo San Lucas in January with Debra and two other couples. He'd spoken last night to Jeff in Vietnam—Jeff was loving his Peace Corps assignment. His daughter-in-law's pregnancy was going smoothly.

Just think, Mom, you're going to be a great-grandmother! Isn't that exciting?

"I'm curious to know about Aunt Julie's tenant," Charles said. He pushed his empty plate away and leaned back, adjusting his patio chair to face the view. "He's working out?"

"He's been a help." The fork in her hand went heavy. How unrealistic of her to think Charles wouldn't probe about Alex.

"Does he come for the whole day?" Charles's gaze was fixed on the horizon. A brilliant orange band traced the line where sky and water met.

"Pretty much." Norma glanced over Charles's shoulder at the sleeping Harry Winston, his head resting on the *Marie Claire* like a pillow.

"Physical therapy doesn't take all day."

"He also runs errands, fixes lunch, takes care of the cat, does some baking every now and then," Norma said, leaving out the part about the pool lessons and the weight room. "He made brownies earlier today, if you want one."

"I brought tiramisu from the market." Charles's face was half in shadow. "How much longer do you think you'll be having him around?"

"That depends on my knee." She shot another look at Harry Winston—lucky cat, how carefree he looked—then over at the horizon. The sky above the orange band deepened to lapis lazuli.

"I found him snooping in Kevin's closet earlier," Charles said.

"Snooping?" She sat up, indignant that Charles would sully the Blue Hour with such a provocative word.

"He was looking at your old prom suits." He gave her a meaningful look, as if goading her to concede that Alex had been doing something wrong.

"I'd hardly call that snooping." She speared her last bite of salmon, not at all appreciating his depiction of those suits as *old*.

"I didn't realize you kept those suits in the house," Charles said. "I thought they were in storage with the rest of your designs."

"Every now and then someone—a design student, a journalist—will ask if they can have a glimpse of those suits," Norma said, giving her stock answer. In fact, she hated the idea of exiling those suits to a warehouse. "I can forgive Alex for being curious."

"But why was he poking around in that closet in the first place? He *said* he was looking for your Wi-Fi router." Charles couldn't have sounded any more doubtful—or more derisive. "Said he wanted the password for his phone."

"Is that all?" She ate the salmon on her fork, relieved Alex hadn't betrayed her.

"Come on, Mom. The nurse wasn't in Kevin's room looking for that router."

"As a matter of fact, he'd asked me this morning if I knew what my Wi-Fi password was." Norma surprised herself by how deftly she was able to build on Alex's lie. "What *is* the password, by the way? I was embarrassed to tell Alex I had no idea."

"Fashion," Charles said with an edge in his voice. "All lowercase. It's the same password if you ever decide to use the laptop. I set up your user profile before I gave the laptop to you. The router's in Dad's study, underneath the desk."

How about that, Mom? All this James Bond theater about the password, and all you had to do was ask Charlie.

"I still can't believe that Kevin took a boy to prom," Charles went on, taking her by surprise. Charles almost never brought up Kevin with her. "What was his date's name again?"

"Zack Patterson," she said, realizing too late that she should have answered Charles's question with less speed.

"Zack Patterson, that's right. I remember talking with him right here on the terrace at Kevin's graduation party. Nice kid." Charles looked lost in thought, his expression turning reflective. "Do you have any idea what happened to him?"

"I think he went to some East Coast college," Norma said, although, in truth, she had no idea how she knew this.

A memory came to her of Zack standing in her full-length mirror, as stiff as the mannequin in her sewing room, not daring to make the slightest move. It was her idea to swathe him in red, give the kid a boost of confidence. She remembered how Zack's face had lit up when she draped the fabric over his shoulder. Kevin had told her later that he'd never seen Zack more outgoing than when he was wearing that suit.

"Kevin was terrified about attending that school, you know," Charles said.

"No, he wasn't," Norma said, scoffing.

"Oh, yes, he was," Charles said. "An all-boys jock school? He begged me to talk Dad out of sending him there, that's how frightened he was."

"He never said anything to me," Norma said, looking at Charles. "*Did* you talk to your father?"

"What good would that have done? Telling Dad would've only made things worse. That's what I told Kevin." Charles shrugged. "Dad went to that school, so we were both going to that school too. No ifs, ands, or buts."

"But Kevin excelled there." She recalled how Robert had talked about his sons attending that prep school as if he couldn't conceive of another option. It had never occurred to her to challenge him. "He was on the track team."

"Not because he *wanted* to take up running, Mom." Charles

leaned toward her with a significant look. "Because he *had* to take up running. If you didn't play sports at that school, you didn't exist. Or worse—you became a target."

"A target," she repeated. How could she have been unaware of all this? Yet another reminder of how accidental a mother she was.

"But he ended up loving track, didn't he?" Charles's tone perked up. "And by senior year he stopped caring what anyone thought of him. Everyone loved him for it. He helped change that school for the better. Remember his graduation party?"

"Half his class was here on this terrace," she said, her voice low. Memories of that party never failed to pain her.

"He had a bigger party than I did, and *I* was captain of the basketball team." Charles stood up with dirty plates in his hands. "I wonder if I would've sent my own sons to that school if Kevin hadn't done what he'd done. You know, Mom, I don't know how we came to talk about this. How about a piece of tiramisu?"

"What about you, Charlie?" She looked up at him. "*You* were never a target at that school, were you?"

"Me? Oh gosh, no." His face grew sober. "But I saw stuff. Bad stuff. Not that *I* ever participated in any of that, but—looking back on it, I wish I'd spoken up more. I didn't know about Kevin *then*."

"When *did* you know about Kevin?" She had often wondered about this but had never worked up the nerve to ask.

"When he asked me how I thought you'd take it if he told you he was taking another boy to the prom." Charles gave a shrug and a smile, not boastful but not exactly modest either.

"He talked to you first," she said, unsure why this news came as such a letdown. Kevin used to idolize his brother, and perhaps still did. "What did you say?"

"I told him I'd be surprised if you'd be anything but

supportive," he said. Then he rolled his eyes and said, "Ugh, high school. Thank God we're teenagers only once. So, tiramisu?"

"A small piece," she said even though she'd rather have a brownie. "Thanks."

He went into the house with the dirty plates. The orange band of sunlight had dissolved into a pink pencil line. The moon shone pearl white against the cloudless sky. An enchanting evening, not that much different, come to think of it, than the evening of Kevin's graduation party. Norma leaned back in her chair, too nettled to enjoy the Blue Hour.

Charles left at a few minutes past nine. He asked her if she'd like his help going upstairs, but she said she'd rather stay outside and take in the cool air. He did her the favor of not arguing. She watched him go into the house and didn't stir from her chair until she was certain he'd driven away.

Then she rose and headed for the chaise longue where Harry Winston lay, using the walker lest one of the neighbors happened to spot her from a window. Harry squirmed and looked up at her sleepily as soon as she sat down next to him, purring as if nothing made him happier than to have her sit nearby. She opened the magazine and found Alex's sticky note. His handwriting was rushed.

Was it too early to search for Kevin on the laptop? The sunset had settled into evening, but the sky, sapphire blue, was cloudless. A few stars were showing, peaceful in their permanence. Maybe she should sit here and enjoy this moment instead.

What's the matter, Mom? Afraid of what you might find online? Or are you feeling guilty about lying to Charlie?

She pulled herself up on the walker and made her way toward the sliding door, Harry Winston trailing her.

*

Once in the sitting room, she lowered the blinds and brought out the laptop. A hummingbird in her chest thrummed its wings. Could tracking down her son really be as simple as typing his name into a machine? She set the laptop on the circular table, opened it, and pressed the *On* button.

A beep. A whir. A dialog box appeared on the screen, requesting a password. Norma typed *fashion*, and *voilà*, the screen came alive with a stock photo of a country meadow. A pizza-slice-shaped icon glowed in the lower right-hand corner of the screen. She'd seen that symbol before, at cafés and airports. Was that the symbol for Wi-Fi? She scrolled the cursor over the icon and clicked it. Her own name appeared. She clicked on her name. A new dialog box requested a password. She typed *fashion,* hit enter. *Voilà*. She had the disquieting sense of unlocking the gate to a toxic waste dump.

A row of icons spread down the left-hand side of the screen. One of them, if Norma was not mistaken, would lead her to the internet. She clicked this icon. A search engine appeared on the screen. She raised her fingers over the keyboard. The hummingbird buzzed inside her ribcage as if struggling to escape her chest. She typed Kevin's name and pressed enter.

An avalanche of information deluged her screen in 0.79 seconds. Page after page of links leading to all manner of Kevin McKinseys. A Kevin McKinsey in New Hampshire. A Kevin McKinsey in the armed forces. Four Kevin McKinseys in Ireland. Obituaries for Kevin McKinsey: one in Arkansas, one in Wisconsin, two in New York. None of these Kevin McKinseys could be the one she wanted.

Are you surprised, Mom? You had to know I wouldn't make it easy.

She typed in *Kevin McKinsey Oakland*. A link from Kevin's high school appeared in 0.61 seconds. An old yearbook photo—the school must have uploaded their archives—that she herself kept hidden in a drawer, unable to look at without feeling wretched. Next down the page, a link led her to an old article about Kevin McKinsey, the model son of that rising star of the fashion world, Norma McKinsey, making his runway debut. The article had nothing but glowing things to say about this young man's future. A feeling of nausea invaded her senses.

She clicked to the next page. Then another page. And another. But no. Nothing else. That vapid fashion article was the most recent story she could find about Kevin. Had he changed his name? Or had he drifted to the margins, evading the notice of the all-seeing internet?

Told you, Mom. You might as well give up.

She could always hire someone to search for her. A private detective. Did she dare stoop to Robert's level, do what Robert had done to her? No. Kevin would be appalled.

Or would he? Wouldn't Kevin forgive her now—at the age of almost eighty, after that harrowing car accident—for wanting some idea of his whereabouts? What harm would she cause if, say, she typed *private detective Oakland* into that search engine?

The laptop spewed links to local private investigators in 0.53 seconds. Norma had never seen the man who'd followed her movements all those years ago, but she pictured him as a palooka, heavy features, metal-gray eyes. A maw in his chest where his heart should have resided. She'd never hire a goon like that to track down Kevin.

Her eye fell on a link for an all-female PI agency. An all-woman agency? She was abashed to realize that a private detective agency *could* be run by only women. She clicked the link.

An official-looking home page presented itself, the typeface bold and serious. The head PI was one Anne Carruthers, a retired detective who'd served thirty years on the OPD. A menu of investigative services was listed on the right-hand side of the screen. Insurance claims. Background checks. Financial fraud. Missing persons. Norma clicked the missing persons link and read Anne's professional yet heartfelt essay on the agency's record of "reuniting families." *Reuniting families*—the term had an upstanding ring to it. She hovered the cursor over the contact form to reach Anne Carruthers.

Are you sure you want to do this, Mom?

You've given me no choice.

I bet that's what Dad said when he hired that detective to follow you.

The contact form requested—good grief—an email address. Norma's only email was from her business, long forgotten like last year's fashions. Her assistants had used that email on her behalf. What was that email address again? For the love of humanity. Couldn't she stop by the detective's office in person?

All right, then. She needed a new email address. But, of course, she didn't have to set up that address herself. Not while Alex still worked for her. He could doubtless set up an address for her in far less time than she could. No need for him to know— yet—that her leg was better. Let him complete this errand for her, then she'd let him go.

Gee, Mom. Always reaching for excuses to put this off.

Be quiet, Kevin.

CHAPTER 11

PLAYING GAMES

WHAT AN ABYSMAL start to the weekend, this fruitless online search for Kevin. On the day she discovered she could walk again, to boot. She should have been toasting her good health with Charles earlier, not wishing him out of the house. Or she could have called Julie to celebrate the good news. How had she spent her evening instead? Holed up in her sitting room, wading through sludge some search engine had regurgitated. Now she lay in bed, staring up at the ceiling and seething. Charles should never have given her that laptop. This was *his* fault.

Email. How was it possible that she yearned for an email address? But as Charles had said at the rehab center, her friends around the world must all use email by now. Charles certainly did. Julie too, for that matter. Everyone must have email nowadays. Everyone, that is, except herself and Harry Winston, now curled up at the foot of the bed in blissed-out ignorance. This was her comeuppance for banishing computer screens from her life, for enlisting others to work the machines for her.

Did Kevin have email? Probably. That might be a positive development. He might be living too far away for her to reach him in person, or even to call him. He could be climbing the Himalayas or wandering the Sahara or teaching English in some far-flung country. Email might be her only option. But only if she had his email address.

She made her way down the stairs by herself on Saturday morning, looking forward to a peaceful if lonely weekend. The sky beyond the picture windows was a spotless pale blue. An ideal morning to have lunch at an outdoor café, or to stroll one of the hiking trails at Tilden Park down the road. Wild irises and lilacs must be dotting the trails. But she couldn't be seen outdoors without her walker. The flowers would have to wait.

Inviting a friend to the house was out of the question, too. Not if it meant pretending to limp around for a few hours, fussing over a knee that no longer gave her trouble. Even to finish the letter she was writing to her friend in Rome, without mentioning she could walk again, smacked of dishonesty. She'd settle for Harry Winston's company this weekend. Alex could help her set up the email on Monday.

How dispiriting, this having to wait for Alex. She'd run a flourishing business for close to forty years, for heaven's sake. How hard could it be to create an email address? But the thought of opening Charles's laptop made her shudder.

You're waiting because you're afraid, Mom. Afraid of wallowing in the mud like Dad. Afraid of what that PI might find on me.

She was finishing her breakfast at the dining table when the cordless phone by the sliding door rang. Too early for a robocall, especially on Saturday. Charles, again? Who else would have the nerve to call this early? She rose and walked to the telephone.

"Norma!" Julie said. Her voice burst through the phone receiver with the same energy as Harry Winston lunging for a moth on the terrace.

"Jules," she said coolly.

"I thought I'd check in before I run errands," Julie said. "How's the knee?"

"Improving every day." Norma was pleased to have said something truthful.

"Glad to hear it," Julie said. By the sincerity in her tone, she might even have meant those words. "Alex must be a big help."

Aha. This was what Julie was up to. She hadn't called to check up on Norma. She'd called because Charles must have called her first thing this morning, to pump her for information about Alex. Norma hesitated, holding in her vexation.

"I was thinking of paying you a visit this evening," Julie went on. "Should be a fine night for a sunset."

"I don't know." Norma glanced at her knee.

"Are you sure?" Julie's tone was tinged with a note of disappointment. "We can play cribbage on the terrace."

Now, Mom. You know you can't say no to Aunt Julie. Uncle Phil isn't around anymore.

"Okay, come at six," Norma said. "We might as well have dinner too. The meal service left me a lasagna I could never finish by myself."

At six o'clock sharp, the sound of Julie's voice—*yoo-hoo!*—echoed from inside the house. No need for Norma to budge from her chaise longue. On an evening as warm as this one, Julie would know to find her here. Soon Julie stepped through the sliding door, her expression brightening at Norma in her cornflower-blue striped ikat dress, both knees concealed in folds of flowing cotton.

Julie insisted on heating up the lasagna and setting the patio table. Norma let Julie do the work. At dinner, Julie prattled away about her life, her friends, her cockatiels, her latest calls with Kate in Chicago and with Olivia in Tokyo, not once asking Norma any pointed questions. The longer Julie talked, the gladder Norma was to have invited her over. She would have regretted whiling away this gorgeous weekend by herself.

After dinner, Julie cleared the table, put on coffee, and brought out two of Alex's brownies on plates along with a pack of cards and Norma's cribbage board from the study. Phil had given Norma the board for her sixtieth birthday, having carved and polished it himself from a piece of driftwood he'd brought home from a camping trip in Sierra County. To think she cherished a homemade gift her sister's husband had given her twenty years ago, when she'd kept nothing from her own husband—not the rubies, not the emeralds, not even the ring he'd bought her in Paris on their honeymoon, a square diamond nestled in a halo of blood-red garnets, to compensate, he said, for their quickie wedding ceremony. She shuffled the cards and set the deck in front of Julie.

"First cut of the summer," she said with a smile that betrayed none of these thoughts.

Julie cut the cards and drew a jack. Norma drew an eight. Julie shuffled the cards, her eyes straying to the cribbage board with a wistful smile.

"We've been lucky with the weather this week," Julie said, putting two cards face-down for the crib. She arranged her remaining cards and studied them then looked up at the rose-tinged clouds. "You must be out here every night."

"Sure have. Me and Mr. Winston over there," Norma said, looking at the cat. He lay on the chaise longue like a bread loaf, front and back paws tucked in, eyes languorous, watching them in an attitude of total satiation. "Every evening we watch the sunset together. Then he follows me inside for the night."

"Sounds like a nice arrangement," Julie said, laying down the seven of clubs and looking over her shoulder at the cat with a smile.

"Charles was over here last night." Norma peered above her cards at Julie. "He barbecued."

"I know," Julie said with a sigh. "He called me this morning."

"He did? What for?" Norma hadn't expected Julie to answer so readily. She laid an eight on top of Julie's seven and moved her blue peg forward two spaces.

"To ask about Alex." Julie laid her cards face-down on the table and looked at Norma with a frank expression.

"What did he want to know?"

"What kind of person Alex was." Julie picked up her cards and laid a nine on top of the eight, advanced her red peg three spaces. "Since, as he put it, Alex is up here forty hours a week."

Was that a note of envy in Julie's voice? But this was her doing, Alex coming here every day. Norma pursed her lips and played a three.

"You said good things, I hope," she said, glancing at Julie above her remaining cards.

"I said Alex was a respectable man who paid his rent on the first of every month." Julie spoke with a tactfulness she'd no doubt used on Charles this morning. She laid down a four of spades and moved her peg up two spaces. "Thirty-one for two points."

"Rats, you did have a four," Norma muttered.

Better to express irritation about the game than about

Charles's intelligence-gathering. So her hunch was right—Charles had called Julie, prompting Julie to call Norma. She wished she could be wrong about these things on occasion.

"You must be keeping Alex busy." Julie glanced at the remaining card in her hand. "I never see him come home before five."

"Busy enough." Norma laid a queen of diamonds to start the next hand. "I'm surprised he hasn't told you himself about his days here."

"I never see him anymore," Julie said with another sigh. She laid down the six of spades and picked up the cards in the crib. "He probably wouldn't tell me anyway. Patient confidentiality, right?"

Harry Winston jumped into Julie's lap as Julie counted the points in her crib. His purrs reached Norma from across the table. A real pair, those two.

"Howdy, my big orange pal," Julie said, wrapping an arm around the cat. With her free hand she laid the crib cards down and reached for her peg. "Two points in the crib."

"Tell me about skydiving," Norma said, collecting the cards and shuffling them. It must have been looking at the sky in full Blue Hour mode, shifting from cerulean to sapphire, which prompted her to ask Julie that question. "You're still going?"

"If I can find someone to go with," Julie said. The cat brought his paws to the table and sniffed first the brownie on Julie's dessert plate and then the edge of the cribbage board. Julie shooed him off the table and said, "That's a beautiful dress you have on. Is that one of your designs?"

"I wish," Norma said, dealing cards. "But, no, I bought this dress on that trip to Bali I took with Robert a hundred years ago. It's been years since I've worn it. I dug out all my dresses from that trip since they're easy to slip on in the morning."

"That's right, you've *been* to Bali," Julie said, suddenly interested. She played a ten. "You enjoyed Bali, didn't you?"

"Loved it," Norma said, laying down another ten and advancing her peg two spaces. "Heaven on earth."

"My Australia friends emailed me this morning, saying they're thinking about going there next year." Julie laid down a nine. "Instead of snorkeling with them at the Great Barrier Reef, they want me to join them in Bali. Do you think you'd like to go with me?"

"Maybe," Norma said, thinking Phil would want her to go. "I'll shop for more dresses."

"Like you need more dresses," Julie said with a smile. "How's your knee? You must be close to walking on your own again."

"Not…quite." Norma took a sudden interest in the cards in her hand. A five of clubs, the ace of spades. She played the ace and said, "Thirty."

"Not that I'm rushing you. Alex needs a job." Julie beamed and laid the ace of hearts on Norma's ace of spades, then she reached for her red peg. "Thirty-one."

As much as she was looking forward to seeing Alex on Monday, she dreaded having to mislead him about her knee. Alex, as a nurse, and as the one who spent the most time with her, was much more likely than Charles or Julie to figure out that she could walk again. How would he react if he found out she'd lied? He'd surely rather tend to a patient in need. She spent Sunday night writing an errand list that would keep him out of the house all day. The less time he spent observing her, the better.

Monday morning came. By now she'd grown used to him letting himself into the house at seven thirty. The cat, as usual, sprang off the bed at the sound of his footsteps. Alex clinked glasses and plates downstairs while she showered and dressed. The aroma of coffee greeted her on her chair ride down the front stairs. A lemony aroma mingled with the coffee. Even if she did track down Kevin, the house would feel bigger and lonelier without Alex.

He was wiping down the counters in the kitchen area, his hair wet from his shower. A lemon cake in a loaf pan sat on a cooling rack. The lemons came from Julie's tree, he said. If he had any suspicion that her knee was better, he didn't show it. Perhaps he was in no hurry to stop coming here, any more than she wanted him to leave. Why shouldn't she keep employing him? Otherwise he'd be sitting at home, taking care of no one. She gave him her errand list, and off he went.

Now she had the next five hours in the house by herself, no closer to having an email than on Friday night. At least he should be back by mid-afternoon, in time for his pool lesson. She'd ask him about email then.

You better, Mom.

Kevin kept her company at breakfast, wanting to know how the lemon cake was. Brownies on Friday, lemon cake today: how fortunate she must feel to have such an attentive nurse! Did she remember all those times he used to bake cookies for her bridge parties? Of course she remembered. Kevin read the paper with her, flipped through the latest fashions with her, had witticisms to pronounce on every outfit, every accessory, every model's smoldering looks. Never mind pouring out her thoughts in a missive to her Rome friend—everything she wanted to say, she said in her mind to Kevin.

I'm going to find you soon, is that okay? You'll adore the cat I adopted. Your Aunt Julie misses you so much. Uncle Phil has passed away, she could use your company. She wants to go skydiving. Can you believe that? Have you ever gone skydiving, Kevin?

★

Not until three thirty, a good forty-five minutes later than she expected, did Alex return from his errands, arms laden with shopping bags. By four o'clock, he had made coffee and brought a mug for her on the sofa along with a slice of lemon cake. Sunshine glowed behind the drawn shades. Harry Winston settled himself onto the back of the sofa, his usual spot during one of Alex's pool lessons, looking as content as Norma felt now that Alex had returned. If sunset on the terrace was the Blue Hour, right now—from four to five o'clock at the pool table— was the Golden Hour. A time when nothing went wrong.

Alex went to the billiard table and lifted the rack from the triangle of balls, gleaming like a wizard's orbs against the green felt. This was Norma's favorite part of the game, this moment before the break, a time when anything was possible. He leaned over the table with the cue stick, adjusted his arm like she'd taught him, and gave the cleanest break she'd ever seen him do. Then he straightened up and looked at her with a schoolboy's smile. This could be Kevin all over again. An ache rippled through her.

"I hope you won't think I'm prying, but I have to know." He was walking around the table, his eyes focused on the billiard balls. "Who taught you to play pool?"

"My mother-in-law." Robert's mother, Miriam, appeared in Norma's mind, a small woman with neat black curls, thin, high-strung, smoking one cigarette after another.

"Your mother-in-law played pool?" Alex looked up as if surprised to hear Norma had ever had a mother-in-law, let alone a mother-in-law who played pool.

"Better than anyone I've known," she said, reaching behind her to pet Harry Winston. "My husband and father-in-law used to travel for business early on in my marriage. Charles was a baby.

Most days I took Charles to my mother-in-law's. She taught me pool while Charles crawled around in his playpen next to the pool table."

"She must've been an expert," Alex said with a look of admiration.

"I didn't know that at the time," Norma said. "This used to be her table. She bequeathed it to me. As part of her will, she'd written a letter directly to me, in her own handwriting, that I was the only one who played well enough to do justice to her pool table."

"I'd love to watch you play sometime." Alex's smile was polite, but his wide eyes suggested she'd made him think. Perhaps he found it interesting that Miriam had pointedly left her own son out of the bequest. He collected himself and turned his attention to the pool balls. "I swear to God, I can stare all day at this table, but staring won't stop the 10-ball from blocking the 2-ball."

"Let me see." She rose to stand with the aid of her walker, perhaps a shade more ostentatiously than she should have. "Never mind the 10-ball. Find another option. No point wasting time wishing things were different."

"Is that what your mother-in-law would say?"

"As surely as if she were standing right here." Her mind turned to Robert, dead on the terrace. *No point wasting time wishing things were different.*

"Hmm," Alex said, walking around the table, looking for angles. "It's the 3-ball or the 6-ball. I can't decide."

At the rate you're going, Mom, you're never going to ask him about the email.

"Charles tells me you came across my suits," she said, settling onto the sofa again.

"By accident." Alex straightened up with an embarrassed

look, the cue stick slack in his hands. "I was looking for that Wi-Fi password you wanted."

"That's what I told Charles." Norma looked at Harry Winston, now fast asleep.

"Those are the same suits as in your drawings," Alex said, leaning the pool cue against the table. "Aren't they?"

"They are."

"Julie tells me those suits made you famous." He spoke with quiet delicacy, as if he'd been wanting to broach this topic for weeks.

"For the record, I wasn't trying to become famous. My business was solvent. My client base was small but faithful. I was more than content with my career. All I wanted that spring was to design two suits for my son and his date." This was the answer, smooth and succinct, that she'd recounted to myriad journalists over the years. She cut a piece of lemon cake.

"Your other son, you mean." Alex cast a careful glance at her.

"Correct. My younger son. Kevin." Norma surprised herself with her bearing, considering she'd said Kevin's name out loud.

"Did you know he was taking another boy to prom?" Alex picked up the cue stick and surveyed the pool table.

"The prom was his way of informing me of his sexuality." She ate a bite of cake and sipped coffee from her mug. "A couple months before prom, Kevin came into my sewing room, visibly nervous, and asked if I could help him pick out a prom suit. Naturally I offered to design him one instead. He said he didn't want me designing his suit, since his date's family had little money. So I offered to design a prom dress for his date. 'Not a dress for a girl,' he said. 'A suit for a guy.' And that, Alex, is how I learned my younger son was gay."

"That's a novel way to come out to your parents. I told my

own mom over the phone." He turned to her and smiled. "Your son was lucky, to have a fashion designer as a mother."

"Not as lucky as you might think," she said, casting her gaze downward into her mug. "My business occupied many hours of my time. My third child, I used to joke to my friends. A demanding, unforgiving child at that. But I've always operated at my best when I'm working. When Kevin gave me the opportunity to design suits for himself and his date—his boyfriend—of course I rose to the occasion."

"With those sneakers your son painted as inspiration," Alex said.

"Charles told you about those sneakers," Norma said with a faint smile, reminiscing. "All through high school, Kevin would sit at this patio table and paint dots on his running shoes to distinguish himself on the track team. He'd spend hours painting them. How could I not use his habit as a starting point? Electricity flowed through my fingers as I sewed those stars into his suit. Once finished, I said to myself, *This is why I make clothes.*"

"I feel almost bad for those suits, hanging in the dark in your closet," Alex said. He stood by the side of the table, holding the cue stick upright. "They should be on display in a museum or something. As out and proud as the young men who wore them."

"Maybe those suits will again see the light of day," she said, thinking with a stab of guilt about the charity auction. She visualized the handsome figure Alex must have cut as an eighteen-year-old. "What about you, Alex? Did you go to your prom with another boy?"

"I didn't go to my prom, period." He turned and bent down as if to take a shot, but his feet were wrong, he was holding the stick wrong, he was looking at the wrong part of the table.

"Why not?" she said. How handsome he must have been at eighteen. She would have dressed him in dark green velvet, a yellow rose in the lapel, perhaps a *faux* amethyst pin from her rhinestone drawer.

"I was barely out to myself in those days," he said, straightening up. He was studying the pool balls, or pretending to study them.

"You could have gone with a female friend."

"I started at a new high school my senior year." He laid the pool stick on the table and turned to her. "We had moved to Roseville for my stepdad's new job. Things were bad at home between my mom and stepdad. I'd shut myself up in my room most nights, earphones in, not daring to come out until the house quieted down. That's how ugly things had become. So I kept my classmates at arm's length that year. Saved me the trouble of showing anyone where I lived. They were already strangers as it was."

Norma had an unpleasant remembrance of the growing iciness between herself and Robert as their sons grew up. Was that how Charles and Kevin had felt, too? Why Kevin had painted all those shoes, practiced all those hours for the track team? Why Charles had spent so much time with Debra, marrying her not long after college?

"What did you end up doing on prom night?" she asked.

"Kept my grandmother company at the retirement center where she lived." Alex's eyes strayed to the drawn shades, an ironic expression on his face.

"You spent prom night at a *nursing home*?"

"My grandmother meant a lot to me," he said. "My mother's mother. She'd been helping us ever since I could remember, even though she was barely scraping by herself. So I never had a problem spending time with her in that retirement center. And something good came of it. Prom night was the night I decided to become a nurse. I watched the staff going about their business and thought, what a great way to dedicate your life. Helping people. People don't hurt you if you're helping them, right? You know something, Norma, I think I'll go for that 6-ball."

He picked up the pool stick, leaned over the table, and smacked the cue ball with enough force to make her flinch. She remembered what Charles had said about his and Kevin's prep school, the "stuff" he said he'd seen.

"How did your mother feel about you spending prom in a nursing home?" she couldn't help asking.

"She didn't know that night was prom," he said, still looking at the table. "She was too busy waiting tables and dealing with my stepdad that she didn't have time to notice anything I might be going through. I didn't want to add to her worries."

"And your grandmother? Did she know?"

"No."

"You went through that experience by yourself? That's awful."

"I'm in a better place now," Alex said, turning to her with a smile. "So is my mom. She remarried a couple years ago. To a much nicer man than my first stepdad. They moved to southern Oregon, near Medford. It's a huge weight off my shoulders, knowing someone is taking care of her."

"You do call your mother, though," Norma said, softly but sternly. "Don't you?"

"Not as often as I should," he said, glancing away. "I haven't had much good news to tell her lately. I don't like to worry her."

"Call her," she said with finality. "She's worried, no matter what."

A buzz in the living room. A wasp? No, the buzzing came from Alex's phone on the fireplace mantel. He went to the mantel and picked it up.

"Oh, God." He frowned at the phone with an expression of distrust. "It's the clinic I interviewed with last month."

He turned and walked toward the dining area, the phone pressed to his ear. Norma occupied herself with petting Harry Winston, her hands going cold despite the cat's fur. If people he'd already interviewed with were calling him now, they could be calling for only one reason. And, if so, Norma's Golden Hours were numbered.

"Alrighty," he said, walking up to her with a stunned look. "That was interesting."

"What did they say?" Norma gave a polite smile.

"The candidate they'd chosen over me didn't work out." He laid the phone on the edge of the pool table.

"And now they want to hire you?" She reached for her mug. The mug was cold.

"They want me to come in on Thursday for another interview. Even if they hire me, I'll tell them I can't start until you're walking again." He glanced at the mantel clock. "Jesus, it's ten past five. Pratyush is going to wonder what happened to me."

"Leave the pool balls as they are." She drew herself up on the walker. "We can finish the lesson tomorrow."

"Great. Thanks, Norma." His eyes were shining.

"Before you leave," she said, as if the thought had only now occurred to her. "I was wondering if you could do me a favor. Could you create an email address for me on my new laptop?"

"Now?"

"You're right, it's late," she said, already losing her nerve. "This can wait until tomorrow."

"Where's the laptop?" He must have noticed her distress.

"Sitting room. Credenza."

"I'll bring it downstairs."

He turned and left the room before she had a chance to call after him, tell him she'd changed her mind. He returned with the laptop in what felt like seconds. It took him even less time to set the laptop on the kitchen island and establish an email in her name. No retreating now. No excuses, either.

After he left, Norma wasted no time going upstairs with the laptop and using her new email address to complete the online form to Anne Carruthers. Then she stashed the laptop in the credenza and went downstairs. The Blue Hour was as splendid as ever as she ate leftover lasagna and a brownie for dessert. But Norma felt too distracted to appreciate it.

At the end of the evening, when it was time to go inside, Harry remained on the chaise longue, looking disinclined to move. The first evening in which he didn't follow her into the house. As much as she disliked the idea, she knew she couldn't force the cat to spend the night indoors. She went through the doorway, closed the sliding door behind her, and looked over her shoulder to see if Harry had changed his mind. He didn't. For the first time in weeks, she had her bed to herself. It was more room than she needed.

I hope you're ready for what's waiting for you, Mom. See you soon!

CHAPTER 12

A DEPARTURE

ALEX DROVE DOWN the hill with the car windows rolled down and the radio turned up, singing along to Lizzo and not caring about who heard. No more wondering what he might've said wrong in his interviews. No more having to wonder if he'd find another job. He was the same guy now as the guy who'd woken up this morning. But one call from that clinic, and now the sun shone brighter, the air smelled fresher, those green fuzzy dice looked less radioactive, more like freshly sprouted leaves. Not even the duct tape holding up the side-view mirror could dampen his mood. The time he could have saved, the grief he could have spared himself and Pratyush, if only the clinic had had the sense to hire him earlier. But, then, he would never have met Norma. He turned onto his street and parked the car.

Had he really confided in Norma about that gut-wrenching night in Sacramento, watching sitcoms with his grandmother instead of going to prom? He'd never spoken of it to anyone else except Pratyush. Sitting in front of the TV that night, forcing himself to chuckle along with the laugh track, all the while imagining his classmates dancing, laughing, partying into the night. His grandmother's face flickered in his mind. *You're mighty quiet this evening, Alex. Everything all right?*

Too bad the interview wasn't until Thursday. He'd spend tomorrow and Wednesday watching the clock, counting the hours like he used to on Christmas Eve. An interview Thursday, a job offer Friday. Seven months of unemployment would evaporate as if they'd never happened. Wait till Pratyush heard.

The apartment was empty. Was Pratyush working late? Oh, that's right. Pratyush had said on his way out this morning that he was going to dinner and then a rehearsal with his bandmates. Hmm. Maybe Alex should hold off telling Pratyush about the interview. Wait until he had the job offer in hand. And if the clinic dashed his hopes for a second time, then Pratyush's hopes wouldn't be dashed as well.

But the clinic wouldn't do something so slimy. Would they? No, of course not.

Harry Winston didn't race down the main staircase to greet him the next morning. Unusual. He must've spent last night outside. But the cat wasn't waiting on the other side of the sliding door.

Alex slid open the door and poked his head out into the cool morning, hoping the noise would roust the cat from his hiding place. No luck. His food bowl and litter box sat untouched. Perhaps Harry had decided to sleep in with Norma? Alex worked out, took a shower, and made coffee and a batch of blueberry muffins with the fresh mountain blueberries he'd bought at Safeway on the way up here. Still no Harry in the kitchen area. Still no Harry by the sliding door.

Norma made her way downstairs about forty-five minutes

later, drifting into the kitchen in a gray kimono, as Alex pulled a tray of muffins out of the oven. Harry didn't follow her.

"Blueberry muffins?" Norma peered at the muffin tray. "We still haven't finished the lemon cake you made yesterday. Or the brownies you made Friday."

"I couldn't help myself, the blueberries were on sale," he said, bringing down her favorite mug. "Coffee's ready. Is Harry up in your room?"

"Mr. Winston spent his evening out of doors last night." She moved with the walker to the windows and looked out, her lips pursed.

"Oh. Well, I'm sure he'll be home soon." He gave a smile he hoped looked reassuring.

"If he knows what's good for him," she said, in the tart voice of a mom whose teenage son is late for curfew.

"I'll take your coffee outside?" He poured coffee into the mug.

"Honestly," she said as if she hadn't heard him, looking along the retaining wall as if she meant to conjure Harry Winston's presence. "The cat insinuates himself into the house, makes himself comfortable, and then runs off without leaving a thank-you note."

"Don't worry," Alex said with affected unconcern. "Harry's going to pop up out of nowhere any second now."

Wednesday came and still no Harry. Alex knew better than to tell Norma that the cat would soon turn up. No reason to give up hope yet, though. The cat was wearing his sushi-shaped collar, wasn't he?

But the collar had only Norma's address, not her phone number. Would someone take the trouble to drive Harry to this address if they found him? Worse, Alex hadn't had the chance to take Harry to the vet to update his chip information. The earliest the vet could see Harry was late October. How could Alex have known that Harry would vanish so soon?

"If Mr. Winston has gone for good," Norma said, "then at least he's done me the favor of deserting before I've had a chance to grow attached to him."

"I'll stop by the shelter later." Alex could tell from her voice that she'd grown attached to Harry Winston, whether she'd wanted to admit that or not.

"If you insist," she said.

He arrived at the animal shelter to find the desk nurse on the phone. He walked up to the nurse and waited for her to finish her phone call before asking, in his politest voice, if an orange tabby cat by the name of Harry Winston had turned up. The nurse left the desk, returned less than a minute later. Sorry. No cat. Try again tomorrow.

He reached Norma's house at ten minutes past four. No Norma waiting on the couch by the pool table. No Norma on the terrace, either. He walked into the front hall and was halfway up the stairs when he heard her voice coming from her sitting room. Was Mavis styling her hair? No, Mavis usually came on Monday. Norma must be talking on the phone. Her words were muffled, but he could tell by her tone—dry and formal—that she was on some kind of business call. He tiptoed downstairs.

On Thursday morning he showed up for his job interview five minutes before the appointed time. He could've arrived sooner, but he didn't want to seem too eager, too desperate.

The receptionist was one he didn't recognize from his previous interviews, a young woman with prudish gold-framed glasses. She gave him a careless good morning and asked him to sign his name on the guest sheet. The receptionist then ushered him into a small room he'd remembered from his last round of interviews. Mouse-colored walls and carpet. A potted plant in the corner. A wall clock.

Ten o'clock came. Five past ten. Ten past ten. Fifteen. People walked past in the hallway, not looking at him. Alex sat with his back straight, hands folded in front of him. Did he come on the wrong day?

Then the hiring manager walked in with a manila folder in her hand. Alex recognized her from the last time. A tall, thin woman with small glasses and stiff features, her black hair pulled into a ponytail. All business. No apology for being late. She looked at him as if she'd never seen him before. He sat up straighter.

She sat across from him and opened the folder. His resume. Scrawled notes in red marker filled the margins. She asked him the same questions as last time, almost word for word. He strove for enthusiasm in his answers. The nurse closed the folder, thanked him, and left. Was someone else coming to interview him? Or was that it?

A few moments later the HR rep came in and ushered him out, saying in a noncommittal voice that she'd be in touch. When he might receive a call from her, she couldn't say. That had to be the worst interview he'd suffered during this slog of a job search. He stood in the clinic's parking lot feeling ready to throw up.

At Norma's house, a dark blue BMW sedan hogged the driveway. Alex edged his car next to the Beemer. Funny, Norma hadn't said anything about having visitors today. Then a tall, middle-aged, square-faced woman in a black pantsuit came striding out the front door. Her pumps clacked on the pavement. Her short red hair was streaked blonde and cut into a bob, her eyes a cutting ice blue. The woman nodded at him before heading for her car with a no-nonsense step. She slipped into the car and drove off. Who in the world was *she*? He got out of the car and went into the house.

The sliding door was open, letting in the late summer air. He found Norma stretched out on a lounge chair wearing a muslin sundress the color of orange sherbet. Her Jackie O sunglasses hid her expression. A broad-brimmed straw hat shaded the rest of her face. She'd swathed herself in fashion, no doubt for the woman he'd seen leaving the house. She probably hadn't intended for him to cross paths with that woman.

"Alex." Her tone was weary, as if he'd woken her from a nap. He was certain she hadn't been dozing.

"Any sign of Harry Winston?" His eyes turned to a tray table next to Norma's lounge chair with two dirty coffee mugs and two plates bearing crumbs.

"None, I'm afraid."

"I'll check at the shelter again tomorrow." He picked up the tray table. Who made this coffee? Norma? Her visitor?

"Your interview went as expected, I imagine." Norma's expression was impenetrable behind her sunglasses.

"It's hard to say how I did." A throbbing pressed against the back of his eyes. "They didn't seem all that excited to see me again."

"Mark my words," she said with dead certainty. "By this time next week, you will have a job offer."

"If you say so." Alex used a chipper voice, but he had to swallow to keep his voice from catching. "Should I make more coffee?"

"Why not?" Norma spoke with an absent-mindedness that to Alex's ears sounded fake. "That was a jewelry appraiser, in case you were wondering."

"A jewelry appraiser?"

"The lady who was here a moment ago." She looked at him with the sun reflecting off her sunglasses. "You must have run into her on your way in."

"Only for a moment."

"I'm thinking of selling a few pieces to buy a new car," she said. "The insurance money from the accident wouldn't pay for an axle."

"Insurance companies can be that way," he said in an understanding tone.

Only after he went into the house did he stop and think about what Norma had said. The accident was the other guy's fault, wasn't it? Didn't that driver have insurance? Even if he lacked insurance, why would a woman as wealthy as Norma need to hock jewelry to pay for a car? And was that woman in the driveway a jewelry appraiser? That power suit? Those flinty eyes? The way she strode toward her car as if she meant to issue a traffic citation? Alex had no idea what a jewelry appraiser looked like. But it sure as heck wasn't that woman.

For the rest of the day he took his phone everywhere he went, waiting for the clinic's call. Once or twice, he pulled the phone out of his pocket, certain he'd felt the device buzz against his thigh, only to confront the phone's blank screen. Why had they bothered calling him in? What else did they need to make their decision?

By Friday he was on a first-name basis with the staff at the animal shelter. Sorry, no Harry Winston. Four days had passed since Norma had last seen him. Might as well give up.

In the afternoon, he let himself into Norma's house to find her outside on a lounge chair, a magazine on her lap, the coffee-pot and a mug on the table by her side. Her head rested on the cushion as if she were about to doze off. How had she managed to bring that coffeepot out here?

"No point in going to the shelter anymore," he said with a sigh. He grasped his phone in his pocket and resisted the urge to pull it out to check for messages. "I wish I'd taken a picture of the cat, then I could've put up signs."

"You're not allowed to hang signs in this neighborhood anyway," she said, sitting up and yawning as if she'd forgotten she ever had a cat. "No job offer yet?"

"Not yet," he said, chafing inwardly at the sound of the word *yet*. He picked up the coffeepot and Norma's dirty mug.

"They'll call," she said blithely, and then her face grew thoughtful.

She turned a page of her magazine as if to turn the subject. The folds of her ice-blue silk dress spilled over the side of the lounge chair like a frozen waterfall. She'd be walking any day now, wouldn't need him anymore. No cat to take care of. And no full-time job, which meant Pratyush still wouldn't touch him. A return to uselessness. How could he call his mother now?

"Don't feel like you need to keep me until the clinic calls," he ventured, his voice timid.

"But you can't leave yet," she said, looking up at him. "I have a favor to ask."

Her tone was soft but significant. She removed her sunglasses and looked at him with wide eyes. She'd never given him such a direct look before. His hands gripped the coffeepot and mug.

"What kind of favor?" He kept his tone dispassionate, as if he expected to be sent to the post office. But his mouth was dry.

"You know, it's a beautiful day today." She threw a glance over her shoulder at the Bay Bridge in the distance, then touched her hair and turned to him. "Let's take your car for a spin."

"*My* car?" He couldn't picture her riding in the Ford any more than he could picture her wearing a sweatsuit. "It's too small."

"My last car was smaller."

"Your walker won't fit in my trunk," he said, looking at her walker. What kind of a favor required her to insist on leaving the house?

"We won't need the walker, Alex."

With a sigh and an air of world-weary grandeur, she swiveled herself to sit at the edge of the lounge chair, placed her hands on her thighs, and stood up with the majesty of a queen rising from her throne. The hem of her dress pooled around her ankles. Perfect posture. No walker.

"You can walk again," he said, gaping.

"Yes." Norma's smile was as terse as her answer. She lowered her eyes as if examining a tear in the dress.

"How long have you been able to walk?"

"About a week." Her tone was casual, but her eyes stayed lowered.

"You've been faking disability for a week?" He slid his eyes to the walker.

"I wouldn't call it *faking*, Alex." She glanced over his shoulder, clearly unused to being caught out. "More like preparing for my future."

"You still could've said something."

"But then you would have left," she said with a tinge of regret. "And you can't leave yet."

She walked toward him with a steady step and grasped one of his hands with both of her own. A cool hand, but the grip was strong. She looked up at him, her eyes calm.

"What's this all about?" His voice was almost a whisper.

"I need you to drive me somewhere."

"Where?"

"Mendocino County."

"Now?" He gaped at her. Mendocino County had to be at least a three-hour drive from here.

"Not *now*," she said. "Sunday morning."

"And what's in Mendocino County?"

"My son," she said. "Kevin."

CHAPTER 13

BROKEN GLASS

NORMA HAD ALWAYS thought Alex's hands would be warm, soft, capable-feeling. But what was that look he was giving her, the freezing blue in his eyes? He should be ecstatic that she could walk again, not staring at her as if he'd witnessed her rise from the dead. He was giving her the same look Kevin had given her, on that awful night when Robert died.

"I can't stay," he said, more to himself than to her. He turned away from her, sliding his hand out from hers, and went into the house.

"Alex, wait. Please."

Her tender knee kept her from walking any faster. By the time she reached the sliding door, he was standing by the kitchen island, moving blueberry muffins from his mother-in-law's elephant plate to a plain white platter. Thank goodness for the elephant plate, or he might already be out the door. She closed the sliding door behind her.

"Alex, please. I'm sorry I deceived you." When was the last time she'd told anyone she was sorry? Her knee throbbed.

"You didn't deceive me. I deceived myself." He gave her a sidelong look. "The truth is, I didn't want the fantasy to end. This house is addicting."

"Addicting?" A pang ran through her as she uttered that terrible word.

"You have to understand, I didn't even have my own bedroom until I was thirteen years old." He threw an awed glance around the living area. "Coming here was like walking into the castle in a fairy tale. I kidded myself. Turned a blind eye. I let myself believe you needed me."

"But I do need you," she said, taking a step forward. Pain shot out of her knee like hot sparks.

"I'm a nurse, not a paid companion," he said with a dark look. He picked up the elephant plate. "Or a chauffeur."

"If you don't drive me to Mendocino," she said, "I won't be able to go."

"You can walk by yourself," he said, looking at her knee. "Why can't you drive there by yourself?"

"I doubt if my knee can withstand a three-hour drive with my foot on the gas pedal," she said. "Aside from that, I don't want to be alone if—if things don't turn out the way I hope they do."

"Why does it have to be me?" A look of distress showed on his face. "What about Charles?"

"Charles?" She drew back. "If Charles knew what I was up to, he'd do everything in his power to stop me."

"Julie, then."

"She doesn't know what I'm planning either. I don't want anyone in my family to know, not until I've seen Kevin first." Her breath was coming fast. "Alex, you're the only one who knows I can walk again. You're the only one who knows I've found my son. I don't want to hire a car service. I don't want to go through this with some stranger. All I'm asking is this one last favor. And then you can move on to your new job."

"My new job," he said with a snort. He pulled out his phone, checked for messages then slid the phone into his pocket. "They're probably offering that job to the winning candidate as we speak."

"What are you talking about? Of course they'll hire you," she said, thankful the clinic hadn't called yet. If they had, then Alex would most likely be out the door right now.

"I don't want to talk about it," he said.

He went to the sink and rinsed off the plate. A positive sign. If he was that disgusted with her, then he would have walked off without washing it.

"I'm so tired of seeing the same things every day." She glanced around the living area, at her many possessions, the porcelain lamps and vintage-glass candy dishes, the carved masks, the Chagall. "I haven't left this house since I came home from rehab. A change of scenery would do me good. Are you sure you have to go now?"

"Norma—"

"Such a perfect day," she said, looking out the sliding door. "We don't have to travel far. I know a place where we can talk. Please, Alex."

Alex turned off the faucet and leaned against the sink, looking up. Norma looked at him and waited. No way to stop him if he wanted to leave. Then he turned and looked at her.

"We're off the clock," he said. "You're not paying me for this."

"Whatever you say," she said, relief flooding through her.

Alex's car sat in its usual spot in the driveway. Nicks and dings showed in the glaring sun. Spots of rust speckled the rear fender. Was that duct tape keeping the side-view mirror in place? If she'd seen a car like this one parked on her street, she would have called to have it towed. An uncharitable thought, to be sure. So long as the car could run, what else mattered?

He opened the passenger-side door, pulled the front bucket seat forward, and put the elephant plate on the back seat. Once finished, he adjusted the front seat and held open the door like a chauffeur, his jaw square, not looking at her. She walked with a ladylike step toward the car, wishing she hadn't heard the distressing creak the car door had made.

"Thank you." She settled into the car, arranged the hem of her dress around her ankles, and buckled herself in.

He shut the passenger door, walked around the car, and sat behind the driver's seat. The car's interior was spotless, thank heavens, and roomier than her old Porsche. She unconsciously felt along the armrest to move the seat backward then realized the control was manual, not electric. A pair of neon-green fuzzy dice hung from the center rear-view mirror. Her gaze latched onto them. She always appreciated a note of tackiness to enliven a humdrum setting.

"So," he said, turning the ignition, "where am I taking you?"

"Tilden Park. I know a spot that looks out onto the east hills."

He pulled out of the driveway. No cars on the road. She leaned back and looked through the windshield at power lines, eucalyptus trees, the shadow of a hawk or vulture gliding over the asphalt. No need to adjust the seat—she had plenty of room. A few twists and turns along Grizzly Peak Boulevard, and he turned into Tilden Park. The engine whined as the car chugged up the hill.

A couple of minutes longer, and they were there. Only two other cars were parked in the small lot. They got out of the car.

No one else around except themselves. Eerily silent. No chattering insects, no cheeping birds.

"It's hard to believe downtown Oakland is a twenty-minute drive from here," he said, taking in the view. The rolling hills in the distance shimmered in the sun as if they'd been painted with gold leaf, soft and rumpled like discarded silk.

"Here is where I told Robert I was pregnant with Charles." Norma sat down on one of the benches that ringed the parking lot. A heart and two sets of initials—*B.K.* and *J.M.*—were carved into the bench, so faded that they were almost part of the wood grain. "I figured if I told him in a natural setting, I wouldn't feel so scared."

"And is that why you chose this place to talk to me?" Alex's expression was serious but soft. "So that you won't be terrified at what you have to say?"

"Perhaps," she said, feeling the sun on her face. "You're easier to talk to than Robert."

He gave a small smile at this then pulled out his phone and sat down on the other end of the bench. No change in his expression meant the clinic hadn't called. She looked away to give him privacy. Bell-shaped yellow wildflowers grew against the rusted barbed wire fence that separated the parking lot from the hiking trail. How was it possible for sixty years to pass since that day on the bench with Robert?

"That woman you saw in the driveway on Wednesday wasn't a jewelry appraiser," she said, once she thought enough seconds had passed. Thank goodness she was wearing sunglasses, to hide the feeling of shame rising in her. "She was the private detective I hired to find Kevin."

"So that's who she was," he said, sounding not at all surprised.

"She needed all of two days to track him down." Norma focused her gaze on the stands of trees clinging to the hills like tufts of dark green cotton. "He lives in southern Mendocino

County. A few miles north of Gualala. Near the Sonoma County border."

"Does he know you're coming to see him?" Alex looked sidelong at Norma.

"If he did," she said, her voice grave, "then he would probably run and hide."

"How do you know he'll agree to speak to you?"

"I don't." Norma looked at Alex, her expression calm.

"And you still want to go?" A stare on Alex's face.

"I have to try." She sat up straight. "Perhaps if I explain what happened between Kevin and me, then you'll understand why I need to see him."

Alex said nothing. His eyes were fixed on the yellow flowers entwining the rusted barbed wire. She watched him and realized that if she had any hope of securing his help, she would have to give him the unvarnished truth. If he didn't understand her now, probably no one ever would.

"Okay then," he said with a sigh and turned to look at her. "Since we're here."

"I presume my sister told you about the night my husband died," she said. She watched the line of the horizon, as fine as a thread against the blue-white sky.

"Something about a bridge party," he said with a slight look of confusion. No doubt he was wondering what Robert's death had to do with her estrangement from Kevin.

"Julie must also have told you I'd gone to check on dessert." She could easily picture Julie recounting the story, with much fidgeting and a hushed, scandalized tone. "Then she told you I returned to the study and played a hand. And the police arrived a few minutes after that. Am I right so far?"

"Pretty much," Alex said and licked his lips.

"But she didn't tell you about the fight I'd had with Robert on the terrace in the afternoon." A buzzing stirred in her ribcage. She absently reached for the opal around her neck. "Right before my guests came. Did she?"

"A fight?" He gave a slow shake of the head. "Julie didn't say anything about a fight."

"Because she doesn't know that fight happened. No one knows that fight happened. Except me and Robert. And now you."

"You're sure you want to tell me about it?" Alex turned and locked eyes with her, lips parting.

"If you're willing to listen."

A dozen crows soared above their heads like rags hurled into the sky. Norma imagined herself floating high above the trees, watching this woman—a stranger on a bench—about to tell her story. She adjusted her sunglasses, unable to believe what she was about to say, let alone to someone she'd known for only a few weeks.

"Go ahead," he said and gave a slight nod.

"Thank you." She twisted the chain of the necklace between her fingers, listening to her own words as if the stranger were saying them, not her. "The sun had set, but it was light outside. The caterers were in the house, making dessert. My guests were due around seven. Robert was in his lounge chair, drunk. He always hated it when I threw a party for the ladies. And he had a particular reason to be angry with me that day. He'd worked himself up with alcohol on purpose to embarrass me that night."

"My stepdad used to drink at home when he was mad," Alex said.

"But this time I resisted." Her hands trembled as if the moment had happened only yesterday. "I marched up to him and told him if he had any self-respect, he'd call a cab and leave me alone and let me throw my party in peace. His face went so ugly that I didn't recognize him. 'Who do you think you are?' he said. 'I bought this house for you, I bought that view for you, and I can take everything away like *that*.' And he snapped his fingers in my face. I told him I couldn't take his abuse anymore. No longer loved him. And that I wanted a divorce."

"With caterers inside the house and party guests on the way," Alex said, looking horror-struck. "My God."

"He said if I filed for divorce, he'd drag me through hell." A sharp feeling of shame raced through her. "He had pictures, he said."

"Pictures? What kind of pictures?"

"The kind you wouldn't want projected on a screen in open court," she said, her face growing warm.

"You mean … a *man*?"

"You needn't act so appalled, Alex." She drew herself up, clutching her purse. "Yes, a man. A short, ill-advised, passionless fling with a model half my age. The only time I strayed. Upon my mother's soul."

"Your marriage, your business," Alex said, holding up his hands.

"Everyone I knew in those days seemed to be having affairs." Norma sighed. "Bored, rich married women with too much time on their hands. They made having an affair seem as simple as taking up golf."

"Not when there are pictures," Alex said with a nauseated look.

"Those pictures still exist for all I know. They're probably sitting forgotten at the bottom of someone's file cabinet. For years I thought they'd surface. I suppose they still could."

"Your husband had you *followed*," Alex said in an almost awestruck tone. "Now *that's* vicious."

"But Robert never did understand that he was no match for me, especially once my mind was made up." She traced her thumb along the surface of the opal. "I intrigued him, I think, especially at the beginning of our relationship. I think that's why he married me. I was the one woman he couldn't quite possess."

"What did you say, when he threatened to take those pictures public?" He leaned toward her.

"I looked him in the eye and said if he wanted a fight, I'd give him one." She spoke in the deadly tone she'd used on Robert that afternoon—a tone she hadn't realized she was capable of using. "I all but dared him to publicize those pictures. He'd only be humiliating himself, I said. Then I told him I knew the names of half a dozen women he'd had affairs with. And that I'd hire someone to track down every other woman he'd ever slept with."

"He cheated on you too?"

"Almost from the start of our marriage. Just like his father used to cheat on his mother—my mother-in-law, Miriam, the one who bequeathed me the pool table. That's why she taught me pool. She knew what future lay in store for me, she knew Robert would be unfaithful. Simply because he could. He was strikingly handsome, my husband. His looks made me think nothing could be wrong with him. The other women he slept with probably thought the same thing. I've often wondered whether he would have been more faithful if he'd been less good-looking."

"Maybe." Alex looked at his hands as if in disagreement with what Norma had told him. His own husband must have stupendous good looks—*as handsome as the dawn*—yet remained loyal.

"I asked him if he was ready to lose the biggest fight of his life," Norma went on. "If he was ready to disgrace himself in front of everyone. In front of Charles. In front of Kevin. Our grandchildren. I told him there wasn't a judge or a jury who would be sympathetic to him. I told him I'd take him for every cent he had. And then he'd be alone, no family, no money, no nothing."

"My God," Alex said, gaping. "How did your husband react to all of that?"

"I thought he'd knock me to the ground." She recalled Robert's red face, his bloodshot eyes, his expression of unadulterated rage—a woeful parody of the good looks she'd once known. "But then the sliding door opened and out came one of the caterers, all sunny and professional, telling me they'd finished making dessert."

An image of that caterer floated in her memory. A blonde-haired woman in a white shirt and black pants, college-aged most likely, smiling, happily ignorant of the catastrophe she'd interrupted. A woman perhaps new to love and dating, a woman lacking the smallest clue of how some marriages, even marriages begun with diamonds and world travel and an angelic-looking son, sometimes went down in flames. Where was that young woman now?

"Saved by the caterer," Alex said with a sad smile.

"I followed the young lady into the house, naturally." A reeling sensation came over Norma, similar to what she'd felt that afternoon. "And there was the catering team, wiping down the counters, setting out coffee cups, arranging éclairs and petit fours on platters. The sound of my own kitchen faucet never sounded so ordinary—or so loud. Then the ladies came to play bridge, and suddenly I'm hosting a party. For a moment, I thought I'd only imagined that fight with Robert."

"What about Kevin?" Alex cocked his head. "How does he figure into all of this?"

"He was in the house that night. His second night home from his latest stint in rehab. Julie didn't tell you that part of the story either, did she?"

"Because she didn't know Kevin was in the house," Alex said with a slow shake of the head. "Am I right?"

"None of my guests knew," she said with an inward shudder. "He'd made sure to shut himself up in his room, with Magic, his old cat, by the time everyone else arrived. They all knew him from the time he was a boy. There was a time when he had entertained them all. But on that night, he didn't want anyone to know he was home. Not even his Aunt Julie."

"He was in recovery," Alex said in an understanding voice.

"I closed the curtains to the terrace and made sure to steer my guests to the study instead of outside," Norma went on, "even though the evening was warm and clear. I kept looking at the study door, convinced Robert would storm in and make a scene. But he didn't. Somehow, that was scarier."

"So you went outside later, to check on him."

"His hand was still warm when I found him." She removed her sunglasses and rubbed her eyes. "The glass he'd been drinking from lay shattered on the ground, next to his chair. And his message to me was clear. He died out there on purpose, to ruin that view for me forever."

"What do you mean, he died on purpose?" He drew back, frowning. "Julie said he died of a heart attack."

"Heart attack was the *official* determination." She looked at him, the sun hurting her eyes. "But I've never believed it. Robert's final act was one of revenge."

"I don't buy that," he said stoutly. "Coroners don't make up heart attacks."

Easy for him to say, she thought. *He* wasn't the one sitting on that terrace night after night. No point in arguing with him, though. She needed to finish her story.

"I was standing over Robert when I heard the sliding door open." She listened to herself speaking in a low voice, amazed she was giving utterance to these words. "And there was Kevin standing in the doorway. He took one look at his father. Then he looked at me. Then he turned and went inside."

"Jesus," Alex murmured. He gazed out into the distance, at the trees lining the horizon.

"Kevin was already out of the living area by the time I reached the sliding door. I wanted to follow him, but I couldn't. Not with guests in the house. I drew the blinds and dialed 911 from the kitchen phone. Then I drew myself up and went to the game room."

"And bid one heart," Alex said.

"Julie told you that I bid one heart? Her memory is better than mine." Norma massaged her aching forehead. "Everyone looked up from their cards once blue lights flashed into the room. I left them there without looking behind me. After that, I couldn't tell you what happened. It's a blur."

"Delayed shock." Alex's tone was reassuringly kindhearted.

"Memories come to me in bits and pieces, like shards of glass." She listened to the preternatural calmness in her voice, the same calmness she'd used with the police that night. "Officers asking me questions. Strangers in uniforms out on the terrace, taking pictures of the scene. Medics wheeling Robert out on a stretcher, covered in a sheet. Someone leading me to the couch. Piles of uneaten dessert on the kitchen island. Cream puffs, éclairs, petit fours, cupcakes. To this day I don't know what happened to all that dessert."

"And where was Kevin during all this?"

"He'd left the house before the police came." She put away her sunglasses, sighed, and looked at him. "I found his keys later that night in the lock by the side door, the one nearest his room."

"He split?" Alex said with a gasp.

"Yes," she said. "And that, Alex, is the last I saw of my son."

A memory came to her of Magic, Kevin's cat, sitting with wide green eyes on the edge of his bed. Norma might have deserved to be abandoned that night. The poor cat didn't.

"Sounds like you blame yourself for your husband's death," Alex said, his tone compassionate. "And like you think Kevin blames you."

"I don't know if Kevin blames me," she said stiffly. "Him not speaking to me sure feels like punishment."

"Does he know about the fight you'd had with your husband?" His expression darkened. "Does he know about those pictures?"

"He could have overheard us arguing, but his room is nowhere near the terrace." She strove to keep her voice from trembling. "Robert could have told Kevin about the pictures, I suppose. But not likely. Kevin and Robert had had a contentious relationship. They were barely on speaking terms those last couple of days."

"Then what does Kevin blame you for?" Alex looked perplexed. "What crime does he think you committed?"

"I designed two prom suits." A sense of exhaustion passed through her. "That was my crime."

"Those suits in your closet? What are you talking about?"

"I was so pleased with my creations," she went on, "that I couldn't resist going further. I made copies in various colors, displayed them in my shop window. Industry people noticed. Then I was invited to mount a show in Los Angeles—and Kevin walked his first runway. He was thrilled. The fashion world wanted to know more about the young man who had inspired his mother's signature design. Both he and his suit became overnight sensations. Suddenly Kevin was dropping out of college to pursue a modeling career."

"So that suit changed both your lives," Alex said.

"For me, it meant I finally had money I could call my own. I also could claim that I *made* my own fortune. All Robert ever did was inherit his father's real estate business. Watching my ascent from the sidelines was a crushing blow to his ego. So he drank more. Philandered more. Those prom suits marked the beginning of the end of our marriage. And the beginning of the end of the Kevin I knew."

"How so?"

"He thought modeling the prom suit was a first-class ticket to the top," she said, shaking her head at the memory. "I tried to talk sense into him, explain he'd have to work harder if he wanted to make it in the business."

"But he didn't listen," Alex said with a slow nod, as if he were speaking from experience. "Eighteen-year-olds aren't known for listening to their mothers."

"Once the drug of his initial success wore off, he resorted to real drugs," she said, her tone hardening. "Work dried up. His agent dropped him. And suddenly he's twenty-seven years old with three stints in rehab. Flat broke. Friendless. Reduced to living at home with his parents. No prospects for the future."

"That's on him," Alex said. "No one put a gun to his head to take drugs."

"Sometimes I wish I'd designed the suits and left it at that," she said, heaving herself up from the bench without wanting to. Her knee throbbed. "Kevin could've finished his degree, done something productive with his life."

"Give yourself a break, Norma. You're a fashion designer, not a clairvoyant," Alex said firmly. "The only destiny you can control is your own. And sometimes you can't even control that."

The wind had picked up. The leaves in the oak trees rustled like taffeta. What he said made perfect sense, of course. So much sense, in fact, that she wished she could believe him. Perhaps one day she would.

"I have no illusions about what's waiting for me up there," she said. "I'm not expecting a tearful reconciliation. That's not him. Or me for that matter. But I haven't seen him since that night. I just—want to talk to him about what happened."

"And if he slams the door in your face?" Alex said with a wince.

"Then I'll live out my life saying I put in the work," Norma said.

For the next few moments the only sound was the rustling of leaves, the faraway voices of hikers. Alex was studying his hands. Norma couldn't remember the last time she'd felt so needy. She sat back down on the bench.

"Norma, can I ask you something?" He looked at her.

"Go ahead," she said, at this point prepared to tell him anything.

"How many years are there between Charles and Kevin?"

"Eight," she said, not sure why he needed to know this. "I was twenty when I had Charles, twenty-eight when I had Kevin."

"But you said you were having trouble with Robert from the start of your marriage," he said, an intent look in his eyes.

"Then why did we have Kevin? Is that what you want to know?" She sighed. "I wish I could say my second pregnancy was as much an accident as my first, but that wouldn't quite be the truth. I suppose I'd thought having another baby would remind Robert how happy we were when we had Charles. Of course, I realized my error almost immediately after I became pregnant. But then Kevin came. And he was ... what can I say? Raising him distracted me from the less savory side of my marriage. Such a happy little boy, always jumping around, telling jokes, making everybody laugh. He brought out the best in Charles too. Charles, who took everything so seriously. I remember thinking that if Robert and I could produce a boy like Kevin, then our marriage couldn't be all bad."

"It's interesting Kevin lives only three hours away." Alex sighed and smiled at her sympathetically. "If he really wanted nothing to do with you, you'd think he would've chosen to live farther away."

"He probably wants to be near Charles."

"Even so, he has to be aware you might find out where he lived," Alex said, tracing his chin with the tip of his index finger. "If the PI found him so quickly, then it's obvious he's living in the open, under his own name. He has to know you might one day pay him a visit."

He has a point, Mom. I know how much you like to drive a car.

"You think he subconsciously wants me to seek him out?" She'd been wondering about this ever since she learned Kevin was living in Mendocino County.

"That's a stretch." Alex shrugged, inspected his fingernails. "But who knows?"

"No way of knowing unless I see him." A swarm of hummingbirds in her ribcage now. "Does this mean you'll drive me?"

"Uh," Alex said, his voice thick with reluctance. His eyes strayed to the hills in the distance. Then he looked at her and smiled. "Okay, Norma. Let's take a trip."

"Thank you," she said. "You have no idea how obliged I am."

Twenty-five years of waiting, about to come to a screeching halt. By this time next week, Norma would have seen her son again. Where would she be? What would she be thinking, doing? A rush of feeling spread out from her chest, like a dam breaking. Sunday felt like twenty-five years away.

CHAPTER 14

ASSIGNMENTS

SILENCE FILLED THE car as Alex drove Norma home. The Ford's engine didn't ping for once, as if it, too, had been stunned speechless by her explosive story. He turned into Norma's driveway. Her house looked different in the brief time since they'd left. The mystique was gone. He saw the place now for what it was. A haunted house.

She couldn't push the passenger door open. He flushed. If the clinic had hired him like they should've, he and Pratyush might be shopping for a new car this weekend, or at least shopping for a halfway-decent used car that didn't feel ready to burst apart at any moment. How could she expect him to drive her three hours up the coast in this piece of crap? Then it dawned on him. His car was junk! He had an airtight excuse to wiggle out of this assignment.

He went around to the passenger side to open the door. A yank, and the door opened with a screech that she couldn't have failed to hear. She might call off Sunday before he could make his excuses.

"I'll rent a car this weekend," she said, stepping out of the car. She wore slip-on tennis shoes, jarringly white against her blue dress. "Do you have a preference for make of car?"

"Uh, no." He couldn't say what unnerved him more, the announcement of the rental car or the sight of those tennis shoes. He'd somehow missed them, hidden under her long dress.

"I found a website where they'll deliver the rental to the house." For a woman who set up her first computer a week ago, she spoke like an internet prodigy. "Very easy to rent a car nowadays. I won't rent anything too sporty. Nothing that will draw attention."

"Um, yeah…about Sunday…" He grasped the open door, queasiness spreading through him. "It's three hours up, three hours back. I need to talk to Pratyush first."

"Of course." Her look was soft and searching behind her sunglasses. "I regret putting either of you through any inconvenience. But do keep in mind you'll be on the clock. On a Sunday, no less. I used to pay my staff double time if they worked on Sundays."

Double time. Half a month's rent, most likely. And that was only to drive her to see Kevin. What if she reconciled with her son? Would that put her in such a magnanimous mood that she paid Alex triple time? Quadruple time? He wouldn't be making these calculations if the clinic had offered him that job.

"I don't feel good about this," he said.

"Please, Alex." She reached out her hand as if to grasp his forearm, but then she caught herself and drew the hand away. "You'll be leaving my employ soon. Harry Winston is gone. This is the last assignment I'll ever offer you. I promise."

She uttered those words with such feeling that he would have needed a heart of granite to refuse her. He knew her well enough to know that her feelings, however well she disguised them with her outfits and her sunglasses and the ever-changing color of her fingernails, ran deep. His mother would tell him he should drive her to Mendocino for free.

"I don't know how to drive a stick shift," he heard himself say. A sensation passed over him that he was walking through a door more solid than Norma's front door—one that would lock behind him.

"I'll be sure to rent an automatic," she said.

"What time would you like me to pick you up?"

"Seven. That should get us there by ten. The investigator told me that Kevin works a second job as a server in the afternoon on Sundays. I don't want to risk going any later."

"Seven it is," Alex said. He pictured his mother, nodding approval. "See you Sunday."

Norma gave a curt "thank you" and vanished into the house before he had a chance to change his mind. He stared up at the house—oak door, green shutters, spider's-eye windows, laurel leaves brushing the orange-tiled roof. Job or no job, he was ready to put this place behind him.

Julie did him the favor of not being in the backyard by the time he reached home. He walked into an empty apartment. No surprise there—he'd left Norma's house earlier than usual. The clock read twenty-five past four. He had plenty of time to figure out what to say before Pratyush came home from work.

In ten-plus years of nursing, he had never told Pratyush any story a patient had confided in him. But how was he supposed to disappear on Sunday without divulging why? True, Pratyush usually played pickleball early on Sundays. Didn't he say he was playing in a tournament this weekend? Even so, he'd likely be home by one o'clock, maybe earlier. Alex would have to drive like a maniac from Mendocino County to reach home ahead of Pratyush. And only if Norma's meeting with Kevin lasted five or ten minutes—if, say, Kevin wasn't at home, rendering the journey a waste of time, gas, and a rental car. What should he do?

At least Pratyush had a gig tonight at the Thirsty Raven. He'd likely come home at around twenty past five, practice on his cello for a half hour in the basement, and be gone by six thirty. Alex had been to enough of these gigs to know he wouldn't be expected to watch Pratyush's band play. He pulled out his phone and ordered a pepperoni pizza with extra olives, Pratyush's favorite. Alex could only hope that Pratyush would eat, practice, and leave.

As it happened, Pratyush walked through the door even later, almost five thirty. The pizza arrived less than five minutes after that. Alex busied himself with setting the table, playing husband while Pratyush took a shower. The gig, Pratyush explained, was earlier than usual.

He stole glances at Pratyush while they ate. Was there any chance he could drive to Mendocino County and back without his husband knowing? Not likely, but worth a shot.

"So," he said, his eyes on the pizza slice he was sliding onto his plate, "what time is pickleball on Sunday?"

"First games are at eight a.m.," Pratyush said, cutting his pizza with a knife and fork. His whole family ate pizza that way. "They want everyone there by six thirty."

"Dave's picking you up?" Alex was careful to show no emotion.

"His car's in the shop, so he asked if I could drive." Pratyush put down his fork. "You don't need the car Sunday morning, do you?"

"Not if you need it." Alex hoped he didn't sound as disheartened as he felt.

"Good. I thought so. I'm not sure how late I'll be—it depends on how far we go in this tournament." Pratyush showed not the slightest hint of noticing anything amiss with Alex. "If I'm home early enough, we can do something in the afternoon."

"Assuming you're not too tired," Alex said. Pratyush and Dave were good players, they might come home late after all. "We can go hiking in Tilden Park or something."

"As long as we don't have to pay your employer a visit," Pratyush said.

"Oh, stop. You know you want to meet her." Alex forced a smile and picked up his pizza slice. The smell of olives made him sick.

"Not on my day off," Pratyush said. "Or *your* day off from her."

"We'll have to drop by Norma's one of these days. If only so I can show you our house from her terrace."

"This again?" Pratyush chuckled then glanced at the wall clock. "I need to make my gig."

Alex brought the dirty dishes to the sink while Pratyush left to collect his viol. Maybe he'd surprise Pratyush with a visit to the Thirsty Raven tonight. But what if showing up only made Pratyush anxious? Better to stay indoors.

He turned on the faucet and rinsed the dishes, listening to the gurgle of running water. He imagined listening to this water after having a blowout fight with Pratyush. What would they fight about? Money? The Ford? Their lack of intimacy? A chill passed through him as if this catastrophe had already happened. Meanwhile, the water kept running, *rush-rush-rush*. The water must've sounded like this to Norma, the afternoon of her fight on the terrace with her husband.

★

On Sunday morning he feigned sleep while Pratyush slipped out of bed at five thirty. He didn't dare move as he listened to Pratyush change his clothes and slip out of the bedroom, shutting the door behind him with care. Then he turned on his back and exhaled, gazing up in the pitch dark.

The sound of the front door opening then closing. There. Safe to step a toe out of bed. The kitchen clock read a couple of minutes past six. He ate, showered, and dressed. Twenty minutes past. What if Julie called to him from the front door, asking where he was going so early? But her windows stayed mercifully dark.

He made sure he was a few blocks away from the house before summoning an Uber. Were Ubers available this early on a Sunday? Would he have enough time to walk all the way to Norma's if no driver answered? But as fate would have it—good fate or bad fate, he wasn't sure—a driver answered his summons within five minutes. The roads were deserted. The Uber passed peaceful-looking houses, its occupants no doubt warm and safe in bed, windows gleaming in pale blue light. Even the sun seemed to be in no hurry to rise this morning.

One last turn, and the Uber turned into Norma's driveway. Alex thanked the driver and stepped out of the car. An electric-orange Porsche Cayenne SUV sat parked in the driveway. He'd never driven an SUV before. Worse, the car looked big enough, and gaudy enough, to be seen from miles away. *This* was Norma's choice of car to evade notice?

The front door opened. Out came Norma with a black leather purse on her shoulder. She must've been standing at a window, watching for him.

"You're early," she said, looking neither pleased nor displeased.

"Pratyush has our car. I thought I'd need the extra time to find a cab." He looked at the SUV, the orange growing more garish in the blossoming dawn.

"This was the only car the rental people had," she said, giving the car a once-over.

She slid on her sunglasses as if to disavow what she'd done. Or perhaps to hide the haggard look on her face. She likely hadn't slept a wink last night.

"We can always go some other time if you don't want to use this car." A long shot to suggest this, but no harm making a last-ditch effort to squirm his way out of this mess.

"It's paid for through Tuesday." She zipped open her purse and brought out a set of car keys attached to a metal ring. "The rental place has a two-day minimum for premium cars."

She handed him the keys and walked to the passenger's side. Her sand-colored dress jacket and dark brown slacks couldn't look any more understated. Her leather flats were the same mild shade as the jacket. In its consummate blandness, her outfit was every bit as calculated as anything he'd ever seen her wear. The only spot of color was the opal pendant, a bluish-green oasis against her eggshell-colored blouse.

He got into the car and sank into the leather seat. Norma sat with her hands folded over her purse, her purse on her lap. No use in reasoning with her—or worrying about whether he'd have to make the same drive tomorrow. He started the car, and they left.

★

He wasn't used to driving so high off the ground. He'd never driven a Porsche either. This whole experience was new—the buttery-soft seats, the glittering controls, the GPS monitor, and above all, the humming engine undisturbed by pings. The car ran so smoothly that more than once he caught himself driving over eighty miles an hour without realizing it. For the last fifty miles he kept an eye on the speedometer, resolved not to incur a ticket and make Norma late for Kevin.

The roads grew emptier the farther he drove north. Sky grayer, foggier. Norma said nothing all the while, a stolid expression behind her sunglasses. She said nothing when Alex took the appointed exit off the freeway, nothing when the GPS announced they were twenty miles, ten miles, five miles away from Kevin's house. To look at her, he might think she was on her way to brunch.

They reached Kevin's town at a few minutes past ten. Fog hung low in the sky. He drove up the town's main street of brick buildings housing a bar, grocery store, café, and two or three art galleries. Everything looked closed. If any townspeople—or Kevin—were walking by, they'd no doubt stop and stare at the SUV, as flamboyant as a float at a Pride parade. But no one was around. The GPS directed him to take a left at the school. A right at the church. One more turn, and the destination would be on the left.

"Pull over here," she ordered, two blocks ahead of their turn.

"Here?" He pulled over to the side of the road, next to a wild pink rosebush bristling with thorns.

"Yes, here," she whispered, peering out the windshield. "We can't let Kevin see the car."

"Right," he said. "Of course."

What was he supposed to do? Sit and wait while she had her one-on-one with Kevin? He checked his phone—no signal. So much for calling Pratyush.

"Do you see this?" She was cradling the opal in her hand, the chain around her neck. She held out her palm to give Alex a better view of the pendant.

"You wear that necklace every day," he said, thinking now a bizarre time for her to talk about jewelry. The opal looked small in her hand.

"Kevin gave it to me right before he graduated high school, to thank me for making those prom suits." She smoothed the opal against her blouse. "Bought it with money he earned himself, bagging groceries. After he disappeared, I stashed the pendant in my safe. Couldn't bear to look at it. But after the car accident, I had Julie bring me the pendant while I recovered at the hospital. My way of keeping Kevin close to me. I own jewelry worth hundreds of times more than this opal. But I cherish this necklace more than any other piece I own."

Alex looked at the stone. Charming. Modest. He should have guessed the opal had a history.

"Pretty," he ventured to say.

"I shouldn't have worn the necklace today." She glanced out the windshield. "He might think I'm trying to manipulate him."

"You have no way of knowing that."

"Today might be my only chance with him." Even behind the large sunglasses, her look of panic showed plainly. "I can't make the slightest mistake."

"Slip the pendant beneath your blouse."

"I'll still know it's there."

"Your purse, then."

"No. I can't. I can't bear to have Kevin's opal on my person at all." She bowed her head to remove the necklace. "Here, you take it. Please."

She held up the pendant. The opal hovered between them like a tiny star. Alex had no choice but to hold out his hand and let her nestle the chain in his palm. The jewel felt as light as a penny. Hard to believe an object this small could carry so much weight.

"After you leave, I might go to the main street to see if that café has opened yet." Alex dropped the pendant into the front pocket of his green plaid shirt. He suddenly felt hungry.

"Allow me to pay for breakfast," Norma said, unzipping her purse.

"I only want coffee," Alex said firmly and held up his hand. "Then I'll come straight back here."

"Very well, as you wish. If I return and you're not here, I'll wait for you by that rosebush." She zipped up her purse, opened the passenger side door, and gave him a long and searching look, as if this might be the last time she saw him. "Thank you for driving me, Alex."

"Good luck," he said, for the first time feeling glad for taking on this assignment. He buttoned the shirt pocket and patted the coiled necklace against his chest. "And for what it's worth, Norma?"

She turned to look at him, one leg out the door.

"I think you're doing the right thing." He smiled at her, his heart swelling. "However this turns out."

"Here goes nothing," she said, and she stepped out of the car.

He watched her walk away from him. Her clothing blended into the misty light. Even so, her gait marked her as a woman of style. He'd wait for her to disappear around the corner before heading to the café.

Then she stopped short and glanced over her shoulder, as if she thought an evil spirit had followed her. Was she okay? Should he go check on her? But no sooner than that thought crossed his mind, she turned around and walked toward him. Had she forgotten something in the car? Had she decided she wanted to wear the opal after all? He stepped out of the car and waited.

"Something the matter?" he asked, once Norma came close enough.

"What if I'm the opal?" she said. The look on her face behind her sunglasses, severe yet vulnerable, was one he'd never seen before.

"You, the opal? What do you mean?"

"I didn't want to wear the opal because I didn't want to provoke Kevin." She laid a hand on the hood of the car. Her chest went up and down. "But what if *I'm* the opal? What if I infuriate him simply by showing up? What if I set off a relapse?"

"You won't do that," he said, almost as a reflex. But how was he supposed to predict Kevin's reaction?

"All weekend long I've done nothing but pace around the house, rehearsing in my mind what I'll say." How extraordinary to see Norma like this, small and helpless in her sensible suit. "If he turns me away before I utter a single word…I don't know what I'll do."

"No one is forcing you to go in there," Alex said, having trouble believing he'd said that. Three hours of driving, only to turn around as soon as they made it here? But if they left for Oakland now, he might well make it home before Pratyush.

"But you went out of your way to drive me here," she said, her tone despairing.

"I'm the last person you should be thinking about." This was the nurse in him talking, not the guy who wanted to be home ahead of his husband. "This is about Kevin, and what he wants. You've already gone all these years without seeing him. What difference will a few more days make? Call him first, if you have his number. Or write him a letter, asking if you can visit."

"He'd only refuse." Norma looked down the street as if she only now understood where she was. Then she turned to him. "I know. You go see him first."

"What?" Alex stared. "Oh, Norma, I don't think that's a—"

"And tell him I'm out here waiting," she said, talking over

him. "If he doesn't want to see me now, tell him I'll reach out to him by letter."

"Norma, I—"

"We've come too far not to do something." She unzipped her purse and took out the slip of notepaper on which she'd written Kevin's address. "Please, Alex. Please. I'll make it worth your while."

She held out the paper. He took it with an unwilling hand. Then she got into the car on the passenger's side and slammed the door shut. Forget about the café. Forget about making it home before Pratyush. This was his assignment now. He slipped the paper into his pocket and headed toward Kevin's house.

CHAPTER 15

STATUES

A s SOON AS he rounded the corner, safely out of Norma's line
of vision, he leaned forward and put his hands on his thighs.
His stomach felt ready to heave into his throat. *I'll make it
worth your while.* This was exhausting, her dangling money in
front of him. How had he let her talk him into doing this?

Then he stood up, breathed the nippy air, and looked around.
Kevin's street wasn't much. A single block of low-slung houses
stood on either side of a pocked road. Cars sat in driveways. A
kid's bicycle leaned against a swing set. Even so, the place looked
deserted. No one mowing a lawn or reading the Sunday paper on
a front porch. No kids playing on that swing set. Drawn shades
covered most of the windows. And past the houses, the road
petered out into a no-man's-land of rocks and trees, as if the street
itself had lost its will to keep going.

Kevin's house was the third one on the left. The front
lawn looked dry but not overgrown. Potted cactuses sat along
the porch railing like abstract statues. The house itself, a gray

clapboard ranch house with a sloping shingled roof, was the sort of place Alex could imagine himself and Pratyush owning some-day—small, modest, easy to manage—though in a sunnier and less remote neighborhood than this one. Affixed to the yellow-painted door was a brass knocker. He climbed a short flight of steps to the door, told himself everything would turn out all right, and knocked.

Muffled voices came from within the house. Alex pictured himself floating backward, away from the door. The voices grew louder. A man's voice. A woman's voice. A woman's voice? Norma hadn't said anything about Kevin living with a woman. Alex pulled out the notepaper she'd given him, to make sure he hadn't knocked at the wrong address. He stuffed the paper into his pocket as soon as the door cracked open.

It was indeed a woman whose voice he'd heard—as it turned out, a young-looking woman with long brown hair held in place by a brown plastic clip. In her arms was a baby girl who looked to be about a year old. The baby's eyes were as large and blue as her mother's, her expression as icy and watchful. Alex doubted if the mother was over twenty-five. This must be the wrong house.

"Good morning," he said in his most nonthreatening tone. "I'm looking for Kevin McKinsey. Does he happen to live here?"

"Who are you?" The woman's eyes, hard with contempt, flicked over him as if he were a collection agent. The baby squirmed in her thin arms.

"My name is Alex Wolsey." He took a respectful step back-ward and folded his hands behind him. "I'm a friend of Kevin's mother."

"Kevin's mother?" The woman held the baby closer as if he might infect it.

"I was hoping to talk to him." His mouth had gone so dry

that he had to keep his tongue from sticking to the roof of his mouth. "Is he home?"

"Nope." The obstinate set of the young woman's mouth made him think of a teenager in the principal's office, denying everything.

"Do you have any idea when he might be back?" He kept a patient gaze on the young woman. His only way to win her over, or at least have her stop loathing him, was to project friendliness.

"I don't," she said curtly, "and if you don't mind, I'm going to be late for work."

"It's just that we've come a long way to see him," he said, casting his eyes down. At least he could say to Norma that a total stranger, not Kevin, had slammed the door in his face.

"We?" The woman's pale lips parted, revealing a line of crooked teeth. "Who's we?"

"Hey, Iris, who's that you're talking to?" A man's voice, low and rich and sonorous, called from inside the house.

"Some guy," the woman said over her shoulder, her eyes fixed on Alex. "Says he's a friend of your mother's."

Alex looked above the woman's shoulder into what might be a kitchen. Behind her appeared a tall, bleary-looking man in a pair of moss-green sweatpants and a white V-neck undershirt. His eyes were large and dark, the same as Norma's. His look of reserve was Norma's, too. Alex now had a face to fill the empty oval of Norma's prom suit drawing. A feeling of disappointment ran through him, a sense that the mystery was gone.

"What's this about?" Kevin McKinsey's gaze was solemn and penetrating—another inherited trait from his mother.

"My name is Alex Wolsey," Alex said, straightening up. "I'm a friend of Norma McKinsey's. You must be Kevin."

"I am." Kevin drew himself up.

"Nice to meet you," Alex said with as much sincerity as he

knew how to put in his voice. "Your mom is wondering if you might have a moment to speak with her."

"She's here?" Kevin exchanged a glance with the young woman, stepped onto the porch. An angular face, long nose, high cheekbones. The face of a model.

"She's waiting in the car."

"Which car?" Kevin walked to the top of the stairs, arms crossed.

"We're parked around the corner," Alex said.

"You left my mother sitting in a car?" Kevin uncrossed his arms, turned, and gave him a look both accusing and disbelieving.

"She didn't want to come until I made sure you were okay about seeing her." Alex used a polite if distant tone. "I can drive her to your door now."

The baby whimpered and squirmed in the young woman's arms. Alex glanced at the young woman. Talking to Kevin was grueling enough as it was, let alone in front of this hostile stranger and her fussing baby.

"I need to go," the woman said in a low voice to Kevin, shifting the baby in her arms. She stepped onto the porch.

"Okay. See you tonight," Kevin said. Their tired-looking expressions had Alex thinking that every day must be a struggle for them.

"I'll stick around if you want." The woman was looking straight into Kevin's eyes, a look of concern on her face. "I'll call Lucy now and let her know I'm running late."

"I'll be fine," Kevin said. The uncertainty in his voice suggested otherwise.

"You're sure?"

"Yes, I'm sure," Kevin said with more confidence this time, and he patted the woman on the shoulder. His tone was fond but held a tinge of impatience, the way a child might react to an overprotective mother, even though he must be double the woman's age.

"Promise you'll call if there's trouble," the woman said.

"There won't be trouble," Kevin said and glanced at Alex as if to confirm this. Alex nodded his assurance, embarrassed his presence had caused such consternation.

"You be nice to him," she said to Alex. She shifted the baby again in her arms.

"You have my word." Alex smiled at her. "I never did get your name this morning."

"Iris." The woman blinked, caught off-guard.

"Nice to meet you, Iris. I'm sorry for making you late this morning." Alex liked this young woman, even if she wanted nothing to do with him.

He was about to ask Iris if she needed help putting the baby in the car, but this task, it turned out, already belonged to Kevin. He followed Iris down the stairs to a small blue car parked in front of the house and opened the rear passenger door. Alex couldn't help noticing the caring look on Kevin's face as he took the squirming child from Iris and placed her into the car seat, buckling her up. Was Kevin the little girl's father?

Once Iris drove off, Kevin turned and plodded up the stairs to the house. The caring expression he'd given Iris and her baby faded, returned to its original guardedness. He walked past Alex to the open front door as if he meant to walk into the house and shut the door behind him. But then he stopped and turned to look out onto the street, as if his curiosity had gained the better of him.

"So," he said, his look grave but not necessarily unfriendly. "My mother is sitting in a car around the corner."

"She is." Alex felt a keen awareness that everything he was about to say would be analyzed and assessed.

"Must've been a tough journey for her. Charles tells me she's using a walker."

"Not anymore."

"She can walk on her own?" Kevin turned to face Alex, a frown creasing his forehead. "Since when?"

"Couple days," Alex said. His insides became weak.

"Has she told my brother this?" Kevin's expression, already mistrustful, turned grim.

"She might've," Alex mumbled.

"But you can guess, can't you?" Kevin looked at him head-on. "Listen, Alex, I know my mother well enough to know she'd never put her trust in some stupe. So stop pretending you don't know more than you do. My brother has no idea my mother can walk again, does he?"

The piercing look in Kevin's eyes bore an uncanny resemblance to Norma's. Alex should've known Kevin wouldn't give him a hearing without exacting a price. If Alex had any hope of winning him over, he had no choice but to tell the truth.

"I honestly don't know what your mom might've said to your brother." As nervous as Alex was, he had enough presence of mind to refer to Norma as *your mom* and not *your mother*. "But he probably doesn't know."

"Which means he doesn't know about your field trip this morning."

"No."

"I swear, I don't know how he puts up with her." Kevin walked to the porch railing, let out a sigh, then turned to face Alex again. "If my mother can walk again, why didn't she drive up here by herself?"

"She didn't think her knee could handle her foot on a gas pedal for a three-hour drive," Alex said. Then, going for a discreet tone, he added, "I also think she wanted the moral support."

"Dude, you aren't here for moral support. You're here because she needed someone to plead her case." Kevin gave Alex a once-over. "You're easy to look at. That's for sure."

"No one is forcing you to see her, Kevin." Blood rushed to Alex's face, both from Kevin's comment itself as well as the insinuating tone he'd used to say it. "If you'd rather not see her, please give me the word and I'll be on my way."

Kevin turned from Alex and grasped the porch railing. His eyes scanned the little street. His triceps flexed as he leaned on the railing. His profile made Alex think of an ancient statue, the marble chipped and worn, but no less compelling. Or perhaps he looked more compelling in this faded state?

"Fine then," he said. "You might as well come inside."

He walked past Alex and disappeared through the doorway. Alex stared after him. What else could Kevin have to say to him, in the house no less? He stepped toward the open door—and then he froze. The opal. Still in his front shirt pocket. Jesus Christ. No running to the car to give it back to Norma now. He straightened up and walked into the house.

He followed Kevin into a modest eat-in kitchen with a blue linoleum floor and a red cuckoo clock on the cream-painted walls. Except for a stack of dirty dishes in the sink, the place looked presentable. Nothing for Norma to disapprove of. The air was chilly—a telltale sign of financial difficulties. Alex had grown up knowing all about heating bills.

He expected Kevin to pull out a chair at the old-fashioned Formica kitchen table. Instead, Kevin led him down a short hallway to a family room. Picture books sat stacked on a low table. On the floor by the table sat a bead maze, the colored beads looking unnaturally cheerful for such a dismal day. A small stuffed pink elephant was wedged between the cushions of a fake-leather chair. A favorite toy, perhaps. But Alex didn't dare focus on the elephant or the bead maze or any other single item in the room, lest he give the impression of taking mental notes to report to Norma. He stood politely by the doorframe with his hands folded in front of him. This was Kevin's show. Let him speak first.

Kevin walked to the picture windows and raised the blinds. Harsh light flooded the room. Then he turned to face Alex. Dark shadows showed beneath his eyes. Alex visualized him making a dazzling entrance with his boyfriend at that long-ago prom.

"Welcome to my home," Kevin said. He spoke in a low voice, but his words shattered the room's silence. "You must be the nurse."

"Yes. I've been helping your mom since her car accident." An unpleasant thrill pulsed through Alex at being called *the nurse*—no doubt the term Charles used to describe Alex to Kevin. "I assume you know what happened."

"My brother told me." Kevin's gaze made Alex's cheeks grow warm. "Just like he told me my mother had hired a male nurse."

"Oh," Alex said, keeping his expression and tone neutral. If he disliked the way Kevin had called him *the nurse,* then he disliked even more Kevin's emphasis on the word *male.*

"My brother also tells me you live in our Aunt Julie's back unit." Kevin's thin shoulders were framed by wan light.

"I do," Alex said, glancing away. Kevin's habit of facing him straight-on was too disconcerting. "Your aunt recommended me to your mom."

"How is she?" A promising shift in Kevin's tone. "Aunt Julie, I mean."

"She's fine," Alex said. Perhaps this was why Kevin had invited him into the house—not to talk about Norma, but to talk about Julie. "Your brother must've told you about your Uncle Phil passing."

"He did."

Kevin gazed out the window with a stubborn expression. The window gave out on a plot of grass hemmed in by a wooden fence. A crow perched on the fence, its silhouette like black construction paper against the murky sky. Alex could easily entertain Kevin with stories about Julie—her constant fretting, her chattering cockatiels, the blue-footed booby carving she'd given him. But if Kevin wanted to know how his aunt was doing, then he could pick up the phone and call her. Kevin might or might not have done wrong by his mother. No question he'd done wrong by his aunt.

"I'm sure Julie would love to hear from you." Alex was certain that he was speaking the very words passing through Kevin's head right now.

"I always wanted to live in Aunt Julie's back unit," Kevin said, turning to look at Alex. "I used to call that unit the tree house, because the apartment was half-hidden behind her lemon tree."

"That tree is still there. I make things with the lemons all the time. Cookies, cakes, marmalade."

"Must be convenient."

They looked at each other. The sight of the stuffed pink elephant—sweet and joyful, existing only to please—filled Alex with sadness. He looked at Kevin, not knowing what else to say. To think that Kevin grew up in that marvelous house in Oakland. Had everything anyone could ask for. How had he wound up isolated here, instead of that apartment behind Julie's house? How had Alex, with all the hardships he'd experienced growing up, wound up in that apartment instead?

"How old are you, Alex?"

"How old am I?" Alex said, taken by surprise. "I don't understand what my age has to do with anything."

"The way my brother described you, I'd assumed you were older," Kevin said, flicking his eyes over him. "Closer to my age."

"I'll be thirty-six next March," Alex said, still not understanding why Kevin needed to know this. "I've been a nurse for over ten years, if that's what you're concerned about."

"I don't care about your nursing experience. Your age is the issue." Kevin was looking at him straight-on again. "I'm sure my mother would love nothing better than for me to settle down with someone."

"Any mother would want that," Alex said, offended for Norma's sake. "Your own mother knows I'm married."

"To a man?"

"Yes," Alex said, tracing his thumb along his wedding ring. "For what it's worth, Kevin, you're being awfully unfair to your mom. She didn't come here with an agenda. She just wants to see you."

Kevin turned to look out the window again. The crow on the fence was gone. The fence line made a sawtooth against the blank sky.

"How is she?" Kevin gazed into the distance, his expression softening.

"Doesn't Charles fill you in on how she's doing?" By now Alex was resolved to say as little as possible about Norma to Kevin.

"My mother doesn't tell my brother anything," Kevin said, turning to Alex with an ironic look. "Your visit is a prime example."

"She's sitting in a car two blocks away from this house." Alex spoke in the respectful but firm tone he sometimes used with—and associated with—a patient's difficult relatives. "Say the word, and I'll drive her to your door. And then you can ask her yourself how she's doing."

"I don't know if I can do that," Kevin said. A tense look flashed in his eyes.

"You're lucky you have this chance to speak to her," Alex said, not caring how stern he sounded. "She was almost killed in that car accident. How would you feel if you didn't see her today, and then something happened to her? Would you want to live with that for the rest of your life?"

He put his hand on the back of the fake-leather sofa, to steady himself from what he'd said. Kevin was looking at him with wide eyes and an open mouth. If Kevin turned him down, Alex could at least tell Norma that he'd done his best.

"Fine." Kevin's tone was peevish and grudging. "I'll talk to her."

"You're sure?"

"Just go and bring her here," Kevin said in a shaky voice, "before I change my mind."

"Great. Thanks. You're a good guy, Kevin." And Alex turned and hurried out of the living room, down the hall, through the kitchen, out the door, and into the street before Kevin had a chance to call after him.

He made sure he was far enough away from the house, in the shade of a Monterey cypress growing on a neighbor's front lawn, before he stopped to compose himself. The sky had grown brighter, the clouds less sinister. Did he dare think the improving weather was a good omen? Every day here along the coast must be fog in the morning, sun in the afternoon. But why not indulge in hope? He'd carried out the task Norma had recruited him to do. The rest was up to her.

CHAPTER 16

MAZES

THE LONGER NORMA waited for Alex, the more time lost its meaning. This was the accident all over again—her sitting stuck in a car, waiting for help. On the other hand, his prompt return would likely have meant that Kevin had refused to speak to him. Alex might be sitting across from Kevin at Kevin's kitchen table right now, entreating him to give his mother a chance. Maybe Alex would succeed in bringing Kevin to the car. The three of them could drive to the main street together, have lunch. Why couldn't that happen?

Minutes crawled by. Alex was nowhere in sight. Perhaps Kevin had invited him inside only to detain him with a point-by-point explanation for why he despised his mother. *You want to know what it's like to be that woman's son?* Her heart thrummed. She opened her purse for her heart pills. The purse held a cheap travel watch, her reading glasses, her keys, and a money clip holding her driver's license, a credit card, and two hundred-dollar bills. For all the care she'd taken last night to pack this spare travel purse, she'd forgotten to include her pills. For the love of humanity.

She took deep inhales, deep exhales. That would be rich, for her heart to fail before she had her chance to talk with Kevin. Eventually, the buzzing died down.

Nerves. Only nerves. Sorry, Mom. You can't sneak your way out of this that easily.

Fatigue set in. She closed her eyes, intending to rest them, and then snapped awake. She'd nodded off without realizing. How irksome to feel drowsy *now*, after a restless, sleepless night.

At last, Alex rounded the corner. Wouldn't he have more spring in his step if he had good news? Then again, what was he supposed to do? Race toward the car pumping his fist in the air? He walked with the equanimity of someone who had conveyed her message and now had a message to convey to her. She stepped out of the car, leaving the passenger door open, and braced herself.

"And?" She clutched her purse, determined to maintain her *sangfroid* no matter the verdict.

"He's waiting for you." Alex's tone was calm but somber, as if he'd been communicating with a ghost.

"Then he'll see me." An electric charge ripped through her. She must have been expecting in her subconscious that Kevin would turn her down.

"That's what he said."

See, Mom? You had to know I wouldn't turn you away.

"Okay, then," she said, strapping her purse over her shoulder.

"Would you like me to drive you to his door?" Alex pulled out the car keys from his front pocket.

"Kevin can't see this car. Not yet, at least." She slammed the door shut. "Besides, the fresh air will do me good."

"Suit yourself," Alex said and gave her an encouraging smile.

"His house is on the left, almost at the end of the block. Look for the cactuses. You can't miss them."

The misty air stirred her awake. Her heels clicked against the sidewalk as she headed toward Kevin's house. A reassuring sound, full of confidence, purpose. Someone looking out a front window might wonder who the white-haired lady was, dressed elegantly, if rather staidly, in her beige jacket and coffee-colored slacks—clothes she'd spent half of Saturday picking out. Thank goodness she'd given the opal to Alex—the jewel would have shown too conspicuously.

The house on the left, in the spot where Alex had indicated, looked as far removed from Kevin's old life—and away from her own life—as he could have found. Perhaps she shouldn't feel discouraged by this. In a place this isolated, he must have chosen to hide from everyone in his former life, not only her. His old friends—the ones who had smoothed his glide path toward addiction—would never deign to visit him here.

She stopped in front of the house and looked up at the shaded windows. A modest frame, a slanted roof, an old-fashioned front porch that could fit two rocking chairs. The cactuses Alex had mentioned weren't in the front yard as she'd assumed but sat in glazed pots along the porch railing. Their upraised branches resembled a line of cheerleaders waving their arms. Anyone passing by here—if anyone ever wandered this far—would know that someone interesting lived on the other side of that door.

I like those cactuses, Kevin. They're witty.

Mom, you've been talking to me in your head ever since your car accident. It's time to talk to me for real.

Eight steps to the porch. Her footsteps made a distressingly hollow echo as she climbed. One of the stairs was rotting—how shameful of her to notice. But the front door was painted an inviting shade of yellow, pale and warm like shortbread cookies.

Twenty-five years of waiting, capped by an interminable weekend—poof. She put away her sunglasses, smoothed the front of her jacket, and reached for the brass knocker.

The sound of the knocker echoed through the house. Silence. A wait, though probably not as long a wait as she imagined. Then came the sound of muffled footsteps. More silence, as if the person on the other side of the door were rallying himself. The door creaked open. And there, in the doorway, stood Kevin.

His wavy hair had the same touches of gray at the sideburns as Charles. Wrinkles lined his eyes and around the sides of his mouth. He wasn't smiling, but he didn't look disgusted either. Norma needed a moment to realize the middle-aged man in front of her—fifty-two years old on May seventh—was in fact her younger son. If she accomplished nothing else today, at least she could say Kevin was still alive.

"Mom," he said. His hand gripped the side of the door. Rough-looking hands, with a pencil-thin line of grime around the nails. Was his face thinner than twenty-five years ago? But his face had always been thin.

"Kevin." She kept her tone cool, her heart swelling at the sound of *Mom*. She reminded herself that she hadn't expected him to hug her.

"Looks like you found me," he said.

"Yes. Looks like it." She drew her purse close to her, aware that one wrong word might end this meeting before it started.

"I knew you'd show up sooner or later." He spoke with resignation but also with respect, the way he used to concede a hard-fought pool game. "I always knew you'd pry my location out of Charlie."

"So Charlie *does* know where you live." As much as Norma would have liked to use Charles as her cover, she knew that wouldn't be fair. "He never admitted even that much to me."

"I suppose I should've guessed that. Since he probably doesn't even know you're here." A wary look appeared on Kevin's face. "Am I right, Mom? Charlie doesn't know I'm here?"

Norma glanced down at her purse. Then she looked up and slowly shook her head. A less than auspicious start to this reunion.

"If Charlie didn't give you my address," he said, "how did you learn it?"

"Does that matter?"

His expression shifted from wariness to disillusionment. *Yes, Mom, it does matter.* But confessing the truth would almost certainly mean banishment. Something rumbled inside her chest.

"At least Charlie's off the hook now," he said with the faintest of smiles. "He never liked keeping that information a secret."

A dreadful pause. An intense urge came over her to say something. She glanced over her shoulder at the potted cactuses.

"I like those cactuses," she said. "They're witty."

"Huh? Oh. Thanks." He cast a glance over her shoulder, in the direction of the cactuses. Then he looked at her and said, "How is Charlie?"

"I thought he kept in touch with you." She'd forgotten that it was Kevin who'd first called Charlie by that nickname, at the age of eight. Charles, in high school, used to read Peanuts comic strips to Kevin at bedtime, expressing sympathy for Charlie Brown.

"That doesn't mean I know how Charlie is." Kevin threw another glance over her shoulder. "Whenever I ask him, he says he's never better. He's always 'never better.' He can't be never-better all the time, can he?"

"He lives in a comfortable home, he's devoted to Debra, and his first grandchild is due in November. I presume that makes him as happy as anyone."

Her answer hung in the air in all its glibness. She'd never

stopped to consider that Charles, for all his good behavior and adherence to the rules, might be as lost as Kevin.

"He told me about your car accident." Kevin glanced at her good leg. Evidently, he couldn't tell which leg had been injured. "Says he can't believe you made it through in one piece."

"Your brother exaggerates," she said with a dip in her voice. So Kevin knew. All those weeks of wishful thinking in the hospital. She glanced at the doorway above Kevin's shoulder. "May I come in?"

He hesitated, but then he opened the door wider and stepped backward, giving her space to pass through. She crossed the threshold into his kitchen, heartened she'd made it this far. Wet dishes dripped in a drying rack next to the sink—she pictured him scrambling to wash them before she knocked on his door. Beer bottlecap magnets glinted on the fridge. The opalescent lining of an abalone shell caught light in the windowsill. On the kitchen table sat wooden salt-and-pepper shakers carved and painted to look like Steller's jays. Modest, charming. Nothing she should feel embarrassed about. All the same, her face went warm—for thinking his kitchen might embarrass her.

She followed him down a hallway to a family room. The room's pleasant disorder reminded her of his bedroom as a teenager, clothes and books lying about. But today's disorder was one a toddler would make—toys, picture books, stuffed animals. A toddler? The PI had said nothing about Kevin living with a toddler. But how else to explain the stuffed pink elephant on the easy chair? The green-and-red caterpillar on the picture book on the coffee table? The bead maze on the carpet? Was Kevin someone's father?

"If I knew I was having company, I would've tidied up," he said. He must have taken Norma's surprised look as an expression of judgment, of disapproval.

"I'm glad you didn't," she said with a careless twist of her purse strap. If she'd given him more notice, he would have swept all these toys out of view. "Sorry to trouble you, but would you mind bringing me a glass of water?"

"You all right?"

"I'm thirsty is all," she said. The room went dim then bright again.

As soon as he left the room, she settled onto the sofa. A ring stain on the coffee table peeked out from beneath the picture books. He must have bought this table used, along with the easy chair across the room, that plastic toy chest beneath the window, this couch on which she now sat. She bent down to the bead maze and slid a red bead along a twisting green wire. The beads made a comforting click, like billiard balls.

"Here you go, Mom." He placed a glass of ice water on a cork coaster on the coffee table.

"Thank you."

She took the water and sipped. Kevin went to the easy chair and made to sit, but he stopped and remained standing. He wore a pair of jeans and a presentable, if faded, blue pinstriped dress shirt. The creases along the sleeves suggested he never wore it. On his feet were loafers, not slippers. Black dress socks. He must have scrambled to change into these clothes after he'd sent Alex to fetch her.

"You have a little one in the house," she said, nodding at the bead maze.

"My roommate has a one-year-old daughter." He seemed about to say more then stopped and bit his lower lip.

"I used to keep one of these in the sewing room." She leaned down and moved a yellow bead along a purple wire. "It was the only toy that would occupy you long enough so I could work. But at least you could occupy yourself. Charles would fuss if I so much as looked the other way."

"I know, you've told me," Kevin said with a note of self-consciousness. He glanced at the bead maze. "I'm helping raise her."

"You are?" Of all the fates she'd conjured in her mind for Kevin, parenthood hadn't been one of them.

"I enjoy taking care of her, to be honest," he said and gave a slight shrug. "Gives me structure. Gives me purpose."

Twenty-five years ago, he hadn't been able to take care of himself, let alone take care of a child. So those toys, these picture books, could reasonably be construed as a propitious sign. But she still had to ask the question hanging over her, the question that had haunted her from the moment he dropped out of her life.

"You're clean?" Her throat went dry.

"Twenty-five years and counting." He gave a slight smile and nodded, eyes softening.

"Good." A shudder ran through her chest, as if her heart would cave in. She reached for her water.

"Charlie tells me you recently adopted a cat."

"It's more like the cat adopted me." She was surprised to hear that Kevin knew of Harry Winston—and cared enough to ask about him. No point in telling him that the cat had run away.

"You were with Magic when she died?" A telltale strain—guilt, perhaps?—came through in his voice.

"She died in my lap," she said. "At home. Peacefully. Her ashes are buried at the base of the laurel tree out front."

"She should've died in my lap, not yours." Relief spread across his face. "Thank you for taking care of her those last couple of years. And taking care of her all those times I was in rehab."

"Of course."

Magic's round black head had stuck out of Kevin's electric-blue track jacket the day he'd brought her home as a kitten from high school running practice. He'd found her on the side of the road. Her green eyes were round with terror as she surveyed her new home. So Kevin *had* felt regret for abandoning Magic.

"Your nurse friend seems nice," he said. His eyes turned to the picture window.

"He is."

"Charlie doesn't care for him," he said with a touch of confiding wickedness, a vestige of the Kevin she'd once known. He turned from the window to face her. "I bet you know this."

"Your brother has expressed his opinion to me," she said, allowing herself a small smile. No harm indulging in a little conspiracy with Kevin.

"Charlie also told me he caught the nurse poking around in my closet. Said he was checking out my old prom suit."

"Goodness, your brother *has* been keeping you apprised," she said in a tone of mild indignation for Alex's sake. "For the record, Alex was looking for my Wi-Fi router."

"It's none of my business what he was looking for."

"That suit still belongs to you," she said, thinking of the tidy sum Kevin would make if he sold that suit. No doubt he could use the money. "Along with your old running shoes. I can ship them here anytime you want."

"All yours, Mom." Kevin chuckled. "It was so otherworldly, listening to Charlie go on about my prom suit. As if he were talking about someone else's clothes. I haven't given that suit a thought in years."

Should she be angered or saddened by these words? Her hard work, borne of love, the suit that had changed their lives, had been reduced in her son's mind to a moth-eaten memory. How could either of them have known the suit would lead them to this chilly room, here in this remote place? All but strangers to each other?

"Do you have any idea," she said, sitting up, "whatever happened to Zack Patterson?"

"Zack Patterson?" Kevin blinked as if shaken out of his thoughts.

"Your prom date."

"You always were good with names, weren't you, Mom?" A faint smile showed on his lips. "As a matter of fact, I do know what happened to Zack Patterson. We connected online a few years ago."

"Is he well?" she asked, once she realized Kevin wouldn't elaborate.

"If his posts are any indication," he said, "then yes, he's well. He's married. Lives in Atlanta. His photo's on my phone somewhere. Do you want to see what he looks like nowadays?"

"Sure," she said, aiming to sound less interested than she was.

Kevin picked up his phone from the coffee table and scrolled through it. The casual way he held his phone was uncannily like Alex on the morning Norma had first met him, searching for a pet shelter for Harry Winston.

"Here," he said, holding out the phone. "Zack's on the left."

She took the phone. The man who could have been her son-in-law beamed from the photo in an unbuttoned lavender aloha shirt, leaning against a sea wall amid palm trees and a purpling sky. His face was rounder, his hair thinner, but he was recognizable. His arm was wrapped around another man, dark-haired with cinnamon-colored eyes. An azure sea spread behind them like a prize ribbon. Was this looker the same skinny, bashful kid she'd dressed for prom? Had the bold red suit she'd insisted he wear contributed even tangentially to his destiny, as depicted in this splendid photo? A lump grew in her throat.

"He looks happy," was all she allowed herself to say.

She handed Kevin the phone. He glanced at Zack Patterson's photo and placed the phone face down on the table. What must he think of Zack now? He sat on the edge of the easy chair next to the stuffed pink elephant. How melancholy, how worn-out her son looked.

"Mom," he said, hands folded in his lap. "Why did you come here?"

"We never talked about that night," she said, matching his direct question with a direct answer of her own. A dazed feeling came over her, a refusal to believe this was happening.

"You want to know why I walked out?" He leaned back in the chair, eyes shining.

"Did you think I had something to do with it?"

"Had something to do with what?" He sat up straight, a shocked look on his face. "Dad's death?"

"The way you looked at me from the sliding door," she said, her jaw tensing. "As if you were accusing me."

"Of what? Killing Dad?" His expression went from shocked to flabbergasted. "My God, Mom."

"I never saw you after that night," she stammered. "What was I supposed to think?"

"I can't believe you'd think that. I don't know what else to say." He looked as if he'd received a blow to the chest.

"Then, if not that, why did you disappear?"

His face grew thoughtful. A square of sunshine appeared on the carpet next to him.

"I overheard you and Dad arguing earlier that day," he said, his expression like stone.

"I see." She traced her finger along the zipper of her purse. "Yes, about that."

"I don't want to know, Mom." Kevin held up his hand. "Besides, what difference does it make now?"

"You can at least know I have remorse for what I did." This was humiliating, to talk about a long-ago affair with a man around Kevin's age, perhaps even younger. "My only indiscretion."

"For real, Mom? Only *one*?" An astounded expression appeared on his face. "I would've thought you'd had more."

"More? What made you think that?" She drew back, a squeezing in her chest. "You mean to say you knew about your father?"

"Didn't everyone?"

"Everyone? Like who?" The squeezing in her chest tightened.

"I don't know." He glanced away, then looked at her. "Listen, Mom, if you came all the way up here to talk about *this*—"

"You're right, you're right. Let's drop the subject."

Her eyes strayed to the bead maze, lustrous in the gray light. *Everyone knew.* Her friends? Charles? Julie and Phil? The notion was too mortifying to contemplate.

"So there I was, two days home from rehab," he said. "Caterers swarming all over the house."

"My bridge party," she said in a monotone.

"I'd gone outside through the side door to take a walk. That's when I heard you and Dad arguing from around the corner of the house. I went straight back inside and shut myself in my room, blocking my ears and craving drugs all over again. I would've fled right then and there. But then the doorbell rings, and it's your lady friends, and suddenly you're throwing a party. I could hear you through the door. Chatting away with your girlfriends as if nothing happened."

"I couldn't throw them out at that point," she said defensively.

"I lay on the bed with Magic, feeling trapped." He was staring off into space as if he were reliving that night. "A couple hours go by. The house goes quiet. My room is stifling, so I open my bedroom door and then the side door, to let in some air. A clear night, nothing but stars. Then I hear a glass break. All night I'd been listening for Dad, waiting for him to blow up. As soon as I heard that glass break, I thought to myself, this is it, it's showtime. But I didn't expect to see what I saw."

"I didn't expect that either," she said, her voice trailing off.

"And that's when I said to myself, I'm done. Done with that house, done with Dad, done with you, done with everything." He was looking down, using the thumb of one hand to caress the palm of the other. "I wouldn't have kept sober if I'd stayed."

"And so you left."

"I took a bus to LA and crashed on friends' couches." He glanced at her then looked down. "Found a program down there. Discovered landscaping. Moved up here. To this day I thank God I never slid backward. Over time I began to feel transformed, as if my former self was nothing but an empty suit. A suit I'd cast off."

A suit I'd cast off. Like the one hanging in his old closet, mummified in plastic. How could she have thought he'd ever want that suit again?

"I never told Charlie about what I saw and heard that day," he said.

"I thought so," she said softly.

"I figured if I didn't talk about it, I could pretend it never happened. That was my key to survival, Mom. And why I never returned. I didn't want to risk everything I'd worked for."

"And now?" Terror rocketed through her. "Do you feel like you're risking everything now, with me sitting here in front of you?"

"I don't know," he said, looking down at his hands. "I hope not."

But, by his tone, he might as well have said yes. No point in prolonging this conversation if Kevin regarded his own mother as toxic. She gathered her purse and glanced around the room, blinking away tears. Her eyes lit on the bead maze.

"Does the little girl enjoy playing with those beads?" A ludicrous question, but she couldn't let go, not if this would be her last moments with her son.

"Sometimes." He stood up and then picked up his phone. "Uh, Mom. Work's in less than an hour."

"I'd like to visit you again sometime." She tightened her fingers around her purse, remembering her pills weren't there.

"Can I call you first?" His eyes darted around the living room, a discomfited look on his face.

"If you prefer. The house number hasn't changed," she said. Of course, he'd never call her. "I'd better go myself. Alex must be wondering about me."

She rose and reached for her water glass, dripping with condensation, and pressed the glass against her throbbing wrist. A chill zigzagged up her arm and through the rest of her body, seizing her heart. She took a sip. The frigid water nauseated her. The square of sunshine grew stronger. White light filled the room. Kevin turned into a blur. The furniture faded. The maze beads vanished as if sinking into snow. She heard the thud of the water glass on the floor before she realized it had slipped from her hand.

"Mom?" Kevin called out to her as if from the other side of a snow drift. "Mom!"

The room solidified into a block of white before shifting to black. Her chest felt as light as a void. She fumbled for the arm rest, the coffee table, then reached her hand forward, groping in darkness. Kevin's voice grew fainter, calling out *Mom*. And then—nothing.

CHAPTER 17
RECKONING

ALEX'S STOMACH GROWLED. How long had Norma been gone since she left to see Kevin? He should've gone for that coffee when he'd had the chance. At least no one was around to wonder what he was up to, loitering in the carrot-colored car.

If she believed in smartphones, he could text her to say he'd gone to grab something to eat. But even if he could text her, would he? She might be deep in conversation with her son by now. A text would annoy her. Or ruin everything.

Food, food, food. Did he dare abandon his post? He abhorred the idea of her waiting for him, standing by herself by that rose-bush. But who knew how much longer she'd be? She might've forgotten him by now, swept away by the joy of her reunion. He started the car, thinking he'd buy a sandwich or a burrito on the main street and be back in five minutes.

Red lights flashed in his rear-view mirror. An ambulance. He kept the car in park, ready to make a U-turn once the ambulance turned a corner. But the lights grew larger, headed straight toward him. No. Oh, Christ no.

The ambulance whizzed past. Scarlet light beamed into the rental car like a splash of blood. Then the ambulance rounded the corner onto Kevin's street. Norma. It had to be. Alex started the car and, with a squeal of tires on asphalt, followed the ambulance.

The ambulance sat in front of Kevin's house with its red lights flashing. Curtains rustled in the windows of nearby houses. A front door across the street cracked open, a head peeked out. His worst fears, confirmed. He parked across from Kevin's house and got out of the car.

Whispering voices issued from Kevin's wide-open front door. Alex resisted the impulse to go inside, offer his services. Soon the paramedics, two tall, burly guys, wheeled out Norma. She was sitting up on a stretcher, her eyes fluttering. An oxygen mask distorted her face. Then Kevin came out of the house, his expression tense and white. He locked the front door and bolted down the front steps without looking Alex's way.

"What happened?" Alex called out.

"I don't know," Kevin said, stopping and turning to face him. "Heart, I think."

"Jesus." Alex turned to one of the paramedics lifting Norma into the ambulance. "Where are you taking her?"

"Santa Rosa."

The young man's leisurely tone was reassuring. If her life were in danger, the paramedics would be acting with more urgency—and driving her somewhere closer than Santa Rosa, almost two hours away. He craned his neck over the side of the stretcher, hoping to catch her eye. Her eyelids fluttered closed.

"Thanks," he said. The paramedic climbed into the van next to Norma, while his partner shut the door and headed for the driver's seat. He turned to Kevin. "I'm following them. Do you want a ride?"

"I'll take my own car." Kevin cast a look of revulsion at the rental car.

"Really, it's no problem."

"I'm driving to work later." Kevin turned to leave but stopped to watch the ambulance make a U-turn and drive off. Then he looked at Alex. "You don't have to stay, though. My brother's meeting me at the hospital."

"Ah." The idea of seeing Charles today filled Alex with dread. If he left for Oakland now, he might make it home a few minutes ahead of Pratyush. But how could he abandon Norma? "No, I'd like to be there for your mom."

"Suit yourself," Kevin said.

Then he turned and strode toward a small white pickup truck. Alex turned and dashed around the corner to the rental car, got inside, and slammed the door. The gas tank was more than half full. He revved the car and banged a U-turn. This day could yet turn out well. No reason to give up hope yet.

The sky became clearer the farther south he drove. He strained to drive within the speed limit, allowing both the ambulance and Kevin's car to race ahead of him. Had Norma remembered to bring her heart pills? Alex should've reminded her.

Kevin must've rejected her. A happier outcome wouldn't have led to this seventy-mile trek to an emergency room. What if Norma asked Alex to stay overnight in Santa Rosa? What would he say to Pratyush then?

The dashboard clock read eighteen minutes past one by the time he pulled into the hospital parking lot. No chance of making it home before Pratyush. Did he have time to text him? Better check on Norma first. He sighed and glanced at the gas gauge. Less than half a tank. His stomach rumbled. He hadn't eaten since six.

The waiting room looked like every waiting room he'd ever known, packed with stressed-looking people shifting uncomfortably in hard plastic chairs. Kevin was sitting by the plate-glass window giving out onto the parking lot, his body partially turned as he stared outside with a listless expression. His look exemplified what Alex called Emergency Waiting Room Face—the bored, dazed attitude of someone who couldn't believe where he was and wished he were anywhere else. He walked up to Kevin.

"How's your mom?" Alex glanced around. No free chairs to be had.

"They stabilized her. Now they're running tests." Kevin kept looking out the window at the passing cars. His reflection was misshapen in the plate glass.

"Are you hungry? Can I bring you something from the vending machine?"

Kevin kept staring outside as if he hadn't heard Alex's question. A young woman sitting next to Kevin gave Alex a dull scowl, lost interest in him, scrolled through her phone. An uncomfortable feeling grew in Alex's stomach, a sense Kevin had airbrushed him from his line of vision.

"My brother should be here any minute," Kevin said, glancing over his shoulder at Alex. "Don't say I didn't warn you."

"Kevin," Alex said, with as much feeling as he could muster, "you have no idea how sorry I am about this—"

"I'm sorry too, Alex." Kevin turned to face him with a deadly, contemptuous look. "I'm sorry I let you talk me into seeing my mother. I'm sorry I let her into my house. I might even be sorry for all the terrible events that have led to this moment. But none of that will change a thing. Now, if you don't have the good sense to make yourself scarce before my brother comes, then go sit somewhere I don't have to look at you. Before I say something I'll really be sorry about."

Alex turned and headed for the men's room and splashed cold water on his face. His cheeks burned as if Kevin had slapped him. He wished he could walk out of this place and drive home and pretend today never happened. But Norma wouldn't want him leaving without her.

Why should Charles take his frustrations out on him? For all Charles knew, Norma had kept Alex in the dark about her trip's purpose. Could Alex look Charles in the face and say he had no idea he was driving Norma to Mendocino County to see her estranged son? But he could already imagine what his mother would say. *No, Alex. You can't.*

Lunch was a plastic container of cheese and crackers. The cheese bore a similar shade of orange to the rental car—a color that most likely never occurred in nature. His muscles tightened every time the sliding glass doors opened. Charles needed to show up soon. Put an end to this excruciating wait.

Up in Santa Rosa with Norma, he texted Pratyush. *Long story.*

About twenty minutes later—it felt longer—Charles walked through the doors. He wore a carnation-pink golf shirt and shamrock-green golf pants whose vividness clashed with his pallid face. Alex made to rise. But Kevin had already risen from his seat and was walking over to Charles.

The two brothers talked in hushed voices. A couple of minutes passed. Then Kevin patted Charles's shoulder and strode through the sliding doors. Was he leaving already? No time to process that. Charles was now looking Alex's way. His red-eyed expression made Alex want to dissolve, melt into a puddle on the shiny white floor. He stood up and awaited his punishment.

"Charles," he said in a professional voice once Charles stood in front of him. "Good to see you again."

"Do you have a minute?" Charles's ashy face made his eyes appear that much more bloodshot. "Outside?"

"Um, sure."

Charles turned and strode for the exit without waiting to see if Alex was following him. The doors parted as if in fear Charles would plow through the glass. Alex followed him outside, the sunshine making him squint. Charles's arms swung beside him as he walked. His broad shoulders and back muscles shifted and strained beneath his golf shirt. Then he stopped at his SUV, parked a few yards away from the entrance, and spun around. He could be any one of those jocks who used to intimidate Alex in high school, self-important and entitled. *Remember*, Alex told himself. *You're Norma's nurse, not Charles's.*

"Okay," Charles said, his tone cutting. "Would you mind explaining to me what this is all about?"

"Your mother wanted to see your brother," Alex said, then regretted saying it. Shifting the blame to Norma felt craven, even if what he'd said was true.

"How did she find out where he lived?" Charles's eyes were cold, hard, uncompromising.

"I don't know." No need to enrage Charles with a truthful answer.

"You didn't help her look for him?"

"I only drove the car," Alex said and swallowed.

"Why didn't you stop her?"

"It wasn't my place to stop her."

"Why didn't you call me then?" Charles crossed his arms.

"I couldn't go behind your mother's back like that," Alex said.

"Sure, you couldn't." Charles shook his head and looked around the parking lot. "Man, I can't believe I'm standing here. First I spend the morning stuck in godawful traffic, driving home from Tahoe. Then I'm summoned to drive an hour and a half up here. I am sick, sick, *sick* of the inside of my car right now."

A vibration against Alex's thigh. Pratyush. Another reckoning.

"For what it's worth, I don't think your mother's chest pains are life-threatening." Alex spoke with all the sincerity in his power, ignoring the buzzing cell phone.

"I *know* they aren't," Charles said acidly. "They never are."

"What do you mean, they never are?" Alex reached into his front pocket, grasped his phone as if the device were a talisman, an object to protect him from Charles. The phone stopped buzzing.

"Nothing's wrong with my mother's heart." Charles gave a caustic look. "The pain is all in her head. Her doctor told me so."

"But—but—she takes pills," Alex said. "I've refilled her prescription myself."

"You have, have you?" Charles went slit-eyed. "Well, Mr. Nurse, would you like to know what you filled a prescription for? Aspirin. That's all those pills are. She drove the doctor bananas insisting she had heart trouble, so he wrote her a fake prescription. What kind of pills does my mother think she's taking?"

"Acebutolol," Alex said, letting this revelation sink in. Embarrassing—indeed humbling—to realize he hadn't figured out on his own that those pills were aspirin.

"Sounds official," Charles said, grim-faced.

"If she doesn't have a heart problem," Alex said, his cheeks burning, "what do you reckon happened to her this morning?"

"You're asking *me*? Weren't you there?" Charles's expression was one of naked contempt.

"I was waiting in the car outside." Alex's spine stiffened to the jealousy in Charles's tone. Did Charles think *he* should've been the one to do the driving this morning?

"I'm as confused as you are, Alex." His voice was thick with frustration. "All I know is I pull into my driveway after almost five hours on the road, my phone rings, and it's my brother calling out of the blue to say our mother is lying passed out in his living room."

"She may not be on heart pills, but she didn't fake what happened to her," Alex said. The cheese and crackers sat like lead in his stomach. "Kevin wouldn't have called the ambulance otherwise."

"Let's put that aside for a second." Charles pinched the bridge of his nose and looked upward, as if he wanted the sun to engulf him. Then he brought his hand down and looked at Alex. "Tell me about how you and my mother showed up unannounced at my brother's door. You drove her in your car?"

"Your mother's car."

"My mother doesn't *have* a car."

"She rented one."

"Specifically for this trip?"

"Yes." Alex turned his eyes from Charles, making sure to avoid glancing at the Porsche SUV. A bright blue Doritos wrapper sat crumpled on the sparkling asphalt.

"That must've been her plan all along," Charles said mostly to himself. "Rent a car, hire a driver."

"A driver?" Alex looked up.

"My mother never needed your nursing skills, Alex." Charles gave him a disdainful once-over. "What she needed was for you to help her see Kevin."

"I don't know anything about that," Alex said. Charles's words sounded disturbingly close to the mark. "She asked for my help this weekend, so I helped her."

"You know something, Alex? I want to help her too." His tone was a mix of sadness and exasperation. "If she'd let me."

"Maybe she found it easier to lean on someone outside of

her family," Alex said. "I go through this sort of thing with my own mother. Lots of parents don't want to burden their children."

"She had no trouble burdening my brother this morning." Charles looked around the parking lot with a disoriented expression. "I'm the only one left to take care of her. And she shuts me out. So does Kevin. They're two of a kind, those two. Not that *they're* aware of that."

Alex looked at Charles, realizing the truth of what he'd said. Poor Charles. Neither Kevin nor Norma had done him any favors, keeping secrets from him. Alex remembered the story Julie had told him of Charles playing sheriff, protecting his cousins from harm. His stomach ached with guilt.

"Why don't you go home," he said, sensing a softening in Charles's attitude. "I'm the one who brought your mom up here."

"She's coming home with me." Charles glared at him, a dull and ominous look.

"But I have her rental car. If you want, I can drive her home, drop off the car, and then drive her to your place in my car."

"Forget that," Charles said, his jaw squaring. "Now you listen here, Alex. I'm driving my mother home in *my* car. You're driving my mother's rental to *her* house. And *then* you're leaving me alone. And leaving *her* alone. I never want to see you again. Do you understand?"

"Yes," Alex said, bowing his head.

"I don't want you sticking around here either," Charles said. "You've done enough."

"Okay."

"You can slip the keys to the rental car through the mail slot." Charles's voice was more subdued this time, as if he were already regretting how harshly he'd spoken. "I'll return the car myself."

"Got it." Alex's voice was shaking. "I'm really sorry about this, Charles."

"Just let me take care of my mother," Charles said, holding up his hand. "She's my mother, not yours."

He turned and strode toward the hospital doors.

Parked cars around Alex came into focus. The sun burned his nape. His head and eyes throbbed. He pulled out his phone and saw Pratyush's missed call. Pratyush didn't leave a voice message, but he did send a text.

You ok?

How to answer him? The way Alex had botched everything up, he didn't deserve to have Pratyush or anyone else ask him how he was. Once Pratyush heard the story, comprehended the scale of Alex's folly, he'd shake his head and go solemn. *Why didn't you tell me?*

I'm fine, will be back in 1 hr or so, he typed. Then he slipped the phone in his pocket and walked with a heavy step toward the rental car.

CHAPTER 18

COMING HOME

H E PULLED INTO Norma's driveway and got out of the car. The air was less scorching here in Oakland than it had been in Santa Rosa. He gazed at Norma's house, car keys biting into his palm. The green-shuttered windows stared out impassively. He went to the front door and slipped the keys through the slot, thus ending the first and most likely last time he'd ever drive a Porsche. Should he leave behind the front door key, too? Sure, why not? He'd never step foot in that house again.

He pressed his hand against his front shirt pocket, felt the opal against his chest. How to return the necklace? Through the mail slot? But what if Charles—or, worse, Norma—found that necklace lying tangled on the floor? Alex couldn't hurt her like that.

Better to take the necklace home and figure out a way to return it safely to her. She'd given him the opal for safekeeping, after all. He'd use that excuse if Charles ever came pounding on his door, accusing him of theft.

He didn't have to wait long for an Uber to whisk him home. Plenty of open parking spaces near Julie's house. No sign of the Ford. Where could Pratyush be at this hour? But Alex had no right to ask himself such a question.

Julie's blinds were up. She was usually home at this hour on a Sunday. Was there any possibility Charles had called his aunt, informed her of Norma's crisis? Unlikely. And Alex had no intention of telling her himself. Norma wouldn't want him telling her sister about what had happened today. If what Charles had said was right and Norma had no heart condition, then she might well come home tomorrow and pretend to Julie that nothing was wrong.

Hopefully, Julie wouldn't be outside right now, lounging on her deck or watering her plants. He walked down the drive to his unit. No Julie in sight. His first lucky break of the day.

Fallen lemons littered the driveway. He'd been giving Norma so much of his attention that he'd grown lazy about clearing them. Of course, they weren't *his* lemons, but still. Poor Julie, all by herself with no one to give her a hand. He'd collect as many lemons as he could tomorrow and make a batch of cookies, all for her.

Julie's canvas bag rested against the recycling bin under her deck. He walked up to the bin, frowning. The bag leaned against a deck post, one strap sagging like a broken flower stem. She must've put the bag down for some reason and forgotten to take it into the house with her. He couldn't leave the bag sitting out here, could he? Wouldn't he have to face her sooner or later, anyway? Here went nothing. He picked up the bag and trudged up Julie's steps.

The blinds to Julie's sliding door were up. He peered into the empty kitchen and rapped on the glass. The cockatiels squawked, loud enough to make him flinch. Julie's footsteps sounded from within the house. He resolved to make this errand short and sweet.

Julie came to the door and pulled it open. Her blue blouse and white slacks, plus her pink lipstick, suggested she'd just returned home from somewhere. Her eyes widened at the sight of her bag in Alex's hands.

"I found this under the deck." He held up the bag.

"Oh, *that's* where I left that foolish bag," she said with a despondent look. "I swear, I'd misplace my own head if it wasn't attached to my neck."

"I misplace things all the time," he said, grateful to know that Julie, at least, still needed his support.

"My arms were full of groceries, so I put the bag down." She took the bag from him and held it close to her like a lost child. "The phone was ringing as I was coming through the door. You want to know who the caller was?"

"Who?" A freezing sensation filled his veins.

"Kate." Julie's voice was low and disgruntled.

All righty then. So long as the caller hadn't been Charles or Norma, he could handle anything. He readied himself to be a thoughtful neighbor.

"The conversation didn't go well?"

"I told her about skydiving," she said. "Asked if she'd like to join me when she's here over Thanksgiving. Boy, was that a mistake. She spent the past half hour refusing to believe me, then lecturing me on how foolish I was being. Said I was too old to consider such a thing. We hung up on such bad terms, now I don't know if she's coming for Thanksgiving. I'm not sure if I even *want* her to come. All she'll do is yammer about how this house is too big for me to handle by myself."

"Aw, Julie, I'm sorry to hear that," Alex said, forgetting about his day. "Does that mean you're not going through with the skydive?"

"I want to go," she said and sighed. "But I've run out of people to ask. Kate was my last resort."

"You'll find someone, I'm sure," he said, looking away with a dart of guilt. Not guilty enough to change his mind about skydiving himself.

"Thanks for bringing in my bag," she said, her voice weary.

How was he supposed to leave her now? Poor Julie and her killjoy daughter. An impulse seized him, and he drew himself up and looked at her.

"You know what, Julie? I hope you go through with that skydive," he said in his most unwavering voice. "Even if it means you have to go by yourself."

"You do?" She drew back as if this idea had never occurred to her.

"Absolutely," he said, nodding. "Phil thought you could do it. So do I."

"Maybe," she murmured. She looked down for a moment then looked up with shining eyes. "Thank you, Alex. I needed to hear that."

So what if her skydive was none of his business? So what if the thought of skydiving scared the daylights out of him, as it no doubt scared the daylights out of Julie's daughter in Chicago? Someone had to take her side. His smile widened, and he turned to go down the deck stairs.

"Oh, and Alex?" she called out.

"Yes?" He turned to face her from the top step, expecting her to thank him again.

"Do you have any idea where Norma might be today?"

"Norma?" He gripped the stair railing.

"I've been trying to reach her all weekend," she said with a slight frown, "but she's not picking up. I can't even get through to her answering machine."

He felt an impulse to tell her everything. But how could he

tell her without betraying Norma's secrets? Better to stay out of it. Let Norma be the one to tell her what had happened.

"Last time I saw her was Friday," he said, pretending to be as stumped as she was.

"Oh, okay. I'm sure she's fine." Julie spoke as if she were trying to convince herself. "You're seeing her tomorrow, aren't you?"

"Actually, Friday was my last day with her." His lie had a sour taste to it. "She can walk again."

"She *can*?" Julie gaped. "How long has she been able to walk?"

"Since, well, Friday," he said, the sour taste growing stronger. "That's when she told me she didn't need my services anymore."

"Maybe I'll give her a buzz now," she said, more to herself than to him.

"I'd better be going," he said, turning. "Pratyush should be home any minute."

But Pratyush wasn't at home. Of course he wasn't, or else Alex would've seen the Ford parked out front. It was fitting for Pratyush to be somewhere else. Alex deserved to wait.

A cheap-looking trophy, no bigger than a jar of peanut butter, sat on the coffee table. He walked over and picked up the trophy. A plastic silver cup sat on a square base bearing a green plastic plaque in the shape of a pickle. MOST FABULOUS BACKHAND, the plaque read. He put down the trophy, thinking of the fun Pratyush must've had today without him.

His stomach rumbled. Did he have time to go out and grab a bite before Pratyush walked through the door? But he couldn't bear the idea of his husband walking into an empty apartment.

A dirty mug and a cereal bowl sat in the kitchen sink. How unlike Pratyush, to leave dirty dishes like that. No, wait. Those dishes weren't Pratyush's, they were his own breakfast dishes from this morning. They'd been sitting in the sink all day. He went to the sink and reached for a sponge.

The sound of footsteps on the front steps reached him as he stood at the sink with the faucet running. His insides seized up. He squeezed another drop of soap into his coffee cup, willing himself not to turn around. Whatever scolding Pratyush gave him, at least it would soon be over.

"Hey," Pratyush said from behind, his tone casual.

"Hey," Alex said over his shoulder, scrubbing his cereal bowl.

"Have you had dinner yet?"

"Not yet," Alex said and turned off the faucet.

The sudden silence jolted him. He slung the dishtowel over his shoulder and turned to face Pratyush. Pratyush looked as handsome as ever in his blue striped shirt and snug beige pants. How could Alex have thought to sneak out on him today?

"I was thinking of going over to Telegraph for fish tacos." Pratyush didn't sound as angry as he should've been.

"Fish tacos, sure," Alex said and forced a smile. "I see you won a trophy."

"Oh, that," Pratyush said with a roll of the eyes. "That was a joke."

"I'm sorry I missed watching you win it."

Alex turned to dry his cereal bowl.

"So," Pratyush said, his tone more curious than critical. "Mendocino County."

"Yep," Alex said with a sigh and turned to face Pratyush again. He couldn't pretend to dry the bowl forever.

"How'd you wind up there?"

"Norma rented a car," Alex said dully. "I took an Uber to her house and drove her from there."

"Why didn't you say you needed the car this morning?"

"I wouldn't trust driving that car all the way to Mendocino County." Alex swallowed and glanced downward. "But that's not the whole story. The truth is I didn't want to tell you where I was going."

"Why not?"

"I, uh…" Alex turned and felt ready to retch into the sink, despite his empty stomach. "You know, Pratyush? I honestly don't know why not."

There. The words were out. He turned on the faucet and ran his hands under the water even though his hands weren't dirty. No way to wipe off what he'd said.

He felt the weight of Pratyush's hand on his shoulder. Then Pratyush's other hand reached around him to turn off the faucet. His breath felt warm and steady against the nape of Alex's neck.

"Turn around," Pratyush said in a low voice into Alex's ear.

Alex turned around, his eyes on Pratyush's collar. Pratyush wrapped his arms around him, drew him close. He buried his face into Pratyush's shoulder and breathed in his warmth. Then Pratyush pulled away from him and ran his fingers along Alex's front shirt pocket.

"What's this?" He unbuttoned the pocket and reached inside.

"Long story," Alex murmured.

Pratyush brought out Norma's pendant and held it up to the light. The blue and pink veins in the milky-green stone looked as innocuous as the threads in a baby's blanket. A pensive gaze showed on Pratyush as he regarded the necklace.

"This belongs to Norma?"

Alex nodded.

"It's okay, Alex." Pratyush lowered the necklace into Alex's shirt pocket. "I just want to know what happened."

He took Alex by the hand and led him to the living room couch. So warm and soft, his husband's hands. Once seated,

Pratyush snuggled close to Alex, clasped his hand. Not at all what Alex had expected. Far more than he deserved.

"I don't know where to begin," he said.

"Begin at the beginning," Pratyush said. "Why did you go up there?"

The warmth of Pratyush's hand traveled up Alex's arm and through his body. Pratyush traced his thumb along Alex's wedding ring. The words came slowly at first and out of order as well. More than once Alex had to backtrack, repeat himself. Eventually, he managed to recount the entire story. His talk with Norma at Tilden Park. The drive to Mendocino County. The opal. Convincing Kevin to see his mother again. The race to the hospital. Charles berating him in the parking lot.

But that wasn't the whole story, was it? So he kept talking. The haircut, the home gym, the pool lessons, the prom suit. By the time he finished, his body felt lighter, hollowed out.

Pratyush said nothing when Alex finished. A thoughtful expression, a hard glint in his eyes. Alex was used to Pratyush having to think before he said anything.

"I'm sorry, Pratyush," he said, a sick feeling in his heart. "You have no idea how sorry I am."

"Sorry for what?" A puzzled frown creased Pratyush's face.

"For keeping all this from you. You have a right to be mad at me."

"But I'm not mad," Pratyush said. "Sounds to me you were honoring your patient's privacy."

"I'm also sorry for spending too much time with Norma," Alex said. "She has this way of drawing people in—and I let myself be drawn in. You had a feeling that would happen, didn't you?"

"I remember the people I used to work for," Pratyush said, his voice as soft as cotton. "They're so loaded, it's impossible not to wonder what makes them tick, what they said and did to have as much as they have. On top of that, Norma's a fashion designer—that's a way more seductive profession than most. So, no, I'm not surprised that she drew you in. But I don't want to be too hard on the lady. She's been through a lot. And I haven't forgotten what you and she did for me. Together, you saved me from returning to my old job."

"All the same, I became too involved in her life," Alex said, a quiver in his voice.

"Not because of *her*, Alex. Because of *me*. I've been keeping you at arm's length. I see that now." The glow in Pratyush's eyes was one Alex hadn't seen in a long time. "Alex, I'm the reason why you went to Mendocino County today. You've been using Julie's sister to fill a hole that I created. I don't care that you didn't tell me. What matters is you're with me now."

He undid the top button of Alex's shirt. The second button. The third. His hand reached inside. Warmth spread across Alex's skin. Oh, God. *Now?*

"What are you doing?" His heart thumped.

"Asking your forgiveness." Pratyush kissed him on the cheek. "All day long I've been waiting for you. Your absence today brought home to me how far inside my head I've been these past months."

"I should be the one asking *your* forgiveness… No, Pratyush… No, wait…"

But he sat riveted as Pratyush undid the rest of his buttons, pulled off his shirt, tossed it onto the couch. His heart hadn't beat this fast to Pratyush's touch since…since when? Their first time together?

"Let's forgive each other." Pratyush's face was close to Alex's. "What do you say? Ready to put this behind us? Ready to come home?"

"You realize," Alex said between heavy breaths, "I'm no closer to having a real job today than the day they laid me off."

"I don't care," Pratyush said in the bossy tone he used during intimate moments. "We've wasted enough time as it is."

He looked at Alex and brushed his cheek with the back of his hand. His eyes were wide and knowing, the irises like melted chocolate. He leaned in and planted his lips on Alex's. Did Alex dare believe what was happening? But here was Pratyush standing up. Holding out his hand and helping Alex to his feet, leaving his shirt to lie rumpled on the couch. Leading him into the bedroom with wordless confidence. The setting sun blazed into the room. Pratyush lowered the shades and drew the curtains so that the light turned rosy. His movements made clear he meant to take control, just as he had that first time. And take control he did.

God. If only Alex's friends at that Christmas party had known what Pratyush—that mild-mannered man standing by himself in the kitchen doorway—could do. If only they'd known the passion that simmered beneath that calm, unassuming gaze. This time Alex knew what was coming. What a joy—a privilege—to explore this side of his husband. To be on the receiving end of Pratyush's generosity. Pratyush knew when to speed up, when to slow down, where to put his hands, the exact words to say, murmuring in respectful but blunt terms the things he wanted Alex to do and the way he wanted Alex to do them. The command in his tone. And all the while he fixed a gaze on Alex that made his desire unambiguous. His look all but ordered Alex to forget the past, forget the future, forget his own identity. If only this could go on forever, unrolling like a magic carpet through space and time. Then a flash of light, a momentary blindness, and now Alex lay staring up at the darkened ceiling, returning to himself. He felt a sudden craving for fish tacos.

★

He awoke the next morning at the decadent hour of eight o'clock. Pratyush was already out of the house. Alex's first day off in weeks. His limbs felt heavy as he pulled himself out of bed.

His shirt from yesterday lay rumpled on the couch. The opal! He rushed over and picked up the shirt, felt the front pocket. Still there. He took out the pendant and laid it slowly and carefully into the cup of the pickleball trophy. Then he put the trophy on the mantel, between the framed photo of his mother and the blue-footed booby.

He was measuring out coffee into the coffee maker when his cell phone on the kitchen table buzzed. Who could be calling at this hour? He picked up the phone. The clinic's number glowed on his screen. A memory of Norma from Friday, her voice ringing with certainty, came to him. He smiled to himself. Then he gazed out the window, eyes focused on the white stars of jasmine, and brought the phone to his ear.

CHAPTER 19

CHECKING OUT

THE DAWN LIGHT seeping through the window blinds tinged everything in Norma's hospital room gray. Soggy light bathed the bed sheets, made a ghost of the papery curtain that walled her off from humanity. This must be what purgatory felt like.

What day was it? Sunday? No, Monday. Monday morning. That might be the time on that computer monitor by the bed, but no way could she see those digits without her glasses. Where were her glasses, anyway? Her purse?

This was obnoxious, to wake up in a hospital bed in Santa Rosa instead of her own bed at home. But the doctor had insisted on keeping her overnight. For observation, he said. To observe what? An old woman who'd made a fool of herself?

A hole bored its way into her stomach. The space behind her kneecap emitted a dull ache. Her heart? She laid her hand on her breastbone. No heartbeat she could feel. Had she died? If so, then perhaps this wasn't purgatory. Perhaps this was actual hell. That would be crafty of the Devil, to assign her for eternity to a hospital bed.

But of course this wasn't hell. This was the room in which they'd deposited her last night. That was her heartbeat, pulsing across the computer monitor's screen. She would have to face the day—and Charles—whether she wanted to or not.

A visitor's chair sat empty by the window. Gloomy light touched the leather seat. She pictured an eighteen-year-old Kevin in that chair, a regretful smile on his lips.

It's time I said goodbye, Mom. After all, I don't exist.

But you do exist.

In Mendocino, I exist. Here, I'm just a fantasy. I'm sorry, Mom. Goodbye.

She opened her eyes to stronger light slicing through the blinds. Sleep must have crept up on her without her realizing it. A nurse came in with breakfast on a tray, opening the partition curtains to reveal the room in all its mediocrity.

"Good morning, how are you feeling today?" The nurse's voice was gratingly vivacious.

"Fine, thank you," Norma said, sitting up and smoothing the sheets on her lap. The letters on the nurse's nametag were a blur.

"Would you like me to open the blinds for you?" The nurse was already standing at the window, looking as if she couldn't wait to pull the cord.

"By all means. Thank you."

The nurse raised the blinds to reveal an empty sky. No buildings, no trees. A bleak start to a bleak day.

Her breakfast was a cup of watery coffee and a pancake that could have doubled as a shoe insole. Her plastic fork rasped against the pancake as if she were cutting into a sponge. Even to look at the pancake was enough to make her swear off breakfast forever. She pushed her tray away.

Charles's voice drifted into the room from the open door—low, courteous, genteel. He must be consulting with the hospital staff. The clueless nurse was no doubt recounting the restful night the patient had had. What did that nurse know?

Soon Charles and the doctor came through the door. The doctor looked about fifty, a friendly enough face, inoffensive manners. Charles wore the AstroTurf golf pants he'd worn yesterday. He must have spent the night up here.

"Good morning!" Charles's grin and sunny tone were only a tad less abrasive than the nurse's had been.

"You're cleared to check out," the doctor said. His eyes strayed to the pancake, gouged by her plastic fork. "Have you eaten?"

"I'm not hungry."

"Can we bring you something else?" the doctor said, concerned.

"No. I'd like to go home, please."

"We'll stop somewhere for breakfast," Charles said in happy problem-solving mode. "They've opened a great new diner right around the corner from us."

"No breakfast. Home," she said, her voice dull. "Can someone bring me my purse?"

"Ready to go?" Charles was nothing but smiles out in the lobby in front of the young nurse pushing Norma's wheelchair.

"Where's Alex?" Norma pulled out her sunglasses and slid them on.

"Oakland," Charles said, this time with an edge in his voice.

"You dismissed him?" She looked over her shoulder and leveled her gaze at Charles.

"I told him that since I was here to take you home, he didn't have to wait."

"He was driving my rental car," she said, biting down on her frustration. She mustn't lose patience with Charles in front of the nurse.

"The car should be parked in your driveway," Charles said with an amiable glance at the nurse. "I asked him to slip the keys through the mail slot."

He didn't have to wait. I asked him. What euphemizing nonsense. Charles had doubtless banished Alex yesterday, in the harshest possible terms. She might never see Alex again.

"You didn't have to stay in Santa Rosa overnight," she said. She glanced at Charles's rumpled polo shirt, the creases in his golf pants.

"I don't mind." He looked at the nurse with a twinkle in his eye as if to say, *Can you believe my handful of a mother?* Then, addressing the nurse, he said in a low voice, "I'll bring the car around in a minute."

She sat in grim silence on the drive home. The fog outside the window lightened. The sun should be breaking through any minute now. Same time as yesterday.

They crossed the Richmond Bridge from Marin County to the East Bay. From here, she looked out over water like blue-tinted glass. The San Francisco and Oakland skylines touched the gray-blue horizon. People must be at work in those faraway buildings now, serving some kind of purpose. What was Norma's purpose? Where was *she* headed?

Not home, apparently. Charles took the exit toward his own house in Orinda. Was he thinking about stopping at that breakfast diner first?

Then Charles turned onto his own street, a block of large, prosperous houses that, to Norma, looked drearily the same. By the time they pulled into his driveway, a rageful feeling rose up inside her. Did he ever know when to give up?

"Why are we stopping here?" She couldn't help a hint of snappishness in her voice.

"We thought that, given your condition," he said, looking out the windshield as he put the car in park, "it would be best if you stayed with us for a few days."

"That's what you think," she said, thrusting out her hand to grasp the handle of the passenger door.

"Come on, Mom, you can't be at home by yourself," Charles said, turning off the car. His patronizing tone was doing him no favors. "You've just been released from the hospital."

"With a clean bill of health," she retorted. "What am I supposed to wear? I have no clean clothes to change into."

"I asked Debra to pick up a few things for you."

"You *what*?"

"Only for a couple of nights," he said, sounding less than happy about the arrangement himself.

"A couple of nights," she repeated with derision. Of course Charles meant to use this episode to remove her from her house for good. What kind of sucker did he think she was?

"My God, Mother." He never called her *mother* unless he was angry. "Do you have to talk about staying at our house as if you were serving time in jail?"

"I would be far more comfortable in my own home," she answered, straining for rationality. As angry as she was, she couldn't help hearing the hurt in Charles's voice.

"That house is too big for you," he said. "And you know it."

"Listen very closely, Charles. This is what's going to happen." Norma pressed the button to unlock her door, the sound making a decisive click. "I'm waiting right here while you go inside and collect my things. Then you're driving me home. If you aren't out of that house in ten minutes, I'm walking down to the city center—bad knee and all—and hailing a cab."

"Come on, Mom, can't you be reasonable? It's only for a few nights—"

"You are driving me home, Charles," she said, drawing herself up with icy dignity. "You have no right to keep me here against my will."

He stared at her with almost a smile, as if he thought she was joking. She glared at him with unflinching focus.

"Would you like to go inside for a few minutes at least?" He looked down at his lap, his mouth set in defeat. "Use the bathroom, have a drink of water?"

"I'll wait here," she said and folded her hands over her purse. In fact, she did need to use the bathroom, but she didn't want to risk spending even one second in Charles's house. She looked out the passenger window. The sun broke through the fog.

"I'll be out in a minute," he said.

He took longer than that. Far longer than she would have thought necessary. He must be recounting everything to Debra. Norma could practically hear the impatience in his voice, telling Debra how thickheaded his mother was being.

Eventually, he came out of the house wheeling a pink suitcase that must be Debra's. The idea of Debra rummaging through her drawers and closets set Norma's resentment aflame. She stared straight through the windshield as Charles stowed the suitcase in the SUV. What relief she would feel, as soon as she stepped into her own home.

★

The Porsche SUV hogged the driveway in all its garish glory, a boulder of shimmering amber. Norma took grim pleasure in Charles's gaping mouth, his expression a mixture of marvel and dismay, as he pulled up behind the behemoth and got out. She unlocked her door and stepped out of Charles's SUV as if she hadn't noticed his reaction. He must've failed to glimpse the Porsche in the hospital parking lot yesterday. Or if he had, the notion must never have crossed his mind that the vehicle belonged to her. He opened the back of the car and brought out the pink suitcase.

"Would you like me to return that rental for you?" Charles kept his eyes fixed on her. Perhaps he was hoping to will the car out of existence by refusing to look at it.

"Someone from the rental place is coming tomorrow to retrieve it." She reached into her purse for her keys and walked past him toward the house.

"Okay. And you're sure you'll be fine in the house by yourself?"

"I see no reason why I wouldn't be." She turned and gave him her best blank look.

"Let me sit with you for a few minutes." Charles flicked his eyes at the oak front door. "You can unpack, and then I can take the suitcase home."

"I'm in no mood for unpacking." She thought of the extra pound of coffee she'd had Alex buy for her last week. A large tray of manicotti—Kevin's favorite—sat in the refrigerator. Hunger gnawed at her.

"Then can we talk about what happened yesterday?"

Her spine stiffened as she glared at him. Charles returned the stare, clutching the suitcase handle.

"What's to talk about?" This was the conversation she had hoped to avoid, when she'd asked Alex, not Charles, to take her to Mendocino County. "Didn't Kevin tell you what you need to know?"

"I heard his side of the story." He walked toward her, suitcase wheels rumbling on the pavement. "Now I want to hear yours."

"I paid my son a visit," she said calmly. "We talked. The next thing I knew, I was being whisked away by ambulance to a hospital. Now I'm home again, like nothing had ever happened. There's nothing else to say."

She held out her hand in such a way that he'd have no choice but to give her the suitcase. He did so reluctantly. The suitcase was heavier to pull than she'd thought. How much had Debra packed?

"That's it?" Charles gave that maddening smirk of his. "Come on, Mom. I want to know what happened with Kevin."

"You do?" She matched his smirk with a tight crooked smile of her own. "Well, here's a notion to consider, Charles. I've been wanting to know what happened with Kevin for twenty-five years."

She turned away from him, unlocked the front door, and went into the house, lugging the suitcase behind her. Her fingers fumbled as she turned off the burglar alarm. The keys to the rental car lay on the floor by the mail slot, next to a couple of fat letters from abroad and the October edition of *Elle*. She bent down to pick up the mail and the keys, bad knee twinging. After what had happened, how could she be doing such mundane things?

"I never wanted to hide Kevin from you," Charles said. He stood in the open doorway, his frame silhouetted by sunlight. "He made me promise not to tell."

"You've known his whereabouts all this time?" She flipped through the *Elle*, keeping her tone casual.

"Not the whole time," Charles said. "For years he'd drop me a line every so often to let me know he was managing. Then he moved to Mendocino County."

"When was that?" She looked up from the magazine.

"About five years ago," Charles said, darting his eyes to the carved giraffe.

"Five whole years," she said in a bitter undertone.

"I swear, Mom, I tried to talk him into reaching out to you." He had a pained look. "Especially after the car accident. But he said he didn't think he was ready to face his past."

"*You're* his past," she muttered, "but he somehow brings himself to see *you*."

"If you can call it that. I doubt if I see him more than twice a year. Even then we don't do much. I meet him someplace halfway between us, Bodega Bay or Jenner. Have breakfast or lunch, maybe a walk along the cliffs by the ocean. But he's always in a hurry to leave. Never lets me pay."

"*I* could stand seeing him only twice a year," she said. Then a thought struck her. "Wait a second. Has Debra ever joined you on these excursions?"

"Once or twice," Charles said with a nervous look. "For what it's worth, the last time Debra saw Kevin, about a year ago, she pled your case. Told Kevin she was speaking to him as a mother. Said refusing to speak to you was cruel. That was the exact word she used—cruel. You should've heard her."

"I wish I had," Norma said, straightening up at this unexpected news. "You'll have to thank her for me."

"Actually, Mom? Maybe you could thank her yourself," he said with a hesitant smile.

He was no doubt telling the truth about Debra. Norma had never thought much of her daughter-in-law, Charles's plain and conventional sweetheart he'd met while a senior in high school. But the scene of Debra working on Kevin appeared in her mind with trenchant clarity. Debra's own three sons would never treat her that way.

"Okay, Charlie," she said and nodded. "I'll be sure to say something to Debra the next time I see her."

"She may not have succeeded in persuading him to call you,

but I could see on his face that her words hit home," Charles said, a hint of pride in his tone. "Kevin always thought highly of Debra."

"Yes," Norma said, her insides shifting. "I know."

Kevin had stood next to Norma at Charles and Debra's wedding, a beaming fifteen-year-old in a silver suit with a pink paisley tie. Debra had flashed him a silly smile as she glided past him toward the altar in her needlessly elaborate wedding dress—an off-the-rack hodgepodge of misguided opinions, designed by some LA upstart Norma had never heard of. Kevin's photo of that smile now sat framed on Charles and Debra's fireplace mantel. Outside of Charles, Kevin had been Debra's best friend in this family.

"I know Kevin didn't give you what you were hoping for this weekend, but at least he's alive and sober," Charles said. "And lives relatively nearby."

"You deserve the credit for that," she said with a prick of envy. "He certainly didn't move to Mendocino County to be near *me*."

"Oh, Mom." Charles looked at the giraffe, the chandelier, the black-and-white floor tiles. Then he nodded at Debra's suitcase. "Would you like me to carry that upstairs? I can at least do that for you."

"Sure, Charlie." Weariness stole over her. "Thanks for driving me home."

★

After he left the house, she took a long shower and then headed to the kitchen. The tray of manicotti she'd ordered sat wrapped in foil on the bottom shelf, right where the meal service had left it. On the shelf above the manicotti tray, a bottle of Veuve Clicquot lay on its side. What was she thinking, having champagne delivered to the house before she was sure that Kevin would be here to clink glasses? She hauled out the manicotti tray and turned on the oven. Now where were the baking dishes?

The service had told her the tray could feed twelve people. Who was going to eat all this? Who would drink the extra coffee stored in the cabinet, use the brand-new towels hanging in the bathroom next to the home gym, sleep beneath the fresh sheets she'd asked the cleaning staff to put on Kevin's bed? A pipe dream. All of it.

An alternate weekend—the weekend she'd wanted—unspooled in her mind. Alex driving them both home in the Porsche SUV, Kevin in the back seat. The family sitting around this huge Italian meal, celebrating Kevin's return. Who was sitting around the dining table? Charles. Debra. Their middle son Louis, a software designer, living with his girlfriend nearby in Walnut Creek. Julie, of course. Kevin's roommate and her baby girl, now that Norma knew they existed. And Alex and his husband with the mellifluous name. She'd long wanted to meet that husband of Alex's. But now, she dreaded ever looking Alex in the eye again.

CHAPTER 20

NIGHT

D EBRA'S PINK SUITCASE sat by the credenza in the sitting room. Norma opened it and brought out eight blouses, five pairs of slacks, three sweaters, her plum-colored nightgown, her bathrobe, and at least half a drawer of underwear. For the love of humanity. Norma would have packed less for a grand tour of Europe.

But she was being too hard on Debra. For all she knew, Debra was the reason why Kevin hadn't kicked her out of his house yesterday. Was her visit only yesterday? She put away her clothes with careful deliberation.

Wasn't there something else she meant to do while she was up here? Oh, of course—write a final paycheck to Alex. She went to the escritoire, pulled open the top drawer, and brought out her checkbook and blue-enameled pen.

There. Check written. Alex would no doubt blanch at the sum. But she might as well be generous. To whom else could she give her money?

Then there was Kevin's opal, still in Alex's possession. He must be wondering how to return that necklace. He wouldn't risk putting it in the mail. Nor would he give the pendant to Julie to pass along to Norma. Otherwise, he'd have to explain how the jewel ended up in his possession. He was too discreet to risk doing that. What would he do then? Drive up here? Ring the doorbell? Her insides clenched at the thought.

She reached into the bottom drawer of her writing desk and brought out one of her best notecards. The card bore a detail from Corot's *Lady in Blue*. Alex didn't have to know that she never sent one of these notecards unless she was sending a vital message. In the same exquisite penmanship that she'd used for the check, she wrote:

Dear Alex,

Please find enclosed my payment for your services rendered this past week. I wish to thank you sincerely not only for assisting me on Sunday but for all your work this summer. As part of the payment, please also accept my opal pendant—

She put down the pen. Letting him keep the pendant was one thing, but to state in her own handwriting that he could keep it? Her hand trembled as she screwed the pen cap.

Better to mail Alex's check, or perhaps give the check to Julie, in a plain envelope. She'd rather be impersonal than fraudulent. If he ever drove up here with the pendant and rang the doorbell, she'd pretend she wasn't at home. She'd put a padlock on the side gate. That should give him the message.

Now look what she'd done—she'd spoiled one of her best notecards. To think she'd once found happiness—and a future for herself—in the sight of this small yet intimate painting at the Louvre, the mysterious lady in blue, a relaxed but serious pose, face half in shadow, reflecting. She tore up the notecard, threw it into the wastepaper basket, and went downstairs to check on her manicotti.

The aroma of pasta sauce and melted cheese reminded her how famished she was. She checked the oven. A few more minutes before the food was done. She turned her attention to the day's mail. In addition to the *Elle*, she'd received two letters, one from her friend Rosalie in Nice and one from her friend Michiko in Osaka. On another day she might have been delighted to receive these letters. Today, she couldn't bring herself to open either one.

How about a round of pool? The pool balls sat in their triangle like chicks in a nest. She pictured herself at the edge of the couch and Alex bending over the table, figuring out his next shot, while Harry Winston basked in the sun on the top of the couch. In this fantasy, Alex missed a shot and stepped away from the table to let his opponent—Kevin—take his turn. She walked to the edge of the table and picked up the cue stick. No, she couldn't bring herself to play. She put down the cue stick and headed for the kitchen.

She ate her manicotti at the island without tasting it. The setting sun beamed through the windows even though the stove's digital clock read only a few minutes past five. She might have lost Kevin. But she still had the Blue Hour.

She put her dirty dishes in the washer and was about to go outside with the *Elle* when the cordless phone by the sliding door rang. Charles, again? He must be concerned she'd fallen down the stairs or something. She was about to let the phone roll into voicemail until she remembered she'd disconnected the voicemail two days ago, to forestall anyone—namely, Charles or Julie—from disturbing her on the eve of her trip to Mendocino County. The phone rang a fifth time. A sixth time. What if the caller wasn't Charles, but Julie? Their mother had always taught them to let the phone ring eight times before hanging up. On the eighth ring, she picked up the phone.

"Hiya, Norma!" Julie's voice was mercifully happy-go-lucky. "There you are!"

"Jules. It's been a while."

"Over a week, but who's counting?" Her cheerful tone suggested that Alex, bless him, hadn't told her about Sunday at Kevin's house. "I tried leaving a message, but voicemail wouldn't pick up."

"I need a new machine, this one's been misbehaving," Norma said, fixing her gaze on the magazine cover. A large-eyed woman with crow-black hair cut into bangs stared morosely at her. "What have you been up to?"

"Busy, busy, *busy*," Julie said. "I spent all day Saturday packing up most of Phil's clothes for Goodwill. Pants, shoes, shirts—everything. I found stuff I don't remember him ever wearing."

"About time," Norma said, settling into a dining chair.

"That's exactly what I imagined him saying to me. *About time*." The pride in Julie's tone had a heartbreaking ring to it. "I don't know what I was so afraid of."

"You didn't throw away all of Phil's clothes, did you?" Norma herself had disposed of everything of Robert's, down to the last cuff link, within two months of his funeral.

"I saved the denim shirt he liked to wear while gardening. Plus his favorite aloha shirt. You know, the one with the pineapples and the flamingos?"

"Of course I remember." Norma pictured Phil grilling hamburgers in that aloha shirt. A charmingly tacky fashion, like the neon-green fuzzy dice in Alex's car. She knew that denim gardening shirt too.

"Now that I have extra room in my closets, let's go shopping," Julie said. A waggish tone as she added, "Especially since I hear you're *walking* again."

"You've been chatting with Alex," Norma said, by now

gratefully convinced that Alex had said nothing to Julie about Kevin.

"I sure have," Julie said, "and I couldn't be happier. Did he call you today with his own good news?"

"What good news?"

"About his new *job*."

"Alex got a job?" Norma stood up.

"With that clinic, the one that turned him down a couple months ago," Julie said. "Can you believe it?"

"No, I can't," Norma said, remembering the pep talk she'd given Alex. She was glad to hear she'd been right about *something* last week.

"They called him first thing this morning with the offer. He starts a week from today." A pause on the line, as if Julie were thinking twice about what she'd said. "Guess he didn't have a chance to call and tell you."

"He doesn't have my phone number," Norma said with a twinge of regret. "Besides, he has no obligation to inform me. He's no longer in my employ."

"And I have some *other* news to tell you." Goodness, but Julie was in high spirits—higher than anything Norma had witnessed since Phil's death. "It's official! I'm going skydiving!"

"You found someone to go with you?" Norma stared out the window, unsure if she'd correctly heard what Julie had said.

"Nope," Julie said in a tone of supreme self-satisfaction. "I'm going by *myself*. One week from Sunday. I can't describe in words how excited I am."

"You're kidding," Norma said, too astonished to speak in more than a whisper.

"It was Alex who encouraged me to go solo. Such a thoughtful guy—he brought me a plate of lemon cookies this afternoon, to celebrate landing that job. Anyway, the more I thought about what he said, the more I thought, heck, why not? Why should I have to deprive myself if no one else has the guts to take the plunge with me? Phooey on them, I say."

Norma wasn't used to hearing Julie speak so fearlessly. And Norma was no doubt part of the *them* Julie was wishing phooey on, even though, strictly speaking, Julie had never asked her to go skydiving. She must have assumed—accurately—that Norma would have rejected the idea out of hand.

"Where will you be skydiving?" Norma asked. The gears in her mind churned toward a plan, one she couldn't quite discern.

"Sonoma County."

"I'll drive you."

"Aw, Norma," Julie said, her voice uneasy, "you don't have to do that."

"But what are you going to do?" Norma said, growing impatient. "Drive all the way to Sonoma County, leap out of a plane, and then drive back to Oakland like you were coming home from church?"

"Yes, but—how can you drive me? You don't own a car anymore."

"I'll drive *your* car," Norma said in her grandest voice. "And after you've finished, I'll treat you to lunch in Sausalito or Tiburon. Somewhere on the water. Given what you're planning, you'll be ready for a square meal."

"Oh, wonderful! Wonderful! We're going to have so much fun!" Joy lit up Julie's voice. "But the dive isn't for another two weeks. How about we go out to dinner sometime this week? You know, to celebrate you walking again."

Norma couldn't say no to this, though in her current state all she felt like doing was lying down and sleeping for days and days. But Julie had worn her down. Her indefatigable cheer would wear down anyone. She said she'd call Julie later in the week.

Then she went outside with her magazine to calm herself down with the sunset.

She luxuriated in the familiar comfort of her favorite chaise longue. The magazine felt reassuringly heavy on her lap. Her terrace. If only this moment could last forever, the declining sun, the fading light, the sky blushing pink then blue then purple.

Leaves rustled on the other side of the retaining wall. Harry Winston? Probably not. Perhaps she should bring out Harry's treat bag anyway, tempt whatever creature was lurking in the gathering dusk. But then the rustling stopped.

The evening grew dark and cold. Might as well turn in. She sat up, her knee emitting the slightest of aches. The black sky left her with an empty feeling in her chest. Kevin, gone. Alex, gone. Julie recovering from her loss of Phil, planning trips to Bali and jumping out of airplanes. Charles and Debra about to become grandparents. What was left for Norma? More magazines? More sunsets?

Perhaps Charles was right. Perhaps the time had come for someone else to admire the Blue Hour from this terrace. The emptiness inside her chest grew. If only her stubborn heart had done the sensible thing over the weekend and quit working. Life would have been easier for everyone that way.

Her eye caught a pinprick of red light in the sky. The red planet? Then the light moved in a straight line. Not a planet—an airplane. Her mind turned to Julie and her skydiving project. Unfathomable that Julie would throw herself out a plane like that one, that far up. She rose, her leg aching. The airplane moved farther and farther away until the winking red light vanished, swallowed by the velvet night.

What if she not only drove Julie to Sonoma, but went on the skydive with her? Jumped out of the plane herself? Her heart would surely fail to withstand that jump. If so, she could pass out of this life without fuss, as easily as stepping off a curb. Her estate would mostly go to charity: Charles didn't need the money, and Kevin, she now was certain, didn't want it. No one would have to know she'd intended her demise. No one needed to feel guilty she was gone. To disappear in a sea of blue. Yes. And for the first time since her return from Kevin's house, Norma felt happy.

CHAPTER 21

PERFORMANCES

L OOK OUT, DOWN *Under!! I'm going skydiving!!!!!*
Julie smiled at those words glowing on her screen. Her
clacking on the keyboard was the only sound in the house.
She clicked the *Send* button and leaned back in the desk chair. It
was already Wednesday morning in Australia. Florence and Isla
in Geelong might be composing a congratulatory response this
very minute. Julie hoped so, if only to prolong her time at the
computer in the dark warmth of Phil's study. To sit at his walnut
desk, surrounded by his books on the shelves, enveloped in the
warm gold of the floor lamp, was about as close as she could
manage to having him by her side. She leaned forward on her
elbows, watching for an incoming email.

A few moments later, her smartphone rang. A call from
Australia—wow! She leaped from the chair to answer the phone.

"It's not too late, I hope?" Norma's voice was on the other
line, more animated than what Julie was used to.

"Not at all," Julie said, glancing at the little clock on the bookshelf above her head. Twenty past nine. Norma almost never called past eight.

"What are your plans for Friday?"

"None yet," Julie said reluctantly, unsettled by the gaiety in Norma's voice.

"Good. I've made dinner reservations for us at seven." Norma spoke in the firm tone she used when she had specific plans in mind. "We're going to Malachite."

"Malachite?" Julie glanced up at the ceiling. Was she supposed to know this restaurant?

"On Piedmont Avenue," Norma said, as if this was the obvious answer. "My friend Diana's son's new restaurant. I thought I told you about it."

"You might've." Julie crossed the room and perched herself at the edge of Phil's leather easy chair, one he'd bought at a flea market for fifty bucks and restored himself.

"I helped the son design the waiters' uniforms. He's been offering me a table to thank me since before the accident. I thought I'd call in the chit."

"Goodness." Julie had trouble regarding herself as any restaurant's VIP guest. "When should I come pick you up?"

"You're not picking me up. The restaurant is a five-minute drive away from your house." Norma spoke as if she'd already thought of everything. "I'll take a cab to your house first. Then we'll cab it to Malachite."

"*Two* cab rides?" Julie scratched the back of her head. "Ma would call that wasteful."

"And you driving out of your way to my house isn't wasteful?" Norma spoke in a stately but playful voice. "Sorry, Jules. You're leaving your car in the garage on Friday. Period. Otherwise, you won't be able to have a cocktail with me. You can't let your old sister drink alone, can you?"

"I suppose not." Now she knew Norma was up to something. Norma never referred to herself as *your old sister*. "What time were you thinking of coming over?"

"Six."

"Even though the reservation isn't until seven?" She gazed at the tall bookcase Phil had built. On the shelf nearest her, the ledgers she'd kept for his carpentry business sat next to a row of do-it-yourself home project books, the spines well-worn, the pages sprouting Post-it notes.

"We'll have champagne on your deck," Norma said. "A bottle of Veuve Clicquot has been taking up space in my refrigerator for weeks."

"Sure, okay. See you then."

She hung up with Norma and settled into Phil's chair. That was one peculiar conversation. If Phil were here, he'd look over the edge of his newspaper, his bifocals low on his nose, and say, *Your big sis wants something*. What might that something be? Was Norma aiming to run into Alex? But she could phone Alex at any time. Why would she want to run into him by accident? Had something happened between them? If only Phil were here. Now Julie was stuck having to solve the mystery by herself.

Friday turned out to be one of those blazing autumn days with the afternoon sun low in the sky, as if to remind Julie to enjoy the good weather before winter set in. The first Halloween decorations popped up around the neighborhood—pumpkins on front steps, a puppet ghost hanging from a porch lamp, cutout bats taped to a picture window. She'd enjoyed the day so much, in fact, that it wasn't until past five that she remembered that Norma would be here in less than an hour.

Her refrigerator was empty. Did she have time to run to the

store before Norma came? If she didn't leave now, then Norma might show up, find Julie away from home, and go knock on Alex's door. Julie couldn't do that to Alex, could she? She found her car keys and left.

The store had Castelvetrano olives, her favorite. What about Humboldt Fog cheese? Yes! A display of Harry Winston's favorite cat treats by the register—why not? A joyous surprise, this unplanned errand. Was this how grief would leave her, in little pleasures like this?

She drove home and came out of the garage to find Alex walking down his front steps, holding a foil-wrapped plate. His blue twill shirt and round rose-tinted sunglasses looked brand new. Striking, blooming, stylish. Norma's influence? If Norma's plan really was to run into Alex, she'd better show her face soon.

"You're looking festive," she said with a smile.

"Couldn't help treating myself, now that I landed that job." He held up the foil-wrapped plate. "Lemon squares, courtesy of your tree."

"I see that. Thanks again for those cookies. I ate the last one today with my afternoon coffee." She glanced over her shoulder at the tree, bristling with lemons. "Where are you headed on this fine evening?"

"Friends in the neighborhood are having me for dinner. Pratyush has a gig tonight, so I'm representing the both of us."

"Norma's coming at six if you can stick around," she said, glancing at her watch.

"She's coming? Here?" Alex looked taken aback by this news. He drew his plate closer to his body.

"We're going out to eat tonight." She wondered why a visit from Norma would take Alex by such surprise.

"Oh. Huh." His expression grew thoughtful behind his sunglasses.

"I've just come from the market with wine and nibbles." She held up her canvas bag. "Care to join us for a few minutes?"

"My friends are expecting me at six," he said, pulling out his phone to check the time.

His answer came a second too soon—enough for her to suspect he'd invented that excuse. He hesitated and glanced at his front door. She watched him and hoped he'd change his mind about leaving. She'd been wanting to see for herself how he and Norma interacted.

"Not even for a minute?" she said. "I'm sure Norma would love to congratulate you on your new job."

"I'm already running late," he said, sounding more genuinely regretful. He slipped his phone into his front pocket. "Have fun tonight. What restaurant are you going to?"

"It's on Piedmont Avenue. Something with an M. Mallomar. Mallard Duck. Malla-something."

"Oh—Malachite," Alex said, his puzzled expression clearing. "You've eaten there?"

"God, no. Way too rich for our blood. But I've read about Malachite. Super trendy, I hear. I've seen their sign from the street. The place is only a few doors down from the Thirsty Raven. Pratyush's gig is there tonight, by the way. In case you want to surprise him with a visit."

"Maybe we will." But she couldn't picture herself hanging out in some bar—especially since she'd be with Norma.

"Gotta run," he said with a smile. "Say hi to Norma for me, okay?"

He headed down the driveway before she had a chance to wish him a good evening. His step seemed quicker than usual. As if he were fleeing.

A thought occurred to her as she was putting the cheese and olives into the refrigerator. What if Norma's cab pulled up as Alex was walking away from the house? Would he stop and talk to her? She closed the refrigerator door, dashed to the living room, and peered out the picture window. A tomato-red cab slowed down in front of her house. No sign of Alex. Maybe he'd spotted the cab and went the other way.

Out came Norma in a cream-colored jacket with outsized black buttons and black bell-bottom slacks, stepping with confidence onto the sunlit street as if to proclaim that her accident was long forgotten history. The promised bottle of champagne, its gold wrapper shining like lamé in the fading light, nestled in the crook of her arm. Already Julie sensed something off with her sister. She went to the front door and opened it.

"I happened to be by the window when the cab came up," Julie said with exaggerated trepidation. "Look at *you*, walking again."

"I wanted to wear Cuban heels tonight," Norma said, kissing Julie on the cheek, "but my knee is refusing to cooperate. That's why I'm wearing bell-bottoms, to conceal my feet. I detest these flats I'm wearing."

"Don't worry, you can't see them," Julie said, without the slightest idea what a Cuban heel was. She glanced at the bell-bottoms, thinking they must be one of Norma's own designs.

"I told the driver to swing by here at five of seven," Norma said. "That should get us to our reservation fashionably late."

She'd decked herself out tonight. A blue topaz ring, blue topaz earrings, a matching brooch in the shape of a lotus flower, her diamond watch. Even so, she looked incomplete. What was lacking?

"You missed Alex, I'm afraid," Julie said. She was wearing a white blouse and navy slacks, her wedding rings her only jewelry. Hopefully the restaurant wouldn't send her home to change.

"Too bad," Norma said with a vagueness that might or might not be sincere. She held up the champagne bottle. "He could've shared bubbles with us."

"He's seeing friends tonight for dinner, otherwise he would've stayed," Julie said, leading Norma to the kitchen. She wondered if Norma's cheer was somehow connected to Alex's strange behavior earlier.

"Next time." Norma's expression darkened for a moment then lightened. "It's nice to be standing inside your house again."

"It's nice to see you standing, period," Julie said, putting the champagne into the fridge. Funny, she didn't remember seeing a champagne bottle in Norma's fridge two weeks ago, when they'd had lasagna and played cribbage on the terrace.

"How are these lovebirds?" Norma walked toward the cockatiels. Rick jumped off his perch and clung to the side of the cage, showing off his crest. Ilsa hopped away from Norma, regarding her with a beady eye.

"Demanding as ever," Julie said, bringing out olives and cheese. "I have some snacks to go with that champagne. And since they were near the register, I bought some treats for Harry Winston."

"Oh," Norma said with a falling voice. Her eyes strayed to the shiny purple bag on the counter.

"What?" Julie felt her heart squeeze.

"Harry Winston ran away." Norma shrugged with what looked like false disregard. "He vamoosed just a few days after your last visit. Alex looked for him at the shelter, but he never turned up. Not much else to say. I guess Alex never told you."

"No, he didn't," Julie said, looking down. She thought of her good mood two hours ago when she'd bought those treats. "I'm so sorry, Norma."

"You have nothing to be sorry about," Norma said. "I'm more annoyed about it than anything."

"But I'm the one who encouraged you to take Harry in," Julie said. Sadness grew inside her chest. "I'm the one who named him."

"Now don't go blaming yourself," Norma said with a small smile, patting Julie on the forearm. "In the short time he stayed with me, he brought me joy. It's enough."

She spoke with more feeling than Julie was used to hearing from her. Her gaze was mellow but penetrating. Her blue topazes glistened as if they were close to tears. When was the last time Julie had laid eyes on those topazes? Years? And now she saw what was missing from Norma's outfit. The opal. Kevin's opal. An icy thrill rushed through her, despite the day's heat.

"Okay, little sister," Norma said. "Enough gloom and doom. Let's have champagne. A toast to Harry Winston. Now how about we have a glass on the deck, enjoy the last of the light."

"Sure," Julie said without enthusiasm.

The sun had slipped behind the roofline of Alex and Pratyush's rental unit. The light framing the roofline was tinged pink and orange. The blue was deepening. True, the view from Julie's modest deck was nothing compared to Norma's view from her terrace. But could Norma boast the lilting notes of Pratyush's cello, now emanating from behind the rental unit?

"Where is that music coming from?" Norma put down the champagne bottle on Julie's small patio table and looked out over the deck railing.

"That's Pratyush. Alex's husband," Julie said, setting a plate of cheese and olives along with two glasses next to the bottle. "He always practices cello before one of his gigs."

Norma placed her hands on the deck railing and looked at the rental unit with a fascinated expression, as if she'd forgotten all about the champagne. Julie stood back, watching Norma. For the next several minutes they listened to the music. The notes from Pratyush's cello hung in the air like droplets of mist.

"I thought he played bass viol in a jazz combo," Norma said, turning to Julie.

"He likes to practice cello first. Keeps his mind limber, he says. He trained as a classical cellist as a kid, you see. Was in a youth orchestra and everything. Alex says Pratyush's parents had astronomical expectations for him."

"They can't be happy he's playing gigs in dive bars."

"Pratyush's father passed away a couple years ago, Alex tells me," Julie said in a low voice, to keep any neighbors from overhearing. "And his mother, Alex says, is the nicest lady you'd ever want to meet. At this point, she's probably happy Pratyush is playing *something*. And has Alex to take care of him."

"I wish *my* sunsets came with a soundtrack." Norma gave Julie a fleeting look of envy. "You must sit outside here every time he practices."

"Would you like to meet him?" Julie gestured toward the rental unit. "I'm sure he wouldn't mind if we popped over and said hello."

"As tempting as that sounds, I'd rather not disturb his practice. I'd hate to interrupt a free performance." Norma looked at the rental unit with a pensive air.

"His gig tonight is near our restaurant," Julie said.

"The Thirsty Raven," Norma said, turning to Julie with a smile.

"You know the Thirsty Raven?"

"Alex told me once his husband frequently plays there. Maybe, after dinner, we can drop by and watch his band play."

"Alex suggested that too. But I don't think Pratyush's band goes on until late." Julie could already envision the grave look on Pratyush's face if he saw his landlady and her sister at his gig.

"Even better," Norma said with a jovial brush of Julie's arm. "We can tell him before he takes the stage that we enjoyed his free cello concert."

The glint in Norma's eyes made her curiosity to meet Pratyush plain. No doubt Alex had told Norma all about him, sparked her desire to check the man out. Was Pratyush—not Alex—the reason why Norma had wanted to stop by here before heading for the restaurant? Had she hoped to see Alex and Pratyush together? The doorbell pealed, breaking Julie out of her thoughts.

"Our cab," Norma said, glancing at her watch. "He's early. Champagne will have to wait, I'm afraid."

"Next time you're over," Julie said, relieved that Norma hadn't made her take a glass. She'd need to stay sober if she wanted to know what Norma was up to.

CHAPTER 22

THE GIFT OF GRIEF

THE CAB SLOWED to a stop in front of a narrow little building, wedged between a consignment store and a yogurt shop. Julie squinted. *This* was the fancy restaurant? The place looked more like an abandoned dentist's office.

The driver turned on his hazard lights, hopped out, and opened the passenger door with a flourish. Norma allowed the driver to escort her out of the cab with the grace of an actress attending a red-carpet event. Julie took the driver's hand, emerged from the cab, and spotted *Malachite* stenciled in small green letters with gold edging on the plate glass. This must be what made the restaurant trendy. Only the people who *knew*—and had good enough eyesight—could locate it.

Inside was more promising. Plates and glasses gleamed in muted candlelight. Two wine bottles rested in a silver holder at the end of the bar. A young man—tall and handsome with short curly black hair—walked up to them and introduced himself as Nathan, their server. He led Norma and Julie to a table for two by the window. Julie had the impression that she'd sneaked into a private club without a valid ID.

"What do you think of the young man's attire?" Norma asked once the server walked to another table.

"Uh…the shirt's nice," Julie said. The patrons at that table were casting glances at Norma, undoubtedly wondering who the celebrity was. "Does it matter what he's wearing? It's too dark in here."

"My thoughts exactly," Norma said, nodding.

She surveyed the restaurant with an amused, disbelieving expression, as if to reassure Julie that, for all her wealth and fame, she hadn't forgotten their working-class roots. Not the slightest glance at the patrons eyeing her. A familiar sensation came over Julie, one she often felt when she was out in public with Norma: that the woman decked out in diamonds and topazes across from her was someone else's sister.

The waiter came with menus printed on cheap brown paper. The entrées were anything but cheap. Phil would have scanned the prices and said, *What—is the food gold-plated?* Julie swallowed the laugh in her throat. She studied her menu.

"We're offering a special cocktail tonight," the waiter said to Norma with a smile. "Drinks are listed on the other side of the menu."

Norma returned the waiter's smile and removed her cat-eye reading glasses from her black leather handbag. Julie slipped on her own glasses and turned the menu over. No need for optical assistance to read the cocktail listed at the top—a concoction entitled *The Norma*. Gin, vodka, Lillet—whatever that was— pomegranate juice, twist of lime. A cocktail named after her sister. Seriously. The evening, already weird, was growing weirder.

"Do I want to know what your mixologist thinks I taste like?" Norma looked up at the waiter with a flattered smile.

"I've heard nothing but raves from everyone who's had one," the waiter said, returning the smile.

"If that's the case," Norma said, "then the Negroni I've been craving all summer will have to wait. Jules, will you join me in ordering my namesake cocktail?"

"Gin doesn't always agree with me," Julie said, her eye skimming tamer choices. Kir royale? Aperol spritz?

"One sip won't kill you," Norma said and turned to the waiter. "Two Normas."

"You're in a good mood this evening," Julie said with a nervous laugh after the waiter had gone.

"I feel ten pounds lighter on account of the charity." A look of satisfaction spread across Norma's face. "I called them yesterday morning. They're excited to have my designs for their holiday auction. You're okay with me donating your wedding dress to them?"

"*I* have no plans to walk down the aisle again," Julie said lightly. Maybe she'd go to the auction herself, soak up the attention as one of Norma's earliest models.

"I'm also donating the prom suits," Norma said almost as an afterthought, turning over her menu to the entrées and pushing in her glasses. "Good, they have New York steak. I haven't tucked into a steak since before the accident."

"Wait, what?" Julie looked at her sister, startled. Norma kept her eyes on the menu. "You're donating the prom suits?"

"Why not?" Norma said, looking up with a frown as if she couldn't understand Julie's shock.

"You once told me you'd never part with those suits."

"What good are they doing me, hanging in my closet? I'm sick of keeping that room temperature controlled." A dismissive wave of Norma's hand, light-blue nails glinting in the candlelight.

"Goodness, you'd think these menus had been cut from grocery bags."

"Two Normas," the waiter said with a smile, arriving with a tray.

He served their drinks, leaving Julie to contemplate a martini glass brimming with a sunset-hued liquid. Norma clinked her glass against Julie's, eyes twinkling. This didn't bode well, this abrupt change of heart about the prom suits. No use asking her more questions though. She lifted her glass and took a sip. The drink's elaborate tartness invaded her senses, unleashing an icy flood through her veins. An apt liquid representation of her sister.

Nathan the Flirty Server brought out a notepad, ready to take their orders. Norma ordered the steak, medium rare, paired with a glass of pinot noir. Julie ordered halibut and resisted Norma's efforts to order a Chardonnay to go with it. Was getting her sauced part of Norma's plan?

Their dinners came. Naturally the chef, the son of Norma's friend, came out to pay his respects. Julie let Norma do the talking. Then she dawdled with the halibut while waiting for Norma to spring more revelations on her. But Norma's attention was all for her steak.

People passed by on the other side of the plate glass. Not one looked Julie's way. Maybe the restaurant was visible only to those folks privileged enough to eat here. She went warm with embarrassment to consider the notion that *she* belonged to this privileged class.

The waiter cleared their table and came with dessert menus. Looking at the choices made Julie's teeth ache. Maybe Norma would let her escape with a cup of black coffee.

"Everything looks delectable," Norma said, leaning over the menu with her glasses low on her nose, "but on a night like this, only chocolate will do. What will you be having?"

"I don't know," Julie said, already losing her nerve. "Coconut bread pudding?"

"Fine. If you insist on spurning the Correct Flavor," Norma said. "Oh, I forgot to mention. I'm going skydiving with you next Sunday."

"Ye-es," Julie said with a sense of foreboding. "You'd mentioned on the phone you'd drive me to the place."

"Not just to drive you, Jules." Norma put down her menu and gave Julie a puckish look from across the table. "I'm jumping out of that plane with you."

"What?" Julie's mouth hung open. Norma's smiling but serious expression made it clear that Julie hadn't heard her wrong.

"I found your skydiving place online and made a reservation." Norma scanned her menu then looked up again, as if surprised to find Julie staring at her.

"You found the place online? You're using the internet nowadays?"

"Yes, with that laptop Charles gave me," Norma said with a smile. "I don't know what I was so afraid of. *Very* convenient. And aren't those search engines efficient? All I had to do was type "skydiving" and "Sonoma County" into the engine, and the name Wild Blue Yonder came up immediately. I called the number, confirmed which dive you were on, and— *voilà*—signed myself up."

"I had no idea you were interested in skydiving," Julie said, whispering across the table. Why was she talking as if this news were top secret?

"I'm accompanying you for Phil's sake. *He* wouldn't want you going by yourself."

"Yes, but—"

"Yes, but nothing," Norma's expression was glowing, close to euphoric, her earrings glittering like fairies' wings. "It's settled."

"Ladies?" The waiter came up to them, pad at the ready. "What will you have for dessert?"

"*Pôt de crème au chocolat,*" Norma said, handing the waiter her menu. "And a coconut bread pudding for my darling baby sister."

Julie ended up eating more of that pudding than she thought she could manage. By the time she and Norma cleared their plates, all she wanted to do was go home, crawl under the covers, and process everything her sister had said. If only she hadn't had that cocktail. If only her brain were clear enough to piece the clues together. Ah, here came the waiter with the bill. Turned out Norma's friend's son had comped them for everything but the drinks. Norma insisted on tipping on the full amount.

"One last request, young man," Norma said as she put away her credit card, leaving her purse open. "Could you kindly direct us to the Thirsty Raven?"

"Across the street, about a block past the movie theater." The waiter glanced at Norma's jewels as if to say, *Are you sure you want to go there?* "Look for the purple neon sign in the shape of a raven."

"Thank you, kind sir," Norma said. "My compliments to your mixologist. And this is for you. I'll be certain to let the chef know that you do justice to that outfit you're wearing."

She reached into her purse and held out a crisp hundred-dollar bill between her fingernails. The waiter hesitated, smiled, and took it. Then Norma turned to Julie with a radiant expression as soon as the waiter walked away.

"You want to go to the Thirsty Raven *now?*" Julie stared at Norma.

"Call me overly inquisitive, but I can't resist a desire to meet

Alex's husband," Norma said with that telltale glint in her eye. She glanced at her watch. "Besides, it's only ten of nine."

"I don't think it's a good idea," Julie said, her chest deflating. "Pratyush won't appreciate us being there."

"For the love of humanity, Jules. The man is a musician. An artist. A *performer*. I've never met a performer who didn't want an audience." A smile spread across Norma's face. "Come on, Jules. Let's have fun. You're acting worse than an old lady."

"I *am* an old lady," Julie said. She resisted adding, *And so are you!*

Four men and a woman were smoking on the sidewalk outside the flung-open doors to the Thirsty Raven. Jumbled voices blasted from inside the bar. At this point, Julie wouldn't put it past Norma to chat up those young people, maybe even bum a cigarette off them. Instead, Norma flashed a smile and excused herself into the bar. The smokers watched her as if wondering whether the lady had wandered into the wrong place. Julie, at a loss herself, followed her sister inside.

The place was packed. And loud. Julie felt as if she'd walked into a throbbing wall of sound. Pumpkin lights dangled from the ceiling, cobwebs covered the windows, a gigantic purple tarantula crawled up one of the walls. A small stage stood by the far wall between two flat-screen TVs showing a baseball game. Pratyush and his band weren't here yet.

In the middle of the bar, in the orangey glow of the pumpkin lights, sat a pool table. Two young men stood around the table holding cue sticks, studying the billiard balls. A couple other young men watched them with expressions that straddled interest and boredom. Norma glided toward the table like a moth drawn to a flame. The young men stopped playing at the sight of her and stood up.

"Please don't allow me to interfere," she said in the unthreatening tone of a kindly grandmother. "I'd be honored to play the next game with the winner."

"We're only goofing around," said one of the young men, a muscular fellow with thick dark hair and dark eyebrows, wearing a navy-blue UC-Berkeley T-shirt.

"Then will you indulge a lady with a game?" Norma's tone was gallant, disarming. "Winner buys the loser and his friends a beer."

She looked at the young man's friends with beaming self-assurance. The guys swapped looks and smiles. *Okay, why not?* The young men collected the balls and racked them up with self-conscious fussiness. A kid with freckles presented his cue stick to Norma as if handing her a scepter. Heads turned toward the pool table—people at the bar, people clustered near the TV screens. Julie could only admire how her sister, at the age of nearly eighty, could enthrall a roomful of strangers.

"Shall I break?" Norma smiled at the dark-haired man in the UC-Berkeley shirt.

"After you, ma'am," the young man said, a mystified grin on his face. That was probably the first time he'd ever addressed a woman as *ma'am.*

A look of determination glimmered in her eyes as she surveyed the table. The room, though noisy, became less so, as if she'd whispered a rumor into the crowd. Even the bartender, a bald man with a tattoo of a king cobra slithering up his bulging arm, stopped to watch her break. Julie held in a sigh. She'd seen Norma do this enough times to know how this piece of theater would play out.

Norma leaned over the table, aimed her stick, and launched the cue ball. The triangle of colored balls exploded like fireworks.

The white cue ball, glowing orange from the lights, rolled to the exact center of the pool table. Julie peered at the faces of the young men—some awestruck, some dumbstruck—glancing at each other as if they'd be talking about this moment for months to come. But Norma betrayed no awareness of their astonishment. The key to celebrity, she had once told Julie, was never to wait for a crowd's validation.

"Two of those solid balls went in," Norma said to her opponent. "You take solid. And go first."

The young man blinked at her, as if she'd shaken him awake from a fainting spell, and stepped up to the table. He managed to sink the orange 5-ball, bringing relief to his face and the faces of his friends. But he missed the middle pocket for his 1-ball, and Norma, with a sigh of breezy resignation, took up her cue stick and proceeded to sink all seven striped balls and then the 8-ball with cold-blooded precision. The feat took her all of five minutes. Her opponent, his friends, and the crowd that had gathered around the pool table broke into applause. Julie clapped along with them. What else could she do?

This must be how sparks had flown between Norma and Robert on the night they met. Julie, in high school at the time, had made Norma recount the fairy tale over and over again. A house party thrown by the boyfriend of one of Norma's friends. Robert strutting around the pool table, acting like a cocky prince. Norma, only eighteen and home from her stint in Paris, stepping forward and challenging him to a game. He'd trounced her, of course. But Norma had captivated him, no doubt, in the same way she'd captivated these young men tonight.

"Thank you for the indulgence, sir," Norma said to her opponent, laying down the cue stick. She turned to the bartender and called, "A round of beers for these gentlemen. And would you happen to know when tonight's entertainment will begin?"

"Band should be here any minute," the bartender said. His voice was gruff, but his smile was like a schoolboy's.

"Thank you, sir." Norma's eyes glittered like her blue topazes. "When you've poured these children their beers, I'd like a Negroni. Beefeater gin and Carpano Antica if you have it."

"Beefeater, Carpano. Check and check," the bartender said, his smile broadening. Even the cobra slithering up his bicep looked charmed.

"And a beer for my sister. The least alcoholic you have." Norma turned to Julie with a victorious look. "For the love of humanity, Jules. You didn't think I'd drink alone, did you?"

Pratyush showed up a few minutes later, bass viol slung over his shoulder. He and his three bandmates took the stage and began setting up. The reserved man Julie almost always saw wearing plaid shirts and tan work slacks was now wearing snug blue jeans, black cowboy boots, and a tight black T-shirt that set off the silver threads in his dark hair along with two well-formed biceps. He looked nothing like the mild-mannered neighbor she knew.

"The fellow holding the bass," Norma said in Julie's ear, over the noise of the bar. "That must be Pratyush."

"Yep, that's him." Julie noticed the flair with which Norma pronounced Pratyush's name.

"He has *sprezzatura*," Norma said, tapping her chin. Her fingernails glinted bluish orange in the pumpkin lights.

"Sprezza-what?" Julie assumed Norma meant some fashion designer, most likely for Pratyush's boots or maybe his T-shirt.

"*Sprezzatura*. It's Italian. It means having a sense of fashion while pretending to care nothing about fashion." Norma smiled. "What does Pratyush do for work?"

"He's an accountant, as a matter of fact," Julie said beaming. "Every now and then we talk shop."

"An accountant?" Norma nodded approvingly, as if she'd been hoping for that answer. "Good. He's better off that way."

Pratyush's fellow players were a man wearing a derby holding a clarinet, a young woman with bubblegum-pink hair wielding a pair of drumsticks, and a slim woman in a tight black minidress with spaghetti straps and a slit up the side. The band's singer, most likely. Pratyush plucked a few strings into the microphone. The twanging sound echoed off the bar's walls. He adjusted the amp and played again. Pratyush looked at his bandmates and gave each a nod. He must be the band's unofficial leader, about to give the signal for them to play.

That was when Norma set down her Negroni, tilted up her chin, and walked toward the stage. The crowd making a path for Norma, rather than Norma herself, was what caused Pratyush to look up. Julie followed her, feeling powerless to stop her.

"I beg your pardon, sir," Norma said to him. "Your name is Pratyush Barad, I believe."

"It is," Pratyush said, straightening up. His expression was more curious than intimidated.

"I'm Norma McKinsey," she said. When Pratyush frowned, apparently not recognizing the name, her smile broadened. "Julie Pontone's older sister. You and your husband are her tenants, I believe."

"Oh, yes," Pratyush said, nodding and looking at her. His bandmates were giving him sideways looks. "You're Alex's patient."

"*Ex*-patient," she corrected. She glanced over her shoulder at Julie and added, "We had dinner down the street."

"Pratyush, hi," Julie said, wishing she could disappear.

"We heard you were performing here tonight," Norma said,

"and since we were in the neighborhood, we thought we'd pop in. We heard you practicing your cello earlier. Enchanting."

"Alex mentioned you had a gig," Julie said, hastening to explain.

"I have an item for you to pass along to your husband," Norma said. She reached into her jacket's inner pocket and brought out an envelope on which the word *Alex* was written in her inimitable script. Her nails gleamed as she proffered the envelope to Pratyush between her fingers. "A final check for his services."

"Oh—thank you," Pratyush said with a surprised look, and then he took the envelope with a frown and slipped it into his front jeans pocket.

"I've also come to apologize."

"Apologize?" Pratyush held the bass viol upright. "Apologize for what?"

"Why, for occupying so much of your husband's time this summer," Norma said, making a show of surprise.

"No problem, Mrs. McKinsey. I'm used to Alex working long hours." Pratyush glanced at his bandmates again then smiled.

"Please. Call me Norma." She had a gentle look in her eyes. "I've also been wanting to place a face to the name. Alex talked a great deal about you."

"He did? I had no idea." Pratyush turned to his bass, almost as if he were grasping a crutch. "I hate to rush you, but we'd better start playing before the bartender throws us out of here."

"He wouldn't dare," Norma said, and she turned to Julie with a broad smile, her eyes shining.

Norma must be imagining Pratyush—or someone like him—not as Alex's husband, but as Kevin's husband. A man who could have protected Kevin from so much heartache. Poor Norma. For everything she had, it would never be enough without both her children by her side.

Pratyush looked at his bandmates and nodded. They brought their instruments into position. How exciting! Julie enjoyed watching this unexpected, take-charge side of her reserved tenant.

It was too loud in here, though. Couldn't everyone see the band was about to play? Then Pratyush strummed a few notes without a glance at the audience—*very* Norma-like—and the band sprang into action. Hands and fingers moved in unison like a well-oiled machine. Their song was slinky and sexy and nothing at all that Julie would associate with Pratyush. As tired as she was, she was glad Norma had talked her into coming here.

He looked wrapped inside his own world as he played, his fingers working the viol strings, his eyes straying up to the ceiling. Every now and then he leaned toward the instrument as if listening to what his fingers were telling him. His wedding ring on his left hand, high up on the viol's neck, winked gold in the orangey light. This must have been the side of Pratyush that Alex had fallen in love with. Julie sighed and looked around the bar, thinking Alex should be here to watch his husband. Then tears sprang to her eyes.

Tears? Now? She hadn't even been thinking about Phil. Not here, not here. But she couldn't stop the tears from coming. Gosh darn, what a blubbering fool she was. She put down her beer and headed out the door into the chilly night air.

A hand clasped her shoulder from behind. Must be Norma. Julie wiped her face and turned to face her sister, angry with herself for failing to keep herself together.

"Where are you going?" Norma's expression of concern was the most honest look she'd given her all evening.

"I needed air." Julie put a hand to her throat, felt her heart slowing. The hum of the jazz music spilled onto the sidewalk.

"Do you want to go back inside?" Norma gestured toward the wide-open doors.

"You go," Julie said, her temples pounding. "I'll catch a cab from here."

"No, I'll call it a night too," Norma said with a glance at her diamond watch.

"But you were having fun."

"It's okay, Jules. I've had enough noise for one night." Norma looked up and down the street. No cabs in sight. "Do you have your phone on you? The gentleman who drove us here earlier gave me his number."

Julie opened her purse and handed Norma her phone. Norma reached into her purse and pulled out a scrap of paper with the number. Their cabbie, it turned out, had just dropped off a passenger at the airport and would be able to collect them in fifteen minutes. The Thirsty Raven? No problem. Julie watched the streetlight change from red to green.

"Sometimes it comes out of nowhere," she said in a faraway voice, her eyes on the green light.

"What comes out of nowhere, Jules?" Norma clicked off the phone and handed it to her.

"Grieving Phil." Julie dropped the phone into her purse and then looked searchingly at Norma. "I was watching the band play, and then—Phil popped into my head. I don't understand. We were in a bar, for heaven's sake."

"Cut yourself some slack, Jules." Norma laid her hand on Julie's forearm. "He'll be popping into your head for the rest of your life."

"I suppose," Julie said. She rested her palm on her forehead. "God, why does grief have to sneak up on me like that?"

"Be thankful you *feel* grief," Norma said with a rueful look. "It's a gift, you know."

Her words transported Julie to the night of Robert's death— the disastrous bookend to Norma and Robert's first pool game.

Blue police lights streaming in through the windows. Norma rising from her chair. Her stoic face, her lack of tears. She'd likely never felt a moment's grief for her husband, not on the night he died or any of the nights that followed. And that failure to grieve, Julie now saw, was a grief unto itself. She felt an urge to put her arms around her sister. Then the cab coasted up to the sidewalk, ready to take them home.

CHAPTER 23
A PLAN

ALEX WALKED HOME from his friends' house, the night air cool on his face. The moon shone like a half-dollar, bathing the pavement in milky light. He pulled out his phone. A few minutes before ten. What if Norma and Julie were coming home from dinner? What if Norma was at Julie's house? What would he say if they ran into each other?

He stopped and hesitated. If he did run into Norma—at this late hour, probably not—then he'd be pleasant with her, reveal nothing, pretend he wasn't worried. He renewed his stride toward home.

He stopped short as soon as he turned the corner onto his street. A cab was idling in front of Julie's house. Julie stepped out of the cab. Then she turned and leaned into the cab to speak to someone—most likely Norma. He stepped into the shadow of a telephone pole. Then Julie shut the cab door and turned toward her front steps. The cab drove off. Now that Norma was gone, why not have a word with Julie? He caught Julie at the front door, fumbling in her purse for her keys.

"Alex," she said in a weary voice, looking up. "You're home."

"Good dinner?" He hoped his tone sounded clueless enough.

"Good enough," she said with what might or might not have been a forced smile. "How was dinner with your friends?"

"Fun," he said with a smile of his own. "Always good to catch up."

"Glad to hear it. Have a good night." She turned to put her key into the lock then turned back to face him. "Alex, are you going straight to bed?"

"Maybe not right away." He pulled out his phone—twelve minutes past ten. Pratyush would probably be home between eleven and midnight.

"I was about to make a pot of decaf for myself," she said. "Care to join me?"

Did he dare accept her offer? Norma had been well enough to treat Julie to dinner—shouldn't that be enough to set his mind at ease? But Norma must've made Julie anxious. How could he pass up the chance to learn more?

"I have cake," he said, holding up a Ziploc bag of leftover cranberry coffee cake. "It'd be a shame to waste it."

Julie led him through the house to the kitchen, turning on lights as she went. He stood by the birdcage while she measured out coffee. Rick and Ilsa hopped around their perches in agitation, or perhaps excitement, at having company at this late hour. The cockatiels proved a useful diversion.

"How was Malachite?" he said over his shoulder, eyes on the birds. "Is it worth the hype?"

"At my age," she said with half a sigh, "nothing is worth the hype."

"Overrated, then." He turned from the cage to face her.

"The chef is the son of one of Norma's friends." She set two mugs on the table, a Minnie Mouse mug for him, a mug of the Chicago skyline for herself. "We were treated like celebrities."

"Norma must've appreciated that, now that she's out and about." He put the Ziploc on the table and slipped his hands in his pockets.

"Appreciative isn't the word to describe how Norma acted tonight." She poured water into the coffee maker and turned to him with a troubled expression. "Alex...is everything all right with my sister?"

"What do you mean?" He could only hope his voice betrayed no knowledge of a secret.

"She wasn't herself," Julie said, as coffee dripped into the pot. "She was...I don't know how to describe it. Happy."

"Happy is a good thing," he said warily. "Isn't it?"

"Not the version of happy that I saw." She brought the coffeepot to the table and poured a cup for him then for herself. "It felt unreal. Like she was faking happiness."

"How so?" He hoped he sounded dispassionate enough.

"For starters, she was wearing these blue topazes I'd forgotten she even owned," Julie said. "I needed some time to remember how she came about buying them—to treat herself for design work she'd done for the opera way back when. Why she felt like wearing them tonight, on a casual night out with her sister, I have no idea."

"Maybe she felt bad she never wore them," he said, unable to help feeling a tickle of curiosity to see those jewels.

"The jewels are the least of it. Remember me telling you about those prom suits she'd designed for her son and his date? The ones that made her career?"

"Sort of," he said, sitting at the table. Minnie Mouse grinned at him, steam rising from her shiny red bow.

"Norma always said she'd never part with those suits." Julie sat down across from him. "Then she tells me at dinner she's donating them to raise money for charity. Talked as if she couldn't care less about them. Like she was dropping them off at Goodwill."

"Sounds generous of her," he said with a rational voice that he hoped concealed his concern. He pulled out his chair and said, "Should I bring out plates for this coffee cake?"

"Only if you want some. I ate so much tonight, I can't even look at that cake." Julie wrapped her hands around her mug, fingertips pressing against the Chicago skyline. "Guess what else she told me. She's going skydiving with me."

"What?" Alex pulled in his chair and put his elbows on the table.

"I told her a few days ago I'd made a reservation at Wild Blue Yonder—you know, that place in Sonoma I told you about?" Worry lines showed on her face. "She told me over dinner she called the place up herself and reserved a spot on the same dive. We're going a week from Sunday."

"You're kidding."

"And where did Norma and I go *after* dinner?" She nodded as if she already expected him to know this answer. "The Thirsty Raven."

"You saw Pratyush tonight?" Alex sat up, hands cradling Minnie Mouse.

"Pratyush was the reason why we went. Norma wanted to meet him. We'd heard him practicing his cello earlier in the evening. She was very much taken by him."

"She was?" Alex wished he'd been there to witness Norma meeting Pratyush.

"She also gave him an *envelope*," Julie said, leaning forward. "With *your* name on it. I think I heard her tell Pratyush it was a paycheck."

"Oh." He glanced at Minnie Mouse.

"Nothing that happened this evening makes sense." Julie sipped coffee and put down her mug. "Do you have *any* idea why she's acting like this? Did anything happen last week?"

"I helped her with her exercises until she could walk again." He looked into his mug to hide the blood rushing to his face. "And—and—we were so excited she could manage without the walker, that she forgot to pay me for my last week of work, and I forgot to ask her. I'm sure her good mood is because she's back on her feet. She must realize how lucky she is to be walking again."

"Oh, I give up. I'm done trying to figure out my sister." Julie traced her finger along the rim of her mug. "Enough about her. You had fun with your friends tonight?"

An opportunity to change the subject—an opportunity Alex was glad to take. He conversed at length about his pleasant if uneventful evening. Talking about his friends reminded him that he had his own life. A good life. Julie listened with a slight smile as if she wished she'd been with him instead of with Norma. But, no question, it was Julie—and, apparently, Pratyush—who'd had the more interesting evening.

He walked into his apartment feeling as if dinner with his friends had never happened. No going to bed now. Not unless he felt like lying awake in the dark, listening for Pratyush's footsteps. He put away the cake and brought his laptop to the living room. He'd pretend he'd lost track of the time.

Ten or fifteen minutes later, he heard footsteps along the side of the house. The basement door opened and closed, followed by the sound of Pratyush stowing away his bass viol. Footsteps plodded up the back stairs. The kitchen door opened and closed. Alex made a point of slouching on the sofa by the time Pratyush walked into the living room.

"You're up," Pratyush said.

"I couldn't sleep," Alex said, forcing a yawn. His eyes hurt from scrolling through too many Instagram photos. "Good gig?"

"More people than usual tonight. Some kind of baseball game was playing on all the TVs."

"It's playoff season," Alex said, flicking his eyes toward his Instagram feed. "Jim and Eric gave us leftover cranberry cake if you want some."

"Sounds tempting," Pratyush said. "Playing made me hungry."

He disappeared into the kitchen. Alex listened to him opening a cabinet, bringing out a plate. Typical Pratyush. Could he have already forgotten about Norma? Nah, he'd probably seen the light in the living room and knew that Alex had been waiting for him, eager for details.

"So," he said, once Pratyush returned to the living room with a hunk of cake on a saucer. "I hear Julie and Norma saw you at the Thirsty Raven."

"Word travels fast," Pratyush said, yawning. He plopped onto the easy chair and cut into his cake.

"I ran into Julie on my way home from Jim and Eric's. She invited me in for coffee. Apparently Norma was wearing some serious bling."

"She was? I didn't notice." Pratyush set his plate down, rose, and pulled out a folded envelope from his front pocket. "If you saw Julie, then I'm sure she told you about this."

Alex took the envelope. Goosebumps spread down his forearms. He opened the envelope and gasped.

"Okay, then." Alex stared at the check then lifted his eyes to meet Pratyush's.

"A paycheck, she told me." Pratyush sat on the couch next to him and looked at the check in Alex's hand. Then, in a nonchalant tone, he added, "Looks like you exceeded expectations."

"We can't accept this." Alex tossed the check onto the table next to the laptop.

"Yes, we can." Pratyush looked at him as if he'd lost his mind. "That's the down payment for our next car."

Then Pratyush leaned back and sighed as if to say he was too tired to argue any longer. Besides, he had a point. Norma would never let Alex refuse that money—if he ever had the opportunity to see her again.

"You met my patient tonight," he said, leaning his head against Pratyush's shoulder. "What did you think of her?"

"A lot nicer than I'd thought she'd be," Pratyush said, his expression growing thoughtful. "People in the bar were looking at her as if she were royalty. If I were being brutally honest with myself, I might even confess I felt flattered she'd paid me so much attention."

"Julie said Norma was taken with you." Alex smiled at Pratyush's admission of his misjudgment of Norma.

"She would've been taken by anyone married to you," Pratyush said.

Good old Pratyush, shunning praise as a reflex. Alex snuggled in closer, brought his arm around Pratyush's shoulder.

"Five short days ago, I was following Norma in an ambulance to the emergency room," he said. "Now she's gadding about town. What is she up to?"

"Mourning the loss of her son," Pratyush said simply. "She probably doesn't realize it."

Pratyush's words landed with a force that felt like the truth. Alex's mind turned to Julie, no doubt lying awake in bed, worrying about her sister. He felt worn out.

"Norma and Julie are going skydiving a week from Sunday," he murmured.

"They are?" Pratyush looked at him, demonstrating that it was possible, every now and then, to catch him off-guard.

"Julie's been wanting to go skydiving for months," he said, withdrawing his arm and sitting up. "Had been looking for someone to go with her. She even asked me if *I* wanted to go skydiving with her."

"You never told me that." Pratyush drew back and looked at him. "What was your answer?"

"I said no, of course," Alex said in a reassuring voice. "I told her you'd never let me go skydiving."

"You used *me* as your excuse?" Pratyush looked at him with a raised brow.

"Does that upset you?" Alex gave a nervous giggle. "I thought I was doing you a favor. You wouldn't want me jumping out of a plane, would you?"

"You were probably in more danger walking home from Jim and Eric's by yourself tonight," Pratyush said.

"Come on, man," Alex said and laughed again. "Are you saying you wouldn't mind if I jumped out of a plane? Heck, would *you* jump out of a plane?"

"I admit, skydiving wouldn't be my *first* choice to spend a Sunday." Pratyush stroked his chin, fixing his gaze on the pickleball trophy and blue-footed booby on the mantel. "But if two old ladies can skydive, then why not two healthy guys in their thirties?"

Because we might go splat, that's why not. How could either of them dare skydive with both their mothers still alive? And yet a powerful jolt raced through Alex. Skydiving!

"Norma sprang on Julie tonight her plans to go with her," he said. "Called the skydiving people herself. Didn't tell Julie until after she'd made the reservation. I doubt if Julie ever thought to ask Norma to go skydiving with her."

"I can picture Norma jumping out of a plane." Pratyush shrugged. "From what I saw of her tonight, that woman's not afraid of anything."

"Something's going on." Alex traced a circle with his index finger on Pratyush's thigh. "Norma announcing she's skydiving, her wanting to meet you, this huge check… Somehow, it's connected."

"Hmm," Pratyush said growing meditative, and he grasped Alex's hand.

"Then there are Norma's heart pills," Alex said.

"I thought you said those pills are only aspirin."

"But Norma doesn't *know* they're aspirin." Alex realized his own heart was racing. "Why would Norma decide to go skydiving if she thinks she has a heart condition?"

Pratyush thought about this. Silence settled over the room. Was it almost midnight already? Then he looked at Alex with a calm but serious expression.

"Because she means to harm herself." Pratyush's tone was low, raspy, reluctant. "And make it look like a skydiving accident."

"No." A freezing sensation zinged across Alex's nerves. "That can't be right."

"I don't want to be right, Alex." Pratyush looked somber, his shoulders sagging. "But I am."

Alex's thoughts turned to Norma at Tilden Park. Her story about the night her husband died. A heart attack. Her certainty that the heart attack was intentional. Why did Pratyush have to make such frightful sense?

"What do we do?" Alex closed his eyes.

"Is there any chance you can reach her before she goes on that skydive?" Pratyush put his arm around Alex.

"I don't have her phone number," Alex said, opening his eyes to Pratyush's touch.

"We'll ask Julie."

"She'll want to know why we want it," Alex said, shivering.

"What about her son in Orinda?"

"You mean the guy who warned me to stay away from him and his mother?" Alex recalled Charles in the hospital parking lot, his furious look. "I doubt if he knows Norma's planning to go skydiving."

"Someone on Norma's staff, then. The food service. The cleaners. Someone must have her number."

"I only knew the cleaners by sight," Alex said gloomily. He reached to twirl a strand of hair above his ear—and an idea flashed in his head. "I know. Mavis."

"Mavis?"

"Norma's hairdresser. The woman who cut my hair on my first day at Norma's." Alex's eyes strayed to the check on the coffee table. No phone number on the check. "Oh, who am I kidding? Norma keeps her number so super-secret, she probably makes everyone who has it sign an NDA."

"We'll drive to Norma's house tomorrow," Pratyush said.

"Charles is over there all the time." Alex shuddered. "I wouldn't put it past him to call the police on us if he catches us there."

They sat on the couch in silence. The wall clock ticked past midnight. Maybe an idea would present itself in the morning. Norma's front door appeared in his mind's eye—thick, solid, impregnable.

"How about this?" Pratyush said, his voice low and full of purpose. "Do you know the name of the place Norma and Julie are going skydiving?"

"Wild Blue Yonder. It's in Sonoma County somewhere," Alex said and watched in horror as Pratyush pulled away from him to reach for the laptop on the coffee table. "Wait a second—why do you want to know? You want to go skydiving with Norma and Julie?"

"Not just me, Alex. You *and* me." Pratyush sat up on the couch and set the laptop on his lap. "Here's what I'm thinking. We go up with Julie early on Sunday, ahead of the scheduled dive. Make them breakfast or something. I'll distract Julie, leave you alone with Norma. That'll be your chance to talk her out of the skydive."

"But why do we have to skydive?" Alex gaped at his husband calling up Wild Blue Yonder's website online. "Why can't we make them breakfast and leave it at that?"

"Because Norma will be more likely to drop out if we go with Julie in her place." Pratyush put the laptop on the table and picked up the check. "And while we're over there, you can return this to her."

"You said a minute ago that I earned that money."

"That was before I knew Norma has an ulterior motive," Pratyush said with a slightly pained look. "Paying fair wages is one thing. Writing a twenty-thousand-dollar check because you've lost the will to live is another."

"You're sure?" Alex looked Pratyush in the eye.

"The car we have is functional," Pratyush said, his voice resigned. "You're starting your new job on Monday. A new car can wait. Let's live with the duct tape for a few weeks longer."

"Skydiving," Alex said, feeling giddy. "You're sure you want to do this?"

"It's a risk, I know." Pratyush put his hand on Alex's shoulder. "But it's a bigger risk if we don't go through with it."

He brought Alex in for a hug. A warmth, like golden light, poured out of Alex's heart. He pictured himself and Pratyush jumping out of the plane. Their parachutes opening, the two of them floating on air. The earth rising to meet them. A plunge, like their wedding day.

"How do we tell Julie about us going skydiving?" Alex said.

"We'll take a page out of Norma's book," Pratyush said with unnerving decisiveness. "I'll call the place tomorrow and reserve us spaces in Julie's party. Then we'll spring the news on Julie. Tell her she inspired us to join her. Insist that she keep everything a secret from Norma. We need that element of surprise if we want this plan to work."

"What if I can't talk Norma out of going?" Alex felt his chest deflating. "What then?"

"One step at a time," Pratyush said, and he brought his face close to Alex's. "Remember, you can't save Norma. But you *can* encourage her to save herself. I know you can do that, Alex. Because you've already done that. With me. At the BART station. Remember?"

"I'd rather not remember," Alex said and looked away.

"I'd rather not remember either," Pratyush said softly, cupping Alex's cheek with his hand. "But I'll never forget it."

"Pratyush—"

No stopping what was about to happen next. Pratyush's kiss. His hands. His fingers. His voice in Alex's ear. As spent as he was, Alex let his husband take control. He couldn't think of a more thorough or more satisfying way to forget he'd agreed to go skydiving.

Hours later, as he lay awake in bed, Pratyush snoring gently beside him, Alex imagined himself standing in the middle of an open field beneath an arcing dome of pristine blue sky. In the middle of that sky, a human figure appeared. Norma. He envisioned her silvery hair, her Jackie O sunglasses, her crimson dress with the shimmering gold bamboo leaves. A jewel around her neck winked at him. Kevin's opal. He sat up in bed, realizing that he now had a perfect opportunity to return not only the check but that pendant. He looked over at his husband, grateful he'd had the good sense to marry him while he had the chance. Pratyush kept on snoring.

CHAPTER 24

FALLING STARS

NORMA OPENED HER eyes on Saturday morning to sunlight slanting onto her rumpled bedspread. The nightstand clock read 10:14. Her tongue felt like Velcro against the roof of her mouth. Mixing her namesake cocktail with that Negroni had left a putrid taste. Vinegar and flat ginger ale, a hint of rotting orange peel.

She hauled herself out of bed, took two Tylenol, wrapped herself in a plain white dressing gown—a color of repentance—and went downstairs. She was in the middle of measuring out coffee when the telephone rang. Charles, it had to be. Did she dare pick up? She hadn't reconnected her voicemail since last weekend. *I tried calling you last night, Mom. Couldn't leave a message. Where were you?* The phone rang a fifth time. A sixth time. Not Charles, Julie. Norma picked up the phone on the eighth ring.

"Hey ho," Julie said, her voice as piercing as one of her cockatiels. "Just calling to check in. Sleep okay?"

"Okay enough," Norma said, flicking on the coffee maker. The Tylenol hadn't yet kicked in.

"Those drinks were something else, weren't they? I thought my hangover days were over." Julie giggled like a teenager at a wedding reception sneaking a glass of champagne. "But don't tell me, *you* feel perfectly fine."

"I will be, once this coffee has finished brewing." Norma opened the fridge and brought out a package of English muffins and a jar of strawberry preserves.

"We should celebrate with drinks when we come home from the skydive," Julie said. "We can sip Negronis and watch the sunset from your terrace."

"I still haven't opened the Campari Joanie had sent me while I was in the hospital," Norma said, realizing with a sudden dread that if her plan succeeded, the celebration Julie was talking about would never occur.

"Which reminds me," Julie said. "Have you given any thought to what you'll wear on the dive?"

"Do I have to give that any thought?" Norma looked at the silk folds of her dressing gown. It was too early for her to figure out what to wear today, let alone what to wear next Sunday.

"Wild Blue Yonder's website has a whole page on what and what not to wear. They suggest lightweight clothing. But lots of layers. Nothing that'll flap or come loose in the wind. I have nothing that fits the bill. Do you?"

No mistaking the hint in Julie's voice. *Let's go shopping! Wouldn't that be fun?* But Norma didn't dare hit the stores with Julie. What if Julie said something to diminish her resolve?

"I have six closets stuffed with clothes." Norma brought her favorite red mug down from a cabinet. "I'm sure I can find something that will work."

"I suppose you're right," Julie said, her voice dropping. Then she added, "But *I'm* wearing something new for Sunday. Let me know if you change your mind!"

Later that afternoon Norma strolled through her walk-in closets, brushed her fingers along gowns and sundresses she'd never wear again. What little she owned in outdoor fashion hung toward the rear of her closet in the spare room behind her evening pieces. Lightweight jackets popped with saccharine colors, ruby red, smiley-face yellow, the lime green of Kevin's first tricycle. Whatever happened to that tricycle? She pictured Kevin as a boy of six, the tricycle shimmering in the sun like a parrot's feathers. His little legs working those pedals, tearing around the driveway. A parrot chasing its own tail round and round. Norma leaned against a clothing rack, ready to faint.

Now, wait—why was she standing in her closet again? The skydive, right. Tangerine orange? Orchid purple? A cheerful color would be wrong for her purposes. But what else could she wear? Gray or beige or—God forbid—*mauve*? Now *that* was a color to stir the bile. No, never. She'd never be caught dead—

Good God. How could she make a joke like that, at a time like this? She looked around as if someone might have heard her thoughts. Forget about finding something to wear for the dive. She exited the closet and shut the door behind her.

Her eyelids felt heavy. Her bedside clock read 4:01. Better to catch a few Zs now and be alert for the sunset and the Blue Hour. She lay down on her bed and closed her eyes.

The bedroom was dark when she opened her eyes again. The nightstand clock read—good God—7:37. She scooted out of bed and went to the window. Not only was the sun gone, but the Blue Hour had passed. The sublime cobalt blue of early evening had darkened to muddy purple. *Mauve.* Only seven more sunsets until the skydive. She sank onto the edge of the bed, feeling tired and old.

✴

Sunday dragged as tediously as Saturday. No phone calls from Julie, at least. No call from Charles, either. Unusual. Almost a week had passed since he'd brought her home from Santa Rosa. He must still be irate with her.

In the late afternoon, she walked into her closet out of boredom. A low dresser she hadn't cracked open in years sat against the far wall. Buried in the bottom drawer was an olive-green windbreaker, long-sleeved cotton shirts in Creamsicle orange, chocolate-colored hiking pants. She'd taken these clothes to the Serengeti with Robert, over thirty years ago now. He'd been having an affair with the wife of one of the couples they'd gone with. Norma didn't learn that until later.

A memory arose of her sitting in the shade, by herself, while a clan of hippos lazed across the river from her tent. Birds flitted in tree branches; insects buzzed in her ear. Not one of those creatures, large or small, had paid her the least attention. Not one had cared who she was or what she was going through with Robert. She'd worn those earthy colors to blend into the background. Wasn't that what she wanted more than anything now? To fade away? To erase herself?

She made a strong pot of coffee after dinner. The sun was high in the sky when she brought a mug to her lounge chair, determined to stay awake. Day deepened into dusk. She stared at the sky, not blinking.

Her heart thrummed. The same vibration she'd felt at Kevin's, a buzz like a hummingbird's wings. Her ribcage felt ready to crack open. She reached into her sweater pocket for her heart pills.

Why take a pill? If her heart gave out now, she wouldn't have to skydive. Wouldn't that be a more convenient outcome for everyone? She closed her eyes and waited.

The thrumming subsided. She opened her eyes to a navy-blue sky. Still sitting there. Still alive.

She took a three-hour nap in the afternoon on Monday. Unprecedented for her to sleep that long. But she managed to pull herself out of bed and struggle to her lounge chair while the day was light. The sun's orange disc touched silver-blue waves and let itself be swallowed up. A soft pink ribbon stretched along the horizon. The evening sky deepened so imperceptibly that Norma couldn't pinpoint the exact moment the Blue Hour began. The moon came into focus. Here and there points of silver light showed like pearls sewn in velvet. As a child, she used to imagine fairies preparing the sky for night, sowing the heavens with stars and planets. This was the scene in which she wanted to enfold herself on Sunday. She regretted she hadn't worn blue on that safari.

Why not design a blue shirt herself? She could take a cab tomorrow to the fabric store and buy what she needed. Her sewing machine and supplies sat in the sewing room upstairs, growing lonesome with disuse. She'd fashion for herself a slice of heaven the charity could later auction off as the last piece world-famous designer Norma McKinsey ever made. She sat up and breathed in the night, feeling more awake than she'd felt in days.

The store stocked a cotton polyester blend in sapphire blue. She bought a few yards along with silver thread and blue elastic rib fabric for the collar and cuffs. Her teenage self stirred inside her, alive with ambition. It surprised her to realize that she could still feel the craving to excel.

The orange safari shirt proved an excellent model for her to shape the fabric. The feel of fresh cloth between her fingertips was like meeting an old friend. She pulled off the protective plastic of her Singer. How apropos, to design her last piece on the first sewing machine she'd ever owned.

She was laying the orange shirt over the blue cloth on her worktable when her desk phone rang. This must be Charles, thanks to his unfailing ability to call when she least wanted to talk. Norma listened and waited. A fifth ring. A sixth ring. After the eighth ring, she picked up the phone.

"Norma, there you are," Julie said, sounding winded as always. "Looks like you haven't bought a new answering machine yet!"

"I've been busy," Norma said, keeping her focus on the orange shirt.

"Busy? Busy doing what?"

"Designing a top to wear on our skydive," Norma said, figuring she might as well admit what she was doing.

"You're making something to wear?" Julie sounded shocked. "You always said after you sold the business that you'd never design anything new."

"That was before I made plans to jump out of a plane." Norma marked the blue cloth with a pleasant heft of chalk. "Six closets full of gowns and dresses and casual summer clothes but nothing to wear for a skydive. The one occasion I never thought of."

"What will your new top look like?" This could be Julie as a girl, elated and impatient.

"Wouldn't you rather be surprised?" The corners of Norma's mouth curled up despite herself.

"Fine, fine," Julie said. The cheerfulness in her tone made Norma shiver. "Now that the day is almost here, the butterflies are hatching in my stomach. Nervous?"

"Less nervous than I thought I'd be." Norma thought she'd given the low-key answer Julie might expect of her.

"The website says we should have something in our stomachs ahead of time," Julie said. "So as not to become lightheaded while diving."

"We'll stop for breakfast on our way up there." Norma brushed chalk off her hands. Her fingertips were cold.

"I was thinking I could bring breakfast to your house," Julie said, a shade too eagerly. "We can eat on the patio if it's warm enough."

"Won't breakfast be cold by the time you come?" Norma imagined greasy sausage and rubbery pancakes. It unnerved her to think of pancakes and sausage as her last meal. But what difference did it make?

"We can heat breakfast in your oven. Or I'll cook breakfast on your stove. Come on, Norma, it'll be easier that way. More fun too!"

"Okay," Norma said, beaten down by Julie's relentless good mood. "Why not?"

"How about I show up at seven thirty?"

"Seven thirty? That's way too early," Norma said, suspicious.

"I know," Julie said, "but we can't go up on that plane on a full stomach either. You don't want to lose your breakfast at eighteen thousand feet, do you?"

"Fine, Jules. Come at seven thirty." Norma hadn't counted on setting her alarm for the last day of her life.

"Great." Julie's tone was as lively as Norma's silver thread. "I still can't wrap my mind around this! So exciting, isn't it?"

Norma bit her lip. Exciting was unearthing a vintage brooch at the Clignancourt flea market in Paris. Or beholding a herd of grazing wildebeests on an African plain. Or opening *Vogue* and savoring her first favorable notice after toiling for years in obscurity. But this? The feeling pulsing through her now was the opposite of excitement. A feeling of lethargy. A desire for everything to be over.

"That's one way to put it," she said.

She cut the blue cloth, stitched the seams. Her sewing machine chattered away. A needed diversion, this shirt. So much more absorbing than dwelling over Sunday. So long as she could focus on the task at hand, she could pretend the skydive wouldn't happen. Work slowly, work slowly.

Why not some handmade stitching to adorn the collar and waist? Her needle was like a dolphin skimming along the soft blue cloth, diving and jumping, leaving a wake of silver stitches. Beguiling. But why stop there? Why not sew a few stars into the blue? One star, two stars. Another and another. Painstaking work, but she couldn't stop. Over the next couple hours she sewed a trail of stars that floated down from the right shoulder and pooled along the waist. She imagined a fairy sowing stars, preparing the night sky. Electricity flowed through her fingers. *This is why I make clothes.*

As she beheld her near-finished work on her trusty mannequin, she recalled something Alex had said on the day Mavis had cut his hair. How, on the morning of his wedding day at the salon, joy had taken him unawares. Perhaps this was the feeling coursing through her veins now. Not only joy itself, but the surprise that she *could* feel joy, despite everything that had gone wrong. Either way, she would be making her exit on a high note. And, yes, had had the good fortune to know—and recognize—what true happiness felt like. How many people could say that at the end of their lives?

She sewed the last stars into the shirt late on Saturday afternoon. The shirt was about a quarter inch too loose about the waist, but that was no catastrophe. She pulled the shirt over the mannequin and regarded her finished work. Despondency spread inside her, one she always felt whenever she completed a piece.

A memory came to her of an eighteen-month-old Kevin, in denim overalls, playing at his bead maze at the foot of the mannequin. His face one of wondering concentration as he slid a bead along a wire. She imagined him looking up at her and breaking into a smile as if he were glad to see her. A purple bead, a red bead, an orange bead—

The phone next to the sewing machine rang. Norma shook herself awake. Now *this* had to be Charles. She pulled in her chair and picked up the phone.

"Mom! Long time no talk." Forced cheer sounded in Charles's voice. "How've you been?"

"Coming along." Her conversational tone struck her as contrived as Charles's.

"Keeping busy?"

"Busy enough," she said, her eyes on her new shirt. "Your aunt and I went to dinner last Friday."

"Glad to hear it! How is Aunt Julie doing?"

"Managing."

"Man, it's been too long since I've seen her," Charles said, as if he might do something about it for once.

"I'm sure she'd love to hear from you," Norma said, for what had to be the hundredth time since Phil died. Hopefully he'd call his aunt more often, once Norma was gone.

"Yeah, I should." The drop in his voice, one that failed to inspire confidence, was exactly what Norma had expected. "So! I was wondering if you might be free tomorrow."

"Tomorrow?" A leaden feeling dropped from her chest to her stomach.

"Yeah. I have all sorts of time nowadays." An awkward pause. "Debra flew up to Seattle this morning, so I'm here on my own."

"Seattle? What is Debra doing in Seattle?" Norma was thankful for this unexpected turn in the conversation. Her gaze absently traveled down the line of embroidered stars.

"Jonah called us two nights ago," Charles said, drawing out his words. "Maria needs to be on bed rest until the baby's born."

"Is she okay?" Norma turned away from the shirt, alarmed.

"Jonah reports that she'll be fine." The pseudo-unconcern in Charles's voice was anything but reassuring. "The baby too, of course. Still, the docs said it would be best. She's not due for another four weeks."

"Four weeks of bed rest," she repeated, grateful her own two pregnancies had been easy. "And Debra's staying with them?"

"Yeah. Shopping, cooking, stuff like that." A vagueness crept into his tone, as if he wasn't clear about what Debra would be doing for the next month. "Jonah and Maria have a futon in their office for her to sleep on."

"Convenient." She could only imagine how much Debra would have appreciated her mother-in-law moving in with *her* while eight months pregnant. "What about you, Charles? When do you join them?"

"Probably not until after the baby's born," he said, sounding casual.

"Not sooner?" She thought she heard a dip in her son's tone, making the best of being left behind.

"You've never slept on that futon," he said, only half joking. "Hey, maybe we could fly up together when the baby's born. Thanksgiving in Seattle. How does that sound?"

Her grandson's wife—a young woman Norma very much

liked and approved of—was on bed rest. Her first great-grand-child was on the way. How could she go through with that jump tomorrow?

"I'll think about it," she said.

"You have four weeks to decide," he said. "So, are you around tomorrow? I have a ten o'clock tee time, but after that I'm free. How about lunch?"

"One of my girlfriends invited me to her house for brunch," she said, astonished at how smoothly that lie came out.

"Oh," he said. He cleared his throat then added, "Mom, hey. You aren't avoiding me, are you? Because of what happened up in Santa Rosa?"

"I've already forgotten about Santa Rosa," she said, keeping her tone smooth.

"I just want to see you." A note of conciliation colored his voice—or was that tone frustration? "Lunch and nothing else. I promise."

"I have the engagement," she said, this time with regret. That was the trouble with lies—once uttered, they couldn't be rescinded.

"If your plans change tomorrow, give me a call." But he spoke as if he already knew to expect no call from her.

"Thank you," she said. "I will."

The light slanting through the sewing room window was golden by the time she rang off. Sadness thrummed through her like the toll of a cathedral bell—slow, rolling, inexorable. This wasn't the way she'd wanted to leave her oldest son, alone and abandoned in his big house.

She ate dinner and reached the terrace in time to watch the sun sink into the ocean. Robert, if he were here, would doubtless be pleased to know that her last sunset on this terrace had arrived. But she'd defeated him, hadn't she? Twenty-five years of sunsets remained an impressive run.

Au revoir, beau soleil! She derived comfort from the notion that the sun would keep on shining, the stars twinkling, the trees spreading their leaves, long after she was gone. Now for the deepening in the sky—wait, wait—and there it was, the sublime shades of the Blue Hour, stretching from horizon to horizon. She watched and watched and watched, not moving, not blinking, until the light faded to purple, and streetlights glittered from below.

CHAPTER 25

BREAKFAST

THE GLOWING RED digits of the nightstand clock hovered in the darkness next to Norma's head. 11:30. 12:00. 1:00. This was an exercise in delusion, lying here waiting for sleep. Might as well play some pool. She pulled herself out of bed, swathed herself in white, and went downstairs.

She hit balls in the faint light from the lamp hanging over the pool table. No one to watch her, admire her, applaud her. A useless skill, this knack for dispatching numbered balls into pockets. All it did was give her an illusory sense of control. Eventually, she laid the cue stick on the cleared table. Her last game. After decades of faithful service, the table's work was done. Heaven knew the table's fate, once she no longer owned it.

She opened her eyes to the buzzing alarm. No recollection of how she'd returned upstairs, or when sleep had stolen over her. Morning sunlight slanted onto the rumpled bed sheets. She dragged herself out of bed.

Her skydiving clothes waited for her in a folded pile on the bathroom sink. She put on a touch of makeup and a bit of gel for her hair. A calmness spread through her as she pulled on her new shirt. Not too flashy, not too morose. At her funeral, people would no doubt say that she'd done what she loved right up to the last days of her life.

The Sunday newspaper, full of stories that no longer mattered to her, sat on the other side of the front door. She took the paper to the terrace and pulled apart the sections to give the appearance she'd been reading it. Mustn't give Julie any reason to suspect anything amiss, later.

The peal of the doorbell reached her from the open sliding door. Was it already seven thirty? She went into the kitchen. The microwave clock read 7:04. Norma, apparently, wasn't the only one who couldn't sleep last night. She drew herself up and walked with a dignified step to the front hall. She took a long, deep breath. Then she grasped the knob and pulled open the door.

Julie stood in the doorway with a frozen smile. In the crook of her arm sat the Veuve Clicquot Norma had given her. And behind Julie stood—for the love of humanity—Alex and Pratyush, posted on either side of her like sentry guards. Norma stepped backward, her hand clutching the doorknob.

"Surprise," Julie said with a weak smile. She might as well have said, *Don't blame me for them being here.*

"Alex," Norma said stiffly. "Pratyush."

"Good morning," Alex said, his smile as luminous as the sunshine flooding into the house. He held a foil-covered platter in one hand and a paper shopping bag in the other.

"Nice to see you again, Norma," Pratyush said. He carried a small cooler.

"Do come in," Norma said and stepped aside.

She was able to see her visitors better once she closed the front door, blocking out the sun. Alex and Pratyush wore form-fitting cycling jackets, Alex in grayish blue, Pratyush in forest green. Julie was the standout in a shocking pink jacket, canary-yellow stripes running down the sleeves. Everything they wore looked brand new. Julie had apparently found people to go shopping with. Norma locked the door and turned up her chin, shifting into hostess mode, fortifying herself for the act of her life.

"I didn't realize you'd be joining us for breakfast," she said to Alex with as much composure as possible.

"*Joining* you for breakfast? We're *making* breakfast." Alex held up the foil-covered platter. "Chocolate chunk muffins, *madame*. We also brought bacon and eggs. Coffee too, on the off chance you're running low. And Pratyush will be making his mother's famous orange pancakes."

"With a dash of turmeric for color," Pratyush put in.

"Did we forget to mention something?" Alex stroked his chin and made a show of thinking. Then he looked at Norma and smiled. "Oh, that's right! We're crashing your skydive."

"You're what?" Norma turned to Julie. "They're diving with us?"

"They asked if they could tag along," Julie said with a trembling smile.

"There were spaces left on the plane?" Norma said. A dull feeling of apathy spread through her, a sense she was losing control of the day.

"*Plenty* of space," Alex said with an edge of false bravery in his voice. "Who'd a thunk?"

Not Norma. Not Julie either, by the affected smile on her face. If only Norma could have a few moments to herself to let this revelation sink in.

"Come, let's have breakfast," she said, turning toward the living area.

"This is quite a home you have, Norma," Pratyush said once they reached the kitchen. He set the cooler on the counter and walked to the sliding door. "This must be the view Alex has told me so much about."

"Yep," Alex said, putting down his shopping bag and plate of muffins on the kitchen island. He pulled off the foil. "Pratyush doesn't believe me when I tell him you can see our house from here."

"You *can't* see our house from here," Julie said, laughing as she put away the champagne bottle.

"Seriously, Alex," Pratyush said, turning from the sliding door. "Do you insist on having this argument in front of the ladies?"

"Norma will back me up." Alex crumpled the foil into a ball as he gave her a smile. "You can see Julie's house and our back unit from here, can't you?"

"It never crossed my mind to look." Norma was too flustered to say anything else. Her lack of sleep last night was catching up to her.

"Let me make pancakes," Pratyush said with an eye roll. He turned toward the kitchen.

"Not until we settle this matter." Alex walked up and grasped Pratyush's arm and then looked at Norma and Julie. "Ladies, if you'll excuse us."

Alex and Pratyush went out through the sliding door. Norma measured coffee into the coffee maker, now and then glancing out the windows. Alex and Pratyush stood at the retaining wall, Alex pointing toward downtown, Pratyush saying something in response. A burst of laughter from Alex, a patting of Pratyush's backside. The easy intimacy of a settled married couple. Norma turned to the coffee maker, unable to watch them.

"You're okay they're here, right?" Julie darted her eyes to the sliding door.

"Why wouldn't I be okay?" Norma brought the coffee carafe to the sink.

"I wanted to tell you they were coming. But Alex *insisted* on keeping it a secret." Julie sat on a stool by the island. "I *told* him you weren't a fan of surprises."

"He meant well. But now we have an occasion on our hands." Norma filled the carafe with water, listening to the dignified coolness in her voice.

Alex and Pratyush let themselves into the house. The triumphant look on Alex's face, contrasting with the harried look on Pratyush's face, made clear their dispute remained unresolved. Norma brought the carafe to the coffee maker.

"And?" Julie asked with raised eyebrows.

"Not. Even. Close." Pratyush's deadpan was *tour de force*.

"I don't care what he says. *I* can see our houses," Alex said in a needling tone, smiling sweetly at his husband.

"Sure you can," Pratyush said with a sigh that suggested that perhaps he too had had enough of Alex's good mood. "All this arguing has made me hungry. Norma, may I join you at the counter?"

"By all means," she said, stepping aside and reaching into the cabinet above the sink for mugs.

"That's quite the shirt you're wearing," Pratyush said. "One of your own creations?"

"I designed it this week," Norma said in a careless tone, bringing down mugs. Pratyush's astuteness was only slightly less inflaming than Alex's sunny mood.

"My mom would love to own a shirt like that," Pratyush said with a slow nod. "She goes to aerobics class three times a week. She's paid top dollar for sportswear that's nowhere as stylish as what you're wearing."

"There you go, Norma," Julie said with a smile. "You're ready to launch your next clothing line."

"Those days are behind me, thank you very much," Norma said with a tautness to end the subject.

"Here, Pratyush," Alex said, going to one of the cabinets, apparently catching Norma's drift. "Let me find you what you need for those pancakes."

He brought out a white ceramic mixing bowl and a nonstick griddle that Norma had never seen before in her life. And that was only the beginning. Out came plates and bowls and measuring cups, a set of measuring spoons, a hand-held grater for Pratyush to zest oranges. Until now, Norma had only a vague idea of their existence. She kept her eyes on the coffee's drip-drip-drip into the pot.

Alex pulled out a red checkered picnic tablecloth from a shopping bag and brought it outside. Eggs and bacon sizzled on a sheet pan inside the oven. Meanwhile, Pratyush mixed batter and flipped pancakes with the same élan he'd applied to his bass viol at the Thirsty Raven. An orangey fragrance filled the kitchen. Out on the terrace, Julie set plates, silverware, and yellow linen napkins. Nothing for Norma to do but bring out the coffee and take her place at the head of the table. The sunlight splashed down from a spotless expanse of cerulean sky. The gold trim of Alex's mother-in-law's platter shimmered. She could only hope they'd eat and be on the road as swiftly as possible.

"So, Alex," she said halfway through breakfast, thinking it would be rude not to ask, "how are you settling in at your new job?"

"So far, so good." Alex sprinkled pepper onto his eggs. "Hard work, rewarding, the usual. You should've heard my mother on the phone the other day—she was *so* relieved to hear I have a full-time job that I like."

"I can imagine," Norma said, glad to hear he'd called his mother.

"Right now I'm helping a teenage girl walk again after she broke her leg in a car accident. I should have you come to one of my sessions with her, Norma. You could teach her a thing or two about hard work and determination."

"I'm sure you can handle her all by yourself," she said, realizing that Alex now had a real patient to take care of, someone needier and worthier than herself. Her eyes shifted to his square-cut sideburns. "I see you've celebrated your new employment with a haircut."

"We both celebrated," Pratyush said, turning his head to show off his trimmed nape. "And took Julie with us."

"We wanted to look spruce for the skydiving pictures," Julie said, running her fingers through her feathery hair. "Your favorite hairdresser took care of us first thing yesterday morning."

"You went to Mavis?"

"We took over her salon," Alex said, smiling. "Mavis opened the place early when we told her why we wanted the haircuts. Julie and I had our hair cut by two other hairdressers. Mavis *insisted* on cutting Pratyush's hair."

"Not that I could tell you why," Pratyush said, looking unruffled. A sly look at Alex, and then he added, "She was full of questions for me, though."

"Such a fun morning," Julie said, putting down her cup of coffee. "Like a celebration. And I adore Mavis's tattoo."

"Mavis has many tattoos," Norma said. "Which one are you talking about?"

"The one right here." Julie tapped the spot below her collarbone. "You know, the one of pink hearts floating out of an airplane? I took one look at that tattoo and thought, now I *have* to buy a pink jacket. I want people on the ground to think a valentine is floating down from the sky."

"Either that," Norma said with an appraising look at Julie's jacket, "or you'll be mistaken for a flamingo who's been blown off course."

"God, I hope not," Julie said and laughed. "I'm sorry you weren't with us at the salon, Norma. And for the shopping afterwards. You would've had a ball."

"Maybe she can join us next time," Pratyush said with a shrewd look, or so it seemed to Norma. He reached for one of his golden-orange pancakes—a superior pancake, in both taste and texture, to the taste-free shoe leather Norma had been served at the Santa Rosa hospital.

"You mean we'll go skydiving again?" Julie said to Pratyush.

"If not skydiving then something else," Pratyush said and threw a smile at Alex. "If you keep going for long enough, then there's always something else."

"Mavis charges more than we're used to," Alex said to Norma, "but I wanted to celebrate my new job. And celebrate today, too. Right? How many times in our lives are we going to go skydiving?"

"We won't be the same when it's over, that's for sure," Julie said, looking from Alex to Pratyush to Norma.

"Would anyone like more coffee?" Norma said, unable to take much more of this. She reached for the near-empty carafe.

"None for me," Alex said, putting a hand over his mug. "I'm jittery enough."

This was exhausting, this breakfast. The relentless cheer of Julie and Alex and Pratyush would wear out anyone. Yet Norma couldn't deny a warm feeling spreading through her. Was the feeling joy? If so, why not let herself feel it? Her body felt lighter, ready for the jump.

"I shouldn't have had that last piece of bacon," Julie said, laying her fork on her empty plate. She patted her stomach. "They'll have to strap an extra parachute on me."

"I'll take care of the dishes," Pratyush said with suspicious alacrity, standing up and stacking plates.

"Let me help," Julie said, rising.

"We're in no hurry, are we?" Alex asked this of Julie, his tone artfully casual.

"We're not expected at Wild Blue Yonder until ten thirty," Julie said. She put down her empty plate and looked at her watch.

Alex turned to Norma and said, "Can I talk to you privately for a second?"

"What for?" Her spine stiffened.

"A couple of things," he said with an offhand tone Norma wasn't buying.

"Take all the time you need," Julie said in all innocence. "After we load the dishwasher, I can show Pratyush the house."

"I like that idea," Pratyush said, his hands full of breakfast dishes.

"Shall we talk in the living room?" Norma asked Alex.

"Would you mind if we talked upstairs? It'll be less noisy that way."

"Certainly," Norma said and rose from the table.

Fine. Let Alex say what he had to say. Let this be the end of it. She headed into the house without turning to see if he was following. But she knew he was there.

"So," she said, standing by her circular table with one hand grasping the back of a chair. "What's all this about?"

"I have something to return to you," Alex said.

He reached into his rear pocket and brought out a pale blue

slip of paper. The check she'd given Pratyush at the Thirsty Raven. That would explain why the check had never cleared. His smile broadened as he held out the folded paper between his front fingers, as if to imitate her.

"Is there an issue?" She cast an uninterested look at the check.

"Yes. A big issue." He laid the check on the table in front of her. "The amount is way too high."

"I disagree. I paid you for your last week of work, plus double time for working on a Sunday."

"More like double time multiplied by ten," he said, his eyes meeting hers. "That amount would be excessive if I'd driven you across the country."

"You spoke on my behalf to my son. You followed me to the hospital when you didn't have to," she said, aware of the tremor in her voice. "I have paid people far more money, for showing far less dedication, than what you did for me two Sundays ago."

"Pratyush and I have talked it over. We're not accepting this check." Alex gave a slow shake of the head. "I won't let myself be paid for a favor I would've done for any friend."

"We're friends now?" She traced her thumb along her index fingernail.

"I wasn't your nurse when I took you to see your son." A soft light appeared in his eyes. "I can't cash that check with a clean conscience."

"If you won't accept the payment," she said, too vexed to press the issue further, "then I can't force you to take it."

"Thank you." He glanced at the check and added, "I can suggest a compromise, though. Instead of writing a check to me, perhaps you'd like to donate to Oakland Cares for Youth."

"Oakland Cares for Youth? I'm unfamiliar with that charity."

"Mentoring and tutoring disadvantaged kids," Alex said. "Pratyush's nonprofit. They always need funds."

"Let me find my checkbook," she said, turning toward her escritoire.

"How about writing me a check later?" He gave her a smile that bordered on the impudent. "I don't feel like skydiving with a check in my pocket."

"Of course."

Only after she spoke did she understand what had happened. For her to write a new check to Pratyush's nonprofit, she would have to come home *from* the skydive. She looked at him with the distinct impression that he'd outwitted her.

"Thanks a million. Pratyush and his charity will be forever grateful to receive that money," he said, this time with a more sincere smile. "I also have this for you."

He reached into the pocket of his cycling jacket and brought out a small envelope. From the envelope he pulled out Kevin's opal pendant. The jewel twinkled in the sunlight like a sea-colored teardrop. He laid the pendant on the circular table. Norma could only stare at it, her throat tightening.

"Thank you," she managed to say.

"Norma." Alex glanced down at the pendant then looked up at her with a directness that few people ever dared with her. "Why are you going on this skydive?"

"To support my sister." An unpleasant feeling rattled through her. "Of course."

"You could've told Julie months ago that you wanted to go skydiving with her." He folded his arms. "But now, all of a sudden, you decide to go? What gives?"

"That was always my plan, to accompany her if she failed to find a skydiving companion." She tilted up her chin. "Phil meant the world to Julie. *He* was the one who wanted to go skydiving with her. I'm doing this as much for Phil's sake as I am for Julie's."

"I had no idea you held Phil in such high regard." Alex's expression was proof he didn't believe her brazen lie.

"If I had had the good luck to marry a gentleman like Phil Pontone," she said, her voice bitter, "perhaps I'd still be happily married today."

Her words hung in the dead silence. Then an echoing chime came from below. The doorbell? Now?

"Are you expecting anyone else this morning?" Alex turned toward the door with a look of disquiet.

"Charles is golfing this morning. Maybe he decided to swing by here first." She was eager for an excuse to escape these uncomfortable questions—even if it meant facing Charles.

"Wait." Alex's bold tone stopped her from heading to the door. He walked around her to the intercom and pressed the button. "Hey, Julie?"

"Alex!" Julie's voice was as bouncy as gumballs spilling out of the intercom. "You want me to answer that?"

"Would you mind?" His eyes were fixed on Norma.

"No problem," Julie said, and Alex let go of the intercom button.

"Oh, no," Norma said, a terrible thought seizing her. "Please don't tell me."

"Tell you what?"

"Charles. The skydive. You didn't tip him off, did you?"

"Of course not," he said, open-mouthed. He looked appalled and maybe even offended that she would suggest such a thing.

"I don't know how I'm going to explain skydiving to him," she said, sick to her stomach, "if that really is Charles at the door."

"Tell him you invited us over for breakfast before we left on our skydiving trip." Alex's voice was calm and serious.

"I'm going skydiving too," she said, not quite following.

"Not if you don't *want* to go," he answered with a meaningful look. "*We* can take Julie."

"And is that why you're here?" She stared at him. "To take my place?"

"Think of your heart episode two weeks ago," he said. "You have to know that skydiving isn't safe."

"The doctors have consistently found nothing wrong with my heart," she answered, her voice thin.

"And the heart pills?" He put a hand on his hip. "You take those for kicks?"

"I haven't taken a pill in weeks." She stood up straight, wishing she were taller. "You can't prevent me from going on that skydive, Alex. You have no medical reason to stop me."

"Then look me in the eye and tell me you think your heart can withstand the jump." He looked certain she'd lack the gall to lie to his face.

"I wouldn't go if I didn't," she said, using all her willpower to look straight at him.

He eyed her as if he wanted to say something more. She glanced out the window, unable to continue holding his gaze. Then she looked at him again, and his features softened. How could she have thought that she could pull this off easily?

"Norma, can I ask you something?" His tone was gentler now.

"Go ahead."

"Did Kevin say to you outright he wanted nothing more to do with you?"

"He might as well have," she said with resignation.

"What do you mean, 'he might as well have'?" He peered at her. "What did Kevin specifically say to you that morning?"

"I don't recall his exact words." Norma stumbled over her

own words as she spoke. "Something along the lines of he didn't know what he wanted."

"So then he didn't say out loud that he wanted you out of his life," Alex said, his face brightening. His eyes shifted to the pendant. "That makes sense."

"What makes sense?"

"For two weeks I've been imagining a young Kevin buying this pendant for you." He walked up to the table and traced his finger along the necklace's delicate chain. "I couldn't believe the teenager who'd made such a gesture would ever kick his own mother out of his house. But he didn't kick you out, did he? All he said was he didn't know what he wanted. That means you still have a chance."

A chance? What an absurd and patronizing notion. A bilious taste filled her mouth.

"That's kind of you to say," she said, swallowing her vexation.

"I can see how you might think Mendocino County represents an ending." Alex's eyes shone like aquamarines in the morning light. "But what if Mendocino County wasn't an ending, but a beginning? Your estrangement with him is what's over. You and he *did* talk. Now something new is about to take its place. Something that may yet end well."

"My eightieth birthday is in less than two months," she said, allowing herself to take a rebuking tone with him. "I don't have time to wait."

"I saw how hard you worked to walk again, Norma. That was all you." He glanced at the opal then looked at her with a little smile. "I know you know how to persist. Come on, Norma. Isn't your family worth persisting for?"

She lacked the words to describe the wrongness of what he'd said. This whole morning had become a sorry muddle. What did he care if she reconciled with her son or not? Her eyelids grew heavy. Then she snapped to attention at the crackle of the intercom.

"Norma!" Julie's voice was high and urgent. "Come downstairs! Quick!"

CHAPTER 26

SWEENEY AND TODD

Norma turned and left the sitting room. Her stomach quivered. Who else but Charles would ring her doorbell at this hour on a Sunday? She quickened her pace to the top of the stairs.

Julie beamed up at Norma from the wide-open door, her hand on the knob. Pratyush came into the hall from the corridor. In the doorway stood a tall, thin young man in a red zip-up sweatshirt and black knitted cap, stubble lining his jaw. His rumpled clothes looked as if he'd slept in them. Norma had never seen this man before. She descended the stairs and sized up her visitor, already disliking him.

"Yes?" She spoke with a razor-thin tone of civility.

"Our visitor," Julie said, her smile widening, "would like to know if this is the *Winston* residence."

"The Winston residence?" Norma looked from Julie to her visitor, in no mood for riddles.

"Oh. My. *God*," Alex called out from the top of the stairs. "You mean the *Harry* Winston residence?"

"So this *is* the right house." The young man glanced around the hall.

"You have Harry Winston?" Norma said. She wouldn't decide whether his presence in her doorway was good news or bad news until after she verified Harry's return.

"He's in my car now," the young man said. He took a tentative step into the house, as if worried he might be walking into quicksand.

"Oh, Norma," Julie said overjoyed, "isn't this the most fantastic news you ever heard?"

Leave it to Harry Winston to pick the most inconvenient possible time to stage his return. Leave it to Julie to say the exact words, with that precise cadence in her tone, to set Norma's teeth on edge. But wasn't the cat's recovery an event Norma herself had longed for? If this young man had shown up at her door two weeks ago, would she have ever thought to go skydiving?

"The cat isn't alone," the young man said in a careful voice. He removed his cap to reveal scruffy brown hair. "His brother is with him."

"His brother?" Julie said, gaping. "Harry Winston has a *brother*?"

"Wait a second," Norma said, eyeing the young man. "You're the man from Los Angeles, aren't you? Harry Winston is *your* cat."

"Yes, ma'am, he is," the young man mumbled, as if confessing a crime. "Or used to be."

"And now you want to give both your cats to *me*?"

"Here's the thing," the young man said, rolling his ski cap into a ball between his hands. "It's something of a story."

"Go ahead," she said dryly. "I don't need a novel."

"I'll keep it short, I promise." The young man darted his eyes to the chandelier then looked at Norma. "A couple of years ago I was down in LA, working on my degree. I was bored and lonely, so I adopted two orange kittens. Brothers. Sweeney and Todd."

"Sweeney and Todd," Norma repeated with a downturn in her voice.

"The shelter named them," her visitor said, wincing as if he understood how hokey those names were. "Anyway, I enjoyed having them around while I worked at home. They'd chase each other around my apartment, have little tussles. But I didn't realize how much work—and expensive—two cats could be."

You don't say, Norma felt like telling him. What an irresponsible young man. And what possessed him to don a sweatshirt and ski cap in seventy-degree weather?

"I moved up here last year to finish grad school," the man continued. "Then Sweeney slipped through an open window and ran away."

"By Sweeney," Norma said, "you're referring to Harry Winston."

"Yes, Harry Winston," the young man said, turning to Julie as if in search of a friendly face. "I kept them as indoor cats, so no collars."

"The shelter found a chip on him," Alex said. He was standing at the foot of the stairs now. "The address was an apartment and a phone number in LA."

"Yeah," the young man said with an embarrassed look. "I changed my number when I moved up here. Never thought to re-register those chips."

"What is your address now?" Norma asked, thinking he must live in an in-law unit a few houses down the road.

"Off Alcatraz Avenue," the young man said. "Other side of Telegraph."

"What?" Alex said, eyes widening. "That's further away from here than our house."

"That's so far," Pratyush added, "you probably couldn't even *see* that house from up here."

"According to GPS, my apartment is eight-point-nine miles away," the young man said, giving Pratyush a slightly baffled look. "On the drive I kept thinking, *How did Sweeney find his way all the way up here?*"

"Maybe he sneaked onto someone's pickup truck that drove up here," Julie suggested.

"But he couldn't have hitched a ride back home to Alcatraz Avenue, could he?" Pratyush said, wrinkling his brow.

"That's true. He must've gone home on foot." Julie looked thoughtful for a moment and absently tugged at her windbreaker's zipper. "This is so touching, isn't it? You all thought he'd vanished for good. Instead, Harry Winston braved traffic and raccoons and God knows what else, all so he could reunite with his brother."

"That *is* touching," Pratyush said. "My own brother is a good guy, but I wouldn't brave traffic and raccoons for *him*."

"Now I'm moving to Toronto for my PhD," the young man said with a worried look. "I can't take the cats with me. No one I know wants them, and I'd hate to return them to the shelter. So I thought that since you must be missing Sweeney—Harry Winston—you might want to take Todd too."

"We'd never *think* of separating Todd from Sweeney," Julie said. She turned to Norma with a doe-eyed expression so flagrantly manipulative that Norma had to slip her hands into the pockets of her hiking pants to hide the clenching of her fists. "You'll take the two cats in, won't you, Norma?"

Norma glared at Julie and assessed her options. How could she deprive her sister, and Alex and Pratyush for that matter, of the happy ending they craved? But who would take care of the cats tomorrow? The days and weeks and months after that? Did this mean she shouldn't go skydiving?

"I'm Norma McKinsey," she said to her guest, extending her hand.

"David." The young man shook her hand with a less-than-firm grip. "David Johnson."

"Should we call Harry Winston 'Sweeney' now?" Julie asked, turning to Norma.

"We can't," Alex said. "In this house, he's Harry Winston."

"Make Sweeney his middle name," Pratyush suggested. "Or use the initial. Harry S. Winston."

"Harry S. and Todd Winston," Alex said and laughed. "Esquire."

"You'll take them?" David gave Norma a hopeful look.

"Bring the gentlemen in for now," she said. "It's far too hot for two cats to swelter in a car."

David Johnson exited the house. Sunlight flooded into the hall from the gaping door. Julie swapped ecstatic if unbelieving looks with Alex. Expectation charged the air.

Then David appeared at the doorway holding two crates. A plaintive mewl from one crate, silence from the other. The man set each crate down and unlatched the wire doors to each.

Twitching whiskers appeared at the mouth of one crate. Then a long-haired orange cat with verdigris-shaded eyes tiptoed into the light. This must be Todd Winston, a slimmer, more skittish, less indolent version of his brother Harry. Todd looked at Norma and let out a howl as if he were as agitated to behold her as she was to behold him.

In a few moments Harry Winston emerged from his own crate. His sushi-shaped collar confirmed that this was no looka-like imposter. He cast a sleepy look around the room as if he failed to grasp—or care about—everyone's shock, disbelief, and jubilation. Norma had grown so used to thinking of his disappearance as permanent that to regard him now, observing his audience with a quintessentially feline lack of self-consciousness, was like contemplating a mirage.

"You're one piece of work, Harry Winston," Alex said, crouching down and extending his hand.

Harry came up to Alex and rubbed his nose against Alex's knuckles then lay down on a patch of sunlight on the floor and writhed around on his back. His spreading stomach indicated no lack of nourishment on his eight-point-nine-mile journey to Alcatraz Avenue.

"And you must be Todd," Julie said, crouching down and extending her finger.

But Todd ignored Julie and went up instead to Pratyush, rubbing his nose against his leg. Pratyush bent down to pet the cat.

"Pratyush!" Julie said. "I thought you were allergic to cats."

"Allergic? I'm not allergic. What made you think I was allergic?" Pratyush stood up and looked at her, puzzled.

"Alex told me you were allergic," Julie said and turned to Alex.

"You *are* allergic." Alex stood up and stared at Pratyush, his expression one of total surprise. "Aren't you?"

"*Mom* must've told you I was allergic," Pratyush said with a wave of the hand. "I think I sneezed once while petting the neighbor's cat. That became her excuse whenever one of my sisters asked if we could adopt one."

"If I'd known *that*," Alex said with an apologetic look at Norma, "then I might've taken Harry off your hands a lot sooner."

"Good that you didn't," Julie said stoutly. "Harry belongs here."

"You're fine with taking them both?" David Johnson gave Norma a hopeful look.

"I don't have much choice, do I?" But Norma's grudging tone masked the relief—yes, relief—flowing through her. "All right, Mr. Johnson. I'll take the gentlemen off your hands."

"Oh thanks, thanks so much," David said. Then he turned to the two cats with a sad expression. "Well, boys. Looks like this is the end of the road for us. Be good to the nice lady, okay?"

"I'd invite you in for coffee," Norma said, softening toward her guest, "but I'm afraid we have an engagement."

"Get this," Julie said, grinning. "We're all jumping out of a plane this morning!"

"Jumping out of a plane?" Charles said, his large frame blocking the open door. "Who's jumping out of a plane?"

Charles stepped into the hall, his face ashen. Julie, Alex, and Pratyush glanced at Norma, as if they were hoping for her to save them. But what could she say to wipe that scowl off Charles's face? The look of betrayal in his eyes? She glanced at Julie, feeling as hapless as everyone else.

"Hiya, Charles," Julie said, smiling at him as if this were any other family gathering. "Long time no see."

"Mom?" Charles turned to Norma with an incredulous look. "What is going on here?"

"This nice young man here brought Harry Winston home," Julie said, gesturing toward David Johnson. She pointed at Harry, now rubbing his nose against Alex's leg, and Todd, crouched between the base of the giraffe and the stairwell. "Over there is Harry's brother!"

Charles threw a scathing look at the cats, then a scathing look at Alex. Alex busied himself by crouching down and scratching behind Harry's ear. Norma's hands went cold. They must have had words in Santa Rosa.

"I'm Pratyush," Pratyush said, stepping between Charles and Alex with an outstretched hand. "Alex's husband. You must be Charles."

"How do you do," Charles said, with an utter lack of sincerity. But shaking Pratyush's hand, being called upon to display good manners, had defused his anger enough for Norma to exhale.

"We're about to take your Aunt Julie skydiving," Alex said, straightening up. He shot a glance at Norma. "Your mother invited us over for breakfast before we left."

His suggestion from a half hour ago. Norma now had a perfect excuse to stay home. She could tend to the cats, read the Sunday paper, write that check to Pratyush's nonprofit.

"That's right," she said to Charles. She gave Alex a thankful look and said, "I'll help acclimate Todd to his new home."

"Wait a minute," Julie said to Norma. "You aren't—?"

"You caught us right as we were about to leave," Alex said to Charles.

"What?" Julie said, disconcerted.

"Aunt Julie, what is he talking about?" Charles stared at Julie then turned to face Norma. His eyes strayed to Norma's hiking pants. Then his expression hardened. "Oh, my God—Mom? *You're* going on this skydive?"

"I—well, yes. That was my original intention," she said, pursing her lips.

"So you *didn't* have brunch plans today?" Charles gaped at her with a wounded look in his eyes. "You *lied* to me on the phone last night?"

"Now, Charles, you needn't come down so hard on your mom," Julie said. Her voice was partly admonishing, partly beseeching. "Skydiving was *my* idea. Your Uncle Phil had always wanted to go, and I couldn't find anyone else to go with me, and, um, we didn't want you to worry, and, um, uh—"

"Stop. Stop. Please stop, Aunt Julie." Charles put up his hands then rolled his eyes to the ceiling. "So this is my reward for canceling golf and coming to check in on you."

"I'd better leave," David Johnson said in an undertone to Julie, glancing at the open front door.

"Let me walk you to your car," Julie said to him. "If you give me your email address, I can let you know how the cats are doing."

"Or you could text me, texting is faster than email," David said, and he and Julie left the house, shutting the front door behind them.

"And, Norma," Alex said, gesturing toward the corridor, "how about if Pratyush and I go and bring out the litter box and food bowls for the cats? C'mon, Pratyush."

The hall was darker now that the front door was closed. Larger, too, now that Norma was alone with Charles. Harry followed Alex and Pratyush down the corridor, but Todd remained crouched by the giraffe, looking up at Norma with wide, fearful eyes. She felt an urge to scoop the poor cat up and comfort him. Instead, she turned to Charles and braced herself for an onslaught of reprimands.

Charles stared at her as if he no longer recognized her as his mother. His mouth opened as if to say something, but no words came out. No doubt he was searching for the exact words to describe his disapproval—and skepticism—of a woman her age going on a skydive. Maybe she should jump out of that plane after all, to spite him.

"So." His tone was measured but judgmental. "When were you planning to tell me you were going skydiving?"

"Tomorrow," she said and swallowed.

"You couldn't have told me last night?"

"You would have tried to stop me."

"Unlike your nurse friend who's going with you," he said, throwing a venomous look in the direction of the corridor.

"For your information," she said with an edge in her voice, "Alex is on *your* side. He was doing his best to dissuade me from going, literally minutes before you arrived."

Charles sighed again. Then he wandered to the stairs, put a foot on the bottom step, and leaned against the newel post. Something was on his mind, something that had nothing to do with cats or skydiving.

"I talked to Debra this morning," he said, his tone glum. He turned to face her.

"Is everything all right in Seattle?" She couldn't imagine much had changed since last night's phone call.

"Maria is uncomfortable," he said, "but otherwise they're managing."

"You really should consider joining them."

"And do what? Besides get in everyone's way?" He shook his head with an expression of disappointment. "Then I come here and find you and Aunt Julie have your own plans. And you lied to me about them! Man, sometimes I feel like I don't belong in my own family."

His wounded expression brought home to Norma how she'd let him down—not only this weekend, but perhaps his entire life. Her thoughts turned to Kevin standing on his doorstep, asking her how Charles was. This must be what Kevin had meant.

"He was a nice young man, wasn't he?" Julie shut the door behind her and looked from Charles to Norma, holding up a wrinkled manila envelope. "He gave me Harry and Todd's medical records. They turned three on June first. Where are Alex and Pratyush?"

"Bringing out cat things," Norma said, realizing she'd have

to reach her ninetieth birthday, at least, if she wanted to outlive those two cats. She cast a side glance at Charles.

"Everything's set," Alex said, coming into the hall with Pratyush. He rubbed his hands together. "Food, water, litter box, cat scratcher. Harry's on the pool table if you're looking for him, Norma. I didn't have the heart to move him. Julie, are you ready to go?"

"She is," Charles said, turning to Alex and drawing himself up. "So is my mother. *She's* going skydiving today too. Isn't that right, Mom?"

"Um," Norma said.

"I sure hope you're going," Charles said with a look of fierce satisfaction. "Because I'm going with you."

A shocked silence rippled through the room.

"On the skydive, you mean?" Norma managed to say.

"If *you're* all going," Charles said, turning to her with a daring little smile, "then why not?"

"For one thing, it's probably too late to reserve a spot on our plane." A feeling came over Norma of her plans going haywire.

"Not necessarily," Pratyush said, stepping forward. "When I made the reservations for Alex and myself a few days ago, they said they had plenty of availability. Do you want me to call them, ask if there's an extra space?"

"Yes. Call them now," Charles said with a sociable if abrupt smile at Pratyush.

Pratyush was scrolling through his phone, looking for the number, before Norma realized she was holding her breath. Julie and Alex looked like they were holding their breath, too. But Charles looked more stunned than any of them. His expression was one of stoicism and regret, one that no doubt concealed the hope that no extra spot would be forthcoming. But Norma—to her surprise—realized she wanted Charles to accompany them.

It was high time he did something impulsive. Especially with his wife out of town.

"Good morning, this is Pratyush Barad," Pratyush said in a sonorous baritone. "I'm with a party attending a skydive at your establishment this morning. Another person wishes to join our party. Would there happen to be an available spot?"

A pause. Pratyush's expression revealed nothing. Then he gave a "thank you" and rang off. Everyone was looking at Pratyush. Even Todd Winston was watching him wide-eyed.

"Well?" Charles's face was tense.

"You're in," Pratyush said and slipped his phone into his pocket.

Charles looked dumbfounded. But he had to know how foolish he'd look if he begged off going now. Good, Norma thought. Great, in fact. Leaping out of a moving airplane might be the medicine Charles needed. And would serve Debra right for traipsing off to Seattle without him.

"Okay then," Charles said, cranking up that thousand-watt smile of his. "Let's go skydiving."

"We'll need two cars now," Julie said. "Would you mind driving to Sonoma, Charles?"

"Happy to," he said. A serenity came over his features, as if he'd already made peace with his decision. "Who's riding with me?"

"I will," Pratyush said. He turned to Alex and said, "You can drive Julie and Norma in Julie's car."

"Sure," Alex said, looking relieved that his husband had spared him an hour's drive with Charles.

"Thanks, Alex," Julie said. "I'm no fan of the freeways."

"Okay," Norma said in a raised take-charge voice. "All of you need to go outside so I can set the alarm."

Everyone filed out of the house. Alex went out last, flashing

Norma a smile before he closed the front door, plunging the hall into shadow. As soon as she was alone, Harry Winston appeared and trotted up to her. She bent down and pet him as he rubbed against her leg. Todd watched from behind the giraffe's legs. This was a miracle, to feel Harry Winston's fur beneath her fingers. And Todd—ah, Todd, her new charge! She'd earn his trust later. If there was a later.

There was nowhere in the hall to leave their medical files. Everyone would have to wait while she put the files away in the sitting room. She went up the stairs faster than perhaps she should have. Her knee was aching by the time she reached the landing.

The opal pendant lay on the circular table, glowing green, pink, and milky blue in the sun. She couldn't leave the necklace lying there exposed, could she? What if the cats wandered up here, used the pendant as a toy? Did she have time to stash the jewel in the safe? No, everyone was waiting.

She put down the manila folder and picked up the pendant. The opal shone in her palm. An image of Kevin came to her, the bashful look on his eighteen-year-old face on the day she'd found the sloppily-wrapped jewelry box in the center of her pool table. Her heart quickened with joy, just as it had on that day. With a quick motion she put the chain round her neck. The opal glowed like a guiding star against the embroidered galaxy on her shirt. A thrill ran through her veins. Then she zipped up her windbreaker and hurried downstairs.

CHAPTER 27

THE BLUE HOUR

CHARLES WAS ALREADY pulling out of the driveway by the time she locked the front door behind her. With Pratyush in the car with him, Charles would have no choice but to drive straight to Sonoma County instead of panicking, changing his mind, and going home. Good. She strode up to Julie's Honda in the driveway, Alex in the driver's seat, Julie in the back seat, the car already running.

The drive to Wild Blue Yonder felt woefully short. A long concrete walk led to two low-slung prefabricated buildings in the middle of a sprawling field. Picnic benches with umbrellas sat next to one of the buildings. The air was hotter here than in Oakland. Norma felt the hummingbird buzzing in her chest. Was that enough for her to excuse herself?

They walked through the front door of the larger of the two buildings. Inside, the place looked like a dentist's office: plastic chairs, framed landscape photos on the walls, a pleasant-featured blonde-haired woman behind the counter. Julie and Pratyush went to the counter to check everyone in. The woman behind the counter gave Charles a clipboard. Those must be the disclaimer forms that Norma had submitted online. Charles sat in a chair next to her and started checking off boxes. It was then that the buzzing wings passed across her heart. She clasped her chest and said, "Oh, wow."

"Mom?" Charles looked up.

"I think," she said, rising from her chair. "I don't know what's happening."

Wasn't this mortifying, for her heart to betray her like this, for the second time in two weeks? The buzzing in her chest was now burning. Wide-eyed looks showed on the faces around her. Any moment now, the light in this waiting room would fade, and she'd open her eyes in a strange hospital bed.

A hand grasped her forearm. She looked up, assuming it must be Alex checking her pulse. But the hand belonged to Charles. He was looking straight at her, an intent but kind expression on his face.

"Mom," he said, his voice patient, "can I have a word with you outside?"

"Outside?" The burning in her chest was already beginning to subside. "I suppose so."

"We'll only be a second," Charles said in an undertone to Julie, and he swapped a look with Alex before leading Norma out the door.

Charles walked a few feet on the concrete walk alongside the building, away from the front door, before turning around and facing her. A couple of lacquered Adirondack chairs sat on the concrete, no doubt for spectators to watch parachuters land. Norma could establish herself on one of these chairs while everyone else dived.

"What's the matter?" He looked at her, squaring his jaw. "Not feeling well?"

"My chest," she said, putting her hand to her sternum. The

opal pressed against her palm. "I forgot to bring my pills. But go on ahead, no need for an ambulance. I'll be fine."

"Mom? Those pills?" He spoke in the tone of someone about to break unwelcome news. "They're not what you think they are."

"What do you mean?" A disquieting sense rose up in her.

"They're nothing but generic-brand aspirin." He gave a small smile and turned up his palms. "The doctor told me so. You don't have a heart condition, Mom. Okay? You don't."

Aspirin? Nonsense. Of course she had a heart condition. But Charles's frank tone—no coaxing, no admonishment—demonstrated he hadn't conjured this from thin air. Could he be right? A fake prescription? Fictitious heart trouble? Good grief. All those times she'd reached for those pills she'd been kidding herself, making a fool of herself, and Charles had known all along. Her face flushed.

"I see," she said, looking down. A hollowness grew in her chest, but her heart must be in there somewhere, beating away.

"I'm not sure why I told you that." Tension showed on his face. "I guess I thought you deserved to know. You can sit the dive out if you want to. But you can't blame your heart. You can't blame me, either. Because I've told you the truth."

How easily he could have let her keep on deluding herself. He could have let her sit in the safety of that Adirondack chair—and then withdraw from the dive himself, using her as his excuse. *Don't want to dive, Mom? Totally okay. Why don't I stay here and keep you company?* For all his worrying about her, he still thought she could pull off this skydive. How could she renege now?

"Charles? Norma?" Julie's head poked out of the front door. "We need to watch the safety video before they let us go up."

"One second," Charles said. Julie nodded and disappeared into the building. He turned to Norma with a hopeful expression. "Mom? Are you coming?"

Charles reminded her of Robert right now. The young Robert, that is. The dashing man who used to believe in her. The one who used to think she could do anything if she set her mind to it.

"Very well then," she said, drawing herself up. She endeavored to sound more formal than sentimental; otherwise, Charles might not recognize her. "We have a plane to catch."

"Great," he said, his smile widening. He held open the door for her.

"Charlie?"

She turned from the door, reached out, and touched his forearm. He looked at her, surprised. She was surprised at the gesture herself.

"Thank you for telling me about those pills," she said.

"Oh, Mom," Charles said with a smile and a roll of his eyes.

In the chilly darkness of Wild Blue Yonder's audiovisual room, Norma settled into a folding chair paying only minimal attention to the safety video, aware with calm certainty that no precaution, no contingency measure, would save her if her parachute failed to open. The dead silence in the room, once the video concluded and the lights came up, could only mean that everyone else must be thinking the same thing. But of course the parachutes would open. A framed certificate in the waiting room boasted a 100 percent safety record. She had no reason to think that track record wouldn't hold.

They went outside to meet the professional divers who would be escorting them. Norma's diver was a blocky young man with orange-rimmed sunglasses and wind-whipped blond hair. His broad smile, easy and self-confident, displayed a set of unnaturally white teeth. He bore a funny resemblance to someone from her past. She couldn't think who.

"I'm Connor Mack," the young man said, holding out his hand. "Are you ready for the adventure of your life?"

"Mrs. McKinsey." Norma shook his hand, answering his strong grip with one of her own. "I've had enough adventure for one life, Mr. Mack. But here we are."

"Well…all right!" Connor Mack said, a smile plastered on his face. "Rest assured, Mrs. McKinsey, you're in good hands. I've done over a thousand jumps."

Now she realized—with a tingle running down her spine—whom this young man resembled. That model half her age, the one from over twenty-five years ago. The one in those pictures—if, in fact, those pictures still existed. Joseph was his name. Joseph…what was his last name again? Oh, what difference did that make? God only knew where he was now.

"Man, it's hotter than I expected," Charles said, removing his beige jacket, revealing a gold golf shirt. He turned to his diver and asked, "Is it too late to take this off?"

"Nope," the diver said. "You can put it in the coat room where you left your phones and purses."

"Won't it be too cold when we go up there?" Julie shot a concerned look at her diver.

"I've done two dives so far this morning. You'll be fine," her diver said. He winked and added, "Besides, you won't be up there for long."

"Gosh," Julie said and laughed.

"You have the right idea, Charles," Alex said, taking off his cycling jacket. He wore a long-sleeved orange shirt with a front pocket. "Pratyush, do you want me to bring in your jacket too?"

"Why not?" Pratyush said, removing his jacket to reveal an oxblood T-shirt stretched tight across his chest.

"You might as well take mine in too," Norma said, and she unzipped and removed her windbreaker.

"Norma!" Julie cried. "Your pendant!"

"Oh." Norma closed her hand over the opal, realizing her error too late.

"You can't wear that on the dive," Alex said, his eyes widening.

"It'll be fine under my shirt."

"No, it won't," Julie said, her mouth open.

"Fine. I'll leave the opal in my purse in the coat room," Norma said grudgingly, taking off the necklace.

"Just so you know," Connor said in a kindly voice, "Wild Blue Yonder isn't responsible for lost or stolen items."

"Our phones are in that room," Charles said. "Aren't our phones safe?"

"They *should* be," Connor said. "Someone is usually behind the desk to watch that coat room. No one has ever lost their phone here, as far as I know. But someone *did* lose their wedding band a couple months ago. We turned that room upside down looking for it. No luck."

"You can replace a phone," Pratyush said to Norma. "But you can't replace that necklace."

"For the love of humanity. Now what?" Norma rubbed the opal with her finger. What was she thinking, slipping on that necklace before leaving the house? She glanced at Alex's shirt pocket.

"Not this time," Alex said with a smile and a shake of the head, laying a hand over the pocket. "The necklace won't be any safer here."

"I should've worn my other hiking pants," Pratyush said. "Those pockets have zippers."

"*My* new jacket has an inside pocket with a zipper," Julie said. She unzipped her pink windbreaker and displayed the pocket.

"You still plan to wear that jacket on the dive?" Norma was already feeling warm in the sun.

"Definitely," Julie said. "I want to be a *valentine*."

"All right then," Norma said, holding out the necklace. "You can be the keeper of the jewel."

"You're sure?" Julie threw an alarmed glance at the opal.

"You're the one who started this, Jules," Norma said, her voice kind but impatient. "Put out your hand. Time's wasting."

She laid the pendant in Julie's outstretched palm. Julie's frightened expression looked as if she'd been entrusted with the Koh-i-Noor Diamond. Why did she always have to dither so theatrically?

"All of you are my witnesses," Julie said, holding out her palm with the opal. She unzipped her pocket. "You are watching me put Norma's pendant into the inside pocket of my jacket."

"We're watching, Aunt Julie," Charles said with a smile.

"You are now witnessing me zip up this pocket," Julie said, zipping the pocket with solemn deliberation. "Did everyone see *that*?"

"For the love of humanity, Jules," Norma said. Alex and Pratyush swapped amused looks.

"Thank you," Julie said, patting her side as if to confirm the opal was still there. "As some of you know, I have a track record of misplacing things. Norma, if we reach the ground and that necklace is somehow not in that pocket, then the opal has slipped into another dimension."

"I'll retrieve it as soon as we land," Norma said.

Now they were ready. The plane, waiting at the opposite end of a field behind the main building, elicited gasps and nervous laughter. Norma wasn't fazed. She'd flown in smaller planes with Robert on safari. What *did* make her blanch was the rollup door toward the plane's front. The door from which she'd presumably be expected to plunge. A door that big, on a plane that small, brought the dive that much closer, made it feel that much more concrete.

They posed for photos in front of the plane before boarding. Norma stood between Julie and Charles. The resulting photograph, when developed, would most likely be the photograph local TV stations would use if the plane crashed. But her face went warm at that thought. The safety certificate, the safety certificate. Hadn't Connor said he'd been on a thousand dives?

To distribute everyone's weight evenly, Charles and his diver would go into the plane first, followed by Alex, Pratyush, Norma, and finally Julie closest to the door. The dives would occur in reverse order: Julie first, Charles last. Norma and Connor crawled into the tube-shaped airplane where Charles, Alex, and Pratyush waited with their divers, nestled in a row like shopping carts. Once she settled in her seat in front of Connor, he bound herself to him with reassuringly strong straps. For the next half hour or so, she realized with a shiver, her life would depend on him.

Then Julie and her diver took their seats in front of Norma. Having Connor behind her and Julie's diver in front of her felt like being wedged between two filing cabinets. Her goggles pressed uncomfortably against her face. She could be sitting on her terrace right now, with Harry and Todd Winston keeping her company. How in the world had she consented to go through with this?

The engines revved up. Then came a rushing sensation, followed by a feeling of weightlessness beneath her seat. She brought herself to peer out the porthole-sized window to her left. Trees and hills shrank before her eyes, swallowed up by bluish-white sky. She felt an odd absence of fear. What good would fear do her now?

Soon the plane leveled to cruising altitude. A sixth diver, one not tethered to anyone, rolled up the door at the front of the plane. Howling air blasted into the cabin. Then the young male diver in front of Norma, the one strapped to Julie, yelled into Julie's ear, "Ready?"

"Yes! Yes! Yes!" Julie screamed over the whipping wind, giving the thumbs-up sign.

"Yay, Julie," Alex shouted from behind. "Ju-lie! Ju-lie! Ju-lie!"

A steady chant of *Ju-lie!* erupted from the rear of the plane—Charles and Alex and Pratyush along with their divers. Julie and her diver duckwalked to the edge of the door. A light next to the door flashed red. The diver spread out his arms and clutched the sides of the doorway. Beyond Julie spread a field of saturated blue. Julie was laughing as if she'd been told the funniest joke of her life. Even now, Norma couldn't fathom that her sister was about to leap out of an airplane.

The light by the door flipped from red to green. The diver rocked backward, rocked forward. Julie kept laughing, her eyes wide with euphoria behind her clear plastic goggles. Then—whoosh—only sky showed beyond the open doorway. Julie and her diver had disappeared.

"All right, Norma, are we gonna do this or what?" Connor shouted this into Norma's ear, above the roaring of the plane's engine, icy wind whistling in her ears.

"I didn't come up here for the scenery," she shouted in Connor's ear. *Or to be outdone by my little sister.*

"Be sure to smile for the camera," Connor shouted. "You're in for the time of your life."

"Nor-ma! Nor-ma! Nor-ma!"

Connor duckwalked Norma toward the gaping door until her toes were in line with the plane's edge. The ground below—way below—crawled like a film in slow motion. Her side vision caught Connor's hands in chartreuse gloves, grasping the sides of the airplane door. Where were the cameras? Would they take a good shot of her wearing her handmade shirt? Her chanted name floated somewhere above her head: *Nor-ma! Nor-ma! Nor-ma!* Her body tilted backward. Tilted forward. Backward. Forward. And then—

★

No drop in her stomach. No fear, either. Only a sense of serenity prickling through her veins like freshly melted snow. Creamy sky stretched into infinity. A halo of electric light glowed along the horizon. The planet spread out in a green-and-brown patchwork against the turquoise sea, shrouded by crawling wisps of clouds. Time itself seemed to stop, ceased to matter. Everything she had lived through—marriage and childbirth, career and fame, toil and pressure, loss and heartbreak—was nothing but a prelude to whatever future waited on the ground below. A true Blue Hour.

A jolt. Now she was upright, as if she were sitting on a trapeze bar. She looked upward and glimpsed a canopy of royal purple above Connor's impossible smile. Her parachute. The icy adrenaline of the freefall gave way to a deep warm feeling of fulfillment. She'd never take another heart pill again.

Slowly, slowly, she drifted toward an apron of green spreading below her feet. People on the ground stood and watched her descend like partygoers awaiting the guest of honor. Julie looked like a pink gumdrop, waving to her with huge sweeps of her arms. Norma's feet brushed against grass, and then she found herself on her rear end, Connor parked behind her. The ground felt strange and new.

She was glad to be free of her tethers to Connor. A forty-five-minute romance. No repercussions this time. If she *were* inclined to go into the fashion business again, a photo of her skydiving in her latest design would make for an irresistible ad.

"Norma, Norma," Julie said, rushing up and grasping both Norma's hands. "Was that the best thing ever?"

"If that's what you want to call it." Norma's feet still felt they were floating on air. "I have no other words."

"And I still! Have! The pendant!" Julie proudly patted her side. "Do you want it now?"

"Wait till we go inside," Norma said. She'd probably drop it and lose it in the grass, her fingers were trembling so much.

"Look, look!" Julie said, pointing up. "Pratyush!"

Pratyush floated to earth with his diver beneath a crimson parachute. His expression showed little emotion, his gaze as calm and observant as it had been at the Thirsty Raven. Once on the ground, he shook his diver's hand as if the diver were his cabbie, dropping him off at the curb. A paragon of *sprezzatura*.

Not long after came Alex, floating toward the grass, strapped to a gray-bearded diver. He was smiling ear to ear, looking like a kid who'd ridden his first roller coaster. Once he reached the ground and unstrapped himself from his diver, he walked up to Pratyush and threw his arms around him. Norma looked at them and blinked to keep her eyes from misting over.

And, finally, Charles. A fleck of gold dust appeared as if from behind a blue curtain. Charles's parachute was the same shade of gold as his shirt. His expression, as he drifted closer to the ground, was one of utter amazement. Norma could only watch her son with satisfaction. After everything she'd gone through this year, she still had her Charlie—the son who stuck by her with a loyalty she'd done too little to deserve.

Charles's feet touched the earth. His feet skidded over the grass like a baseball player sliding into home. Once free of his straps he clasped his diver's hand with both his own hands, thanking the man profusely. Then he turned to Norma as if he'd been awarded a trophy.

"*Man*, that was something," he said with his mouth hanging open, his chest rising and falling. "Let's do that again."

Then he stumbled. He was having trouble finding his footing. He gave a game but crooked smile, as if trying to demonstrate to the world—and perhaps to himself—that he felt fine.

"Charlie?" The nervousness in Norma's tone caught everyone else's attention. "Are you all right?"

"Never better, never better," he said, wiping his forehead with his hand. His breathing was ragged. "A tingle in my jaw, that's all."

"Your jaw?" This came from Alex, taking a step toward Charles.

"I don't know, I don't know, I don't think so." The smile was vanishing from Charles's face. He had a confused expression. He ran his fingers down one arm, down the other. "I'm sure it's nothing."

His hands were now on his chest, mouth open. Sweat broke out on his forehead. Norma swapped looks with Julie. The panic on Julie's face might as well be the same horror spreading through Norma.

Alex walked with purpose toward Charles, who was swallowing gulps of air. Alex's hand unbuttoned and reached into his shirt pocket. He pulled out a small plastic bag. Norma squinted. Were those pills in that bag?

"Take these," Alex said. He shook out two white pills from the bag into his palm and held them out to Charles.

"What are they?" Charles looked at Alex's palm then at Alex.

"Aspirin," Alex said in the tone of a seasoned nurse. "You're having a heart attack."

CHAPTER 28

CHARLIE

NORMA COULDN'T SAY when the ambulance started moving. The vehicle was as cramped as a broom closet. Her fold-out seat next to Charles's stretcher, squeezed between the door and a low white chest bearing a red cross, was more constricting than the plane's. Charles's skin was like wax, his forehead damp. This was what a real heart attack looked like.

The paramedic on the other side of the stretcher didn't look too perturbed, though. The monitor next to Charles beeped in soothing rhythm. If Alex were standing in that paramedic's place, he'd no doubt tell her that Charles would recover. But what if he didn't?

"Mom," Charles said. His voice was faint, his breathing labored. His arm was hooked to an IV drip.

"Charlie," she said, leaning forward.

"Call. Kevin." He patted his pants pocket as if looking for his phone.

"Let's not worry Kevin now."

"I was supposed," he said, his eyes half-closed, "to call him. Tonight. Can't find my. Phone."

"I have your phone, Charlie." She pulled out the device from the pocket of his jacket. But should she call Kevin? He wouldn't want to hear her voice under any circumstances, let alone these circumstances. She grasped the phone, her mouth going dry.

"The phone is asking for a password," she said, hoping this would save her.

He recited the four-digit code. One breath for each digit. This was absurd, Charlie wasting oxygen to recite a password for a call she shouldn't make.

"What should I say?"

"Just tell Kevin," he said and took a long breath. "Tell him..."

His eyes fluttered shut. She looked at the monitor; the machine's beeping stayed steady. The phone felt like a rock in her hand. Where was she supposed to locate Kevin's number on this contraption?

"Ma'am, would you like me to find the man you're trying to call?" The paramedic, a muscular man with short, braided hair and a tattoo of a peace sign on his inner forearm, looked at her sympathetically.

"Please." Norma, feeling old and incapable, held out the phone. "His name is Kevin McKinsey."

"No problem," the paramedic said, taking the phone and looking at the screen. "Hmm. Someone named Debra has been leaving messages."

"Debra is his wife."

"She left three calls in the past two hours," the paramedic said. "No messages."

"I'll call her later," Norma said, biting down on her irritation. For the love of humanity, if the woman was so concerned with

Charles's welfare, then why did she leave him to make a nuisance of herself in Seattle?

"Okay." The paramedic scrolled through the phone. "Here's the number you want, ma'am."

"Thank you," she said and took the phone. She had enough presence of mind to add, "I'm Norma McKinsey."

"Grady," the paramedic said. He gave an optimistic smile that made her think of Alex. "Don't worry about your son. Signs are good he'll make it."

She gave the paramedic an appreciative nod and turned her attention to Charles's phone. Kevin's information was all there—name, number, email, home address. She blanched to think of the money she'd paid for material that existed in this pocket-sized machine for free. She couldn't believe she'd be hearing Kevin's voice again, only two weeks after she thought he was out of her life for good.

"Charlie, *there* you are," Kevin said on the other end of the line, his tone clipped and urgent. "Have you talked to Debra yet?"

"Kevin, it's your mother," she said, sitting up straight behind her seat belt.

"Mom?" Surprise and suspicion sharpened Kevin's voice. "Why are you calling me on Charlie's phone?"

"He asked me to call you." She looked at Charles on the stretcher with his eyes closed, head lolling to one side.

"He did? Why?"

"He can't talk right now." She glanced at the monitor. "What's this about Debra? Everything all right in Seattle?"

"Maria's in labor."

"She's *what?*"

"Her water broke late this morning," Kevin said. "Debra's been trying to reach Charlie all day. Where is he?"

"That's the thing," Norma said, her breath coming fast. "There's been an episode."

"Episode?" Kevin's voice was startled. "What kind of an episode?"

"With his heart."

"A heart attack?"

"We're not sure yet," Norma said, "but that's what we think it might be."

"Charlie had a *heart* attack?"

"But he'll be fine," she added, keeping her voice level. "No need to be alarmed. Or to tell Debra at this point. Not until we know more."

"Where is Charlie now?"

"We're on our way to the hospital. I'm in the ambulance with him."

"Which hospital?"

"I—I don't know." A sense of free-falling, the same feeling she'd thought she'd have while skydiving, came over her. "Excuse me, Grady? Where are we headed?"

Petaluma, Grady told her. Over a two-hour drive south from Kevin's house. She relayed the information.

"Petaluma?" Kevin sounded taken aback. "What are you and Charlie doing in Petaluma?"

"Charlie can explain later."

"I'll be there as fast as I can."

He rang off before she had a chance to say he might as well stay put. Would he call Debra now? She stared at the phone in her palm.

"Kevin." This was Charles, his eyes barely open. He spoke with a wisp of breath. "What did. He say?"

"He's meeting us at the hospital." She laid her hands over

Charles's phone on her lap. No need to strain his heart further with news from Seattle.

"No. He can't," Charles said through labored breaths. "He works. Sundays."

"Stop worrying about Kevin. Okay, Charlie?" Norma leaned forward, straining against the seat belt, and grasped Charles's clammy forearm. "And stop talking. Please. Think about yourself for once."

Think about yourself for once. She'd never spoken those words to Charles before. Perhaps if she had, his life would have turned out differently. He was forever the older brother, watching over Kevin better than Robert ever had. He'd been taking care of people his whole life. His wife. His children. Kevin. And herself. She shrank in her seat.

Grady and another paramedic wheeled Charles into the emergency room. Norma followed. She must've looked as bewildered as she felt, because a young woman with long dark hair and a kindhearted expression offered Norma her seat. She thanked the woman and sat down. Exhaustion washed over her.

In a few minutes Alex came through the door by himself. Norma rose and walked up to him. He'd driven over in Charles's SUV, he said. Pratyush and Julie should be here in five minutes.

"What's the word on Charles?" His tone was brisk and no-nonsense.

"I don't know for sure." She glanced at the nurse's desk. "He was lucid on the ride over here."

"Good thing we caught it early."

"Good thing *you* caught it early." Her eyes traveled to Alex's unbuttoned shirt pocket. The flap was half-tucked. "Do you always carry aspirin with you?"

"I thought aspirin might come in handy today," he said and glanced away.

"Charles told you, didn't he?" She gave him a direct look. "About my so-called heart pills?"

"In Santa Rosa," he said, turning to face her again.

"I should have known." She listened to the humility in her tone, one she ought to use more often. "You wouldn't have let me skydive if you thought my heart problem was real."

"I did think your suffering was real," he said, his voice compassionate. "I was worried you were skydiving for the wrong reasons."

How long ago all that felt, the dark week leading up to this moment. How deluded, how selfish, how flat-out wrong she'd been. Her mind turned to Charles lying motionless on the stretcher. How could she have thought she had nothing to lose?

"Charles had me call Kevin from the ambulance," she said, her voice hoarse.

"And?" Alex cocked his head, his eyebrows pricking.

"He's on the way." She glanced around the waiting room. "Maybe we should clear out before he shows."

"And leave Charles by himself?" Alex frowned.

"But Kevin," she said weakly.

"Don't give me 'but Kevin,' Norma." Alex leaned forward with the intent look of her equal. "If there's one thing you and Kevin can agree on, is that you both care deeply about Charles. The two of you need to be here for him. Not only today, but from here on out. You're not going anywhere, Norma. And you and Kevin are leaving your differences out there in the parking lot. Understood?"

He gestured with his thumb toward the plate glass window. Norma couldn't remember the last time anyone had spoken to her so bluntly. But he'd said what she needed to hear.

"Yes," she said. "Understood."

"I'll wait outside for Pratyush and Julie." He sighed as if exhausted by what he'd said. "You must be hungry. Can I bring you something from the vending machine? A bag of chips? A candy bar?"

"I don't know." Her stomach was growling. "A Kit Kat?"

"I'll see what they have."

She reached into her purse as a reflex, but he was already heading toward the vending machine. Of course, he'd never let her give him money for a candy bar. But she already owed him too much.

Each bite of the Kit Kat reminded her how ravenous she was. Pratyush's pancakes had been over eight hours ago. She hoped Harry Winston and Todd were managing in the house without her. Perhaps Harry was teaching Todd how to yank down the blinds in her sitting room.

She wished she had her Sunday paper, sitting unread at home. The celebrity magazines on the communal table—creased pages, screaming headlines, the airbrushed faces of flash-in-the-pan starlets—no doubt carried the germy fingerprints of countless readers. She studied the faces of the other people in the waiting room. A young man in a dusty blue cap sat in the corner with a drained expression. A father, mother, and daughter sat across from her, whispering in what sounded like Chinese. A mournful-looking white-haired woman stared listlessly out the window. She didn't know who they were yet felt connected to these people, all of them here for a loved one's sake.

In a few minutes Pratyush and Julie walked through the sliding door. Norma caught Julie's eye and stood up. Alex and Pratyush hung back while Julie rushed up to Norma and embraced her. Norma should have known Julie must be feeling a crushing sense of responsibility for what had happened. Norma hastened to assure her that Charles would likely pull through.

"Oh thank goodness, thank goodness. And before I forget," Julie said, unzipping her windbreaker. "Here."

She reached into the windbreaker and brought out Kevin's pendant.

"I completely forgot you had this," Norma said, taking the necklace from her.

"And *that's* how things disappear," Julie said, nodding. "I can't bear the thought of you losing it. That necklace is the only piece you own that you didn't pay for yourself, right?"

"Uh, well." Blood rushed out of Norma's heart. "Yes. As a matter of fact, it is."

"Thought so." Julie looked at Norma full in the face and smiled.

From the time she'd asked Julie in the hospital to bring her the opal, she'd wondered whether Julie remembered who had given it to her. Now she knew. Her dithering, maddening, indispensable sister.

"Your new jacket suits you," Norma said, taking in the windbreaker's unabashed pinkness.

"You don't think it's *too* pink?"

"Jules, if there was ever a day for you to wear pink," Norma said, patting her sister on the shoulder, "today is the day."

"Thanks. I thought so too," Julie said with a glow on her face, basking, even now, in the approval of her older sister.

"Oh, and I talked to Kevin in the ambulance on the way over here," Norma said. "He's on his way here as we speak."

She didn't have time to take in Julie's astounded expression. A woman in blue scrubs came into the waiting room and called out Norma's name. Norma slipped the pendant around her neck and walked up to her.

The doctor shook Norma's hand and introduced herself as Dr. Juliana Rivera. Charles had had a pacemaker put in and was now resting comfortably. She explained that Charles's heart attack was brought on by a congenital heart defect. Today's excitement had done him no favors, but the heart attack, in theory, could have happened as easily on the golf course as on a skydive. The doctor asked if Charles was aware that he had this defect.

"My son, to put it mildly, is risk-averse," Norma said. "He wouldn't have gone skydiving today if he'd known he had this heart condition."

"What about your family?" the doctor asked. "Does any family member have a history of heart problems?"

"His father died of a heart attack," Norma said. Thoughts and emotions snaked through her. "At around the same age that my son is now."

"We'll keep him here tonight," Dr. Rivera said, nodding. "I see no reason why he shouldn't be able to live a normal life. No more skydiving, though."

"Once is enough." Norma spoke with a stoic expression. "When can we see him?"

"Now if you want," the doctor said and smiled. "He's in Room 401."

A congenital heart problem? One that Charles had possibly inherited from Robert? If that were true, then Robert's heart attack could've happened anywhere, at any time, whether he'd fought with Norma or not. Was that possible? Did she dare allow herself to let go of the story she'd replayed countless times in her head? She turned and headed for the elevators.

★

Charles lay propped up by the window in a blue hospital gown, the blinds raised to let in golden afternoon light. His color was returning. Norma settled into the chair by his bed, while Julie perched herself at the bed's edge. Alex and Pratyush stood nearby.

"Sorry for dragging out everyone's day," Charles joked, an exhausted look on his face. His gaze settled on Alex. "Thanks for the aspirin."

"Anytime," Alex said and smiled.

Something buzzed in Norma's purse on her lap. She reached into the purse and pulled out Charles's phone. Debra's name glowed on the screen. No putting her off now. Norma turned the phone to show Charles.

"Lord," he said groaning, looking at his wife's name on his phone. "Do I *want* to talk to Debra now?"

"In fact, you do," Norma said and laid the phone on the bed next to him. "She has news."

Charles gave her a look that showed he'd picked up the meaning in her voice. He took the phone and tapped the screen with his index finger.

"Hey, hon. Yeah, sorry, I forgot I had my phone turned off." He glanced out the window with a nervous look. "Yep, all good! *Fantastic* day of golfing."

His eyes darted around, his look settling on Norma. Norma suppressed a smile. Bravo, Charlie. It turned out he *could* tell his wife a baldfaced lie, if the occasion rightfully called for it.

"How's everything in Seattle?" Charles's eyes widened. "She *what?* Oh, man. When? Oh, *man*. Wow."

Norma leaned forward, reminding herself that she had no control over whatever drama had unfolded in Seattle. Now was not the time to show panic or frailty. Good news or bad news, she would have to show strength.

"Okay, okay," Charles went on, his eyes going red. "Listen,

would it be all right if I call you in a few minutes? ...What?... No, I'm fine... I'm, uh, in the car. Be home later this afternoon. Yes, everything's fine, I swear. Great, thanks. I love you, honey. Bye."

He placed the phone on the bedstand and looked up, a jubilant expression on his face. Then he looked at Norma. A knot loosened in her chest, relief spreading through her like water released from a dam.

"Congratulations, Mom," he said, a smile spreading across his face. "You're a great-grandmother."

Ecstatic cries all around. How typical of Charles, to deflect his own good news onto someone else. Norma wasn't having it.

"This is a great day of firsts for *you*," she said, grasping Charles's forearm. "Your first skydive. And, now, your first grandchild."

"And my first pacemaker," he said with a sheepish grin, glancing at his chest.

"What did Maria have?" Julie said, her face rapturous. "Boy? Girl?"

"Boy," Charles said. He shrugged and gave an apologetic smile to Norma.

"A boy, a boy," Julie said in a singsong voice, "Maria had a boy."

"Given the circumstances, I'll settle for a healthy baby," Norma said in all honesty. All the same, she couldn't help a twinge of disappointment. Most of her jewelry would go to charity upon her death. But what about Kevin's opal?

"Our skydive photos are on the Wild Blue Yonder website," Pratyush said, inspecting his phone. "Would anyone care to look?"

"I would," Julie said eagerly and took Pratyush's phone. Her face fell. "Everyone *else* looks good."

"For the love of humanity, Jules," Norma said and took the phone from her sister.

There was Julie, her mouth wide open in either surprise or wonder, looking very much like a valentine against the deep blue sky. Alex's photo showed him grinning ear to ear. A serious but amazed look appeared on Pratyush's face. Charles was his usual dashing self, looking heartbreakingly unaware of the calamity awaiting him below. And Norma? No expression at all. No one would know what she was thinking as she descended. The stars on her shirt shimmered with marketable appeal.

"Outstanding," she said, handing Pratyush his phone. "I'll have enlargements made and hang them in my corridor, to replace my old dress sketches that are headed for auction."

"You want to replace those sketches with photographs of *us*?" Julie gave an apprehensive look. "Oh, Norma, you can't do *that*."

"I can. And I will," Norma said with an expression of total serenity.

"Let's talk about photos later," Alex said. He exchanged a look with Pratyush then brought out Charles's car keys and set them on the bedstand. "In the meantime, we should let the patient rest. Norma, what do you say? Ready to go home?"

"I'd like to stay until Kevin comes," she said, looking at the wall clock. It was past four already.

"Me too," Julie said, a hopeful look on her face. "I'd *love* to see Kevin again."

"Another time, Jules," Norma said as gently as possible. "I'm only staying to keep Charles company. Once Kevin arrives, I'll go home myself."

"Don't worry, Aunt Julie," Charles said. "As soon as I'm out of here, I'm taking you to see him. He asks about you all the time."

"Alex and Pratyush can drive you to my house in your car,"

Norma said. "I'll take Charlie's car home. You don't mind, do you, Charlie?"

"All yours," he said.

"Perfect. I'll come in the morning and bring you home." She turned to Alex and Pratyush. "Gentlemen, what are your plans for this evening?"

"Laundry," Pratyush said with a shrug.

"For the love of humanity, *laundry*," Norma said, drawing out that last word with good-humored disdain. "How about this? Instead of going home, how about you remain at my house and order dinner? There is an excellent Chinese restaurant down the road—Julie, you know which one I'm talking about. Order whatever takeout you want, and I'll reimburse you. I'll join you for dinner later. And we can crack open that bottle of champagne in the fridge. You have my housekey, don't you, Julie?"

"I don't," Julie said with a moment's worry. "I was afraid I'd lose it."

"Then take mine," Norma said, pulling out her keys from her purse. "I won't be that far behind you."

"Fine, I won't wear socks to work tomorrow," Pratyush said and turned to Alex.

"I can lend you socks," Alex said. He then turned to Norma with a smile. "We'd love to have Chinese takeout with you tonight. I've always wanted to watch the sunset from your house."

"Oh, you *have* to watch the sunset from Norma's terrace," Julie said, slapping her hands on her knees. "You've never *seen* the sunset until you've seen it from her terrace."

"All right, Julie, no need to oversell it," Norma said.

"Should be a beauty of a sunset tonight," Charles said, glancing out the window. "Mom has a special name for it. What do you call it again, Mom?"

"The Blue Hour." Norma hadn't realized that Charles knew this.

"And I'm stuck here with this crappy view," Charles said, his tone good-humored. "Aw, *man*."

"I'll throw a bash for you and Debra when she comes home." Norma was already looking forward to throngs of guests enlivening her house. "To celebrate the newest McKinsey. Everyone here is invited."

Was it only this morning that she'd pulled herself out of bed, thinking today would be the last day of her life? Fate, apparently, had devised other plans for her. No way to explain it. No *need* to explain it. Might as well keep on living.

A peaceful feeling filled the room once Julie, Alex, and Pratyush had gone. Norma sat by Charles, the two of them watching a 49ers football game on TV. How was this for a role reversal, him in the hospital bed, her in the guest chair?

"So, Mom," he said during a commercial break, his eyes straying to the window. "Now that we've gone skydiving, what are we going to do for an encore?"

"Something less strenuous on your heart," she answered, her eyes following Charles's gaze. The sky, framed by the window, looked innocent, benevolent.

"Is Aunt Julie still planning to go snorkeling at the Great Barrier Reef?" Charles's expression went distracted, as if he were imagining the wide world beyond that window.

"Actually, she's had a change of plans. Her Australian friends, the ones she met in Ecuador, want her to meet them in Bali next year. She asked if I'd like to join her. I hadn't given the idea serious thought, but… Do you think you could talk Debra into going to Bali?"

"You know how she feels about long flights." He sighed. "But if she doesn't want to go, maybe I can tag along with you and Aunt Julie. You wouldn't mind, would you?"

"Of course not. You can carry our luggage." How deliciously strange it felt to kid around like this on the day Charles had had a heart attack—indeed, to kid around with Charles at all. "But Bali can wait. Let's bring you home in one piece first."

Bali, hmm. She could buy more ikat dresses. Perhaps extend the vacation to Tokyo, to see her niece Olivia. She'd always wanted to study in Japan, would likely have spent more time there if she hadn't gotten pregnant with Charles. She could stock up on innovative Kit Kats and visit old friends. Show her favorite places to Charles and Julie. And let Alex and Pratyush stay at her house while she was away, to enjoy the Blue Hour and take care of Harry and Todd Winston. The television switched back to the football game.

"There is so much I haven't told you," she said, watching the screen. Second and goal for the 49ers.

"About what?"

"About me. And Kevin." She looked at Charles. "And your father. I had wanted to protect you from the truth. That was a mistake. I see that now."

"I'm listening." He had the look of someone whose lifelong suspicions were about to be confirmed.

"You've had enough stress for one day," she said gently. "But I promise to tell you everything once we're home."

The door opened.

Kevin walked up to Charles's bedside, not looking her way. He wore a denim shirt and tan corduroy pants—no doubt his real Sunday clothes. This was exactly what she'd wished would have happened after her own car accident: Kevin rushing to see her without equivocation, without judgment. She watched him not watching her.

"Charlie?" Kevin stood by the bed with a lost, overwhelmed expression, a scared little boy. "What happened?"

"A mild heart attack, no big deal," Charles said with a soft smile. He tapped his breastbone. "They put in a pacemaker, now I'm okay. End of story."

"How did you wind up here in Petaluma?" Kevin threw a pained glance at Norma, unable, apparently, to pretend she wasn't sitting there. Evidently, she was part of the *you* of Kevin's question.

"Funny you should ask that," Charles said and then looked at a loss for words. He turned to Norma. "Mom? Would you like to tell Kevin how we wound up here?"

Now Kevin had no choice but to look at her more fully—and for her to return his look. Their eyes met. He glanced down. At first she assumed he couldn't bear the sight of her, until she realized his eyes had lit on the opal, shining against the embroidered stars of her blue shirt.

"We went skydiving this morning," she said in a blasé tone.

"Skydiving?" Kevin stared. "What possessed you two to go skydiving?"

"Your Aunt Julie inspired us," Norma said with a quickening in her pulse. She'd progressed from the *you* of his previous question to the *you two* of this one.

"Aunt Julie went with you?" Kevin's look went from disbelieving to dumbfounded.

"Other way around, bro. We went with *her*. Skydiving was *her* idea," Charles said with approval. "She's already on her way home—you missed her by a few minutes. But she wants to see you. Pick a time, and we can meet in Bodega Bay. Sometime soon. Okay?"

"Okay."

"Good," Charles said and smiled.

Kevin's expression darkened, as if deep in thought. He must be worrying about them for a change, instead of them worrying about him. Norma looked down at her unpainted nails and listened to the football announcers on the TV, nattering on about the game.

"Have you spoken to Debra yet?" Kevin said to Charles.

"We're grandparents," Charles said, smiling and nodding at his phone. "A boy. Everyone's fine."

"Awesome. I'm happy for you, Charlie."

Kevin gave a long exhale, his eyes misting over. He laid a hand on Charles's arm. He'd probably say more if Norma weren't in the room. Why not make a graceful exit now, let the brothers have their *tête-à-tête*? She should count herself lucky that her two sons remained close.

"I should be going," she said, rising from her chair.

"So soon?" Charles said. He spoke as if she were breaking up a party early.

"The others are waiting for me at home." She glanced at the wall clock. Then she turned to Kevin and in a businesslike voice said, "You'll stay with him a while?"

"Until they make me leave," Kevin said, his tone civil.

"I'll be here first thing tomorrow," she said to Charles.

"Sounds good." Charles looked from Norma to Kevin, a boyish smile spreading on his face. "*Man*, I can't tell you how glad I am to see you both here."

"Of course," Kevin said without hesitation.

"Today was something, wasn't it, Mom?" Charles looked out

the window with an expression of wonder. "Look at that sky. We were up *there* this morning. I can't wrap my head around that."

"Neither can I," she said softly. "I'll mention Bali to Aunt Julie tonight."

"Bali?" Kevin asked.

"Charlie will tell you all about it," she said, and after a nod and quick smile, she turned toward the door.

"Mom," Kevin called out.

She turned and faced her younger son.

"What's that you're wearing?" His eyes darted to the opal, then he looked up at her. A look passed across his face, shy and flattered, that reminded her of his eighteen-year-old self.

"A good luck charm," she said, holding the jewel between her thumb and index finger.

"I can't believe you still have that." Kevin spoke with a wondering look, as if he were remembering the day he'd given the present to her.

"You didn't think I'd give it away, did you?" She gave Kevin a small smile and then turned to Charles. "I'll see you tomorrow, Charlie."

An unusual feeling spread inside her ribcage as she headed down the corridor to the elevator. Not the buzzing she'd been feeling over the past few days. Warmth. A spreading of her heart. Pride. Relief. Joy. She'd walked out of a room with Kevin in it, instead of Kevin walking out of the room on her. Now it was his turn to come to her, to show up at her own door one of these days.

And he would show up. He cared too much for Charlie to do otherwise. Charlie was the thread that united them. A thread that was one heart attack away from snapping. But, still, it was a start.

She put her hand to her chest, felt the opal against her breastbone. Why did Charlie's first grandchild have to be a boy?

But—wait—what about the little girl up in Mendocino County? The girl Kevin planned to raise? If Kevin ended up adopting that girl, then the girl would become the granddaughter Norma had always wanted. She might even be tempted to leave a few dollars for the girl's education, to go along with the jewel. Kevin would probably appreciate that. She pictured herself writing a letter to this granddaughter, on one of her best Corot notecards, in her most elegant handwriting. A missive to accompany the bequest.

Your father gave me this pendant many years ago. He was only eighteen when he gave it to me. It is one of my most cherished possessions. It makes my heart glad to pass this along to you.

She spotted Charlie's SUV in the lot and strode toward it. Her chest grew warmer and warmer, her heart wider and wider, as wide as the dimming sky above her head. The sun was well on its descent toward the horizon. If she drove fast enough, she might be able to catch the Blue Hour with Julie and Alex and Pratyush, with Harry Winston on her lap and Todd curled up on a lounge chair. But no need to hurry. The sky would be there for her tomorrow, sublime and infinite, asking nothing of her in return.

www.ingramcontent.com/pod-product-compliance
Lightning Source LLC
Chambersburg PA
CBHW030233120726